MUTINY

MUTINY

A KYDD NOVEL

Julian Stockwin

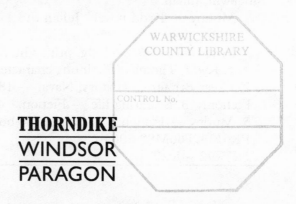

THORNDIKE
WINDSOR
PARAGON

This Large Print edition is published by Thorndike Press®, Waterville, Maine USA and by BBC Audiobooks, Ltd, Bath, England.

Published in 2004 in the U.S. by arrangement with Scribner, an imprint of Simon & Schuster, Inc.

Published in 2004 in the U.K. by arrangement with Hodder & Stoughton.

U.S. Hardcover 0-7862-6682-1 (Adventure)
U.K. Hardcover 0-7540-9530-4 (Windsor Large Print)
U.K. Softcover 0-7540-9418-9 (Paragon Large Print)

The text of this Large Print edition is unabridged.
Other aspects of the book may vary from the original edition.

Set in 16 pt. Plantin by Liana M. Walker.

Printed in the United States on permanent paper.

British Library Cataloguing-in-Publication Data available

Library of Congress Cataloging-in-Publication Data

Stockwin, Julian.
    Mutiny : a Kydd novel / Julian Stockwin.
        p. cm.
    ISBN 0-7862-6682-1 (lg. print : hc : alk. paper)
    1. Kydd, Thomas (Fictitious character) — Fiction.
2. Great Britain — History, Naval — 18th century — Fiction.   3. Seafaring life — Fiction.   4. Sailors — Fiction.
5. Mutiny — Fiction.   6. Large type books.   I. Title.
PR6119.T66M88 2004b
    823'.92—dc22   2004050147

MUTINY

The Articles of War, 1749

If any person in the fleet shall conceal any traitorous or mutinous practice or design, being convicted thereof by the sentence of a court martial, he shall suffer death. . . .

Prologue

"Damme, but that's six o' them — an' they're thumpers, Sir Edward!" The massive telescope that the first lieutenant of HMS *Indefatigable* held swayed in the hard gale, but the gray waste of winter sea made it easy to see the pallid white sails of line-of-battle ships, even at such a distance.

Captain Pellew growled an indistinct acknowledgment. If it was the French finally emerging from Brest, it was the worst timing possible. The main British battle fleet had retired to its winter retreat at Portsmouth, and there was only a smaller force under Rear Admiral Colpoys away in the Atlantic, off Ushant to the north, and the two other frigates of his own inshore squadron keeping a precarious watch — and those an enemy of such might could contemptuously sweep aside. Heaven only knew when the grudging reinforcements from the Caribbean would arrive.

"Sir —" There was no need for words: more and more sails were straggling into the expanse of the bay. Silently, the officers continued to watch, the blast of the unusual easterly cold and hostile. The seas, harried by the wind, advanced toward them in combers, bursting against their bows and sending icy spindrift aft in stinging volleys.

The light was fading: the French admiral had timed his move so that by the time his fleet reached the open sea it could lose itself in the darkness of a stormy night. "A round dozen at least. We may in truth say that the French fleet has sailed," Pellew said dryly.

The lieutenant watched eagerly, for the French were finally showing after all these months, but Pellew did not share his jubilation. His secret intelligence was chilling: for weeks this concentration of force had stored and prepared — with field guns, horses and fodder — and if reports were to be believed, eighteen thousand troops. If the entire fleet put to sea, it could have only one purpose . . .

"Desire *Phoebe* to find Admiral Colpoys and advise," he snapped at the signal lieutenant. However, there was little chance that Colpoys could close on the French before they won the open sea. In the rapidly dimming daylight, the swelling numbers of men-o'-war were direful.

"Sir! I now make it sixteen — no seventeen — of the line!"

A savage roll made them all stagger. When they recovered it seemed the whole bay was filling with ships — at least the same number again of frigates; with transports and others there were now forty or more vessels breaking out into the Atlantic.

"*Amazon* is to make all sail for Portsmouth," Pellew barked. It would reduce his squadron to a pitiable remnant, but it was essential to warn England while there was still time.

Yet the enemy sail advancing on them was not a line of battle, it was a disordered scatter — some headed south, shying away from the only frigate that lay across their path. Strings of flags rose from one of the largest of the French battleships, accompanied by the hollow thump of a gun. The gloom of dusk was fast turning to a clamping murk, and the signal was indistinct. A red rocket soared suddenly, and the ghostly blue radiance of a flare showed on her foredeck as she turned to night signals.

"So they want illuminations — they shall have them!" Pellew said grimly. *Indefatigable* plunged ahead, directly into the widely scattered fleet. From her own deck colored rockets hissed, tracing across the windy night sky, while vivid flashes from her guns added to the confusion. A large two-decker trying to put about struck rocks; she swung into the wind, and was driven back hard against them. Distress rockets soared from the doomed ship.

"Can't last," muttered Pellew, at the general mayhem. The driving gale from the east would prevent any return to harbor and the enemy had only to make the broad Atlantic to find ample sea-room to regain composure.

The mass of enemy ships passed them by quickly, disdaining to engage, and all too soon had disappeared into the wild night — but not before it was clear they were shaping course northward. Toward England.

Chapter 1

"Bear a fist there, y' scowbunkin' lubbers!" The loud bellow startled the group around the forebitts who were amiably watching the sailors at the pin-rail swigging off on the topsail lift. The men moved quickly to obey: this was Thomas Kydd, the hard-horse master's mate, whose hellish open-boat voyage in the Caribbean eighteen months ago was still talked about in the navy.

Kydd's eyes moved about the deck. It was his way never to go below at the end of a watch until all was neatly squared away, ready for those relieving, but there was little to criticize in these balmy breezes on the foredeck of the 64-gun ship-of-the-line *Achilles* as she crossed the broad Atlantic bound for Gibraltar.

Kydd was content — to be a master's mate after just four years before the mast was a rare achievement. It entitled him to walk the quarterdeck with the officers, to mess in the gunroom, and to wear a proper uniform complete with long coat and breeches. No one could mistake him now for a common sailor.

Royal blue seas, with an occasional tumbling line of white, and towering fluffy clouds brilliant in southern sunshine: they were to enter the Mediterranean to join Admiral Jervis. It would be the first time Kydd had seen this fabled sea and he looked forward to sharing interesting times ashore with his particular friend, Nicholas Renzi, who was now a master's mate in *Glorious*.

His gaze shifted to her, a powerful 74-gun ship-of-the-line off to leeward. She was taking in her three topsails simultaneously, probably an officer-of-the-watch exercise, pitting the skills and audacity of one mast against another.

The last day or so they had been running down the latitude of thirty-six north, and Kydd knew they should raise Gibraltar that morning. He glanced forward in expectation. To the east there was a light dun-colored band of haze lying on the horizon, obscuring the transition of sea into sky.

The small squadron began to assume a form of line. Kydd took his position on the quarterdeck, determined not to miss landfall on such an emblem of history. His glance flicked up to the fore masthead lookout — but this time the man snapped rigid, shading his eyes and looking right ahead. An instant later he leaned down and bawled, "*Laaaand* ho!"

The master puffed his cheeks in pleasure. Kydd knew it was an easy enough approach, but news of the sighting of land was always a matter of great interest to a ship's company many weeks at sea, and the decks buzzed with comment.

Kydd waited impatiently, but soon it became visible from the decks, a delicate light blue-gray peak, just discernible over the haze. It firmed quickly to a hard blue and, as he watched, it spread. The ships sailed on in the fluky southeasterly, and as they approached, the aspect of the land changed subtly, the length of it beginning to foreshorten. The haze thinned and the land took on individuality.

"Gibraltar!" Kydd breathed. As they neared, the bulking shape grew, reared up far above their masthead with an effortless immensity. Like a crouching lion, it dominated by its mere presence, a majestic, never-to-be-forgotten symbol: the uttermost end of Europe, the finality of a continent.

He looked around; to the south lay Africa, an irregular blue-gray mass across a glittering sea — there, so close, was an endless desert and the Barbary pirates, then farther south, jungle, elephants and pygmies.

Only two ships. Shielding her eyes against the glare of the sea, Emily Mulvany searched the horizon but could see no more. Admiral Jervis, with his fleet, was in Lisbon, giving heart to the Portuguese, and there were no men-o'-war of significance in Gibraltar. All were hoping for a substantial naval presence in these dreadful times . . . but she was a daughter of the army and knew nothing of sea strategy. Still, they looked lovely, all sails set like wings on a swan, a long pennant at the masthead of each swirling lazily, a picture of sea grace and beauty.

Flags rose to *Glorious*'s signal halyards. They both altered course in a broad curve toward the far-off anonymous cluster of buildings halfway along at the water's edge. As they did so, the gentle breeze fluttered and died, picked up again, then dropped away to a whisper. Frustrated, Kydd saw why. Even this far out they were in the lee of the great rock in the easterly; high on its summit a ragged scarf of cloud streamed out, darkening the bay beneath for a mile or more. He glanced at the master, who did not appear overly concerned, his arms folded in limitless patience. The captain disappeared below, leaving the deck to the watch. Sails flapped and rustled, slackened gear rattled and knocked, and the ship ghosted in at the pace of a crawling child.

Kydd took the measure of the gigantic rock. It lay almost exactly north and south some two or three miles long, but was observably much narrower. There was a main town low along the flanks to seaward, but few other buildings on the precipitous sides. On its landward end the rock ended abruptly, and Kydd could see the long flat terrain connecting the Rock of Gibraltar to the nondescript mainland.

It wasn't until evening that the frustrating easterly died and a local southerly enabled the two ships to come in with the land. Kydd knew from the charts that this would be Rosia Bay, the home of the navy in Gibraltar. It was a pretty little inlet, well away from the main cluster of buildings farther along. There was the usual elegant, spare stone architecture of a dockyard and, higher, an imposing two-story building

17

that, by its position, could only be the naval hospital.

Rosia Bay opened up, a small mole to the south, the ramparts of a past fortification clear to the north. There, the two ships dropped anchor.

"Do you see . . ."

Kydd had not noticed Cockburn appear beside him.

"Er, no — what is it y' sees, Tam?" The neat, almost academic-looking man next to him was *Achilles*'s other master's mate, a long-promoted midshipman without the proper interest to make the vital step of commission as a lieutenant, but who had accepted his situation with philosophic resignation. He and Kydd had become friends.

"We're the only ones," Cockburn said quietly. "The fleet must be in the Med somewhere." Apart from the sturdy sails of dockyard craft and a brig-sloop alongside the mole in a state of disrepair, there were only the exotic lateen sails of Levant traders dotting the sea around the calm of Gibraltar.

"Side!" The burly boatswain raised his silver call. The captain emerged from the cabin spaces, striding purposefully, all aglitter with gold lace, medals and best sword. Respectfully, Kydd and Cockburn joined the line of sideboys at the ship's side. The boatswain raised his call again and as the captain went over the bulwark every man touched his hat and the shriek of the whistle pierced the evening.

The captain safely over the side, the first lieutenant remained at the salute for a moment, then turned to the boatswain. "Stand down the watches. We're out of sea routine now, I believe."

The boatswain's eyebrows raised in surprise. No strict orders to ready the ship for sea again, to store ship, to set right the ravages of their ocean voyage? They would evidently be here for a long time. "An' liberty, sir?" he asked.

"Larbowlines until evening gun." The first lieutenant's words were overheard by a dozen ears, sudden unseen scurries indicating the news was being joyfully spread below.

At the boatswain's uneasy frown, the lieutenant added, "We're due a parcel of men from England, apparently. They can turn to and let our brave tars step off on a well-earned frolic, don't you think?"

Kydd caught an edge of irony in the words, but didn't waste time on reflection. "Been here before?" he asked Cockburn, who was taking in the long sprawl of buildings farther along, the Moorish-looking castle at the other end — the sheer fascination of the mighty rock.

"Never, I fear," said Cockburn, in his usual quiet way, as he gazed at the spectacle. "But we'll make its acquaintance soon enough."

Kydd noticed with surprise that *Glorious*, anchored no more than a hundred yards away, was in a state of intense activity. There were victualing hoys and low barges beetling out to the bigger ship-of-the-line, every sign of an outward-bound vessel.

The old fashioned longboat carrying the senior hands ashore was good-natured about diverting, and soon they lay under oars off the side of the powerful man-o'-war, one of a multitude of busy craft.

"*Glorious*, ahoy!" bawled Kydd. At the deck edge a distracted petty officer appeared and looked down into the boat. "If ye c'n pass th' word f'r Mr. Renzi, I'd be obliged," Kydd hailed. The face disappeared and they waited.

The heat of the day had lessened, but it still drew forth the aromas of a ship long at sea — sun on tarry timbers, canvas and well-worn decks, an effluvia carrying from the open gunports that was as individual to that ship as the volute carvings at her bow, a compound of bilge, old stores, concentrated humanity and more subtle, unknown odors.

There was movement and a wooden squealing of sheaves, and the gunport lid next to them was triced up. "Dear fellow!" Renzi leaned out, and the longboat eased closer.

Kydd's face broke into an unrestrained grin at the sight of the man with whom he had shared more of life's challenges and rewards than any other. "Nicholas! Should y' wish t' step ashore —"

"Sadly, brother, I cannot."

It was the same Renzi, the cool, sensitive gaze, the strength of character in the deep lines at each side of his mouth, but Kydd sensed something else, something unsettling.

"We are under sailing orders," Renzi said quietly. The ship was preparing for sea; there could be no risk of men straggling and therefore no liberty. "An alarum of sorts. We go to join Jervis, I believe."

There was a stir of interest in the longboat. "An' where's he at, then?" asked Coxall, gunner's mate and generally declared leader of their jaunt ashore — he was an old hand and had been to Gibraltar before.

Renzi stared levelly at the horizon, his remote expression causing Kydd further unease. "It seems that there is some — confusion. I have not heard reliably just where the fleet might be." He turned back to Kydd with a half-smile. "But, then, these are troubling times, my friend, it can mean anything."

A muffled roar inside the dark gundeck took Renzi's attention and he waved apologetically at Kydd before he shouted, "We will meet on our return, dear fellow," then withdrew inboard.

"Rum dos," muttered Coxall, and glared at the duty boat's crew, lazily leaning into their strokes as the boat made its way around the larger mole to the end of the long wall of fortifications. He perked up as they headed toward the shore and a small jetty. "Ragged Staff," he said, his seamed face relaxing into a smile, "where we gets our water afore we goes ter sea."

They clambered out. Like the others Kydd reveled in the solidity of the ground after weeks at sea. The earth was curiously submissive under his feet without the exuberant liveliness of a ship in concord with the sea. Coxall struck out for the large arched gate in the wall and the group followed.

The town quickly engulfed them, and with it the color and sensory richness of the huge sunbaked rock. The passing citizenry were as variegated in appearance as any that Kydd had seen: here was a true crossing place of the world, a nexus for the waves of races, European, Arab, Spanish and others from deeper into this inland sea.

And the smells — in the narrow streets innumerable mules and donkeys passed by laden with their burdens, the pungency of their droppings competing with the offerings of the shops: smoked herring and dried cod, the cool bacon aroma of salted pigs' trotters and the heady fragrance of cinnamon, cloves, roasting coffee, each adding in the hot dustiness to the interweaving reek.

In only a few minutes they had crossed two streets and were up against the steep rise of the flank of the Rock. Coxall didn't spare them, leading them through the massive Southport gate and on a narrow track up and around the scrubby slopes to a building set on an angled rise. A sudden cool downward draft sent Kydd's jacket aflare and his hat skittering in the dust.

"Scud Hill. We gets ter sink a muzzler 'ere first, wi'out we has t' smell the town," Coxall said. It was a pothouse, but not of a kind that Kydd had seen before. Loosely modeled on an English tavern, it was more open balcony than interior darkness, and rather than high-backed benches there were individual tables with cane chairs.

"A shant o' gatter is jus' what'll set me up prime, like," sighed the lean and careful Tippett, carpenter's mate and Coxall's inseparable companion. They eased into chairs, orienting them to look out over the water, then carefully placed their hats beneath. They were just above Rosia Bay, their two ships neatly at anchor within its arms, while farther down there was a fine vista of the length of the town, all cozy within long lines of fortifications.

The ale was not long in coming — this establishment was geared for a fleet in port, and in its absence they were virtually on their own, with only one other table occupied.

"Here's ter us, lads!" Coxall declared, and upended his pewter. It was grateful to the senses on the wide balcony, the wind at this height strong and cool, yet the soft warmth of the winter sun gave a welcome laziness to the late afternoon.

Coins were produced for the next round, but Cockburn held up his hand. "I'll round in m' tackle for now." The old 64-gun *Achilles* had not had one prize to her name in her two years in the Caribbean, while *Seaflower* cutter had been lucky.

Kydd considered how he could see his friend clear to another without it appearing charity, but before he could say anything, Coxall grunted: "Well, damme, only a Spanish cobb ter me name. Seems yer in luck, yer Scotch shicer, can't let 'em keep m' change."

Cockburn's set face held, then loosened to a smile. "Why, thankee, Eli."

Kydd looked comfortably across his tankard over the steep, sunlit slopes toward the landward end of Gibraltar. The town nestled in a narrow line below, stretching about a mile to where it ceased abruptly at the end of the Rock. The rest of the terrain was bare scrub on precipitous sides. "So this is y'r Gibraltar," he said. "Seems t' me just a mile long an' a half straight up."

"Aye, but it's rare val'ble to us — Spanish tried ter take it orf us a dozen years or so back, kept at it fer four years, pounded th' place ter pieces they did," Coxall replied, "but we held on b' makin' this one thunderin' great fortress."

"So while we have the place, no one else can," Cockburn mused. "And we come and go as we please, but denying passage to the enemy. Here's to the flag of old England on the Rock for ever."

A murmur of appreciation as they drank was interrupted by the scraping of a chair and a pleasant-faced but tough-looking seaman came across to join them. "Samuel Jones, yeoman outa *Loyalty* brig."

Tippett motioned at their table, "We're *Achilles* sixty-four, only this day inward-bound fr'm the Caribbee."

"Saw yez. So ye hasn't the word what's been 'n' happened this side o' the ocean all of a sudden, like." At the expectant silence he went on, "As ye knows — yer do? — the Spanish came in wi' the Frogs in October, an' since then . . ."

Kydd nodded. But his eyes strayed to the point where Gibraltar ended so abruptly; there was Spain, the enemy, just a mile or so beyond — and always there.

Relishing his moment, Jones asked, "So where's yer Admiral Jervis an' his fleet, then?"

Coxall started to say something, but Jones cut in, "No, mate, he's at Lisbon, is he — out there." He gestured to the west and the open Atlantic. Leaning forward he pointed in the other direction, into the Mediterranean. "Since December, last month, we had to skin out — can't hold on. So, mates, there ain't a single English man-o'-war as swims in the whole Mediterranee."

Into the grave silence came Coxall's troubled voice. "Yer means Port Mahon, Leghorn, Naples —"

"We left 'em all t' the French, cully. I tell yer, there's no English guns any further in than us."

Kydd stared at the table. Evacuation of the Mediterranean? It was inconceivable! The great trade route opened up to the Orient following the loss of the American colonies — the journeys to the Levant, Egypt and the fabled camel trains to the Red Sea and India, all finished?

"But don't let that worry yez," Jones continued.

"And pray why not?" said Cockburn carefully.

" 'Cos there's worse," Jones said softly. The others held still. "Not more'n a coupla weeks ago, we gets word fr'm the north, the inshore frigates off Brest." He paused. "The French — they're out!" There was a stirring around the table.

"Not yer usual, not *a-tall* — this is big,

forty sail an' more, seventeen o' the line an' transports, as would be carryin' soldiers an' horses an' all."

He sought out their faces, one by one. "It's a right filthy easterly gale, Colpoys out of it somewhere t' sea, nothin' ter stop 'em. Last seen, they hauls their wind fer the north — England, lads . . ."

"They're leaving!" The upstairs maid's excited squeal brought an automatic reproof from Emily, but she hurried nevertheless to the window. White sail blossomed from the largest, which was the *Glorious*, she had found out. The smaller *Achilles*, however, showed no signs of moving and lay quietly to her anchor. Emily frowned at this development. With no children to occupy her days, and a husband who worked long hours, she had thrown herself into the social round of Gibraltar. There was to be an assembly soon, and she had had her hopes of the younger ship's officers — if she could snare a brace, they would serve handsomely to squire the tiresome Elliott sisters.

Then she remembered. It was Letitia who had discovered that in *Achilles* was the man who had famously rescued Lord Stanhope in a thrilling open-boat voyage after a dreadful hurricane. She racked her brain. Yes, Captain Kydd. She would make sure somehow that he was on the guest list.

The next forenoon the new men came aboard, a dismal shuffle in the Mediterranean sun. They had been landed from the stores transport from England, and their trip across wartime Biscay would not have been pleasant.

Kydd, as mate-of-the-watch, took a grubby paper from the well-seasoned warrant officer and signed for them. He told the wide-eyed duty midshipman to take them below on the first stage of their absorption into the ship's company of *Achilles* and watched them stumble down the main-hatch. Despite the stout clothing they had been given in the receiving ship in England, they were a dejected and repellent-looking crew.

The warrant officer showed no inclination to leave, and came to stand beside Kydd. "No row guard, then?"

"Is this Spithead?" Kydd retorted. Any half-awake sailor would see that it was futile to get ashore — the only way out of Gibraltar was in a merchant ship, and they were all under eye not two hundred yards off at the New Mole.

The warrant officer looked at him with a cynical smile. "How long you been outa England?"

"West Indies f'r the last coupla years," Kydd said guardedly.

The man's grunt was dismissive. "Then chalk this in yer log. Times 'r changin', cully, the navy ain't what it was. These 'ere are the best youse are goin' to get, but not a seaman among 'em . . ." He let the words hang. By law the press-gang could only seize men who "used the sea."

He went on. "Ever hear o' yer Lord Mayor's men? No?" He chuckled harshly. "By Act o' Parlyment, every borough has to send in men, what's their quota, like, no choice — so who they goin' to send? Good 'uns or what?" He went to the side and spat into the harbor. "No, o' course. They gets rid o' their low shabs, skulkers 'n' dandy prats. Even bales out th' jail. An' then the navy gets 'em."

There seemed no sense in it. The press-gang, however iniquitous, had provided good hands in the past, even in the Caribbean. Why not now? As if in answer, the man went on, "Press is not bringin' 'em in anymore, we got too many ships wantin' crew." He looked sideways at Kydd, and his face darkened. "But this'n! You'll find —"

Muffled, angry shouts came up from below. The young lieutenant-of-the-watch came forward, frowning at the untoward commotion. "Mr. Kydd, see what the fuss is about, if you please."

Fisticuffs on the gundeck. It was shortly after the noon grog issue, and it was not unknown for men who had somehow got hold of extra drink to run riotous, but unusually this time one of them was Boddy, an able seaman known for his steady reliability out on a yardarm. Kydd did not recognize the other man. Surrounded by sullen sailors, the two were locked in a vicious clinch in the low confines below decks. This was not a simple case of tempers flaring.

"Still!" Kydd roared. The shouts and murmuring died, but the pair continued to grapple, panting in ragged grunts. Kydd himself could not separate them. If a wild blow landed on him, the culprit would face a noose for striking a superior.

A quarter-gunner reached them from aft and, without breaking stride, sliced his fist down between the two. They fell apart, glaring and bloody. The petty officer looked inquiringly at Kydd.

His duty was plain, the pair should be haled to the quarterdeck for punishment,

31

but Kydd felt that his higher duty was to find the cause. "Will, you old haul-bowlings," he said loudly to Boddy, his words carrying to the others, "slinging y' mauley in 'tween decks, it's not like you."

Kydd considered the other man. He had a disquieting habit of inclining his head one way, but sliding his eyes in a different direction; a careful, appraising look so different from the open honesty of a sailor.

"Caught th' prigger firkling me ditty bag," Boddy said thickly. "I'll knock his fuckin' toplights out, the —"

"Clap a stopper on it," Kydd snapped. It was provocation enough. The ditty bag was where seamen hung their ready-use articles on the ship's side, a small bag with a hole halfway up for convenience. There would be nothing of real value in it, so why —

"I didn't know what it was, in truth." The man's careful words were cool, out of place in a man-o'-war.

Boddy recoiled. "Don't try 'n' flam me, yer shoreside shyster," he snarled.

It might be possible — these quota men would know nothing of sea life from their short time in the receiving ship in harbor and the stores transport, and be curious about their new quarters. Either way, Kydd realized, there was going to be a hard beat to windward to absorb the likes of these into the seamanlike ship's company that the *Achilles* had become after her Atlantic passage.

"Stow it," he growled at Boddy. "These grass-combin' buggers have a lot t' learn. Now, ye either lives wi' it or y' bears up f'r the quarterdeck. Yeah?"

Boddy glared for a moment then folded his arms. "Yair, well, he shifts his berth fr'm this mess on any account."

Kydd agreed. It was a seaman's ancient privilege to choose his messmates; he would square it later. There was no need to invoke the formality of ship's discipline for this. He looked meaningfully at the petty officer and returned on deck.

The warrant officer had not left, and after Kydd had reassured the lieutenant-of-the-watch he came across with a knowing swagger. "Jus' makin' the acquaintance of yer Lord Mayor's men, mate?" Kydd glanced at him coldly. "On yer books as volunteers — and that means each one of 'em gets seventy-pound bounty, spend how they likes . . ."

"Seventy pounds!" The pay for a good able seaman was less than a shilling a day — this was four years' pay for a good man. A pressed man got nothing, yet these riffraff . . . Kydd's face tightened. "I'll see y' over the side," he told the warrant officer gruffly.

At noon Kydd was relieved by Cockburn. The bungling political solution to the manning problem was lowering on the spirit. And Gibraltar was apparently just a garrison town, one big fortified rock and that was all. England was in great peril, and he was doing little more than keeping house in an old, well-worn ship at her long-term moorings.

Kydd didn't feel like going ashore in this mood, but to stay on board was not an attractive proposition, given the discontents simmering below. Perhaps he *would* take another walk around town. It was an interesting enough place, all things considered.

Satisfied with his appearance, the blue coat of a master's mate with its big buttons, white breeches and waistcoat with cockaded plain black hat, he joined the group at the gangway waiting for their boat ashore. The first lieutenant came up the main-hatch ladder, but he held his hat at his side, the sign that he was off-duty.

"Are you passing through the town?" he asked Kydd pleasantly.

Kydd touched his hat politely. "Aye, sir."

"Then I'd be much obliged if you could leave these two books at the garrison library," he said, and handed over a small parcel.

Kydd established that the library was situated in Main Street, apparently opposite a convent. It didn't take long to find — Main Street was the central way through the town, and the convent was pointed out to him half-way along its length. To his surprise, it apparently rated a full complement of sentries in ceremonials. There was a giant Union Flag floating haughtily above the building and a sergeant glared at him from the portico. Across the road, as directed, was the garrison library, an unpretentious single building.

It was a quiet morning, and Emily looked around for things to do. On her mind was her planned social event, as always a problem with a never-changing pool of guests. Her brow furrowed at the question of what she would wear. Despite the tropical climate of Gibraltar, she had retained her soft, milky complexion, and at thirty-two, Emily was in the prime of her beauty.

There was a diffident tap on the door. She crossed to her desk to take position and signaled to the diminutive Maltese helper.

It was a navy man; an officer of some kind with an engagingly shy manner that in no way detracted from his good looks. He carried a small parcel.

"Er, can ye tell me, is this th' garrison library, miss?" She didn't recognize him: he must be from the remaining big ship.

"It is," she said primly. A librarian, however amateur, had standards to uphold.

His hat was neatly under his arm, and he proffered the parcel as though it was precious. "The first l'tenant of *Achilles* asked me t' return these books," he said, with a curious mix of sturdy simplicity and a certain nobility of purpose.

"Thank you, it was kind in you to bring them." She paused, taking in the fine figure he made in his sea uniform; probably in his mid-twenties and, from the strength in his features, she guessed he had seen much of the world.

"*Achilles* — from the Caribbean? Then you would know Mr. Kydd — the famous one who rescued Lord Stanhope and sailed so far in a tiny open boat, with his maid in with them as well."

The young man frowned and hesitated, but his dark eyes held a glint of humor.

"Aye, I do — but it was never th' maid, it was Lady Stanhope's travelin' companion." His glossy dark hair was gathered and pulled back in a clubbed pigtail, and couldn't have been more different from the short, powdered wigs of an army officer.

"You may think me awfully forward, but it would greatly oblige if you could introduce me to him," she dared.

With a shy smile, he said, "Yes, miss. Then might I present m'self? Thomas Kydd, master's mate o' the *Achilles*."

Chapter 2

It had been an agreeable day, Kydd decided. Cockburn had joined him later and they had wandered along the busy back streets, sampling exotic fruit and fending off importunate gewgaw sellers. They returned on board and Kydd opted to stay on deck, knowing that Cockburn would want to get out his quill and paper to scratch away, his particular solace.

The evening had turned into night, and Kydd stood at the mizzen shrouds. Yellow lights twinkled in the darkness, faint sounds of the land floated across the water: a donkey's bray, an anonymous regular tap of a hammer, the ceaseless susurration of activity.

Possibly their indefinite stay in Gibraltar would not be wholly unpleasant, he reflected. Then he recalled the dire news of the invasion fleet and that Renzi, in *Glorious,* was on his way to join in a titanic battle for the very life of England, while his own ship was left here as a poor token of English power.

Logically, he knew that helpless worry was of no use to his country, and he tried resolutely to turn his mind to other things. The ship: as soon as they took delivery of a spar, they would resling the cro'jack yard across the mizzenmast, and he would then make his plea for a double cleat truss, for this would conveniently also act as a rolling tackle.

His thoughts returned to the present. Here he was, a master's mate, a warrant officer. It was something he couldn't have dreamed of being in years past; it was the pinnacle of achievement for a common sailor to have a crackling Admiralty warrant in his sea chest. While he wasn't a real officer — *they* held a commission from King George — as a master's mate he was held in real respect aboard. He messed with the midshipmen, it was true, but he was senior to them and could curb their schoolboy antics as he felt inclined. At the same time, he was squarely part of the ship's company — a seaman and a professional. His social horizons were theirs, but he was at the top and owed no one before the mast except the master any deference; he could look forward to long service at this comfortable eminence.

Yet there was one aspect of this existence that was a continuing source of regret. Nicholas Renzi had not only shared his adventurous and perilous sea life, but had opened so much to him that was deep and true, and from him he had learned the habits of reason and principle in many a companionable night watch. He remembered the passionate discussions in the South Seas over the precepts of Rousseau, the intensity of Renzi's convictions informed by Locke and Diderot — all worthy of an enlightened mind. And Renzi's effortless acquaintance with the beauty and art of words, which touched a part of the soul that nothing else could.

But Renzi was now also a master's mate; even a sail-of-the-line would only have one or two. This made it unlikely that they would ever again serve together.

His eyes cast down to the dark water. At least up to now they had been on the same station and could occasionally visit. They had divided their stock of books in Barbados, now long since read, but to exchange them he must wait until they met again . . .

Moody and depressed, he was on the point of going below when he thought of the garrison library. Perhaps the kind lady in charge would understand and allow him a volume or two; then he would apply himself and later astonish Renzi with a morsel of philosophy, or an arcane and wonderfully curious piece of natural science. He brightened.

Emily was cross with herself. Mr. Kydd had come to her, and she had ended up tongue-tied, like a silly girl, letting him walk away. And this morning she would have to face the odious Mr. Goldstein again to inform him that the committee did not see fit in this instance to contravene their inviolable rule that tradesmen, however eminent, were not eligible to join the library.

She fussed a row of learned journals into line, then heard a diffident knock. Brushing aside the Maltese helper, she strode rapidly to the door and opened it with a sweet smile. "Why, Mr. Kydd!" He was just as she recalled, the same shy smile. Emily inclined her head gracefully: she would not be discommoded this time.

"Er, I was wonderin', miss, if there's any chance I might borrow a book 'r two?"

His eyes were so open and guileless — if he had seen much, it wasn't in salons or drawing rooms. "Mr. Kydd," she said coolly, "this library was created after the Great Siege by the officers of the garrison who did not want to endure such another without they had food for the intellect. This is their library by contribution."

Kydd's face fell. Emily suppressed a smile: he was so adorably transparent.

"Naval officers have nobly contributed as they can," she continued, "and the committee have therefore declared them equally eligible for borrowing privileges." She picked up a book and pretended to scrutinize its pages.

Kydd didn't respond, and when she looked up, she was surprised to see rueful resignation. "Then I'm brought up wi' a round turn — I'm a master's mate only." At her puzzled look, he added, "A warrant officer."

Her face cleared. "We don't care what kind of officer you are, Mr. Kydd. You may certainly join our library."

Kydd's smile returned and Emily responded warmly. "Now, let me see, what do we have that will interest you . . ."

It was a nice problem: there were officers who earnestly sought educational tomes, others who reserved their enthusiasm for accounts of the wilder excesses of the fall of Rome, yet more who would relentlessly devour anything on offer. Kydd did not seem to fit any of these.

"May I suggest the Gabinetti, *Customs and Cultural History of the Iberians*? It might prove interesting for someone come to this part of the world."

Kydd hesitated. "Er, I was thinkin' more ye might have one b' Mr. Hume — I have a hankering t' know more about what he says on causality." Mistaking her look, he hurried to add, "Y' see, I have a frien' who is more in th' metaphysical line, an' will much want t' dispute empiricism wi' me," he finished lamely.

"Oh," Emily said. "We don't get much call for that kind of thing, Mr. Kydd, but I'll do what I can." There was a dark old leather volume she remembered behind the desk by Hume, but she hadn't the faintest idea what it contained.

"Ah, here you are," she said brightly, "David Hume, *An Enquiry Concerning Human Understanding*."

Kydd took the little book and leafed through it reverently. His hands were very strong, she noticed. "This will do, thank ye, miss," he said.

"Splendid!" Emily said, with relief. "And it's Mrs. Emily Mulvany," she added.

Kydd gravely acknowledged her, his old-fashioned courtesies charming. At the door he turned to bid her farewell. "Oh, Mr. Kydd, I may have omitted to let you know, we are holding an assembly and you are to be invited, I believe," she said, as off-handedly as she could manage. "I am sure you will find it congenial after your long voyaging." It would be a fine thing to display such a prize — and so interesting a man. Emily's thoughts were bubbling. Gibraltar was small and unchanging and she'd never met someone like Mr. Kydd before. Imagine — discussing philosophy with his friend under the stars, yet ready at a moment's notice to engage the enemy in some dreadful battle. And his great feat in rescuing the diplomat in a tiny boat on the open sea. He'd certainly led a much more exciting and romantic life than a soldier. She watched him depart. A man's man, he was probably restless, hemmed in by the daily round of the Rock. It would be an interesting challenge to keep boredom at bay for him . . .

The invitation came the following morning, a plainly worded card, beautifully penned in a feminine hand and addressed to "Mr. Kydd, on board HMS *Achilles*." It was the first social invitation he had ever had, and he fingered the expensive board with both pleasure and surprise. Mrs. Mulvany was obviously of the quality and he'd thought that she was just being polite when she mentioned the assembly.

An assembly, he knew from a single previous experience in Guildford, was a fairly informal social gathering — but then he remembered that it involved dancing . . .

"M' friend," he said to Cockburn, after showing him the invitation, "do ye help me, I must refuse. I'm no taut hand at th' dancing, an' I'll shame the ship. C'n ye give me some rousin' good reason I cannot attend, or —"

"Thomas, you *must* attend," Cockburn said, his face shadowed at this familiar token of polite society he was most unlikely to see himself. "An absence would bring dishonor on both you and the service!"

"But I can't dance, I never learned," Kydd said, in anguish. He would far rather face an enemy broadside than make a fool of himself before tittering ladies.

"Ah." Cockburn had grown up with the attentions of a dancing master and had no apprehension himself of the dance floor; in fact, he rather enjoyed the decorous interplay of femininity on gentlemanly ardor.

"My folks were never much in th' social line," Kydd said forlornly.

"Then I shall be your teacher!" Cockburn declared impulsively.

"Wha— No!" Kydd blurted. A moment's fantasy flashed by of Emily's slim figure bobbing in delight at his dancing skills, her attractive ringlets springing out in the mad whirl, a blush on her cheeks as . . . "Could ye? I don't —"

"Of course. It's, er, it's rather like your redcoats doing their drill, and they learn it easy enough."

The dog-watch saw them both repair down to the dim cockpit on the orlop, the area outside the surgeon's cabin, the purser's and the midshipman's berth.

Cockburn looked around warily, then addressed himself to Kydd. "In the matter of a cotillion, it is of the first importance to place the feet so . . ." he said, as he gracefully adopted the pose. Kydd did so, looking down doubtfully. "You look at the lady, not your feet — is she not to your liking, sir?"

Kydd's head lifted, and he strained to be graceful. A muffled splutter came from the shadows and he wheeled around. "Clap a stopper on y'r cacklin', damn y'r whistle," he snarled, "or ye'll be spending y'r dog-watches in the tops!" A midshipman slunk back into the shadows.

Cockburn persevered. The gloom and thick odor of the orlop did nothing to convey a ballroom atmosphere, and there were ringbolts on the deck, here above the main hold. "The measure is stepped like this — one, two, three and a stand, and a one, two, three and a four . . ."

The surgeon's cabin door opened noise-lessly, and Cockburn was aware of muffled footfalls from forward, an appreciative audience gathering in the shadows. "No, Tom, you've forgotten the 'four' again," he said, with some control, for Kydd had tripped and sent him staggering. His pupil had a memory as short as . . . "It won't answer, not at all," he said to the crestfallen Kydd. He muttered under his breath, then had an idea. "Please to pay attention — I will now make this clear enough for the meanest intelligence." Kydd looked at him resentfully.

"Er, the first is to make sail, then we haul our wind to the starb'd tack, and wear about before we drops anchor to boxhaul around, like this." The relief on Kydd's

47

face was plain. "Then we tack about twice against the sun and heave to for a space, let the lady get clear of our hawse, and we are under way again, this time to larb'd . . ."

"Shouldn't be more'n a half hour," the lieutenant said, through his towel, finishing his personal preparations for a rendezvous ashore. "Lobsterbacks like marchin' around, up 'n' down, that sort of thing, then they flog the poor wight an' it's back to barracks."

"Aye, sir," Kydd said, without enthusiasm. He had agreed to take the lieutenant's place in an army punishment parade to represent *Achilles* as a major ship in the port.

"Mos' grateful, Mr. Kydd. As long as you're at the Alameda by five bells . . ."

Kydd clapped on a black cockaded hat, and settled a cross-belt with its distinctive anchor shoulder plate over his white waistcoat. The rather worn spadroon sword he had borrowed from Cockburn was awkward in the scabbard; it was so much longer and daintier than a sturdy cutlass. A glance reassured him that his shoes were well shined — the gunroom servant needed coaxing of a sort but was a knowing old marine.

With two marines as escort stepping out smartly ahead, Kydd found his way to the Alameda, and halted the marines.

The Alameda was a remarkably large parade ground that would not be out of place in the bigger army establishments in England. It was alive with ranks of marching soldiers, hoarse screams sending them back and forth. Splendidly kitted sergeant majors glared down the dressing of the lines and bawled in outrage at the hapless redcoats. The discordant blare of trumpets and the clash and stamp of drill added to the cacophony, and from the edge of the arena Kydd watched in wonder for what he should do.

A sashed, ramrod-stiff figure with a tall shako detached himself from the mêlée and marched up, coming to a crashing halt before Kydd. His eyes flickered at Kydd's polite doffing of his hat and strayed to the marines motionless behind him.

"Sah! With me. Sah!" He wheeled about abruptly and marched energetically across to a ragged square of men across the parade; Kydd saw with relief that a few were in navy rig.

"An' what happens next?" Kydd asked a weathered marine lieutenant. The other navy representatives nodded cautiously or ignored him in accordance with rank.

The man's bored eyes slid over to him. "They brings out the prisoner, the town major rants at 'im, trices him up t' the whipping post, lays on the lashes, an' we goes home." The eyes slid back to the front in a practiced glassy stare.

Kydd saw the whipping post set out from the wall they were facing, an unremarkable thick pole with a small platform. He had grown inured to the display of physical punishment at sea, seeing the need for it without a better solution, but it always caused him regret. He hoped this would not take long.

The parade sorted itself into a hollow square behind them. Within minutes a small column of men appeared from the farther side of the parade ground. They were accompanied by a drummer with muffled drum, the slow *ta-rrum, ta-rrum* of the "Rogue's March" hanging heavy on the air.

The prisoner was a blank-faced, scrawny soldier without his shako. The column halted and turned to face the post. From the opposite corner of the parade ground, a small party appeared, led by a short, florid officer strutting along bolt upright.

"Actin' town major," murmured the marine.

The peppery army officer looked about testily, ignoring the prisoner. Slapping his gloves against his side irritably, he stepped over to the assembled representatives. "Fine day, ge'men," he rasped, his flinty eyes merciless. "Kind in ye to come."

The eyes settled on Kydd, and he approached to speak. "Don' recollect I've made the acquaintance?" The tautness of his bearing had a dangerous edge.

"Thomas Kydd, master's mate o' *Achilles*, sir."

The eyes appraised him for a moment, then unexpectedly the man smiled. "Glad t' see your ship here, Mr. Kydd — uncertain times, what?" Before Kydd could speak, he had stalked off.

The essence of the business was much as the marine had said. The town major tore at the prisoner's dignity with practiced savagery, the hard roar clearly meant for the parade as a whole. The offense was the breaking into of an army storeroom while drunk.

Stepping aside contemptuously, he ordered the anonymous brawny soldier with the lash to do his work. It was a lengthy and pitiful spectacle — the army had dif-

51

ferent ideas of punishment and, although delivered with a lash that was lighter-looking than a navy cat-o'-nine-tails the blows went on and on, thirty, forty and finally fifty.

At the conclusion, in a flurry of salutes, the attendant officers were dismissed. Kydd avoided the sight of the wretched victim still tied to the whipping post and declined the invitation to a noonday snifter. He wanted to get back aboard to sanity.

"Ah, you there — Jack Tar ahoy, is it?" A resplendent sergeant major, tall and with four golden stripes, was heading rapidly toward him. "Me boy!" the soldier bawled. He came closer, his smile wide. "A long time!"

Soldiers leaving the parade ground went respectfully around them while Kydd stared and tried to remember the man.

"Why, it's Sar'nt Hotham, if m' memory serves!" The desperate times on Guadeloupe came back vividly.

"Not any more, it ain't," Hotham boomed, the effortless authority of his voice still the same. "Color Sar' Major Hotham will do fer you, m'lad." His happy satisfaction turned to curiosity. "An' what're you now, then?"

"Master's mate Tom Kydd, it is now."

His hand went out and was strongly gripped. "Thought you wuz dead, Tom," Hotham said, more quietly.

"No, got t' the other fort on the west, got taken off b' *Trajan*," he said.

He hesitated, and Hotham picked up on it. "I'd admire ter have yer as me guest in the barracks fer a drink or so. Then we c'n take a look at th' fortress, if yez got the time."

Line wall and bastions, counterguard and casemates, innumerable heavy gun positions and watchful sentries everywhere. Gibraltar was nothing if not a mighty fortress. The garrison even had its barracks, Town Range, in the center of the town, which was itself behind massive walls and ramparts.

"We gets a ride on th' ration wagon, you'll see somethin' 'll make ye stare." Hotham flagged down the small cart pulled by mules. They sat together on the back, legs dangling, and the cart wound slowly up a steep zigzag track.

The view rapidly expanded, an immense panorama of misty coast, dusty plains and sea. Kydd was fascinated.

The cart stopped at a gate, which was

neatly set around a large hole in the side of the Rock. Hotham dropped to the ground briskly and, nodding to the curious sentry, motioned Kydd inside.

Coolness, a slight damp and the peculiar odor of unmoving air on old stone enfolded him as they strode into the bowels of the Rock of Gibraltar.

"Watch yer bonce," Hotham warned, his own tall frame stooped, but Kydd was used to the low deckhead of a man-o'-war. The tunnel drove on, then widened, and suddenly to the left there was a gallery with bay after bay, and in each a twenty-four-pounder gun facing out of an aperture in the rock. The gallery was bright with daylight, and a cheerful breeze played inward.

"See 'ere, cully," said Hotham, edging toward the opening on one side of the first gun. Kydd stared out at a dizzying height from the sheer face of the north aspect of the Rock. Far below was a flat plain that issued from the base, curving around until some miles farther on it dissolved into mainland.

"Spain, cully!" Hotham declared, waving outward.

"Where?" These guns could fire far, but not to the hills.

Hotham grinned. "There!" He pointed

directly down to the flat plain. No-man's-land, and only some half a mile away. So close — an enemy in arms against Britain, continuously ready to fall upon them if there was the slightest chance. Kydd tried to make out movement, figures on the hostile side of the lines, but to his disappointment could not.

"We got a hunnerd 'n' forty like this'n," Hotham said, patting the twenty-four-pounder, "an' thirty-twos, coehorns, even our own rock mortars. Nothin' ter fear, really, we ain't." Kydd wondered what it must be like to look up at the sheer heights of the Rock, knowing the firepower that could be brought down on any with the temerity to test the impregnability of Gibraltar.

Kydd was no more than halfway returned to his ship when he heard the first gun, a low *crump*, from somewhere above him. He craned to look, scanning the skyline, but there was only dissipating smoke. Suddenly, below him, there came the heavier thud of an answering gun.

Kydd hurried on. Within minutes there were signs of agitation, shopkeepers emerging to look about nervously, water carriers halting their donkeys in confusion.

A young seaman acknowledged Kydd, just as the measured thump of a minute gun started from somewhere in the harbor. Guns opened up in other parts of the Rock and the sudden soaring of a rocket from below was quickly followed by others.

Achilles! It could be nothing less than an urgent general recall. Kydd *had* to make it back: there was peril abroad and his deepest instincts were with his ship. At the Ragged Staff gate there was a scrimmage for boats; Kydd and others quickly packed into the launch. Bedlam erupted all along the Rock — guns, church bells, shouting and confusion.

"What's th' rout, then?" one sailor demanded.

"Spanish. Sighted t' the east, mebbe a dozen or more sail-o'-the-line, comin' on like good 'uns an' straight for us!"

The Spanish Mediterranean battle fleet was usually skulking far away in Cartagena, but they had heard of the English evacuation of the Mediterranean and knew Gibraltar was at the moment defended only by an old 64, a handful of unrated ships and local craft. Were they now going to take revenge for nearly a century of humiliation — and finally liberate the Rock?

Achilles was frantic with activity. She couldn't go to quarters until sail had been bent to the yards as she was still in refit. But a single ship? The enemy fleet would now be in sight from the point, a sinister straggling of tiny sail spreading over half of the eastern horizon.

Kydd's battle quarters was on the main gundeck, but for now he was at the fore-mast, frantically driving men to send up the long sausages of sails to seamen on the yard. The new hands, landmen all, were pale and frightened at the prospect of battle and needed hard pressing. Kydd grew hoarse with goading.

"*Haaands* to unmoor ship!"

The boatswain's mates pealed out their calls, but Kydd knew they had two anchors out, which would take time to buoy and slip — it was a race against time.

From his station at the catheads, Kydd kept an eye on the point. The eastern side of Gibraltar was sheer and inaccessible, and any invading force must come around to this side, sweeping aside with concentrated cannon fire the single ship of significance before beginning their landing.

First one or two, then a dismaying cloud of heavy men-o'-war appeared from beyond the point, keeping well out of range, however, of the guns perched high up on the Rock. Kydd's heart beat fast. The last cable buoy splashed into the water. They were now free to sail out to meet the enemy.

The ship cast to larboard and, under all plain sail, stood out from the harbor. The urgent thundering of the drum to quarters sounded, and Kydd snatched a last look at their opponents, then closed up on the main deck, briefly regretting having to face the battle in his best rig. Gun crews with unskilled landmen, shot not brought up to the garlands from the lockers, gunners' party sewing cartridges like madmen. It was the worst conceivable timing for a Spanish descent, with Admiral Jervis and the fleet far in the north, but Kydd accepted that the sacrifice of their ship had to be made. They could not stand aside meekly and allow Gibraltar to fall.

"They've hauled their wind!" the voice of the forward midshipman shrilled, withdrawing from a gunport. "Headin' north!"

Kydd brushed a gun crew aside and peered out. The Spanish had not completed the turn into the Bay of Gibraltar. They had simply braced up and headed north, past — and away. After the urgent recall to his ship, Kydd felt a sense of frustration. But then the lieutenant of the gundeck, staring hard at the enemy ships, said coldly, "They're making for Cadiz. Together they will outnumber even Jervis, heaven help us!"

The cro'jack was got up into the mizzen very satisfactorily. Kydd's party in the tops took care of the chain sling and, his suggestion being adopted, additional cleats were secured out on the yard through which the truss pendants could be led to their own thimbles. By this neat solution, the wicked swing of the cro'jack in any kind of beam sea would be effectively damped without the need for rolling tackles from the deck.

Idly he watched his seamen passing the rose lashing, which fixed in place the cushioning dolphin underneath the spar, and relished a sense of satisfaction in a job well done. He had personal experience enough of fine seamanship as a life-preserving imperative never to take the short path.

Cockburn dismissed the deck party and waited for Kydd to descend the shrouds. "Tell me, in what character will you be attending your assembly?"

Taken aback, Kydd hesitated. "I should —"

"You will have noticed 'masquerade' on the invitation, of course."

"But . . ." Kydd had no idea of the oddities of polite society, and could only wait for the elucidation that Cockburn was clearly looking to provide.

"This means that your assembly is in the nature of a fancy dress, I fear."

"I — I —" Kydd struggled for words.

Four days later, at three bells in the first dog-watch, Mr. Kydd and Mr. Cockburn were logged as stepping ashore. What was not noted was the capacious seabag carried by Mr. Kydd, and the haste with which they hurried to a small taphouse in King's Yard Lane.

Minutes after, at a side entrance, the astonishing sight of King Neptune emerged furtively, holding his crown and trident self-consciously, but looking a striking picture with his muscular torso exposed.

"Best o' luck!" Cockburn chuckled, Kydd's seagoing rig safely in the bag.

"Be damn'd!" Kydd growled, but an impish delight was building in him.

The first measures of the dance were as fearsome a trial as bringing in topsails under the eye of the admiral, but the same skills that made Kydd a fine seaman out on a yard came to his rescue and he stepped out the rest of the dance with increasing confidence.

His partners, an improbable wood nymph, a well-nourished Britannia, a shy young swan and a stout milkmaid, all enjoyed dancing with Neptune. The candlelight did well for Kydd's sea-darkened complexion, and he attracted many thoughtful female glances.

He dared a look around the long room: great chandeliers cast a golden light that picked out the sparkles of ladies' jewelry and gentlemen's quizzing glasses. The smell of candles and perspiration was swamped in a generous cloud of fragrances, but there was an unmistakable air of living for the moment. With a stab, Kydd remembered the grave threats out in the wider world that might bring all of this to an end.

Uneasily aware that he could be thought a trespasser socially if the gentlemen around him knew his status, he held firmly to the fact that he had been personally invited. And in the happy chatter around him he could perceive that there were others who in England's polite society could not expect an invitation to such an evening as this. How kind of Emily to invite him. She was a striking woman: tall, self-possessed, she had the disturbing trick of letting her voice change to a low purr in the intimacy of a personal conversation.

Kydd smiled and waved at a laughing mermaid sweeping by.

Emily, thinly disguised as a Spanish temptress, approached him at refreshments. "Do I see you enjoying yourself, Mr. Kydd?" she asked lightly, flourishing a large, colorful fan.

"Aye, Mrs. Mulvany," Kydd said, although his oakum beard was itching and his cardboard crown drooping in the heat.

"Do call me Emily," she protested. "May I, er . . ."

"Thomas it is, er, Emily," Kydd said. "Your husband?"

"Sadly, he cannot be with us tonight. A sweetmeat, Thomas?"

He had become aware that he was the center of attention for several other ladies and turned to address them, but a disturbance at the entrance to the room resolved into the arrival of an imperious young officer, his tall hat tucked under his arm.

The hubbub went on, so he bent impatiently to the resting string quartet, who obliged by sounding a single strident chord. The talking died in puzzlement, and the officer strode to the center of the room. "News!" he declared dramatically. An animated murmuring spread among the guests. "The descent on England . . ." He waited for silence; the last news anyone had had was of the French fleet's sudden sally past Pellew's frigates toward England; all else was speculation. ". . . has been scattered, destroyed!"

Excited chatter burst out and Kydd exclaimed. The soldier turned to face him. "They didn't attempt England — Irish traitors ready to rebel welcomed 'em over there, but it was a gale o' wind from the north, and the troops couldn't land." He took a hurried breath. "Our fleet missed 'em, but the storm sent 'em all ahoo and they're back where they came from, the knaves."

"Ye mean —"

"No invasion, no great battle." The officer flashed a boyish grin at Kydd, bowed to the ladies and left.

In the babble of agitated comment that broke out, Emily took Kydd's arm. "This is Mr. Kydd, and he's mate of the *Achilles*!" she announced loudly. "He shall explain it all to us."

It would be of no use to protest the subtleties of naval rank and rating at this time. A rapidly gathering group of dryads, harlequins and nondescripts were converging on him wanting reassurance. But what *were* the full circumstances? Did "destroyed" mean the French were lost in the weather? "Returning where they came from" implied the invasion fleet was still intact and therefore a mortal danger. What if —

"Ye'll understand a storm o' wind at sea can't be commanded b' any admiral. If it blows, y' can't just —"

"A gale from the north?" The willowy faun had perfect white teeth and a remarkably well-turned ankle.

"Why, this is y'r worst news if you were a Frenchy," Kydd began, to general interest, "a foul wind f'r Ireland, right in y'r teeth —"

"What's it like in a storm, Mr. Kydd? Do tell!" The young swan, fetchingly accented in blue, simpered under her eyelashes. Kydd blushed at the attentions from the attractive young women all around him. Emily frowned and stood closer, her hand still on his arm. Kydd felt it grip him hard.

Instinctively, Kydd knew he had been a success. Cockburn had pressed for details, and he had obliged, entertained by his friend's visible envy. He knew, however, that if Renzi had attended, his natural patrician urbanity would have assured him a place at the center of things. Almost guiltily, Kydd found himself grateful he had not been there.

His thoughts turned to Renzi's situation. He had heard that Admiral Jervis and his fleet were in the Tagus, Lisbon, encouraging the Portuguese, but they were the only force in any way able to meet the French, should they put to sea again. What would happen if both the French and the Spanish should simultaneously emerge and combine did not bear thinking about. And Nicholas was there . . .

In *Achilles*, life settled to a dull routine. Most seamen had seen their means dissipated quickly. As the days turned into weeks their prospects for diversion were not large, and a disquieting pattern asserted itself. Cheap wine and quarrels with soldiers ashore led to meaningless fights in the frustration of endless inaction. Aboard, "hands to witness punishment" was now almost a daily feature, and the atmosphere in the mess decks was turning ugly. The officers found things to do ashore and were seldom in their cabins at night.

Kydd was restless, too, but he found

himself thinking more and more of Emily. Was he imagining it, or did she like him? He reviewed his attendance at the assembly — he was certain he had not let her down, and he was positive she had spent more time with him than with any other; in a glow he remembered her alabaster complexion, the startling blue-green eyes and delicate hands — Emily really was an attractive woman. She hadn't mentioned her husband much . . . Did that mean —

His eyes snapped into focus. The first lieutenant was coming aboard and looking at him curiously as he mounted the brow to the quarterdeck. Kydd touched his hat.

"Ah, Mr. Kydd, I'm desired to give you this." The officer fumbled inside his waistcoat and drew out an envelope, which he passed across, watching for reaction. It was in a hand Kydd recognized. He took it, and placed it carefully inside his jacket without comment.

In the absent master's sea cabin aft Kydd pulled out his letter and hurriedly broke the wafer.

Dear Thomas,

My dear friend Letitia and I usually spend an enjoyable day on Thursdays sketching at Europa Point. Letitia

66

thought that perhaps you might like to join us one time, should you feel so inclined. The prospects to be had of Africa and Europe together do entrance and would exercise the skill of a Girtin or Cozens but we will have such enormous fun.

If this appeals, would you signify to the above address at your convenience. . . .

Kydd let out his breath. What could he read into this? With increasing elation he decided to consult with Cockburn as to the correct routine at a sketching party.

Never having ridden a donkey before, Kydd straddled the beast nervously; its round belly and knobbly spine felt utterly strange. Fortunately its gray ears flicked nonchalantly back and forth without resentment at his gawky mounting, and he perched on its back, feet nearly touching the ground. Feeling a fool, Kydd smiled tentatively at Emily.

"Well, then!" she responded, and tapped her donkey with a polished rattan. The little party wound off southward: Letitia, Emily, Kydd and a weatherbeaten old Moor leading a donkey piled with easels and paraphernalia.

"So good of you to come," Emily said. She was riding sidesaddle, swaying in time with the clopping of the animal's hooves.

"My pleasure, er, Emily." He was aware of Letitia's covert gaze on him; she was a studious, quiet soul without much conversation — might that be due to his presence?

Within half a mile they had left behind the flank of the Rock and emerged onto the flat area at its tip, which Kydd knew, from the navigation charts, was Europa Point, and which he had fixed by bearing as they had approached from seaward.

They made their way to the rocky end of the land where there was a convenient flat ramp, and dismounted, Kydd's rump sore and aching. The ladies in their comfortable white exclaimed at the scene. At their feet, stretching to an immensity, was the deep blue of the sea, but straight ahead in the distance was the purple and gray-blue bulk of a mountain at the side of the spreading width of another coast. "Africa!" announced Emily, with a dramatic flourish.

The Straits of Gibraltar. To the left was the Mediterranean, and the primordial birthplace of civilizations, on the other side was the Atlantic Ocean and the pathway to the rest of the world. Kydd glanced to his right, at the nearby coastline angling away into the distance in a series of bays and headlands. "Spain — Algeciras an' Tarifa," he offered.

Emily turned briefly to check on the silent Arab, patiently spacing out three easels to face the scene, then came to stand next to Kydd, shading her eyes to look over the glittering sea. "And the mountain on the other side," she said softly, "is Jebel Musa in Morocco, which in ancient times they thought was the other Pillar of Hercules." She looked up at him, almost searchingly. "The end of the known world."

Kydd felt an awkwardness, an almost adolescent clumsiness at her closeness, then she moved away to the easels. She sat at the middle one, delicately perched on the three-legged portable stool, making a business of unpacking her kit. "Have you brought anything with you, Thomas?" she asked, in a brisk, practical manner.

"My silver-lead pencil in course," Kydd said, with only a twinge of guilt that it was actually Cockburn's treasured possession, "and a quantity of y'r common run o' Cumberlands." The graphite from that county provided the whole world with fine black-lead pencils.

Emily had out a curious tray of colors, which she fastened to the easel. "I have favored cake water-colors," she said, sounding to Kydd's ears suspiciously professional, "since I saw what Captain Cook's artist did with those breathtaking views of Otaheite." She poured water into a small well, and slung a selection of well-used brushes in a quiver to one side of the easel. She adjusted her wide-brimmed sun hat and addressed her paper with purpose.

Kydd had a sketchbook, unused, that he had acquired from a young midshipman in exchange for the loan of two clean white stockings. He set it up on the easel and selected a Cumberland; he would do the fine work with the silver pencil. Aware of Letitia's furtive glances, he sized the view.

It was not difficult — he had executed innumerable sea perspectives for the master of *Artemis* in the South Seas for inclusion on the margins of sea charts and knew the discipline of exactitude in representation.

With a light breeze and the occasional sound of gulls, it was pleasant work, and their surroundings were conducive to artistic expression. Kydd had soon finished the African coast, and began on the irregular Spanish landscape. This demanded care, for their height-of-eye at this elevation could cunningly deceive, turning square perspectives into slants.

"Oh, my goodness! You are good, Thomas! Look at this, Letitia — he has a very fine hand." He had not heard her approach, and felt the heat of a blush at her words. She bent to admire his work, her femininity briefly enclosing him, then turned to him without drawing away. "You will think my piece so amateur." She giggled.

Taking his cue, Kydd rose and sauntered across to her easel, trying to look at ease. The watercolor was bold, using clear tints not perhaps justified by the hazy wash of sun over far objects, but had a vibrancy that he had not the experience to identify. But the coastlines were sadly out of proportion, the vertical dimension, as was always the way with beginners to a seascape, greatly exaggerated.

"It's — it's wonderful," he found himself saying. Behind him, Emily stifled a giggle. Kydd couldn't think what else to say and stared woodenly ahead.

"I say — I have a most marvelous idea!" He swung around at the sudden energy in her voice. "We shall combine our talents —

you have the strong structure, I shall add color — and together we will produce a masterpiece." She didn't wait for a reply, but ran over to his easel and abstracted his drawing, brought it back and clipped it over her own.

"There! Now we shall see!" Emily selected a broad brush and mixed a quantity of pale blue from the squares of color in the ingenious wooden box. She soon had a color wash in place, and set to with finer brushes on his coasts. Her cunning use of ocher and light purple had his pencil hatching underneath take on a sinister, distant quality, which undeniably brought a dramatic quality to the original.

Engrossed, she persevered at the fine work, her dainty hands perfect for the task. Kydd cast a glance at Letitia, still at her picture; their eyes met, but there was no answering smile.

At last, Emily leaned back and gazed critically at the result. "There!" she said, and stared at it, motionless, for a space. She turned and looked up at Kydd with large eyes and said seriously, "It's really very good, is it not, Thomas? We make quite a pair, I believe."

Kydd felt heat rising, but before he could speak, Emily had snapped shut the box and stood. "I think we have earned our picnic, don't you?"

"God blast ye, Mr. Kydd, what d'you think you're about? You've not overhauled y'r clewlines." The master was choleric. The times for the topsail setting evolution were sadly delayed by Kydd's failure to see that the clewlines were loosened at his mizzenmast at the same rate as the sheets were hauled in.

It seemed everyone was in a state of enervation. Attempts to stir the ship's company to life with harbor exercises were met with sullen lethargy. The *Achilles* of the Caribbean was becoming a fading memory, the cruises to sweep the seas of the enemy, the landings to wrest yet another rich island from the French all in the past. Below, mess-decks were aligning themselves between the real seamen and the unfortunates of the quota.

Kydd could feel the resentment — and the broken-down pride. To be left to rot in port was hard for a good seaman to take, especially when England was menaced by as great a danger as she had ever been.

Evening drew in and, with it, more tiresome carping in the gunroom and petty quarreling on the lower deck. Kydd made up his mind to take a turn along the streets of Gibraltar to get away.

It was impossible to avoid the wine shops at the lower levels of the town, and Kydd pushed past hurriedly, but at one angry shouts climaxed with the ejection of a thickset seaman, who skidded angrily in the dust then staggered to his feet. It was a common sight and Kydd moved to go around the spectacle — but something about the build of the man made him hesitate.

It was Crow — Isaac Crow of the *Artemis*, the hard and fearless captain of the maintop who had been so much a part of Kydd's past — become a wine-soaked travesty of his former self. Kydd steadied him and leaned him against a wall. "Isaac, where —"

"What — well, if it ain't me ol' shipma' Tom Kydd!" Crow chortled. His clothes were musty and ragged, probably all he had left after selling the rest for cheap drink, Kydd guessed.

His expression changed. In an instant his overly cheery features grew pinched, suspicious. "A master's mate, our Tom Kydd, doin' well fer 'isself. Still know yer frien's, then?" He pushed away Kydd's steadying hand and drew himself up. "Th' blackstrap they sells 'ere is worse'n goat's piss."

"What ship, Isaac?"

Crow looked at him for a moment. "*Weazle* brig-o'-war." It was an unrated minor warship, in Gibraltar for lengthy repair. "Gunner's mate, but broke fer fightin' out o' turn."

So now he was a common seaman, disrated no doubt for a frustrated flaring on the mess-decks while his ship was interminably delayed.

Crow stared at Kydd, his face hardening into contempt. "It's gone ter rats — the whole fuckin' navy's gone t' rats. Shite off th' streets is gettin' seventy pound ter be a sailor, while we gets the same less'n a shillin' a day the buggers got back in King Charles's day. What sort o' life is it ter offer a younker t' go to sea?"

There was no answer to that, or to the unspoken loathing of professional seamen with pride in themselves having to share a mess with the kind of men Kydd had seen. "Isaac, mate, y' knows that a ship o' war can't be sailed b' the likes o' those shabs. It takes real seamen — like us!" Kydd felt the rise of anger. "They'll always need us, an' just when are they going t' wake up to it?"

Crow turned on him slowly. "Yer messin' aft wi' the grunters — why should yer worry yerself about us foremast jacks?" He held Kydd with his hard black eyes, then swayed back into the pothouse.

Kydd was taken aback by his words. He wandered for a time, then made his way back aboard before evening gun. Cockburn looked at him curiously, but Kydd did not feel like confiding in him. His origin was as a volunteer and midshipman and presumably, in the fullness of time, he would attract interest and gain a commission as an officer; he had never slung his hammock with the men, and could not be expected to know their true worth and particular strengths. It was something that he would give much to reflect on with Renzi. He could bring things to order in fine style.

Brought on deck by a general rush, Kydd saw from out of the early-morning haze the 38-gun frigate *La Minerve* sailing into the anchorage.

Even the arrival of a single frigate was a noteworthy event, and there were few in *Achilles* who weren't on deck and interested in the smart ship coming to anchor. As she glided in, sharp eyes picked up a most unusual state of affairs: this frigate was wearing the swallowtail broad pennant of a commodore, Royal Navy, in place of the usual sinuous length of a commissioning pennant, placing her notionally senior to *Achilles*.

The first lieutenant's telescope was steadily trained on the frigate's quarterdeck. "I see him — Commodore Nelson! A firebrand if ever I heard of one."

Another lieutenant gave a bleak smile. "I know him — cares only to add to his reputation at the cannon's mouth whatever the cost to others, a vain soul, very vain."

The master's stern face relaxed slightly as he murmured, "Aye, but he cares f'r his men as few does."

The frigate's anchor splashed down and the vessel glided to a stop close enough for them to see every detail aboard, the sails vanishing from the yards in moments, the disciplined rush to each point of activity. The sharp orders and crisp flourishes of the boatswain's calls carried over the water. Even as the admiral's barge pulled strongly shoreward, aglitter with gold and blue in the sternsheets, the launch and cutter were not far behind.

"Seems in an almighty pelt." Cockburn grinned. It was in stark contrast to their own indolence. Recently Kydd had noticed the first green shimmer of weed below the waterline of *Achilles* also appearing on the anchor cable. But that didn't concern him today: Emily had offered to show him the top of the Rock.

It was donkeys again, but this time the party consisted only of Emily, Kydd and the quiet but watchful Letitia. They wound up a long path set at an incline to the face of the Rock. Emily kept up a prattle about the view and the history, all of which enabled Kydd to take his fill of her looks without pretense.

From the top, a rocky spine and smooth parts, the view was every bit as breathtaking as claimed — at this height the ships were models, the town buildings miniatures, but Kydd was more aware of the rosy flush on Emily's cheeks as she pointed out the sights. "Ah, look there, Thomas!" Far below, Nelson's frigate was getting under way, her commodore's pennant lifting in the fluky breeze and with all sail set. "What a picture it is, to be sure." Impulsively, she laid her arm on his.

The frigate was smart in her actions, but was having a hard time in the uncertain wind eddies in the lee of the Rock, paying off in the light airs but nevertheless slowly gaining ground to the northward.

"And are the others coming, too?" Emily

added innocently, taking out her dainty ladies' pocket telescope.

Kydd frowned. The faraway ships she had seen were moored across the bay, in Spanish Algeciras — and they were sail-of-the-line. "No doubt about it — but if y' would allow . . ." She offered him the telescope with no comment, and two mighty enemy vessels leaped into view. If they caught up with the lone frigate, they could blast her to splinters.

"They're Spanish battleships, I'm grieved t' say," Kydd said. *Achilles* had her bowsprit in for survey and was not in any condition to come to the frigate's aid. The Spanish ships had a steady wind in their favor, and had picked up speed; the English frigate's wind was still in the thrall of the huge Rock, and she could not beat back against the southeasterly to escape.

Kydd clenched his fists. This fire-breathing Nelson would not surrender tamely: the pretty frigate would be a shattered, smoking wreck even before he and Emily had had chance to spread their picnic.

"Thomas?" Emily's voice was edged with concern. Kydd stared through the telescope at the spreading drama. The larger

Spanish three-decker was stretching away ahead of the other in her impatience to close with the frigate and, as Kydd watched, her guns were run out.

Then, unaccountably, the frigate slewed around into the wind and came to a stop. Kydd could find no reason for the action. A small boat ventured out from behind her, her crew pulling energetically. It was carried forward by the current toward the Spanish, but stopped halfway. At last he understood: *La Minerve* had come aback while the jolly boat attended to a man overboard.

The leading Spanish battleship shortened sail, slowing to drop back on her consort. Clearly, she thought the move preposterous. There had to be a reason for the doomed frigate to round confidently on her pursuers. Could it be that she had sighted the English fleet coming to her aid?

Kydd could only watch in admiration as the frigate picked up her boat and made off in the strengthening breeze. The Spaniard clapped on sail, but he was too late — the frigate was well on her way.

Kydd punched the air in pent-up excitement. "That was well done, blast m' eyes if it weren't!" he roared, too late remembering the ladies' presence.

Cockburn was uncharacteristically blunt. "She is a married lady. It's unseemly to be seen so much in her company."

Kydd glowered. "An' have I been improper in m' actions?" he asked. "Do I press my attentions? Is she unwilling?" He challenged Cockburn with a stare. "She's invited me t' see so many of her friends, right good of her —"

"She is a married woman!"

"So I'm to refuse her? I think not!"

Cockburn paused. He leaned back and said, in an odd voice, "Do ye know her husband?"

Kydd's face hardened. "She's not discussed him wi' me at any time — must be a poor shab, he doesn't keep station on her more. Mr. Mulvany is —"

"The town major."

A shadow passed over Kydd's face. "Acting town major only," he replied stubbornly. Cockburn kept his silence, but the pressure of his disapproval was tangible. "An' I regret I cannot be aboard t'night. The bishop is receivin' an' I'm invited," Kydd added.

The news of the climactic battle of Cape

St. Vincent broke like a tidal wave on Gibraltar. The anxieties of the past months, the hanging sword of an invasion and devastation, the flaunting of enemy naval power just a few miles away, as they passed in and out of the Mediterranean — *their* sea now — needed a discharge of emotions.

Over the horizon, on St. Valentine's Day, two great fleets had clashed: fifteen British ships-of-the-line and a handful of frigates met the enemy's twenty-seven of the line and a dozen frigates, and had prevailed.

Admiral Jervis had been reported as saying, "A victory is very essential to England at this moment," and had gone on to achieve just that. Details of the battle were sketchy, but wild rumors made the rounds of the daring Commodore Nelson disobeying orders and breaking the line to fall on the enemy from the rear. Apparently he had then personally led a boarding party to the deck of one enemy battleship and from there to yet another in a feat of arms that must rank alone in its bravery.

Gibraltar went berserk with joy — bells, guns, joyous crowds flooding into the street and, finally, an official *feu de joie* ordered by the governor. Six regiments stood motionless on the Alameda parade ground in tight-packed rows, small field pieces at each corner. At twelve precisely, artillery thudded solemnly, then by command the redcoats presented their muskets — and a deafening running fire played up and down the ranks, beating upon the senses until rolling gunsmoke hid the soldiers. The noise stopped, the smoke cleared, and the spectacle was repeated twice more.

On the water, every ship replied with thunderous broadsides; even the smallest found guns to mount and fire. The sailors dressed their ships in flags and there were wild scenes that night in the grog shops.

Kydd responded warmly, but this was tempered by the realization that he had missed what must have been the defining battle of the age. With a stab of dread he realized that Renzi might have been struck down, mortally wounded, thrown overboard in the heat of battle. He fought down the thought, then turned his mind to other things. Emily.

At their last meeting, she had shyly offered a little package, neatly finished with a bow. It was a pair of gloves — kidskin, probably Moorish, but of obvious quality. There was no conceivable need in his station for gloves, but Kydd's imagination grew fevered with conjecture. A gift from her to him: What did it mean?

He found Cockburn with a slim book. "Tam, I'd be obliged f'r the lend of a clean waistcoat, if ye please. That scurvy gun-room servant's in bilboes after a spree ashore." Cockburn looked up, but said nothing. "I have t' go somewhere to-morrow," explained Kydd.

Cockburn laid down his book. "To-morrow, it seems, I shall need my waist-coat," he said, his face hard.

This was nonsense: without means, he was spending all his time on board. "Then y'r other one — I know you have 'un."

"Strangely, it appears that I shall need that also," Cockburn said evenly.

Kydd breathed hard. "An' what kind o' friend is it that —"

"A friend who sees you standing into perilous waters, who fears to see you play the cuckold without —"

"She cares f'r me, I'll have ye know."

"Oh? She has told you? Pledged undying love when not free to do so?"

Kydd clamped his jaw shut.

"I thought so. You are naught but a fool," Cockburn said, in measured tones. "Treading a path where so many poor loobies have gone before." He sighed and returned to his reading. "I can only grieve for your future."

"Be damned t' you 'n' y'r prating," Kydd snarled, and stormed off petulantly.

They started in the cool of the morning, Emily mysterious as to their destination. "It might be Africa — or the bowels of the earth. Or the very summit of the Rock . . . or perhaps all three."

Kydd grunted in bafflement, but was much taken by Emily's outfit; instead of the wide morning dress, it was a more close-fitting garment. Letitia followed behind, leaving the conversation to them.

They emerged onto the upper spine of the Rock, a stretch of rifted rock layers, covered with furze and pungent with goat smell. Emily descended daintily from her donkey and pointed to an irregular small peak. "The highest point of the Rock," she declared.

Silently cursing his clumsiness, Kydd staggered off his beast.

"Governor O'Hara wishes to build a tower on it, which he swears will allow him to look into Cadiz Bay," Emily said, idly twisting her muslin scarf. "The surveyor calls it 'O'Hara's Folly,' but he will not be dissuaded."

Her cheeks appeared rosier at this

85

height, wisps of hair framing her face under the wide straw hat, and Kydd felt desire build. He glanced behind. There was Letitia, still on her donkey, her un-blinking eyes gravely on him.

"They call him 'Cock o' the Rock,'" Emily said, with a giggle, then dropped her eyes.

To cover his embarrassment, Kydd bowed gallantly to Letitia and offered to help her down, but she shook her head mutely and slipped easily to the ground.

From nowhere a dark-complexioned Iberian appeared, taking the donkey bri-dles and fixing Kydd with glittering, un-fathomable eyes. Kydd hastily caught up with Emily, Letitia as usual falling behind.

"This is our destination, then," Emily said. "I do hope you think it interesting."

"Africa? Th' bowels of the earth?" It was nothing more than an undistinguished cleft in a jutting crag.

Emily stepped forward confidently, Kydd at her side. It was a cave of sorts, the outside light dimming the farther they en-tered, their footsteps changing from a tap into an echo as the light died and myste-rious vertical shapes appeared from out of the Stygian blackness.

She stopped to let the Iberian catch up.

He produced candles in colorful pottery holders, and got to work with flint and steel. As each flame leaped and guttered, the golden light spread to reveal a huge vaulted cavern, a magnificent palace of gilded stone.

Emily's candle illuminated her face from beneath in an unearthly radiance, and for a long moment Kydd was lost to her beauty.

"Saint Michael's cave. Such a spectacle — you'd never know that the Rock is hollow from the outside," she said softly, her eyes wide. The cavern smelt of damp soil, and tiny drip sounds were amplified all around.

Letitia shivered, and stepped back, pulling her shawl close.

Emily pointed forward. The path trended down, then reached a lip of rock. "We must climb down there." It continued as another chamber beyond, untouched by their candlelight.

"I — I shall wait here, Emily," came Letitia's small voice. "I have no stomach for these places. Do let's return now."

"Nonsense, Letitia. I mean to show Thomas the inner chambers." Carefully, she laid her candleholder on the stone, and slid over the lip to the blackness beyond. "Come along!" she called imperiously to Kydd.

The inner cave was smaller, longer, much colder. The path dipped sharply, and as they plunged out of sight Letitia's plaintive voice echoed, "Please hurry back — I'm frightened."

Kydd kept up with Emily, the candlelight casting startling shadows that continually moved as if alive. They entered a vast chamber, the sounds of their steps and voices dissipating into the cold, breathy stillness.

Emily stood still, gazing upward, enraptured. She moved farther in, found a broken-off stalagmite and placed her candle on it, letting the tiny golden light lose itself in the distance, as it did, hinting at fantastic shapes in the gloom. "Isn't this the most splendid sight you have ever seen?" she breathed.

Kydd's heart was thumping: this was the first time they had been alone.

Her eyes roamed upward, and Kydd added his candle to hers. The combined light beamed out strongly and grotesque shapes were illumined on all sides. But Emily's face was brushed with gold.

"We're now in the center of the Rock! No one has ever reached the end of these caverns — it is said that they reach all the way to Africa . . ." Her voice was a whisper of awe.

A swell of emotion surged in Kydd — a wellspring of feeling that could not be stopped. It found focus in the soft loveliness of Emily's face. He closed with her, held her, and kissed her in silence.

Her lips were formless with surprise, but she did not resist. His kiss grew deep with passion and she responded, avid and strong, her body pressing against his. They broke apart, hands clasped, staring into each other's eyes.

"M' dear Emily! You — you're . . ." Kydd was shaken with the power of his feelings.

She did not speak; her face was flushed and taut. Kydd still held her hands, and their warmth and softness triggered another passionate upsurge. He pulled her close, but she turned away her face, yet not resisting him.

Baffled, he let his arms drop. "Emily, I —"

"Thomas, please." Her voice was shaky. She disengaged from him, and half turned away. Kydd was unsure of what was happening; he felt gauche and adolescent.

"We — we must return, Letitia is on her

own." She avoided his eyes, but did not try to move away.

Kydd sensed he would lose all if he pressed his attentions now. He picked up his candle. "Yes, of course."

A trim 28-gun frigate materialized out of the morning haze to seaward, slow and frustrated by the light winds. But Kydd was not watching. He'd gone to the master's sea cabin, ostensibly to correct charts for the Spanish coast but in reality to struggle with the wording of a letter to Emily. They had returned safely from the cave, and after a somewhat distant leave-taking, which he put down to necessary caution in front of Letitia, they had parted.

It had now been some days since they had met, and his mind was feverish with thoughts of her. He had to decide if her silence meant that she was waiting for a more bold approach from him, even a romantic gesture. He knew he was not as taut a hand in these waters as he would like, and it was too much to expect a steer from Cockburn, whose cold manner now wounded him.

All he knew was that he was besotted with her. He stared at the bulkhead, seeing her lovely eyes and perfect lips. It was time for action! He would invite her casually for a tour of the ship — after the dog-watches but before the frustrated men started their interminable drinking and fighting.

He scratched his head at the taxing necessity of getting the wording exactly right; it would not do to have his motives misconstrued. "Dear Emily" . . . Damn! Of course he must put something more in the formal way. Another piece of paper. The master did not have many fresh sheets in his cabin desk; he always employed the other sides of used paper for everything except formal work. "Dear Mrs. Mulvany, It would be a right honor to escort you on a visit aboard my ship, HMS *Achilles* 64."

From time to time the officers brought their ladies of the moment on board for a quick and often scandalized peek, and the petty officers and men brought their much more worldly doxies to the fo'c'sle when they had the silver to afford them. *His* lady was much more the prime article, and he could see her now, by the capstan whelps, cool and elegant, asking how the bars were pinned and swifted, then smiling that warm and special smile at him.

In a glow, he continued: "Please signify when you are free, and we will meet wherever you say."

That was all that was needed. After the visit they would step ashore together, and who knew what might then eventuate? Kydd's brow furrowed at choosing the closing words, and he decided on a more neutral cast: "Your devoted friend, Thomas Paine Kydd."

There! He folded the paper, and looked for a wafer to seal it. He rummaged guiltily in the compartments of the master's desk, but found none, or even red wax. The ship's messenger would take the letter readily enough on his forenoon rounds for a coin or two, but Kydd did not want him to read its content. He remembered that the caulkers were at work around the main-hatch. He would use a blob of caulking pitch as sealing wax. Admittedly, it was black instead of red, but that would not trouble a lady of Emily's breeding.

Kydd strolled back to the quarterdeck and saw the little frigate. She was making a cautious approach, probably to warp alongside the New Mole. Lines were passed, capstans manned, and she was neatly brought in.

Distracted, Kydd went below to rouse out a crew for cleaning down after the caulkers, but his mind was not on the job. When he returned to the upper deck he caught a glimpse of a boat rounding under the stern of *Achilles*. It was probably from the frigate, and he watched the bulwark to see who would come over.

With unbelieving eyes, he saw Renzi hoist himself awkwardly aboard, touch his hat to the officer-of-the-watch, and look around. Kydd crossed over to him rapidly and held out his hand. "Well met, Nicholas!" he said happily, but saw that things were not as usual with his friend. There were dark rings around his eyes and the handshake clearly gave him pain. "You're in a frigate now," Kydd offered.

"I am — *Bacchante* twenty-eight, a trim enough daughter of Neptune." A smile cracked through. "Quite fortuitous. *Glorious* was sadly knocked about in the *rencontre* before Saint Vincent and lies under repair at Lagos. I act temporarily in the place of a wounded mariner in the frigate, having the duty but never the glory, I fear." He sighed. "Yet here you lie in the same berth, topping it the sybarite while the world is in a moil — and I took such pains to come here of the especial concern I have for my friend."

Kydd colored, but the pleasure at seeing his best friend was profound, and he didn't rise to the gentle gibe. "You were there in

93

th' great battle, wi' a mort o' prize money t' come, I suspect."

Renzi looked away. "I was, but . . . You shall have your curiosity satisfied, should you be at liberty to step ashore this afternoon, I have a consuming desire to be at peace. Do you know of such a place we can —"

"O' course! We c'n —" Kydd stopped. If a favorable message came from Emily and by his absence he did not respond . . . It was unfortunate timing but —

"Er, Nicholas, I've just remembered, I have an arrangement f'r tonight. It's very important, y' know," he mumbled. Renzi's face fell. "With a lady, y' see," Kydd added hopelessly.

"Then we shall rendezvous on the morrow, and you shall hear my tale then," Renzi said softly.

Kydd watched him leave, with a pang of guilt.

There was no reply by noon, and the afternoon hours passed at a snail's pace; Kydd had donned his best rig, in case Emily wanted to take up his invitation immediately. The ship was in harbor routine. After dinner at noon, those who were allowed, and had the means, quickly made

94

their way ashore, the remainder settled down restlessly.

By the dog-watches he was torn with doubt. Had he been deceived by her manner, mistaken in his conclusions? But there could be no mistaking the need and urgency of that kiss.

The evening had turned into a study of scarlet and orange, the sea darkling prettily, with Thomas Kydd, master's mate, still to be found on deck. Then, after the evening meal, a message came. The coxswain of the gig's crew brought it to him, apologetically mentioning that due to being called away to attend the captain, he had not had a chance before to pass it along — and this from early afternoon.

Kydd ground his teeth and clattered below to the gunroom. The master had returned, so his cabin was no longer available. Savagely, he sent the midshipmen to their berth and, silently cursing the impossibility of getting privacy in a warship, settled to open the message under the eye of the sallow surgeon's mate and his bottle.

He inspected the inscription — "Mr. T. Kydd, HMS *Achilles*" — then split the wafer and hurriedly unfolded the sheet.

Dear Mr. Kydd,

Thank you for the kind invitation to visit your ship. Unfortunately, I have rather a lot of engagements at the present, but will let you know when convenient.

Yours sincerely,
Mrs. Emily Mulvany

He reread, and again, slowly, so as not to miss any subtle clues. An initial wash of disappointment was replaced by logic. Of course, she would be otherwise engaged, it had been kind of her to fit him in before. "Mr. Kydd": cold — or cautious, lest the message fall into the wrong hands? The same might be said of the way she had ended the letter. In any event, he must bide his time.

Nothing could have been better calculated to ease Kydd's frustrations than his meeting with Renzi the following day. True to Renzi's wishes, the pair toiled up the hill to the commissioner's house, then found the path running along the flanks of the Rock. There was a row of fig trees on the upper side, and a vineyard below, with occasional olive trees to afford shade.

"This is particularly agreeable to my

spirit, Tom," Renzi said. They walked on in the warm sun in perfect silence but for the sough of the breeze, an occasional murmur of busyness from the distant town below and their own progress along the dusty ground.

The quiet was calm and companionable. Presently, they came to a flowered area with a fine orange tree in the center and a rustic wooden seat around it, a view of the harbor at their feet.

"Utterly peaceful — the work of man, yet supernal in its effects." Renzi sat and stared at the view, then closed his eyes. Kydd's mind was alive with distractions of the present. Was Emily's letter a delaying tactic while she reviewed her feelings? Should he press his case more clearly, perhaps?

"A lady?" Renzi's lazy murmur cut through his rush of thoughts.

Kydd glanced suspiciously at him, but Renzi's eyes were still closed. "Er, y'r in the right of it — but I beg, tell me of y'r battle. I heard it was a thunderin' good drubbing f'r the Dons."

Renzi opened his eyes and stared into space. "Little enough to say. It was a hard-fought encounter and they had overweening forces, but we prevailed." He looked at Kydd with a sardonic smile. "You would have been diverted by the sight of their *Santissima Trinidad* — a four-decker of a hundred and thirty guns, a leviathan indeed."

As far as Kydd knew, the largest ship in the Royal Navy only had a hundred guns and three decks, so such a monster a third bigger should have made a devastating impact. "Did she — who should say — get among our ships —"

"We took her."

Kydd's eyes gleamed.

"Then we forgot about her, so she rehoisted her colors and retired from the field."

"But Nelson, did he not —"

"The man is a genius of the sea war — daring and courageous with it. He will either die young or find great glory, nothing less."

Kydd fell silent. While great deeds were happening on the open sea, he was wasting his life in port, going nowhere.

Renzi shifted position awkwardly. "Somethin' pains you?" Kydd asked.

"Only a pinking from a splinter across my chest." He turned to Kydd. "You made mention of a lady . . ."

"Er, yes. Her name's Emily."

"A fine name," said Renzi dryly.

"She's very beautiful."

"I have no doubt she has shining parts," Renzi prompted.

"There is somethin' that is stoppin' her showin' her true feelings."

"She believes you are from an inferior station in life?"

"No. That's to say, this is not where the problem lies." He struggled with what had to come next, feeling a chill of doubt for the first time. "You see, Nicholas, right at th' moment . . . she is married." Kydd blushed, then muttered protestations of love.

Renzi's expressionless mask did not change. Then, suddenly, he came to his feet, and paced around the small garden with his hands behind his back, once, twice, then returned to Kydd and stood before him. "It seems to me the lady does not appreciate your true worth, my friend. She probably has cognizance only of the army life, never the navy." He paused for effect, then announced gravely, "I have a plan."

"Yes, Nicholas?"

"You shall be known for a daring, dangerous and romantic sea feat that will have the whole of Gibraltar talking. She will regard you as her adoring hero, her Galahad."

"Ye're chousin' me! *Achilles* is not goin' to sea, there's no chance o' that."

"No, but *Bacchante* is, and she needs men." Renzi leaned forward. "I'm quite certain that the frigate is bound for the eastern Mediterranean. It is not talked about, there is a smothering secrecy, but the application of a little logic suggests much. The master has taken in certain charts of the area, the vessel is under some kind of Admiralty orders, we are a private ship. The Mediterranean is now without a single English sail — why would the Admiralty risk a single valuable frigate in a sea so hostile?" Renzi paused. "It is because they wish to rescue someone, a grandee, perhaps, but one of some consequence."

The romantic possibilities of an audacious rescue of a notable were easy to see.

Renzi went on, "We have abandoned our ports and bases and retreated to Gibraltar, the princes, governors and such ilk long retrieved. No, this is somewhere that is lately under threat, and for that we can discount the petty fiefdoms of the Levant, the decadent Ottomans, the Barbary Coast — none would rate any personage of importance. Italy — now, the French have been pressing them from over the Alps, they have overrun much of the north. Austria is inviolate — for the moment — and I believe it is to Italy we are headed."

A smile broke through; Kydd waited.

"None of the northern kingdoms of Italy has much in the way of diplomatic representation, so my conclusion is that our dignitary is stranded in the nor'east after fleeing over the Alps and, finding that the English are no longer there, having evacuated the Mediterranean entirely."

"Er, what do we find in th' nor'east?"

Renzi rubbed his chin. "Well, there you will find the wild Balkan shore, Ragusa, but also Naples — and Venice."

Chapter 3

Kydd spun the wheel experimentally — there was no doubt that *Bacchante* was a sea witch. Responsive and eager to the helm, she was like a racehorse — and nearly brand-new — as sweet a lady as had ever come down the slip at Buckler's Hard. His practiced eye flicked up to the leech of the main topsail, and he inched the helm over until the hard edge of the sail began a minute flutter. Satisfied, he checked first against the dog-vane in the shrouds giving the wind angle, then the compass.

A broad grin broke on his face, and he caught an amused look, tinged with respect, from the officer-of-the-watch. "Damn fine sailer!" he muttered defensively. It had been a few years since he had last held the helm of a top frigate, and that had been the famous *Artemis*. Unable to suppress a sigh of the deepest satisfaction, he reluctantly surrendered the wheel to the duty helmsman, who was waiting patiently; Kydd had shipped in a vacancy of quartermaster and had the overall responsibility of the conn, his rate of master's mate willingly put aside temporarily.

"Fletcher on th' helm, sir," he called, as was his duty to the officer-of-the-watch, the courteous Griffith.

"Thank you, Kydd." The officer resumed his pacing on the weather side, leaving Kydd to drink in the sheer pleasure of having a live, moving deck under his feet, the sweet curving of deck-lines set about with drum-taut rigging, the urgent hiss of their progress.

Renzi had been right: it had been announced that they were heading deep into the Mediterranean on some sort of venture to bring off a distressed but unknown worthy hiding somewhere on the other side of Italy. Kydd had jumped at the chance to volunteer for the voyage, even though for them every ship that swam must be hostile — and it was not certain they would survive to return.

"Do I find you in spirits, then, brother?" Renzi murmured, from behind him.

Kydd turned to him happily. "Aye, y' do." A chance to be involved in a romantic rescue, the prospect of weeks at sea with Renzi before they returned to Gibraltar, and all happening in this lovely frigate. "A spankin' fine ship!"

"Larbowlines have the last dog?" Renzi's question was necessary, for as master's mate his watches conformed to the officers' while Kydd was back with the traditional two watches of the men. He was hoping he and Kydd could spend a watch companionably together, as in the old times.

"First dog-watch." The forms would have to be observed; while all the ship knew Kydd's origins, he must now wear the blue short jacket and white trousers of a seaman, while Renzi must appear in the coat and breeches of a warrant officer. Kydd would address him as "Mr. Renzi" on watch, and would take his orders, which, in the immutable way of the navy, he would do without question.

They strolled together to the lee side of the ship, Kydd automatically checking the yeasty foaming of the wake as it slid aft to join with the other side in a perfectly straight line into the far distance — the helmsman would hear from him if there were any betraying dog-legs.

"It would seem we are set on a course

to round Sicily and enter the Adriatic, but the captain is under orders to keep in with the coast of Africa to avoid being seen."

Kydd was acquainted with the charts of the Mediterranean and understood the dangers of such a precaution. He glanced up at the red-white-red of their ensign — that of a unit of the Austrian navy, their disguise for this part of the voyage. "Wind fair f'r Malta, five days north t' Venice, another three —"

"Master says the wind's dead foul this time of the year up the Adriatic."

"So that lets us get away fast, after," said Kydd, with a chuckle.

Renzi gave a half-smile. "We have a Venetian gentleman with us in the gunroom who will be our agent. He warns that we're in some measure of danger. The advance of the French into Italy is fast and unpredictable, and he cannot guarantee the loyalties of any."

But in his present mood Kydd could not be repressed. It should be straightforward enough: a fast passage, send the boats in to bring off the fleeing notable, and a rapid exit, to admiration and acclaim in Gibraltar. They were not looking for trouble — it would go ill for the captain were he to rescue the fugitive, then hazard him in a battle.

Renzi swung around as the captain appeared at the main-hatch. He wore a frown of worry, and searched the horizon minutely. They were deep into a hostile sea where every man's hand was turned against them, every sail an enemy. "How does the ship, Mr. Griffith?" he asked at length.

"Well enough, sir — we shifted three leaguers aft, seems to have cured the griping." Kydd and his party down in the hold had heaved aft three massive water casks to raise the vessel's bow, altering her trim such that her stem did not bite so deeply to bring her head to the wind.

"Very well. Do you spare no pains to impress their duty upon the lookouts!"

"Aye-aye, sir."

A broad vista of royal blue water, tinting darker as the evening drew on, was broken at the bows by a school of the small dolphins peculiar to this enclosed sea. They played around the bows of *Bacchante*, more like darting fish than the disciplined phalanx of the oceanic dolphin.

Renzi had his clay pipe going to his satisfaction and stared out into the blue, letting the peace of the evening calm his senses, the ceaseless wash and slop of the slight waves soothing to the soul.

"Y'r battle, it was a close enough thing, you say," Kydd said.

"Elias Petit is no more. A round-shot destroyed him." The gentle, simple mariner, who had shared their mess in the *Artemis*, had been slammed across the deck by the impact of the ball, his innards strung out grotesquely.

Kydd murmured a commiseration.

"And Joe Farthing lost a leg." One of the few original *Seaflowers*, a careful, sober seaman of the best kind, he had been with them in the topsail cutter through all their adventures in the Caribbean. The last Renzi had seen of him was his contorted body carried down to the surgeon's knife with the ugly obscenity of a long splinter transfixing his limb.

"But it was a noble victory, Nicholas."

"Of course it was, my friend, one that will be talked about for all of time."

"Especially your Nelson — boards a ship, takes it, then uses it to board another."

"They are calling it 'Nelson's Patent Bridge for Boarding First-Rates.'"

"Aye, and in Gibraltar the toast is 'To

Nelson fill bumbo/For taking *Del Mundo*.' Wish ye joy of y'r prize money."

Renzi took another puff on his pipe — he had been able to find the tobacco in Lisbon, the light but fragrant Virginia he now favored. "Um, your lady, would it be indelicate of me to ask her particulars?"

"Ah, yes." Emily's image had slipped from Kydd's mind in the contentment of being at sea once more, but Renzi's question brought a pang. "She's very partial to m' company, Nicholas. We've had some rare times visitin' and sketchin' all over the Rock."

Renzi's eyebrows rose.

Kydd's features took on a bashful cast. "In a cave she kissed me — she wants me, I know it."

"And her husband, what is his view of this?"

Kydd threw him an indignant look. "He's not t' be troubled until Emily has settled her mind."

"You've discussed this?"

"Not as who should say," Kydd admitted. "Ladies don't come to it as fast as we men — they need a bit o' sea room t' see where they lies."

Renzi considered. Ashore Kydd was an innocent, and he had got entangled with a

108

married woman. It needed circumspection. His instinct to get Kydd away from the situation had been right, and it would be best to let nature take its course, no matter the cost to Kydd in wounded pride.

The north coast of Africa, low, drab, meandering, with no exciting features in its unrelieved ocher, lay to starboard and would stay there for the next few days. It was the coast of Morocco, Algiers and Tunis — the Barbary Coast that had so often figured in the bloody history of the Mediterranean with slave galleys of Christian captives, unspeakable cruelties and straggling medieval empires. All just a few leagues under their lee.

"Steer small, blast y' eyes!" Kydd growled at the helmsman, all too aware of the consequences of falling off course to fetch up on this shore.

There was little shipping. Trading vessels showed prudence on sighting them; a throng of lateen-sailed feluccas clustered nervously together inshore as they passed, while a pair of xebecs came by from the opposite direction, purposeful and sinister, but showing no interest. They would keep in with the land, sheering out to sea around the fortified coastal cities, conscious that news of an English frigate at large would threaten their mission. But it was an odd feeling, knowing that the coastline to starboard was really the edge of a great desert with the rest of a fabulous continent beyond.

The forenoon wore on, sparkling seas as gentle and soft as could be wished, and it was pleasant sailing weather in the warm breeze. A point of land on the empty coast approached, and course was altered to keep it at a respectful distance. They slipped past toward the long bay beyond.

Kydd glanced in the binnacle at the leeward compass to check that the helmsman was being scrupulous in his heading. When his gaze came up, he knew something was amiss. Some indefinable sense told him that all was not right with the world. The ship was on course, all sails drawing well, the watch alert, nothing changed — yet something had.

His eyes caught those of the lieutenant on watch. In them he saw alarm and incomprehension. Exactly on course and with the same sail set, the frigate was slowing, her pace slackening little by little, no other sensation but a gentle retardation.

Sinbad. Ali Baba casting a spell on them. Something had got hold of *Bacchante* and was dragging her back. The hairs on the back of Kydd's neck prickled; the world was slipping into fantasy. The ship dropped to a crawl, then gently stopped altogether, her sails still taut and drawing. Around the deck men froze.

A shout came from a seaman, excited, pointing over the side. There was a general rush to see and it became instantly clear what had happened. "We're hard 'n' fast on th' sand!" In the green-brown waters a dusting of sand particles swirled lazily around the length of the hull.

The officer-of-the-watch blared out orders for the taking in of sail; the creaking masts were straining perilously, but the grounding had been gradual and gentle and, without the inertia of a sudden impact, the spars had been preserved.

Boatswain's mates hurried to the hatches, their pipes squealing an urgent summons. Sailors leaped up from below, racing up the shrouds, dousing canvas almost as quick as the yard could be laid, until *Bacchante* was naked of sail. The pandemonium subsided and the captain threw urgent orders at his ship's company: grounding a ship brought a court of inquiry, his actions of the next few minutes would determine if it turned into a court-martial, presuming they survived.

The frigate had just passed abreast of a low point of land to enter the long bay beyond and the chart had promised the usual deep water, but the shifting sands of the desert must have blown out into the sea, forming a wicked spit. The usual lightening of the bottom in shoal water had been obscured by the unlucky proximity of a river in muddy spate after rains, and there had been no warning.

It was very bad news. The rock-solid deck underfoot indicated that they were firmly aground; everyone knew that there were no tides to speak of in the Mediterranean, no high tide to float them off. Worse, if the French or a Barbary pirate happened along and saw their predicament, they had but to approach by the stern or the bow of the immobile vessel in full scorn of their broadside, which was helplessly facing outward on each side.

The master was quickly into a boat, and had the hand-lead going steadily as he built up a picture all around the stranded frigate. There would then be only two options: to bump forward over the sandbank, or ease back the way she had come. Soundings confirmed that the shoal shallowed ahead, leaving a heaving-off as the only solution.

The most urgent necessity was to lay out the kedge anchor in the direction they had come; they would then heave up to it with the full weight of the main capstan. This was the best chance to see the ship into deep water again — it was unlikely she had suffered much in taking the ground in sand.

The boatswain had Kydd tumbling into the launch with a full crew of oarsmen. This was the biggest boat aboard, and he took the tiller knowing that his task would be to stream the kedge to its full extent. "Out oars, give way together," he growled, and began a sweep about to pass around *Bacchante*'s stern to the kedge anchor stowage, atop the sheet anchor.

"Belay that!" The boatswain's bellow sounded above. "We takes th' stream killick!" The stream anchor was ten hundredweight of iron, more than double the sinking weight of the kedge, and would bite well in the shifting sandy seabed. Kydd shoved over the tiller to come up on the stream anchor. Already seamen were at work on the outside stowage, bending on a fore pendant tackle to take the weight of the big anchor while casting off the sea lashings.

"Oars," Kydd ordered. There was no

point in closing until they were ready aboard the ship. A yardarm stay tackle was secured to a ring stopper and shank bridle, and the tackles were eased off until the anchor was ready to be got off the bows — Kydd kept a comfortable distance while the weight was taken up.

He watched while a capstan bar was fetched and given to a brawny fo'c'sleman on the foredeck. When the big anchor rose to life, he plied it to pry the fluke clear of the timberhead, pivoting the moving anchor around the other fluke resting on the billboard.

This was the moment Kydd had been waiting for. The massive anchor now lay suspended and clear of the ship's side, the imperfections and hammer marks of the forge visible in the black iron swaying so close above him. He stood in the sternsheets, bringing the boat carefully closer and to seaward. "Cast y'r bight!" A stout painter was passed around the throat at the base of the anchor, and paid out. Kydd's arm shot up as a signal, and the anchor started to dip into the sea, sliding in until only the broad wooden stock and ring showed. Another painter secured on the shank was quickly brought into the boat, and the most difficult part of the exercise approached.

Eased down, the anchor disappeared into the sea, but the first painter was heaved up on the opposite side of the boat. "Right glad it ain't a bower," muttered one seaman — a bower anchor was four times the size and another boat and sweaty labor indeed would have been needed to handle it.

The shank painter brought the stock of the anchor close and, working together, the two lines eventually persuaded the anchor to come to rest beneath the boat, hauled athwart the bottom, only the shank above water. The launch settled low in the water under the weight, the painters were secured to each other and they were ready.

Kydd again held up his arm, and the fall of the stay tackle was eased away until the boat had the full weight. Kydd's eyes darted around the boat — the dripping lines seemed in order, straining over the gunwales. He slid out his knife and, with a sailor gripping his belt, leaned far out and down into the water to get at the seizing of the suspending hawser. A vigorous sawing, and the thick rope fell free.

The deep-laden boat moved sluggishly; Kydd's men tugged at the oars with ponderous results. The sun was now uncomfortably high. They passed heavily down the length of the ship and, as they reached the stern, the end of a deep-sea lead line was thrown to them. This would be their measure of where to let the anchor go, and Kydd cleared it watchfully over the transom as they crabbed their way through the wind and waves.

He glanced back. A cable was being lowered through the mullioned windows of the captain's cabin into the smaller cutter; no doubt it would pass into the ship in a direct line to the lower capstan. That way, there would be opportunity to man the capstans on both decks, doubling the force.

The cutter made good progress, and by the time the lead-line suddenly tautened, the cable was on hand, fully extended and ready to seize to the big forged-iron ring of the anchor. There was no need to wait for a signal from the ship. Kydd took up a boarding axe, and brought it down on the painters straining across the boat.

The severed ropes whipped away, and with a mighty bounce of the boat at the relieved buoyancy, the anchor plunged down. Now it was the turn of others — Kydd knew that the capstans would be manned by every possible soul. Bleakly, he reminded himself of the penalties if they could not win the ship back to deep water.

Laying on their oars, the aching men in the launch waited and watched. The martial sounds of fife and drum sounded faintly; every effort was being made to whip them into a frenzy of effort. Time wore on, but *Bacchante* was not advancing to her anchor. Uneasily, Kydd threw a glance at the shore. The skyline was reassuringly innocent, but for how long?

The sun beat down. A peculiar smell — goats, dryness, sand — came irregularly on the light breeze that fluffed the sea into playful wavelets. It was peaceful in the boat, which was hardly moving in the slight sea, just the odd creak and chuckle of water.

The recall came after another twenty minutes. Kydd did not envy the captain in his decision — the ship was not moving. The next act would be to start water casks over the side, perhaps even the guns. And that would certainly mean the end of their mission, even if the move was successful.

Coming aboard again, Kydd could feel the tension. The captain was in earnest discussion with his officers on the quarterdeck. Renzi was there also; he regarded Kydd gravely, then cocked an eye at the shore. Kydd saw that the low scrubby dunes were now stippled with figures.

"Moors — the Bedoo of the desert," Renzi murmured, as Kydd took in the exotic scene; camels, strings of veiled Arabs still as statues, staring at the ship and more arriving.

Forward, men were grouping nervously. Everyone knew the consequences of being taken on the Barbary Coast. Renzi pursed his lips. "It's not the Bedoo that should concern us," he muttered. "They can't get to us without boats. But your Moorish corsair, when he has his friends, and they make a sally together . . ."

The worried knot of officers around the captain seemed to come to a decision. Stepping clear of them, the boatswain lifted his call, but thought better of it, merely summoning the captain of the hold, a senior petty officer. "Start all th' water over the side," he ordered. Tons of fresh water gurgled into the scuppers from the massive leaguer casks swayed up from the hold.

"Rig guns to jettison." Murmuring from forward was now punctuated with protests, angry shouts following the gunner's party as they moved to each gun, knocking free the cap squares holding the trunnion to the carriage and transferring the training tackle to the eyebolt above the gunport. Now it only needed men hauling on the side tackles and, with handspikes levering, the freed gun would tumble into the sea — and they would be defenseless.

A shout from a sharp-eyed sailor, who had seen something above the dunes along the coast, stopped progress. It rounded the point and hove to several miles off; twin lateen sails and a long, low hull gave no room for conjecture. "We're dished," said Kydd, in a low voice. "There'll be others, and when they feel brave enough they'll fall on us." Another vessel, and then another hauled into view.

The captain's face was set and pale as he paced. The master went to him diffidently, touching his hat. "Sir, the ship settles in th' sand — if it gets a grip even b' inches, the barky'll leave her bones here." He hesitated. "I saw how *Blonde* frigate won free o' the Shipwash."

"Go on."

"They loose all sail, but braces to bring all aback — every bit o' canvas they had. Then ship's comp'ny takes as many round shot as they c'n carry, doubles fr'm one side o' the deck to the other 'n' back. Th' rhythm breaks suction an' the ship makes a sternboard 'n' gets off."

With a fleeting glance at the gathering predators, the captain told him, "Do it, if you please."

The master went to the wheel. "I takes th' helm. Kydd, you're th' lee helmsman." Kydd obediently took position and waited. Sail appeared, mast by mast, hesitantly, shrouds and stays tested for strain at the unaccustomed and awkward situation of the wind taking the sails on the wrong side.

"Mark my motions well. When we move, it'll be dead astern, an' if we mishandle, we'll sheer around an' it'll all be up wi' us," the master warned. A ship going backward would put prodigious strain on the rudder, and if they lost control it would slew sideway and slam the wind to the opposite side of the sails. At the very least this would leave *Bacchante* with broken rigging, splintered masts and the impossibility of getting away from the gathering threat.

Kydd gripped the spokes and stared doggedly at the master. His job, as leeward helmsman, was to add his weight intelligently to the effort of the lead helmsman, and he knew this would be a fight to remember.

Shot was passed up from the lockers in

the bowels of the ship, each man taking two eighteen-pound balls. "One bell to be ready, the second and you're off," the first lieutenant called from the belfry forward.

One strike: the men braced. Another — they rushed across the deck, more perhaps of a reckless waddle. They turned, and the bells sounded almost immediately. They rushed back. Some saw the humor of the situation and grinned, others remained straight-faced and grave.

Twice more they ran. Kydd snatched a glimpse up at the bulging, misshapen sails fluttering and banging above; the men were panting now. The boatswain had a hand-lead over the side, and was staring grimly at its steady vertical trend.

Near him Kydd could hear a deep-throated creaking amid the discordant chorus of straining cordage. He dared not look away — the moment, if it came, would come suddenly. The bells and thumping feet sounded again — and again.

The deck shifted under Kydd's feet, an uneven rumbling from deep within, and the boatswain's triumphant shout: "She swims!"

Forced by the wind, the frigate started to slide backward. The wheel kicked viciously as the rudder was caught on its side. The master threw himself at the wheel to wind on opposite helm, Kydd straining with him, following his moves to within a split second. The pressure eased, but the ship increased speed backward, at the same time multiplying the danger in proportion.

The master's lean face became haggard with strain and concentration as together they fought the ship clear. A fraction of inattention or misreading of the thrumming pressures transmitted up the tiller ropes and at this speed they would slew broadside in an instant.

The rumbling stopped — they must be clear of the sand. Orders pealed out that had canvas clewed up, yards braced around and a slowing of their mad backward rampage. The master's eyes met Kydd's, and he smiled. "That's cutting a caper too many f'r me," he said, in a gusty breath of relief.

Kydd returned a grin, but he held to his heart that this fine mariner had called on him, Thomas Kydd, when he needed a true seaman alongside.

The beat north through the Adriatic was an anticlimax. After re-watering from a clear stream on the remote west coast of Sardinia, they had thankfully rounded

Malta and Sicily at night, through the Strait of Otranto and on into the Adriatic. The stranding had not had any observable ill effects.

They now flew the red swallowtail of Denmark. It was unlikely that any French at sea would interfere with a touchy Scandinavian of a country they were in the process of wooing into their fold.

In the event, they saw no French. But they did, to Kydd's considerable interest, sight all manner of exotic Mediterranean craft. Built low but with a sharply rising bow in line with sea conditions in the inland sea, there was the three-masted bark, with its canted masts, lateen sails and beak instead of a bowsprit; the pink, which could use the triangular lateen sail interchangeably with the familiar square sail on its exotically raked masts, and the more homely tartan coaster.

Once, sighted far off and in with the coast, they saw a galley, fully as long as *Bacchante*, sails struck and pulling directly into the wind. The dip and rise of the oars in the sunlight was steady and regular, a never-ending rhythm that went on into the distance.

They were getting close to Venice at the head of the gulf, and that evening Kydd caught Renzi gazing ahead with an intense expression. "Y'r Venice is accounted a splendid place, I've heard," Kydd ventured.

Renzi appeared not to have heard, but then said distantly, "It is, my friend."

"A shame we can't step ashore. I'd enjoy t' see the sights."

Renzi responded immediately: "In Venice you'd see spectacle and beauty enough for a lifetime." He turned on Kydd with passionate intensity. "There you'll find the most glorious and serene expressions of the human spirit — and in the same place, soul's temptation incarnate, licentiousness as a science, a pit of profligacy! *E sempra scostumata*, if you'll pardon the expression."

Kydd tried to resist the smile pulling at his mouth; at last, this was the Renzi he remembered, not the cheerless introspective he had seemed to become of late.

Renzi noticed and, mistaking its origin, frowned in disapproval. "This is also, I might point out, the Venice of the Doge and his cruel prisons, where torture and death are acts of state and the Council of Ten rules by fear.

"But it is also the Venice of carnival," he continued, in a softer voice. "The masks will be abroad at this very time, I think you'll find, and in the evening —"

"You've been t' Venice before."

Renzi looked away. "Yes." There was a pause before he went on: "In the last years of the peace. You will know it is the custom for the sons of the quality to perform a Grand Tour. My companion and I knew no limits in the quest for education, you may believe."

Kydd waited for Renzi to continue, and saw that it was causing him some difficulty. "I was a different being then, one whose appreciation of life as the aggregate of pain and heart's desire was a little wanting in the article of penetration to the particulars."

Wondering what lay behind the careful cloud of words, Kydd decided not to pursue it. He had not seen Renzi so animated for a long time, but his features were a curious mixture of longing and sadness. Whatever blue devils were haunting him, the proximity of the fabled Venice had awakened life in him once more.

This far north the winds of spring were chill and strong; the frigate closed the Italian coast that night, and launched her cutter. It was too dark to make out much of the lonely figure of the Venetian agent helped down into the boat, but Kydd felt for him, going out alone into the unknown night.

Kydd knew the general area from the charts — a long thin spit of land enclosing a vast lagoon inside it, with the island of Venice in the middle. The agent had insisted they come no closer than the southern corner of the lagoon, the fishing-port of Chioggia, which now lay somewhere out in the darkness.

The cutter's sails went up and were sheeted home smartly, the boat quickly disappearing into the murk. After some hours it returned on time, magically reappearing under their lee having sighted the special red-white-red lanthorns set as a signal, and without the agent. *Bacchante* lost no time in making for the safety of the open sea, to spend the daylight hours in standing off and on.

It was disappointing — the whole mystery of Venice just out of sight, and one they would not see — for in the absence of any English opposition the French were rampaging down Italy in an unstoppable wave and could be anywhere. It was not a place to linger more than was necessary.

They returned that night; the agent

would have news or, better, the important person himself, presuming all was well ashore. They could soon be in a position to crowd on all sail, turn about and fly back to Gibraltar.

Kydd didn't know whether to be pleased at an early return to Emily or dismayed at the prospects of reverting to his fractious, low-spirited ship. Emily's image seemed oddly unreal in his mind's eye, and he was uneasily aware that the hot sap that had risen before was gone.

He sought out his friend, who as usual was to be found on the foredeck with his clay pipe, taking advantage of the frigate's easy motion and looking pensively out to seaward.

"You think I'm pixie led, quean-struck on her?" Kydd blurted, after a while.

Renzi turned to him, amused. "Not as one might say." Did his friend think that he was the first to be infatuated with an older woman? His own past was not one he could hold as an exemplar. In this very place he and his fellow young gentlemen on the Grand Tour had been shamelessly dissolute, uncaring and unfeeling as any young and careless sprig of nobility. But Kydd's honesty and sincerity in his voyage of self-discovery touched something in

Renzi. "Cupid casts his spells unevenly, capriciously, we cannot command his favors. If she has not been blessed in full measure with the same warmth of feeling as yourself, then . . ."

"She has!"

"Oh? You said before that she hadn't declared her feelings for you, had not thrown herself at your feet." Kydd remained silent, frowning. "When you volunteered for this mission, there was no urgent message, no beseeching to keep from danger." He paused significantly. "In fine, *your* ardor exceeds *hers.*"

Kydd reddened but said stubbornly, "She'll be waitin' for me, see if she don't."

"It might be the more rational course to allow her time to reflect. Cool your fervency, steady your pace — haul away, keep an offing, so to speak."

"Aye, I c'n see this, but y' see, my course is set. Nicholas, before we sailed I sent her a letter, a warm letter in which — in which I made m' feelings known."

"Good God!"

"I wanted t' set her right about things. Make sure she knows — makes no mistake about m' passion."

"May I know, er, what you said in this letter?"

It took some embarrassing prodding but the full story was not long in coming. In Kydd's own strong round hand it had opened with flowery darlings, then plunged into hot protestations of undying love, the usual heights and depths, and — was such innocence believable? — a final urging to find it in her heart to break with an unhappy, sterile marriage and flee with him to Paradise.

Renzi shook his head wordlessly. Then he said, "If you sent the letter in the usual way, the husband might have intercepted it."

"I know," Kydd said impatiently. "I took steps t' have it delivered personally."

"My dear fellow — dear brother." Renzi took a deep breath. "Might I point out to you what you have just done? If, as I suspect, your lady is as yet — unformed in her affections, then your letter most surely will cause her great agitation of the spirit, will frighten her like a deer from the unknown."

Kydd did not argue, but stared at him obstinately.

"And the rest is worse. It is a cardinal rule in any affair of the heart, which is, shall we say, on an irregular basis, that nothing is placed in writing, which could, er, be misconstrued by a third party." Renzi held Kydd's reluctant attention. "For the passing on of your letter you will have secured the services of someone close to her, I assume her maid. The letter will most certainly be delivered — but she is not expecting it and it will be placed on a silver salver, as is our way in polite society, together with others, but you are not to know this. Her husband may be in residence, he will be curious at the unknown writing or the perturbation of spirits in his wife as she receives it. In short, my friend, you most certainly will be discovered.

"And if I recollect, it is mentioned that her husband is, in a substantial way, a member of the military."

Kydd paled. "Er, the acting town major, right enough. Do you — would he, d'ye think, want a duel or somethin'?"

Renzi held his stern expression, delaying his response as long as he could in the face of Kydd's anxious gaze. "Well, I am obliged to point out that as you are not accounted a gentleman, he cannot obtain a satisfaction and would not demean his standing in society by a meeting." He sighed and continued gently, "Therefore a horse-whipping is more to be expected, I believe."

There was a shocked silence. Then Kydd drew himself up. "Thank ye, Nicholas, that was very kind in you t' make it all so clear," he said quietly, and made his way below.

That night, the agent was picked up, unaccompanied, at the appointed rendezvous. His news was not good; given in breathless haste as soon as he had made the dimly lit deck, it was overheard by the entire quarterdeck watch and, in the way of things, quickly relayed around the ship.

The grandee, a diplomat, Sir Alastair Leith, had planned to cross the Alps to safety in the independent republic of Venice, but things had gone from bad to much worse. Daring a lightning advance from France across the north of Italy to the other side, the French had taken city after city, putting the Austrians and Sardinians to humiliating retreat. Beautiful, ancient Italian cities, such as Verona, Mantua, Rivoli, were already in the hands of the vigorous and precocious new general, Napoleon Buonaparte, who was now flooding the rich plains of the Po Valley with French soldiers. Soon the Venetian Republic and her territories would be isolated, quite cut off, and the history of this gifted land would be changed for all time.

"You saw the consul, did you not, Mr. Amati?" the captain asked coldly. The ambassador would have long since departed, and English interests would be served by a consul, a local, probably a merchant.

The single lanthorn illuminated only one side of the agent's face and he shifted defensively. "Mi scusi — the city is violent, excited, he is deeficult to fin', Capitano."

"So you were unable to contact him."

"I did no' say that," the Italian said, affronted. He was short, dark and intense, and his eyes glittered in the lanthorn light. "I send a message. He tell me Signor Lith i' not in Venezia — anywhere."

"Thank you."

There was now the fearful decision as to whether and for how long they should wait for him to appear or if they should make the reasonable assumption that he had been overtaken by the French. A frigate dallying off the port would inevitably attract notice, no matter which colors she flew, and in the heightened tensions of war she would soon be the focus of attention from every warring power. Then again, if they sailed away, leaving stranded the delayed object of their mission . . .

The captain paced forward rigidly along the whole length of the deck to the fo'c'sle.

Men stood aside, touching their hats but unnoticed. He returned, and came to a halt near the wheel, then turned to the waiting officers. "I cannot wait here, yet we cannot abandon Sir Alastair.

"Lieutenant Griffith, I'd be obliged if you would go to Venice and there await his arrival. When he appears, it is your duty to hire or seize a vessel, and make rendezvous with me at sea. This will enable me to keep the ship well away from the coast. I propose to wait for ten days only."

Griffith hesitated, but only for a moment. "Aye-aye, sir."

"The master will furnish you with a list of our noon positions for the next fourteen days. I do not have to impress upon you the importance of their secrecy."

"No, sir."

"You will be provided with a quantity of money for your subsistence — which you will account for on your return, together with a sum for contingent necessaries." He pondered, then said, "You may find Mr. Renzi useful, I suspect. And a couple of steady hands — it would be well to have a care when ashore, I believe. Who will you have?"

"Kydd, sir," Griffith said instantly. Then, after a moment's reflection, "And

Larsson." The big Swedish quartermaster was a good choice.

"We must rely on Mr. Amati to find discreet quarters for you — the place will no doubt be alive with spies of every description, and you must be extremely circumspect."

"Yes, sir."

"Then we shall proceed to details."

At Amati's suggestion, a *trabaccolo*, a fat lug-rigged merchant craft, one of many scuttling nervously past in the dark, was brought to with a shot before her bows. Discussions under the guns of the frigate were brief, but English silver was considered a fair compensation for the delay, with the promise of more on safe arrival in Venice.

Bemused and interested by turns, Kydd clambered over the gunwale of the little coaster after Lieutenant Griffith. The crew lounged about the lively deck under an evil-smelling oil lamp, watching stonily, the stout captain fussing them all aboard with a constant jabber of Italian and waving hands. Seabags clumped to the deck, and they were on their own.

Amati was clearly tense, and answered the skipper in short, clipped phrases. "He say he wan' you to unnerstan' it ays forbidden to enter Venezia in th' night. We wait for day."

Griffith grunted. "Very well. Get sleep while you can, you men." The three seamen found a place under a tarpaulin forward, over the cargo in the open hold. This was a tightly packed mass of wicker baskets containing lemons, their fragrance eddying around them as they bobbed to the night current.

They awoke to a misty dawn, off a long, low-lying coast stretching endlessly in each direction. They were not alone: nearly two dozen other coastal traders were at anchor or moving lazily across the calm sea, morning sounds carrying clearly across the water.

Kydd rolled over. He saw Griffith waiting for Amati to finish a voluble exchange with the skipper, but Renzi lay still staring upward.

"So we're t' see this Venice, an' today," Kydd said, with relish.

Renzi's dismissive grunt brought a jet of annoyance. His friend had become vexing in his moods again, dampening the occasion and making Kydd feel he had in some way intruded on private thoughts. "M' chance t' see if it is as prime as ye say," he challenged. There was no intelligible response.

Griffith clambered over to them, steadying himself by the shrouds. "The captain wishes you to be — shall we say? — less conspicuous. Mr. Amati says that there's every description of seaman in Venice — Dalmatian, Albanian, Mussulmen, Austrians — and doubts we'll be noticed, but begs we can wear some token of this part of the world."

He looked doubtfully at Kydd's pea coat and Larsson's short blue naval jacket. The crew members wore the *bonnet rouge,* the distinctive floppy red headgear, and a swaggering sash. The Englishmen paid well over the odds for such common articles, which brought the first expressions of amusement from the crew.

The first diffuse tints of rose and orange tinged the mists when a gun thudded next to a small tower. As one, bows swung around and there was a general convergence on a gap in the coastline at the tower, a cloud of small ships slipping through the narrow opening, the *trabaccolo* captain at his tiller a study in concentration as he jockeyed his craft through.

It was only a slender spit of land, but inside was the Venetian lagoon, and Venice.

The spreading morning vision took Kydd's breath away: an island set alone in a glassy calm, some five miles off, fairy tale in the roseate pale of morning, alluring in its medieval mystery. He stared at the sight, captivated by the tremulous beauty of distant bell towers, minarets and old stone buildings.

The lagoon was studded with poles marking deeper channels and Kydd tore away his attention to admire the deft seamanship that had the deep-laden trader nimbly threading its way through. The *trabaccolo* was rigged with a loose lugsail at the fore and a standing lug at the mainmast, an odd arrangement that had the lower end of the lug swung around the after side of one mast when tacking about, but left the other on the same side.

As they approached, the island city took on form and substance. A large number of craft were sleepily approaching or leaving, the majority issuing forth from a waterway in the center of the island. They tacked about and bore down on it and it soon became apparent that a minor island was detached from the main; they headed toward the channel between, toward a splendor of buildings that were as handsome as they were distinctive.

Kydd stared in wonder. Here was a civilization that was confident and disdainful to dare so much magnificence. He stole a look at the others. The crewmen seemed oblivious to it, faking down ropes and releasing hatch covers; Larsson gazed stolidly, while Renzi and Griffith both stared ahead, absorbed in the approaching prospect. Amati fidgeted next to the captain, visibly ill at ease.

They shaped course to parallel the shore, passing a splendid vision of a palace, colonnades, the brick-red of an impossibly lofty square bell tower. "Piazza San Marco," Renzi said, noticing Kydd's fascination. "You will find the Doge at home in that palace. He is the chief eminence of Venice. You will mark those two pillars — it is there that executions of state are performed, and to the right, the Bridge of Sighs and the Doge's dread prison." He spoke offhandedly, and Kydd felt rising irritation until he realized this was a defense: his cultured friend was as affected as he.

Griffith broke off his discussion with Amati and came across. "You see there," he said, pointing at a golden ball displayed prominently at the tip of the approaching promontory, "the Saluday, where we find the customs house of Venice. We shall be boarded, but Mr. Amati says there'll be no difficulties. They're much more concerned to levy their taxes, and foreign seamen are not of interest to them."

He gave a small smile. "I will be a factor from Dalmatia, Mr. Renzi will be my clerk." Griffith wore the plain black last seen on *Bacchante*'s surgeon. "We may disembark and take passage to our lodgings without interference."

True to anticipation, the revenue officials ignored them in favor of a lively interchange with the captain, leaving them to hail and board one of the flat workboats sculling about.

They clambered into the forward well and settled. "Dorsoduro," Renzi said briefly, eyes on the colorful, bustling shore ahead. "And this, my friend, is the Grand Canal."

It was impossible not to be moved by the unique atmosphere of Venice — a true city of the water. Every building seemed to grow straight up from its watery origins with not an inch of wasted space. Instead of roads there were countless canals along which the commerce of the city progressed in watercraft of every kind in a ceaseless flow on the jade-green waters.

They passed deeper into the Grand

Canal, seeing the mansions of the rich, each with a cluster of gaily colored poles outside, an occasional market, throngs of people going about their business.

A bend straightened, and into view came a bridge, a marvelous marble edifice complete with galleried buildings all along its length. "The Rialto," said Renzi. "You will, of course, now be recalling Shakespeare and his *Merchant of Venice*."

The workboat glided up to a landing platform short of the bridge, and they stepped out into the city-state of Venice. "La Repubblica Serenissima," breathed Renzi. They were on the left bank with its fish markets, peddlers in sashes and pointed shoes, peasant women in brightly colored skirts with pails of water on yokes, shopkeepers yawning as they arranged their cheeses, porters trundling kegs of salted sardines, all adding to the tumult with their florid Venetian dialect.

Amati wasted no time. "Follow!" he demanded, and plunged into the crowd. They fell in behind, their rapid pace taking them into a maze of alleyways between many-colored buildings until they came on a dark and heady-smelling tavern. In the rank gloom was a scattering of foreigners, hard-looking Armenians, Jews, unidentifiable eastern races. The chatter died and faces turned toward them as they slid onto benches at a corner table.

"Da mi quattro Malvasie," Amati snapped to a waiter. "Sir, you stays here — please," he told Griffith in a whisper.

"Where are you going?" Griffith asked suspiciously.

"The consul, Signor Dandolo, he will come soon. I — I must go to my family, they expec' me." His eyes flicked about nervously as he spoke.

Kydd glanced across at the heavy Swede, whose set face gave away nothing. Renzi looked subdued. "He don't want to be seen wi' us," Kydd murmured, only too aware that they were unarmed. Griffith looked troubled.

"We are enjoying a visit to a furatole," Renzi said, with a wry smile, "a species of chophouse, this one frequented by despised foreigners. Eminently suitable as a rendezvous, I would have thought."

Four earthenware pots of coarse wine arrived, a little later fish soup. The sailors tucked in, but the penetrating strength of the anchovy stock dismayed them. Only Renzi finished his bowl, with every evidence of satisfaction. Hard bread was all that was on offer afterward.

Short and stout, but with dark, intelligent eyes and a quick manner, Dandolo arrived. He was dressed in flamboyant reds and greens, and he quickly got down to business. "Signor L'ith ha' still not arrive. You must stay how long, one, two week? Then I mus' find some lodging." His eyes narrowed. "You have money?"

Griffith brought a small purse into view and placed it on the table. It clinked heavily. "Guineas," he said, but kept his hand over it.

Dandolo kept it fixed with his keen eyes. "This Buonaparte is too lucky, he win too fast. All Friuli is in danger of him. There are some 'oo say Venice is too old to keep 'er empire, others, it frighten trade, threaten th' old ways. The Doge is weak and fear the Council of Ten — but now I must fin' you somewheres."

Pausing only for a moment, he turned to Griffith. "Sir, you will come wi' me to the Palazzo Grimani. The *marinaio*, they go to San Polo side —"

"Una camera vicino alla Calle della Donzella, forse?" Renzi interrupted, with a twisted smile.

"Sì." Dandolo looked sharply at him.

"With the foreign sailor. You know this place?"

"Yes." There were amazed looks from the other Englishmen, the sort of admiration reserved for those who had learned something of a foreign language.

"Y'r Grand Tour — ye must have had a whale of a time!" Kydd chuckled.

Renzi grinned shamefacedly. "We stayed at the Leon Banco, on San Marco side. It was considered a dare to spend a night with . . . on San Polo side . . ."

Griffith had been as strict as the circumstances allowed. Renzi, as master's mate, was placed in charge, and they occupied the top floor of a doss-house for merchant seamen, a single dark room with rag palliasses and a scatter of chairs and tables.

Wrinkling his nose at the smell, Kydd crossed to one of the mattresses, threw aside the cover and brought down his fist in the center. He inspected the result: several black dots that moved. He wouldn't be sleeping there that night. Renzi's face was a picture of disgust. Below in the tavern a rowdy dice game was already in progress, a swirl of careless noise that would make sleep impossible.

"So . . ." began Kydd. Larsson kicked

aside some palliasses to make a clear area, then dragged up a table and three chairs.

They looked at each other. "Sir Alastair might come at any time." Renzi's words were not convincing, and Kydd detected a wariness.

"Aye, but must we stay in — this?" he asked.

All eyes turned back to Renzi. He cleared his throat, and folded his arms. "The French are near."

Kydd sat back. Renzi was now going to make things clear.

"Venice is a very old, proud and independent republic, and she has no quarrel with revolutionary France. In the legal sense, therefore, we have as Englishmen a perfect right to be here, no need for disguise, dissembling." He pondered for an instant. "However, it would make sense not to embarrass the authorities if they must deny knowledge of the presence of English citizens to the French. I rather think our best course would be to lie low and see what happens. We must make the best of our circumstances, therefore."

"We stay."

"We must." There was a heavy silence.

"Why is th' agent, Amati, s' skittish, then?"

"Here we have an ancient and well-worn rule of government that is unique to this place. There are no kings, rather they elect one who should rule over them — the Doge. The first one over a thousand years ago, in fact. And there are nobles, those whose names are inscribed in the Golden Book of the Republic, and honored above all." He paused. "But the real power lies at the palace in the hands of the Council of Ten, who have supreme authority over life and death. They rule in secrecy — any who is denounced risks a miserable end in the Doge's prison. This, perhaps, is the source of his terror." Renzi continued: "But on the other hand, even while we are here in durance vile, there are at this moment — and not so very far from here — rich and idle ladies who think nothing of waking at noon, supping chocolate and playing with their lapdogs." He smiled at his shipmates' varied expressions and went on, "Should you desire — and have the fee — you may choose from a catalogue your courtesan for her skills and price."

Talk of this soon palled. The contrast with their present situation was too great.

Almost apologetically, Renzi tried to change tack. "In Venice gambling is a form of art. Should there be a pack of cards, and as we have time on our hands I would be glad to introduce you to vingt-et-un, perhaps, or . . ."

Time dragged. A noon meal in the smoke-blackened *furatole* did not improve the outlook of the three seamen.

Back in the room, Larsson's expression faded to an enduring blankness, and Renzi's features darkened with frustration. Many times he went to the grimy window and stared out over the rooftops.

"I needs a grog," grunted Larsson, challenging Renzi with a glower.

Renzi didn't answer for a time. Then, suddenly, he stood up. "Yes. Below." He left the room abruptly, without his coat.

Kydd jumped up and followed, tumbling down the stairway. *"Garba!"* he heard Renzi shout. It was rough brandy and water; Kydd had no real desire for it, and was unsettled by Renzi's deep pull at his pot.

The third round of drink came. In a low, measured tone, Renzi spat vehemently, "Diavolo!" The others looked at him. "This is *Venice!*"

"Aye, and so?" Kydd asked.

Renzi glared at him. "When last I was here . . ." He stopped. His knuckles showed white as he gripped the stone drinking vessel. Then he got to his feet in a sudden clumsy move that sent Kydd's pot smashing to the floor. Curious eyes flickered from other tables.

"I'm going out!" Renzi said thickly. "T' breathe some o' the air of Venice. Are you with me?"

"An' what about Leith?" Kydd wanted to know.

A quick smile. "Taken by the French long ago," Renzi said contemptuously. "How can he get through a whole army to us here? No chance. We make our time here as bearable as we can. Are you coming?"

Kydd saw that something serious had affected his friend, and resolved to stay by him. "I'll come, Nicholas." Larsson merely shook his head.

The evening, drawing in, had a spring coolness, but this did not deter the swelling numbers joining the hurrying tradesmen, market porters and domestics concluding their working day. An outrageously sequined and powdered harlequin stumbled by, well taken in drink, and an apparition emerged from the shadows wearing a cruel bird's-head mask and flowing blue cape. It trod softly, a thinly disguised Dulcinea on its arm in a red silk swirling cape and a glittering mask.

It was dreamlike and disturbing. No one took any notice of the grotesquerie in their midst. A group of masked revelers turned the corner, laughing and singing to the discordant accompaniment of timbrel and tambourine.

Kydd stood rooted in astonishment. "Is this —"

"Carnivale!" cackled Renzi harshly. "The world is aflame, and all they think of is carnival!"

A couple passed, exchanging kisses, elaborate coquetry with their masks doing little to conceal the naked sensuousness of their acts. Renzi stopped, staring after them. "But who then is to say — in all logic, for God's sake — that *they* are the ones with the perverted sense of the fitness of things, their perspectives malformed, their humanity at question?"

He breathed heavily, watching a figure in a russet cloak approach. The man's mask had slipped, exposing his foolish, inebriated grin as he staggered toward them. Renzi tensed. The figure bent double against a wall and Renzi darted across and toppled him over.

"Carnivale!" he howled triumphantly, tore away the cloak and snatched up the ivory mask. "Se non ha alcunio obiezione," he threw at the fallen form.

Kydd was appalled. "Nicholas, you — you —" But Renzi had thrown the cloak around himself, and pushed forcefully ahead, predatory eyes agleam through the cruel saturnalian mask.

Kydd hurried after him, helpless in the face of the unknown demons that possessed his friend. The narrow maze of streets now looked sinister, threatening. Renzi plunged on. A small humped bridge appeared ahead, spanning a canal. The blaze of a link torch carried by a servant preceded a decorous, well-dressed group, which scattered at Renzi's advance.

They were soon in an ancient square with a dusky red church facing them. Light showed in its high windows. As they thrust across, music swelled from it. Renzi faltered, then stopped. It was a choral piece, the melodic line exquisitely sustained by a faultless choir, the counterpoint in muted trumpet and strings a meltingly lovely intertwining of harmonies.

Kydd stopped, too, as the music entered his soul. Within those moments came a dawning realization that there were regions of the human experience above the grossness of existence and beyond the capability of the world to corrupt and destroy.

He turned to Renzi, but his friend was lost, staring at the church, rigid. Kydd tried to find some words but, suddenly, Renzi crumpled to his knees. The mask fell and Kydd saw his face distort and tears course down.

"N-Nicholas —" He struggled to reach out. Around them the people of Venice bustled with hardly a glance, the harlequins, falcons and the rest in a blur of color and impressions, and all the time the cool passion of the music.

Kydd tried to help Renzi up, but he pulled himself free and shot to his feet.

"Nicholas —"

Renzi rounded on him, his face livid. "Damn you!" he shouted. "Damn you to hell!" His voice broke with the passion of his words.

"M' friend, I only —"

Renzi's savage swing took Kydd squarely, and he was thrown to one side. He shook his head to clear it, but when he was able to see, there was no sign of Renzi.

Chapter 4

━━━━

Images streamed past Renzi, as bittersweet memories flooded back. He pushed past the gay troubadours, weary craftsmen, giggling couples, bored gondoliers — on and on into the Venetian night. His thoughts steadied, coalesced. For someone whose pride disallowed a display of emotion, his sudden loss of control in the square was disturbing and frightening.

His frenetic pacing calmed and he took note of his surroundings. He was heading in the direction of the dark rabbit warrens around Santa Croce and turned to retrace his steps. Then, recalling the soaring beauty of the Vivaldi that had so unfairly got under his guard, he stopped, confused. In truth, he could not go back — or forward.

A memory of what had been returned in full flower. The more he considered it, the more he yearned for her, the calm certitude and steel-cored passion he remembered from before. He had to go to her.

Lucrezia Carradini was married, but that was not of concern before and would not be now; in the Venetian way it was a matter of comment if a lady did not have at least one lover. He racked his brain to recall her whereabouts — yes, it was somewhere near the Palazzo Farsetti on San Marco side.

With rising excitement he made his way to the Grand Canal, taking an indolent gondola trip, then stepping feverishly through the night until he found himself before the Palazzo Carradini. He remembered the ogling brass-mouth knocker, but not the servant who answered the door.

"Il giramondo," he said, as his name — "the wanderer." Would she remember?

Footsteps came to the door. He raised his mask. It opened slowly, and there was a woman before him, in red velvet and a mask. Renzi saw the glitter of dark eyes behind the mask, then it dropped to reveal a delighted Lucrezia. Her vivacity and Italianate presence were just as he remembered. "Niccolò — mio caro Niccolò!" she screamed, and clung to him, her warmth and fragrance intoxicating. He thrust back guilt at the memory of how he had treated her and allowed himself to be drawn into the house.

In the opulence of the chamber she eyed him keenly. "You — you 'ave changed, Niccolò," she said softly. "An' where Guglielmo?"

It were better that his wild companion of the Grand Tour be allowed to live down those days in anonymity, Renzi decided. He was now one of England's most celebrated new poets. "Um, married," he said. "Lucrezia, I —" A flood of inchoate feelings and unresolved doubts roared through his head.

She looked at him intently. "You're still the crazy one, Niccolò — and now you come?"

"If it does not inconvenience," he said.

Little more than a child before, she had now firmed to a woman of grace and looks, and was just as much in possession of her own soul.

"Niccolò . . . it is Carnivale, not s' good to have heavy thoughts now, carissimi nonni." A shadow passed over her face. Then she said impulsively, "Come, we shall 'ave chocolate at Florian's."

"But, Carlo —"

"It is Carnivale. I don' know where he

is," she said impatiently. "We go in th' gondola Carradini."

The family gondola waited by the small landing platform at the water frontage of the house, varnished black with a shuttered cabin in the center. Renzi allowed himself to be handed aboard and the two gondoliers took position noiselessly, gazing discreetly into the middle distance.

Renzi and Lucrezia settled into the cushions of the closed cabin; her features softened to a tender loveliness by the little lamp. The craft pushed off with a gentle sway. Firmly, she reached across and pulled the louvered shutters closed, and then, just as purposefully, drew him to her.

They stepped ashore arm in arm into the magnificence of St. Mark's Square, alive with excitement and color, light and sequins, noise and mystery. There was an electric charge in the air, a feverish intensity that battered deliciously at the senses. They passed by the looming campanile into the arched colonnades of the square, Renzi's spirits willingly responding to the vibrancy of the atmosphere.

Caffè Florian had, if anything, increased in splendor. Outrageously clothed exquisites bowed to each other under glittering chandeliers hanging from polished wood paneling, their subdued voices occasionally broken through with silvery laughter. Renzi and Lucrezia sat together in a red padded alcove.

"Questo mi piace," Renzi breathed, but Lucrezia held her silence until the chocolate came.

Renzi did his best to pull himself together. "Tell me, what of this Buonaparte? Does he threaten Venice, do you think?"

She went rigid. He could see her eyes darting furtively behind the mask, scanning the room. "Niccolò — pliss, never say again!" She lowered her mask so he could see her seriousness. "Venezia, it is not like you remember. It is dangerous times now, ver' dangerous!" He could hardly hear her soft words, and bent forward. She smiled, popped a sweetmeat into his mouth, and continued in a whisper, affecting to impart endearments. "The Council of Ten have th' Inquisition, an army of spies, look everywhere for th' Jacobin." Renzi could sense her tension behind the gay smile. "Ever'where — you never know who."

She slid toward him, close enough that her words could not be intercepted. "Carlo, he brings wine from Friuli, he says French are all over nort' Italy like locust,

155

nothing can stop them, not even th' Austrians." Staring at her drink, she went on, "Montenotte, Lodi — that Buonaparte, he will not be contented with this. And he advance ver' fast — an' all the Veneziani think to do is more spies — and Carnivale!"

Renzi caught her eye. "As it's said, 'Venetians don't taste their pleasures, they swallow them whole'!"

She giggled, then sobered again. "Niccolò — don' you trust anyone, not anyone!"

"Not even you?" he teased.

"You must trust me," she said seriously. Then she cupped her chin in her hands and looked up at him. "Il giramondo — you are ver' strong now, I feel it."

The warmth of the evening fell away in layers, and the cold reality of a gray sea-tossed world penetrated even this conviviality, drawing him back. Reminiscences, hard memories pushed themselves into his consciousness, building a pressure of unresolved forces that he knew he must face.

"Cara Lucrezia, ti voglio appassionatamente, but I fear I'm no fit companion this night . . ."

"I understan' this, Niccolò." She regarded him closely. "What diavolo rides on your back, God know."

"Lucrezia, can we talk somewhere?"

"Th' gondola," she responded, and they rose and left. The gondoliers were on hand, as if by magic, and the chill of the night was kept at bay within the comfort of the cabin.

"You have changed, Niccolò — I don' know," she said tenderly, plucking at his waistcoat as if in doubt of its exotic origins. A wave of feeling broke; he would tell everything, whatever the cost.

He said the words and, looking into her eyes, saw pity, compassion — and insight. She did understand — the transformation of a careless youth to a morally sensitive adult through the harrowing suicide of the son of a farmer, ruined by an Act of Enclosure enforced by his family; the conviction and, more important, commitment to a course of action in atonement.

"My sentence is exile from my world, at sea. The problem lies in that since then I have grown to respect, admire and, if you can believe it, in some ways *prefer* the purity of the brotherhood of the sea."

Renzi had found opportunities for the deepest considerations of the intellect in the long watches of the night, and he could bring to memory many a conversation with

Kydd that he would never admit had settled his own doubts as much as his friend's.

Her hand crept out to seize his. "But this is not your world, Niccolò," she whispered.

A lump rose in Renzi's throat. "I know it. There are times —" How could he show how much he was torn? The sturdy honesty of deep-sea mariners, their uncomplicated courage and direct speaking had to be contrasted with their deep ignorance of the world, their lacking of subtlety to the point of obtuseness. But such a degree of friendship, won in adversity and tested in perils, was never to be found on land where daily trial of character was not a way of life.

He tried to explain — her intent expression encouraged him. He went on to describe the satisfactions: the change in worldview when the horizon was never a boundary but an opportunity, not the same daily prospect and limit but a broad highway to other lands, other experiences. And the different value for time at sea, when discourse could be followed to its own true end, the repose of mind resulting from the realization that time aboard ship would not be hurried, varied, dissipated.

The harsh conditions of his exile compared with his privileged upbringing were not the primary concern — a monk would understand the self-denial involved. In fact, as he examined it, explained it, there came a clarifying and focusing. Kydd. Without any doubt, Kydd's friendship had saved his sanity and made possible the enduring of his sentence. Renzi knew his own mind needed nurture and satisfaction or it would suffer a sterile withering, and he had found both in Kydd's intelligence and level-headed thinking. And they had shared so much together — what they had shared!

But when Kydd had been in another ship he was robbed of this. He was in an island of himself, no one to relieve the days with insight and an acquisitive mind. It was in those dull, repetitive times that the full hardship of what he had taken on was brought to bear. The lower deck of a man-o'-war was plain, unadorned, uncomplicated, but — and this was the cruel, plain fact — it was not the place for an educated and sensitive man.

"Lucrezia, pray help me. My sentence of exile is for five years, and its course is nearly run. So do I — *must* I — return then to my family? Leave the sea and my friends — my true friends . . ." It was harder to bear, now it had been given voice.

The gondola rocked gently in the calm of the lagoon, Lucrezia watching him calmly. But she had no hesitation: "Niccolò, ragazzo, you know th' answer to that," she said gently, stroking his hair. "You have serve your sentence, you can be proud, but you are a gentleman, not low-born. Go to your family an' start life again."

It was devastating — not what she had said, which was unanswerable, but the discovery that he should have known it would have to finish in this way. A great upwelling of emotion came, sudden and deluging. He covered his face as sobs turned to tears — but in the hot rush a cool voice remained to tell him that this was a final, irreversible decision: before the end of the year he would no longer be in the harsh world of the common seaman.

Kydd picked himself up, more dismayed than hurt. He had always admired his friend's fine intellect, but now he had serious doubts about the balance of his mind. Yet to look for him in this libertine madness was not possible — more to the point was how to steer a course back to their lodgings.

He remembered the big marble bridge. "Th' Rialto, if y' please," he asked passersby, and in this way soon found himself on familiar territory. A quick hunting about found their doss-house.

The Swede looked up curiously. "Where's Renzi?" A swirl of smoke and coarse shouting eddied from the dark recesses inside, but Larsson was content to stay with his *garba*.

"He's comin' back," Kydd snapped. "Renzi knows his duty, ye'll find." That much would be certain: if anything in this world was a fixed quantity it was that Renzi would fulfill his duty.

But Renzi did not return that night. Kydd waited in the dark loft, hearing the strange sounds of the Venetian night. He slept fitfully.

Minutes before their due reporting time to Lieutenant Griffith, Renzi returned. He gave no explanation, but seemed far more in control — yet distant, unreachable, in a way Kydd had never seen him before.

"We meet the agent at the Rialto," Renzi said, leading them down to the steps close to the bridge. Amati was waiting for them, and did not reply to their greeting. A gondola threaded through the water toward them, its cabin closed. They stepped aboard and it pushed off to the middle of the Grand Canal.

"Report!" The order came from the anonymous dark of the cabin.

"All quiet, sir," was Renzi's cool reply. "But I have heard reliably that the French are at the approaches to Venice, no more than a few miles. It is to be reasonably assumed, sir, that Sir Alastair has been unfortunately taken in trying to get through their lines."

"Where did you hear this?"

"From . . . I have no reason to doubt my source, sir."

There was no immediate reply. Then, "Venice is a sovereign republic — the French would never dare to violate her territory. We are safe here for the moment. We shall wait a little longer, I think."

Renzi frowned. "Sir, the French commander, General Buonaparte, is different from the others. He's bold and intelligent, wins by surprise and speed. I don't think we can underestimate —"

"Renzi, you are impertinent — this is not a decision for a common sailor. We stay."

"Aye-aye, sir," Renzi acknowledged carefully.

"You will report here at the same time

tomorrow. If you get word of Sir Alastair, I am to be informed immediately."

"Sir."

The gondola reached the landing place, and they disembarked. With barely a muttered excuse Renzi was gone — who knew where? Kydd found himself growing resentful and angry. They were on a mission of considerable importance, they were in danger, and Renzi had deserted them.

He growled at the gawping Larsson to keep with him as they headed back to their quarters, then saw what he was looking at. In a chance alignment of the dark streets, the bright outer lagoon was visible, and at that moment a vision was passing, surrounded by a swarm of lesser craft, a great vessel of dazzling gold and scarlet, moving trimly under the impulse of fifty oars.

"Il Bucintoro!" a passing onlooker said, with pride, noticing their fascination.

The galley glided grandly out of sight, leaving Kydd doubtful that he had actually seen what his senses told him he had.

Undoubtedly there were more such sights and experiences lying in wait all around, enough to have his shipmates lost in envy when he later recounted his adventures. But the French were allegedly just a few miles away, and their duty was plain.

He turned reluctantly toward their noisome lodgings.

The next morning Renzi arrived to meet them at the appointed place, this time with serious news. "Friuli is invaded. Buonaparte has stormed into Carinthia to the north, and his troops have bypassed Venice to strike south."

"Then we are surrounded," a low voice said cautiously from the gondola's dark cabin. "Where did you hear this?"

"From traders that have business in the interior, sir. And you may believe they are —"

"That will be all, Renzi."

"Sir —"

"We leave. Now." There was decision and relief in the officer's voice. "Sir Alastair has obviously been taken. We must depart, our duty done. Mr. Amati, do you please engage passage for the four of us out of Venice immediately? You men muster abreast the Rialto Bridge in one hour with your dunnage."

This time Renzi stayed, fetching his small seabag from the loft and waiting in the shadows with them. "May I know where you've been, Nicholas?" Kydd said gravely.

"No." Renzi's eyes were stony and fixed

on the opposite side of the Grand Canal.

"I'd take it kindly should ye tell me more o' this grand place, m' friend."

There was no response from Renzi. Then his eyes flicked to Kydd and away again. "Later," he muttered.

Kydd brooded. Something was seriously troubling his friend. They should be in no real danger — the French wouldn't dare to interfere in such a noble city, so all they had to do was leave. But they would run from Venice and return to Gibraltar without the glory of a daring rescue . . . He tried to bring to mind Emily's face, but it was shadowed, overlain by the incredible events and sights he'd so recently witnessed. His wandering thoughts were interrupted — a piece of paper had been passed to Renzi.

"This is from L'tenant Griffith. We are to report to this warehouse at once." He led the way toward the waterfront. Just before they emerged on to the quay area they stopped. Renzi stepped forward and banged on the decrepit door of a small warehouse. It opened cautiously and they were pulled inside.

As their eyes grew used to the dark, they saw Dandolo, pacing nervously up and down. There were two others, sitting on

165

the floor, heads down, exhausted. Kydd's nose tickled at the pungent scent of the warehouse, which lay heavy on the air — ginger, spices, tobacco.

"Where iss your officer?" Dandolo pressed. As if in answer, there was a rattling at the door and Griffith stepped in, breathless.

"Sir Alastair?"

"The same," whispered one of the men on the floor.

"Good God! Sir, you must be — but we have you in time."

Dandolo intervened. "We agreed . . . ?"

"Indeed." Griffith fumbled in his coat, and withdrew a cloth-wrapped cylinder. He handed it to Dandolo. It was broken open expertly and a spill of dull gold coins filled Dandolo's hand. He grinned with satisfaction. "We are leaving Venice. Do you wish to claim the protection of His Majesty also?"

Dandolo's eyes creased. "No. I have my plans."

"Is there a way to inform Mr. Amati where we are?" Griffith asked.

Dandolo paused. "If that iss what you wan'."

Griffith crossed to Leith. "Sir, Lieutenant Griffith, third of *Bacchante* frigate, and three seamen. We are sent to remove you from Venice."

"Thank you," Leith said equably, "and this is my man. He has stayed with me since the other side of the Alps. What is the situation, if you please?" Before Griffith could answer, Leith added, "Be aware that the French are advancing with celerity and all the determination of a strong sea tide. There is no time to be lost, sir."

"Our evacuation is in hand as we speak, sir. Our agent is procuring passage for us by any means, and I expect him back by the hour."

"Very good. I will not speak of food and drink — these can wait until we are on board. Now, if you please, be so good as to allow us a period of sleep. We are sorely tried."

"Sir."

There was nothing to do except wait for Amati in decorous silence. Renzi lay on a sack and closed his eyes, but Kydd could not rest. It was expecting a lot of the agent to delay his own hopes of safety for their sake, however high his expected reward. Perhaps he had already slipped away, leaving them to wait in vain for their passage out.

It seemed hours, but Amati returned.

Kydd felt for the little man as he slipped in noiselessly. "I can no' find a passage," he said defiantly.

"What?" Griffith jumped to his feet.

"My dear sir, the man returned, did he not?" Leith said wearily. "Pray tell us, what is the difficulty?" he asked Amati.

"The French, they take Chioggia, Malamocco. Now they ha' control all gate to th' lagoon. No ship can lif. None." He looked up wearily. "No one wan' to try."

Griffith stared at Amati. "So, we have a problem."

No one spoke.

Renzi's expression eased to a half-smile, and in the breathless hush he said, "Sir, you are mindful that we are English —"

"Of course I do — you try my patience, Renzi!"

"— and therefore we shall probably be yielded up by the Venetians as a placating move to the French —"

"Enough! Hold your tongue, you impertinent rascal!"

"— who will without doubt understand us to be here as spies, to be executed perhaps?"

At his words there was only a grim silence. It was broken by a dry chuckle from Leith. "Just so. Nothing less than the truth,

I would have thought." He glanced keenly at Renzi. "Please go on."

"Sir. Our logical course is to hide among the people but, sadly, I fear we would make poor Italians. Disguise is impossible — we would be discovered out of hand. I feel we must find another solution."

"They gotta catch us fust. Let 'em come!" Larsson challenged.

"With no weapons of any kind?" Everyone present knew that an armed party discovered ashore in Venice would have been an intolerable provocation to the Serene Republic. "No. I fancy we are at hazard to a degree."

A rattling started at the door. Kydd and Larsson hastily took position at each side, ready for the final act. The door opened, but instead of soldiers there was a small figure, fetchingly arrayed in a Columbine costume, her face hidden by a white mask.

"What in heaven —" spluttered Griffith.

"You fools!" Lucrezia said, dropping her mask and sparing Renzi a withering look. "Why you still 'ere?"

Leith picked up on the look. "Your acquaintance, Mr. Renzi?"

Renzi ignored the expression of sudden realization on Kydd's face. "Signora Lucrezia Carradini, Sir Alastair Leith."

She acknowledged him warily, sizing up the little party. Her eyes rested on Amati. " 'Oo is zis?" she demanded. Renzi began to explain, but Amati's muttered Italian seemed to satisfy her.

She looked away for a moment. "To hide all you, zis will be deeficult. It may be long time, the French will no' go away soon." It seemed natural that she was taking charge of their fate. Her strong features and resolute bearing made it so.

The men waited. She looked once toward the door, then spoke decisively. "Here I say I store my cargo, a ver' valuable load, to wait the ship. I send men to guard it, no one interfere wi' you now."

Her mask went up as she prepared to leave. "I will fin' you a ship, jus' be patient. And *never* show yourselfs." She turned to Renzi. "You are ze compradore, you worry of its safety, you come back an' check on it many times. But now you mus' come wi' me."

The spicy rankness of the warehouse bore on the spirit but, sailor-fashion, the men turned to, making the best of it. Hammocks were fashioned, screens were rigged and a "mess area" squared away as clean as possible. They tried to ignore the sounds from outside, the chains drawn across the door, the unknown muffled words.

Renzi returned at nightfall with food and drink concealed in a chest, as if an addition to the cargo. He did not volunteer conversation, and the others did not press him. He left quickly.

Leith spent his time with the naval officer, leaving the two sailors to themselves. There was not much conversation in Larsson, and Kydd found himself on edge.

After a restless night and a quick dawn visit from Renzi they had no choice other than to resign themselves to another day of tedium. It was well into the morning when Kydd's senses pricked an alert. "There's somethin' amiss," he said. "Listen . . ."

"I hear nothing," said Griffith irritably.

"That is m' point, sir. There's nothin' going on — everythin's stopped."

"He's right," said Leith.

The troubling stillness continued into the afternoon.

"One o' their papist festivals cleared 'em from their duties" was Griffith's opinion.

Dryly, Leith disagreed. "I rather fancy they'd make more noise, more bells and crowds."

"Then maybe the French have entered?"

"Without protest, cannon fire? Their soldiers would certainly have let the world know if they had, I can assure you." Leith stood up and paced about, the first sign of unease Kydd had seen him display. "I don't like this — at all."

By late afternoon, it was obvious that something was seriously out of kilter. And Renzi had not come with their food.

"We have to know what is afoot. Pray stand by me, you men." Leith crossed to the doors and shook them sharply for attention.

"Sir, the woman —"

"We must be ready to take action — of any kind." There was no response from the outside. Leith shook the door again. Kydd tried to squint through the cracks, but could see no one.

"Her men have gone. We are forgotten."

Griffith stood suddenly. "We have to move. Kydd, climb aloft to the upper storeroom and see if there is an exit for us there." Kydd swung up into the darkness of the partitioned loft above, but found that the warehouse was proofed against thieves and had no discernible openings.

Larsson was tasked to look for a sizable timber for use as a battering ram on the stout doors. Then the chain rattled on the outside. It fell away and Renzi thrust himself in, pulling the door to hastily.

"The gravest news!" He was breathless and looked weary. He let a bundle fall, which Kydd recognized as his seabag.

"We have hours only before the worst and — I — I cannot believe what has taken place!" Renzi's expression struck a deep chill in his listeners.

"And that is?" Leith's tone was steely.

Renzi turned. "Venice is no more! A thousand years of civilization gone! Finished!"

Griffith snorted. "Get on with it, you ninny, make your report."

Renzi ignored him, staring at Leith, whose grave face suggested that he knew what was to come. "The people have been betrayed. The Council of Ten — the Doge — have failed their citizens. They have been deluded, bullied. It is all over for Venice."

He paused and looked away. "The true situation has been concealed. What has happened is that the French general, Buonaparte, has cleverly turned an enemy, Austria, to an ally. How? He cannot strike southward into Italy until he has pacified this hostile country in his rear. So he pacifies it in another way. He gives it Venice."

"Venice is neutral."

"This Buonaparte is truly a genius at war, but as ruthless and unscrupulous as the very devil himself. Yes, Venice is neutral, but he has taken every excuse to paint her the aggressor, the tyrant. Just two weeks ago his commander, Junot, apparently stormed before the Council of Ten with a personal letter from him containing unacceptable demands. Today —" Renzi's voice changed almost to a whisper. "Today the Doge Lodovico called a Grand Council. It was the first the people knew of the danger — they believed themselves neutral in this war. A new letter was read out from General Buonaparte. In it he said that the old ways were to be swept away, a new age of revolution was upon them, and if they objected, he would not be held accountable for the consequences.

"While they deliberated, a dispatch was received from their own consigleri militari that there is French artillery, many guns, ringing the lagoon and ready to reduce Venice to a ruin. The Doge asks for a final vote of submission to the French and suicide for the Venetian state. What he did not reveal was that their spies had reported that, not two weeks earlier, a secret peace was signed at Leoben between Austria and

174

France. The price asked was Venice and her decrepit empire."

Renzi continued quietly, "The vote was taken in indecent haste, passed, and the nobiluomini of Venice fell over each other to get away, turning their backs on their birthright and abandoning their noble obligations to save their skins. Gentlemen, the Serenissima is no more!"

The brooding quiet lay heavy and ominous. When the people of Venice had digested the events, there would be a reaction. Even now far-off shouts could be heard. The French would be forming up to march in, whether to civil chaos or a humbled populace it didn't matter: the end was the same. They only had hours to decide what to do.

"You seem very well informed, Renzi, for a foremast hand," snarled Griffith.

"The lady Carradini, whom I knew — before is well placed in the highest of the land. You can be assured there are few secrets she does not know."

"And tells you?"

Renzi's smile was weary. "She has a *tendre* for me. This is not for us to debate. What is more at issue is the next few hours."

"Have a care, Renzi, you are still under

discipline, even here."

"Sir."

Leith stirred. "I care not for your nautical niceties, gentlemen. Now, are you about to leave us again, Mr. Renzi?"

"No, sir."

Kydd realized the implication of the seabag: Renzi might have had a chance to get away, but he had chosen to see things through with his friends. "Thank ye, Nicholas," he said softly.

The dusty silence was broken by a tiny sound, a wispy slither. The pale edge of a paper appeared under the door, but when Kydd reached it there was no sign of anyone. "Here, m' friend, it's all Dutch t' me," Kydd said, passing it to Renzi.

"Thank you. It says we are to stay here until after dark. Then we will receive a visitor, whom we may account a welcome one. I recognize the hand," Renzi added gravely.

"We wait?" Griffith ignored Renzi, addressing Leith directly.

"Have you an alternative in mind, sir?"

As evening approached the gloom in the musty warehouse deepened. Muffled shouts and random disorder erupted at intervals, a scuffle breaking out not far from the door. The situation was apparently resolved with a grunting, despairing cry, then silence.

There was a feeble oil lantern in the spaces by the wall, but it served to keep the darkness at bay.

Kydd could hardly bear the inactivity, the inability to do *anything*. He yearned for the lift and fall of a deck under his feet, but realized that, with the stranglehold now established by the French, it was probable he would never again know the sensation.

The darkness outside was absolute when their visitor arrived. A hurried double knock and hoarse, "Il giramondo — ehi." Dressed in a black cloak, the man kept his face averted in its hood. "Dovè il ufficiale di marina inglese?" he asked tensely, the eyes glittering within the hood.

"He wants the English naval officer," Renzi said.

Griffith stepped forward to a quarter-deck brace and said crisply, "I am Lieutenant Griffith of His Britannic Majesty's frigate *Bacchante*."

The man hesitated, then seemed to come to a decison. He threw off his hood and snapped smartly to attention. "Tenente di vascello Bauducco — Paolo Bauducco."

"Lieutenant Paolo Bauducco," Renzi

murmured, and in turn made an appropriate introduction of Lieutenant Griffith.

"Prendendo in considerazione la grandezza della marina inglese . . ."

The stream of passionate Italian appeared theatrical in the drab confines of the warehouse, the weak lantern light picking up the occasional flash of rank and decorations under the cloak. Renzi held up his hands to pause the flow, and tried to put across the officer's plea. "Er, it seems that, in deference to the regard he has for the Royal Navy, he wishes to put forward a proposition."

Griffith frowned, but Leith showed instant interest. Bauducco resumed, his ardor transparent.

"Ah, he is a loyal Venetian, and today he was profoundly ashamed of the perfidy of the Doge and his ministers. He learned as well that the Arsenale, the famous naval dockyard and all the ships of Venice, are to be turned over to General Buonaparte."

Bauducco's voice swelled in anger.

"This is intolerable. It seems . . . if I understand him aright, that there are many men in the Venetian service who feel as he does." Renzi cocked his head, as if in doubt of what he was hearing, and continued carefully, "He goes on to say, sir, that this night he and his men intend to rise up against his captain and carry his vessel to sea. Would he be right to put before them that his vessel — a xebec only, but well armed — would then be taken into the sea service of Great Britain against the French?"

There was a disbelieving silence. Griffith recovered first. "Tell him that a British frigate at this moment lies to seaward, and we have but to reach her — and tell him, too, damn it, that his offer is handsomely accepted."

The hours passed in a fever of waiting. They had been warned that when the time came they were not to delay an instant: there could be no turning back. But they were safe where they were — when they broke for freedom anything might be waiting for them out there in the night.

The lantern had sputtered and died from lack of oil, and they had only the shadows of men and terse orders to assure them that deliverance was at hand. They emerged from their refuge, stepping warily behind the unknown emissary, past shuttered and silent buildings, sinister by their very quiet.

In the open, noises of disorder and signs

of a gathering tumult were much clearer on the night air, sounds that were both distant and near, chilling in their portent of chaos to come. They hurried along the claustrophobic streets in a tight group, this way and that, until they reached yet another of the small humped bridges.

On the other side was a rich gondola, its varnished black sides glittering in the illumination of a single streetlight. A pair of gondoliers stood tense and ready. The party tumbled in, and packed into the cabin, falling against each other in their haste. The gondoliers poled off, but not before Renzi, raising the slats of the cabin window to catch a last sight, noticed a figure detach itself from the shadows and a gloved hand lift in silent farewell.

The motion of the craft was purposeful and steady, the men in the cabin having no difficulty in visualizing its track along the narrow canals, then the straight course and lively movement of the open lagoon.

The regular creak and thrust of the gondoliers ceased unexpectedly, leaving the gondola to an aimless bobbing. Renzi peered out. "We're in the lagoon, more to the south, and off the Arsenale — I can see the entrance." This would be where the xebec would break out, through the twin towers of the gate from the internal basin and through the channel to open waters — if the rising were successful.

Few craft were abroad that could be seen in the rising moon, and a motionless gondola was a dangerous curiosity. It couldn't be helped. If attention was diverted to the water by some incident, their fate would be sealed. This was the Carradini gondola and Lucrezia would have paid the gondoliers well for their night's work — but enough?

Renzi checked the flint and steel he had been given. It was essential that they attract the attention of the xebec at the right time or they would be left behind in its desperate flight. It was time, but there was no sign of insurrection or riot in the brightly lit dockyard.

Lifting more of the slats, he scanned the lagoon. At night there was no reason to sail about, the wharves had no men to work cargo and no one to account for movement of the goods. A couple of other gondolas, far off, moving at speed, and some anonymous low riverboats were all that were in sight.

Then from around the northern point of Venice came a larger vessel, a lugger. It altered course directly toward them.

"Trouble," he muttered, and alerted the others. Their die was cast: there was no way they could make it back into the maze of canals before the lugger closed with them.

"Somethin' happenin'." Kydd had been watching the dockyard. Renzi snatched a look. They could not see into the basin, but he could have sworn that a gunflash briefly lit up the front of one of the buildings.

The lugger came on purposefully. But there were men at the Arsenale entrance — and then the bows of a vessel emerged into the channel, indistinct and with no sail hoisted. Renzi hesitated; if this was not the xebec, their one chance . . . but he could just make out the three counterraked masts of such a vessel — and not only that: there was musket firing.

This was their salvation — if he got the light going. Kydd held the wooden tube, the grainy fuse close to Renzi's flint. Renzi struck it once, twice. No fat spark leaped across. Again — this time a faint orange speck.

The xebec won through to open water; it was under oars, but a triangular sail was jerking up from the deck. It angled over.

"For Christ's sake!" The strangled oath had come from Griffith. The flint must have got wet, and there was nothing for it but to keep trying, hard, vicious hits. A bigger spark, but it missed the fuse. Renzi steadied and struck again. The spark leaped, and landed squarely on the fuse with an instant orange fizz. Kydd stepped out into the well of the gondola, and the light caught, a pretty golden shower.

The xebec immediately lay over toward them, but the lugger would reach them well before it could. But then the lugger unexpectedly abandoned its pursuit and resumed its course along the foreshore of St. Mark's.

As the xebec slashed toward them, Kydd laughed. "It thinks th' shebek is takin' us in!" It was the work of moments for the sailors to tumble over the low gunwale and onto the narrow deck, then turn to heave in Leith and his servant. The two gondoliers scrambled up, leaving their smart black gondola to drift away into the night. It was now clear how Lucrezia had secured their loyalty. The lump in Renzi's throat tightened.

Instinctively, they made their way aft to the narrow poop where Bauducco stood searching for signals. "Dobbiamo stare attenti alla catena," he muttered.

Renzi heard the warning, and told the others. "It seems the lagoon entrance to the open sea is chained. If this is so, I fear we cannot break through it in this light vessel."

The dark hummock of land that was Rochetta loomed, and a pair of lanterns appeared on the shore. They danced up and down energetically — Bauducco whooped with joy.

"The chain is evidently lowered for us," Renzi murmured, and the xebec passed through to the darkness of the sea beyond.

They were free.

Chapter 5

The noon rendezvous had been made, the passengers transferred and *Bacchante*'s crew made whole again. Now the xebec was curving in a respectful swash under their lee as they set course for Gibraltar, a lieutenant and midshipman of the Royal Navy aboard this newest addition to King George's fleet.

Kydd saw Renzi at the fore-shrouds, looking back at the wasplike lines of the xebec, and wandered over. The last few days had been too intense, too contrasted, and he needed to make sense of them — but what was bedeviling Renzi, threatening the friendship of years? "So it's all over f'r Venice?"

"I believe so," Renzi responded. His hand twisted the shroud. "Venice is old, ancient, and now extinct as a military power. That is all."

The little frigate stumbled to a wave and

recovered in a hiss of foam. Kydd grabbed at a rope and shot an exasperated look at Renzi. His stiff manner perplexed him. He had done nothing to cause it that he could think of, and it had been the same since Gibraltar. "Nicholas, if there's anything I've done that troubles ye, then —"

"No!" Renzi's fierce response was unsettling. "No. Not you," he went on, in a more controlled tone. "At the least, not in the proximate cause."

"Then —"

"I will tell you — as my friend. As my dear friend."

"Nicholas?" asked Kydd, with a numbing premonition.

"And as one who I know will honor my — position." He composed himself. "This, then, is the essence. You will know that my presence on the lower deck of a man-o'-war is by choice. It is the self-sentence I have assumed to relieve my conscience of a family sin. And you may believe that it has been hard for me, at times very hard — not the sea life, you understand, which has its attractions, but that which bears so dire on the spirit."

It had always been a given, an unspoken acceptance that Renzi would never allow his origins to prevail over his convictions, never let the harsh, sometimes crude way of life on the lower deck affect his fine mind and acute sensibilities.

Renzi continued: "I mean no derogation of the seamen I have met, no imputation of brutishness — in fact, since making their close acquaintance, these are men I own myself proud to know, to call friend. No, it is the absence of something that *to me* is proving an insupportable burden — the blessed benison of intellectual companionship."

His eyes lifted to Kydd's face. "Those years ago, when we met for the first time, it was as if you were a gift from the gods to help me bear my private burden. Now, it seems, the exigencies of the service have taken this solace from me, and I spend my days at sea in isolation, in a bleakness of spirit, day in, day out. The fo'c'sle is not the place for a child of learning. In short, my dear friend, the five years of my exile reaches its end in December and I shall not be continuing this life beyond that point."

Wordless, Kydd stared at him. He had no idea that Renzi had valued their friendship on that plane; he had gone along with the Diderot and the Rousseau to experience pleasure at the display of fine logic and meticulous reasoning as well as for the evident pleasure it gave his friend. As Renzi's words penetrated, he became aware that he had gained so much himself by the friendship. His own mind had been opened to riches of the intellect, he had glimpsed life in polite society, and now it was over. He would become like so many fine old seamen he knew, the very best kind of deep-sea mariner, but rough-hewn, without the graces, inarticulate.

His mind struggled to adjust. So much in his world would no longer be there, but Renzi's was a fine and noble mind and it had no place on the gundeck of a ship of war. "Nicholas, you'll —"

"It is quite resolved. It will be so."

"Then — then you'll go back to y' folks?" Kydd said, trying to hide his sinking spirits.

Renzi paused. "I suppose I will. That is the logical conclusion." They both gazed out on the blue-green waters. "You will always be welcome, dear fellow, should you be passing by."

"Aye. An' if y' wants t' see how the Kydd school is progressin' . . ."

Their keel plowed a white furrow through the empty cobalt blue of the Mediterranean. Renzi had become ever more agreeable, courteously debating as in the old days, delicately plucking a great truth from a morass of contradictions for Kydd's admiration. They mourned the passing of Venice, the chaos of war now engulfing the world, the irrelevance of the individual in the face of colossal hostile forces.

All too soon they sighted the great Rock of Gibraltar rearing up ahead. Kydd would rejoin his ship there and face his fate: a shameful horsewhipping at the hands of a jealous husband. It all seemed so forlorn. His feelings were now a dying ember of what was before, but he would see through what had to come as a man.

Bacchante glided into Rosia Bay, striking her sails smartly and losing no time in sending her important guest ashore. *Achilles* was not at anchor, and Kydd learned that she was in Morocco, at Tetuan for watering.

The mate-of-the-watch had little to do in harbor, and after Renzi had seen to the brief ceremony attending the captain going ashore, he reflected on what had come to pass. There was no doubt that he had made the right decision regarding his future: he had served his sentence fully and he could take satisfaction not only in this but in the fact that he had been not unsuccessful in his adopted profession. Yet the thought of returning to his inheritance, to the confining, predictable and socially circumscribed round, was a soul-deadening prospect after vast seascapes, far shores and the sensory richness of a sea life.

He reviewed the years of friendship he had enjoyed. Not just the times of shared danger, but golden memories of a night watch under the stars far out in the Pacific, with a silver moonpath glittering. Or when he had mischievously taken a contrary stand on some matter of philosophy simply to have Kydd find within himself some sturdy rejoinder, some expression of his undeniable strength of character.

He burned at the remembrance of the logical outworking of one line of philosophy that, but for Kydd, would have seen him end his days in the savagery of a South Sea island. Other instances came to mind, the totality of which led to an inevitable conclusion.

In his core being, he must still be the tempestuous soul he always had been, and his carefully nurtured rationality was an insufficient control. He *needed* Kydd's strength, his straight thinking to keep him stable and, dare he say? the regard that Kydd obviously had for him. Now it was no longer there, only a lowering bleakness.

Then, breaking through his thoughts, he saw a figure slowly emerge on deck from the main hatchway. Rigged once more as a master's mate in breeches and full coat, Kydd looked pale and his movements were deliberate. He came aft to report, as was his duty.

"Steppin' ashore, Nicholas."

"Er, I wish you well of —"

"That's kind in ye," Kydd replied. Both men knew there was nothing Renzi could do in a matter of honor: the kindest thing was to be absent when the inevitable final scene took place.

"Then I'll be away," Kydd said. He held his head high as he stepped over the bulwarks and down to the boat.

It stroked lazily toward Ragged Staff steps; Kydd did not look back. Renzi watched until he was out of sight. A vindictive husband, who wanted to take a full measure of revenge, could make Kydd pay a terrible price for his foolishness.

Kydd returned before the end of Renzi's duty watch. The warm dusk had also seen

Achilles put back into Gibraltar. "Nicholas, do ye have time?"

Renzi's relief was already on deck, so they went to the main-shrouds, out of earshot of the one or two on deck aft. Renzi looked keenly at Kydd.

"It was th' damnedest thing, Nicholas," Kydd said, in a low voice. He looked around suspiciously, but no one was anywhere near. "M' letter — y' remember? Well, seems that Consuela — that's Mrs. Mulvany's maid I gave m' letter to — she gets it all wrong 'n' thinks it's *her* the letter's for, there bein' no names in it a-tall, an' there she is, waitin' for me when I gets ashore."

"So you've been spared the whip?" Renzi said dryly.

Kydd colored. "I have — but it's to cost me five silver dollars to buy the letter back," he said, "and when I went t' Emily's house, her husband was in, invited me t' dinner, even." His face fell. "But when I wanted t' see Emily — say my farewells afore we return to England — seems she was unwell an' couldn't see me."

"Unfortunate," murmured Renzi. Then he straightened. "You're sailing tonight."

"F'r England," Kydd replied, but there was no happiness in his voice.

"*Bacchante* goes to Lisbon where I rejoin my ship," Renzi said. "I — I'm not sanguine that we shall meet again soon, my dear friend." It were best the parting were not prolonged.

"Ye could be sent back t' Portsmouth f'r a docking," Kydd said forlornly.

"Yes, that's true," Renzi replied softly. "Thomas, be true to yourself always, brother, and we shall see each other — some time."

"An' you as well, Nicholas. So it's goodbye, m' friend." The handshake lingered, then Kydd turned and went.

Achilles stood out into the broad Atlantic, questing for the trade westerlies, the reliable streams of air that blew ceaselessly across thousands of miles of ocean to provide a royal highway straight to England.

She soon found them, and shaped course northward. The winds so favorable on her larboard quarter also formed a swell that came in, deep and regular, under her old-fashioned high stern. Up and up it rose, angling the rest of the ship over to starboard and steeply down into the trough ahead. Then, when the swell reached the midpoint of the vessel, her bow rose, bowsprit clawing the sky, and her stern fell precipitously away while, with a sudden jerk, she rolled back to larboard. To a seaman it was instinctive. The fine sailing in these regular seas was easy, the motion predictable. The only concern was that the winds might die away to a tedious flat amble.

These spirited seas saw *Achilles* at her best, an energetic, seething wake stretching away astern, flecks of foam driven up by her bluff bows flying aft to wet the lips of the watch-on-deck with salt, the bright sun casting complex, hypnotically moving, shadows of sails and rigging on the decks.

But there were those aboard who did not appreciate the Atlantic Ocean in springtime. Huddled over the bulwarks in the waist, sprawling on the foredeck in seasick misery, were the quota men who had exchanged the debtor's jail for a life at sea and others who had never had a say in their fate.

The run north was a time of trial and terror for these land creatures. Forced to overcome their seasickness, they learned an eternal lesson of the sea: no matter the bodily misery, the task is always seen through to its right true end, then belayed and squared away. There were some who prevailed over their soft origins and won through to become likely sailors, but there were more who would be condemned forever to be no more than brute laborers of the sea.

By contrast the mariners had their sea ways; the carefully fashioned lids over their oaken grog tankards against slop from the surging movement, the lithe motion as they got up from the mess tables and swayed sinuously along in unconscious harmony with the sea's liveliness, chinstays down on their tarpaulin hats while aloft. There were an uncountable number of tiny details, the sum of which set on one side those who were true sea dwellers, who knew the sea as a home and not as a frightening and unnatural perversion of human existence.

In the several days it took to pass northward along the Portuguese and Spanish coasts and make landfall on Finisterre, *Achilles* tried hard to return to her character as a true man-o'-war after a long and corrosive confinement in port.

"God rot 'em, but they're a pawky lot o' lobcocks!" Poynter, quarter-gunner, glared at the gun's crew standing sweaty and weary after unaccustomed work at training and side tackle on the cold iron.

Kydd could only agree. As master's

mate, he was essentially deputy to the lieutenant of the gundeck and had a definite interest in excellence at their gunnery. "Keep 'em at it, Poynter, the only way."

Hands were stood down from their exercise only when at seven bells the pipe for "hands to witness punishment" was made. The familiar ritual brought men up into the sunlight to congregate in a sullen mass at the forward end of the quarterdeck. Officers stood on the poop while the gratings were rigged below, in front of the men. Kydd stood between, and to the side.

This was not a happy ship: the combination of a God-fearing captain of dour morals and a boatswain whose contempt for the men found expression in harshness gave little scope for compassion.

Kydd glanced far out to seaward, where a light frigate was keeping loose station on them for the run to Portsmouth. She made much of being under topsails only to stay with *Achilles*'s all plain sail. Kydd had known service in a frigate, in his eyes a more preferable ship, but they seldom rated a master's mate.

"Same ones," Cockburn murmured, bringing Kydd's attention back to the flogging and the three pathetic quota men whose crime was running athwart Welby's hawse yet again. The captain's bushy gray eyebrows quivered in the wind, his eyes empty and merciless as he judged and sentenced.

The boatswain's mate waited for the first man to be seized up to the grating, then stepped across. He pulled the lash from the red baize bag and measured up to his task. The marine drummer took position directly above the half-deck, looking inquiringly at Captain Dwyer. In expectation the rustle of whispers and movement stilled — but into the silence came a low sobbing, wretched and hopeless.

"Good God!" Kydd breathed. It was the scraggy little man at the gratings, his pale body heaving in distress.

The boatswain's mate stopped in astonishment, then looked at the captain. Dwyer's eyebrow rose, and he turned to Welby, nodding once.

"Do yer dooty then, Miller," Welby threw at his mate in satisfaction. The drum thundered, and stopped. In the sickening silence the cat swept down, bringing a hopeless squeal of pain. Kydd looked away. This was achieving nothing, neither individual respect for discipline nor a cohering deference for justice in common. Lashes were laid on pitilessly. The ship's company watched stolidly. This was the way it was, and no amount of protest could change it.

Kydd scanned the mass of men. He noticed Farnall, the educated quota man who'd had a run-in with Boddy when he first came aboard. Farnall's face showed no indication of disgust or hatred, more a guarded, speculative look.

The contrast between the grim scenes on the upper deck and the fellowship at the noon meal directly afterward brought a brittle gaiety. Grog loosened tongues and the satisfaction of like company quickly had the crowded mess tables in a buzz of companionable talk and laughter.

Kydd always took a turn along the main deck before his own dinner; after overseeing the issue of grog to the messes, he had an implied duty to bear complaints from the men aft, but the real reason was that he enjoyed the warm feeling of comradeship of the sailors at this time, and he could, as well, try the temper of the men by their chatter.

He passed down the centerline of the ship, the sunlight patterning down through the hatchway gratings, the odor of the salt pork and pease filling the close air of the gundeck. Today there were not the lowered voices, glaring eyes or harsh curses that usually preceded trouble, and he guessed that the useless quota hand had gained few friends.

"Jeb." He nodded at a nuggety able seaman, who grinned back, winking his one remaining eye. No bad blood, it seemed. This was a man Kydd had seen to it drew duty as captain of the heads after he had found him asleep in the tops. He could have taken the man before the captain for a serious offense, but instead he was cleaning the seats of ease each morning before the hands turned to.

As Kydd came abreast the next pair of guns, a seaman got to his feet, hastily bolting a mouthful. It was Boddy. "First Sunday o' the month, next," he said significantly.

"Aye," said Kydd, guessing what was coming.

"An' I claims ter shift mess inter number six st'b'd."

Kydd pursed his lips. "They'll have ye?" It was the right of every man to choose his messmates — and they him. The first Sunday of the month was when moves were made. What was a puzzle was that this was Farnall's mess, a landman's refuge, and he'd heard that Boddy and Farnall had tangled in Gibraltar. He took out his notebook. "I'll see first luff knows," he said.

The indistinct blue-gray bluff of Finisterre left astern, *Achilles* plunged and rolled on into the Bay of Biscay. Kydd's heart was full: they were bound for England, to his home and hearth for the first time after years that had seen him on a world voyage in a famous frigate, in the Caribbean as a quartermaster in a trim little topsail cutter and a full master's mate in a 64-gun ship-of-the-line. He would return to Guildford, a man of some consequence. "Back to th' fleet — no chance of prize money there," he said to Cockburn, a grin belying his words.

The day faded to a brisk evening, then night. The frigate had been called to heel, and her lights twinkled and appeared over to larboard in the moonless dusk. Last-dog-watchmen were called, hammocks piped down and the watch-on-deck mustered. *Achilles* sailed into the night, her watch expecting an uneventful time. The frigate's lights faded ahead before midnight, but an alert lookout sighted them an hour or two later on the opposite side, creeping back companionably.

The morning watch was always a tense

time, for enemy ships could appear out of the cold dawn light and fall upon an unprepared vessel. As with most naval vessels, *Achilles* met the dawn at quarters, ready for any eventuality. A ship-of-the-line with a frigate in company had little to fear, and as the light of day gradually extended, the boredom of waiting saw gun crews dozing, watch-on-deck relaxed, captain not on deck.

The situation caught everyone by surprise. In the strengthening light the comfortable but indistinct loom of the frigate to starboard resolved by degrees into a much larger ship, farther off. Eastman, the master, snatched the night glass from Binney, the officer-of-the-watch, and sighted on the vessel. "Blast m' eyes if that ain't a Mongseer!" he choked. The telescope wavered slightly. "An' another comin' up fast!"

Binney snatched the glass back. "The captain," he snapped, to a gaping midshipman.

Kydd crossed to the ship's side and strained to make out the scene. The larger vessel, ship-rigged and just as large as *Achilles*, was making no moves toward them. The tiny sails beyond were the other ship that Eastman had spotted.

"Mr. Binney?" Dwyer was breathless and in his night attire.

"Sir, our frigate is not in sight. The lights we saw during the night were this Frenchman, who it seems thought ours were, er, some other. There's another of 'em three points to weather." He handed the telescope over.

The morning light was strengthening rapidly and it was possible to make out details. "Frenchy well enough," Dwyer murmured. As he trained the telescope on the ship, her masts began to close, her length foreshorten. "She's woken up — altering away."

"Off ter get with the other 'un," offered someone.

"Yeeesss, I agree," Dwyer said, and handed back the telescope. "Bear up, Mr. Binney, and we'll go after him." He turned to the master. "What's our offing from the French coast?"

"About twelve leagues, sir." Nigh on forty miles; but no ports of consequence near. The captain's eyes narrowed, then he shivered and hurried below.

Kydd clattered down the main hatchway; his place at quarters was the guns on the main deck forward, under Binney. The captain and his officers were now closed up on the quarterdeck, so he and Binney could assume their full action positions.

Low conversations started among the waiting gun crews: a weighing of chances, exchanging of verbal wills, a comparative estimate of sailing speeds — the age-old prelude to battle. Kydd grimaced at the sight of the new hands, nervously chattering and fiddling with ropes. Mercifully, the course alteration to eastward was downwind, the complex motion of before was now a gentle rise and fall as she paced the waves. The landmen would at least have a chance of keeping their footing.

One had the temerity to ask Poynter their chances. He stroked his jaw. "Well, m' lad, seein' as we're outnumbered two ter one, can't say as how they're so rattlin' good." The man turned pale. "Should give it away, but the cap'n, bein' a right mauler, jus' won't let 'em go, we has ter go 'em even if it does fer us . . ." He drew himself up, and scowled thunderously at the man. "An' you'll be a-doin' of yer dooty right ter the end, now, won't yez?"

Kydd himself was feeling the usual qualms and doubts before an action, and when the man looked away with a sick expression, he smiled across at him encouragingly. There was no response.

"Hey, now!" An excited cry came from one of a gun crew peering out of a gunport. "She ain't French, she's a Spaniard!"

Kydd pushed his way past the crew and took a look. The larger vessel, stern to, had just streamed the unmistakable red and yellow of the Spanish sea service. At the same time, he saw that she had not pulled away — but the other ship was much nearer, as tight to the wind as she could.

Poynter appeared next to Kydd, eagerly taking in the scene. Kydd glanced at him. His glittering, predatory eyes and fierce grin was peculiarly reassuring. "Ha!" Poynter snarled in triumph. "Yer sees that? She ain't a-flyin' a pennant — she's a merchant jack is she, the fat bastard!" The stern-on view of the ship had hidden her true character, but Poynter had spotted the obvious.

It seemed that on deck they had come to the same conclusion, for above their heads there was a sudden bang and reek of powder-smoke as a gun was fired to leeward to encourage the Spaniard to strike her colors. Binney couldn't resist, and came over to join them at the gunport. "She's a merchantman, you say."

"She is," said Poynter, who saw no reason why he should enlighten an officer.

The fleeing ship did not strike, and Kydd saw why: the other ship, the frigate, coming up fast must be her escort. The odds were now reversed, however. He did not envy the decision the frigate must take: to throw herself at a ship-of-the-line, even if of the smallest type, or to leave the merchantman to her fate. A frigate escort for just one merchant ship would see them safe against most, but a lone ship-of-the-line on passage would not be expected.

"We'll soon see if we win more than a barrel of guineas in prize money," Binney said significantly.

This drew Poynter's immediate interest. "How so — sir?"

"Why, if the frigate sacrifices himself for the merchantman, we'll know he's worth taking. And if that's so, we may well have a Spaniard on his way to the mines with mercury. I don't have to tell you, that means millions . . ." His words flew along the gundeck, and soon the gunports were full of men peering ahead, chattering excitedly about their prospects. Another gun sounded above, but a stern chase would be a long one especially as *Achilles* had no chase guns that would bear so far forward, and with the French coast and safety lying ahead the Spaniard would take his chances.

The Spanish frigate tacked about; the combined effect of the run downwind and her own working to windward toward them had brought her close — this tack would see her in a position to interpose herself between *Achilles* and her prey.

"Stand to your guns!" bawled Binney. Kydd pulled back from the bright daylight into the somber shades of the gundeck. All was in order, and he nodded slowly in satisfaction as he saw gun captains yet again checking carefully the contents of their pouches, the quill tubes to ignite the main charge from the gunlock atop the breech, the spring-loaded powder horn for the priming.

Kydd had been in ships that had sailed into battle to the sound of stirring tunes from fife and drum, but *Achilles* went into action in a lethal quiet, every order clear and easy to understand. His stomach contracted — as much as from his delayed breakfast as anything. From his position on the centerline he could see everything that happened inboard, but nothing of the wider sea scene. But he could imagine: *Achilles* crowding after the merchantman, the frigate coming across between them, and in the best possible position for her — cutting across the bows of the ship-of-the-line and thereby avoiding her crushing broadside, and at the same time her own broadside would be ready to crash into *Achilles*'s bow and rampage down the full length of the bigger ship.

A cooler appreciation told him that this was not something that an experienced captain would allow, and Dwyer was nothing if not experienced. Going large, the wind astern, there was the greatest scope for maneuverability, and at the right moment he would haul his wind — wheel around closer to the westerly — to bring his whole broadside to bear on the hapless frigate. They would lose ground on their chase, but . . . . "Starb'd first, then to larb'd," Binney relayed. On the quarterdeck the captain had his plan complete: it was seldom that a ship fought both sides at once, and here they would be able to have the unengaged side gun crews cross the deck to reinforce those in action. "Mr. Kydd, I want the best gun captains to starb'd, if you please." Kydd felt the ship turn, the sudden heel making the deck sway before she steadied. He tensed. There was a muffled shout from the main-hatchway, and Binney roared, "Stand by!"

Kydd braced himself, but these were only twenty-four-pounders; he had served great thirty-twos before now. At the gun closest to him, he saw one of the new hands. His eyes were wild and his legs visibly shaking.

The distant shout again, and instantly Binney barked, *"Fire!"*

The crash of their broadside with its deadly gunflashes playing through the smoke dinned on his ears, the smoke in great quantities filling the air. Up and down the invisible gundeck he heard the bellow of gun captains as they whipped raw gun crews into motion.

They had got in their broadside first. Such a brutal assault from two whole decks of guns would utterly shatter the frigate — if they had aimed true. Kydd felt *Achilles*'s stately sway as she resumed her course; this she would not be doing if they had failed.

"Larb'd guns!" Having blasted the frigate to a standstill, they would cross her bows and in turn deliver a ruinous raking broadside, while at the same time be resuming their pursuit.

He folded his arms and smiled. There was little for him to do. Poynter and the other quarter-gunners could be relied on to keep up the fire. His duty was for the graver part of an action — if it was hot work, with casualties and damage, Kydd would need a cool mind acting as deputy to the lieutenant of the gundeck, to see through carnage and destruction to deploying men to continue the fight. But there was no chance of that now.

Reload complete, the crews crossed to larboard and took position. "Stand by!" Gun captains crouched down, the handspikes went to work, the guns steadied and the gunlocks were held to the lanyard. Kydd pitied the helpless frigate somewhere out there on the bright morning sea, knowing what must be coming next.

A cry from aft, and then Binney's *"Fire!"* The broadside smashed out — but a louder, flatter concussion overlaid the sound of the guns. Kydd's half-raised sleeve was rudely tugged away, sending him spinning to the deck. Then, the tearing screams and cries began. He picked himself up shakily, afraid for what he would see when the smoke cleared. His coat had been ripped right up the sleeve, which dragged useless, and as the smoke gave way he saw a gun now lying on its carriage, split open along its length, the upper portion vanished. Wisps of smoke still hung sullenly over it. A small defect in casting deep within the iron of a gun, perhaps a bubble or streak of slag, had been sought out by the colossal forces of detonation and had failed, the rupture of metal spreading in an instant to burst the gun asunder.

The cost to its crew was grievous. Those closest had been torn apart, bright scarlet and entrails from the several bloody corpses bedaubing deck and nearby guns, and all around the piteous writhing of others not so lucky, choking out their lives in agony.

Flying pieces of metal had found victims even at a distance, and sounds of pain and distress chilled Kydd's blood. Binney stood farther aft, swaying in shock, but he appeared untouched, staring at the slaughter.

The gundeck had come to a stop, aware of the tragedy forward. Kydd felt for the unfortunates involved, but there was a higher imperative: out there was an enemy not yet vanquished, who could lash back at any time. There was no alternative: organize fire buckets of water to soak away body parts, rig the wash-deck hose to sluice away the blood but, above all, resume the fight. It was the worst possible luck — the easy success against the frigate was just what would have pulled *Achilles*'s ship's company together and given point to their exercises, but now, and for a long time after, there would be flinching and dread in gun action.

Fearfully, the men turned back to their battle quarters. Kydd went to a gunport and looked out. The shattered ruin of the frigate lay dead in the water, falling behind as *Achilles* remorselessly pursued the merchantman. If their own frigate had stayed with them instead of slipping away during the night, she would be sharing in the prize.

On deck they would be under a full press of sail; a stuns'l on the sides of every yard, all canvas possible spread, it would be a hard chase. *Achilles* was not a flyer but, then, neither was the merchantman, and all the time the coast of France was drawing nearer, already a meandering blue line on the horizon.

It was late afternoon, when the coastline was close enough to make out details, that the drama concluded. On the merchant ship the unwise setting of sail above her royals had its effect: the entire mizzen topmast was carried away, tumbling down with all its rigging in a hopeless ruin. The vessel slewed up into the wind, and within minutes a single fo'c'sle gun on *Achilles* thumped out and in answer her colors jerked down.

★ ★ ★

Even on the main gundeck there was jubilation; a respectably sized prize lay to under their guns, and with not another ship in sight they would not have to share the proceeds. The launch was sent away with an armed party as happy speculation mounted about her cargo. But it was not the mercury, silver and other treasure that fevered imaginations had conjured. When the lieutenant of marines returned, he hailed up at the quarterdeck from the boat: "Sir, I have to report, we've captured a Spanish general, Don Esturias de . . . can't quite remember his whole name, sir." There was a rumble of disappointed comment from the mass of men lining the ship's side. "He's accompanied by a company of Carabineros Reales," he added. "And their pay chest."

An immediate buzz of interest began, headed off by the captain. "My compliments to Don, er, to the general, and I'd be honored to have him as my guest —"

"Sir, the general does not recognize that he's been defeated in the field. He says — his aide says, sir, that he had no part in his own defense, and therefore he will stay with his faithful soldiers in what they must endure."

Dwyer glanced at the first lieutenant with a thin smile. "Do you go to the ship and secure it, the troops to be battened down well — the general, too, if he wants it."

"The pay chest, sir?"

"Leave it where it is for now. Take who you need to fish the mizzen topmast and we'll have a prize crew ready for you later."

A satisfied *Achilles* shaped course north, into the night. By morning they would have the big French port of Brest under their lee; then it was only a matter of rounding Ushant and a direct course to England.

During the night, vigilant eyes insured their prize did not stray. The morning light shone on her dutifully to leeward, a heartening sight for the bleary-eyed middle watchmen coming on deck for the forenoon exercise period.

Just as Brest came abeam and *Achilles* was deep into three masts of sail drill, their prize fell off the wind, heeling over to starboard and taking up a course at right angles to her previous one — toward the land. Above her stern, the White Ensign of England jerked down, and moments later proud Spanish colors floated triumphantly on the peak halyards.

It was a bitter blow. The prisoners had risen during the night and taken the ship, but bided their time before completing their break.

A roar of rage and disappointment arose from *Achilles*, but the run had been timed well, and it was long minutes before the ship could revert her exercise sail to running before the wind. There was no hope: sail appeared close inshore — it was common to see a French ship fleeing before an English predator, and gunboats were always on hand to usher in the quarry. There was no chance they could haul up to their ex-prize in time. *Achilles* slewed around to send a frustrated broadside after her and slunk away, rounding irritably on an interested English frigate of the inshore squadron attracted by the gunfire. Yet again, the fortunes of war had conspired against them.

The next day, in a bitter mood, *Achilles* sighted the gray point of the Lizard, the most southerly point of England, but Kydd's spirits soared. It had been so long, so far away, and now he was returning once more to his native soil, to the roots of his existence. It was only a lumpy blue line on the horizon ahead, but it meant so much.

"Y'r folks are in Scotland, o' course, Tam," Kydd offered, seeing a certain distraction on his friend's face.

Cockburn didn't answer at once, seeming to choose his words. "Yes. In Penicuik — that's Edinburgh."

The ship made a dignified bow to one of the last Atlantic rollers coming under her keel; the shorter, busier waves of the Channel produced more of a nodding. There were sails close inshore, coasting vessels carrying most of the country trade of England with their grubby white or red bark-tanned canvas, and occasionally larger deep-sea ships outward bound or arriving after long ocean voyages.

"You'll be lookin' t' postin' up, or will ye take the Leith packet?" Kydd hugged to himself the knowledge that Guildford was less than a day away by coach from Portsmouth — and this time he'd travel inside.

"Perhaps neither. We won't be at liberty too long, I'll wager." He wouldn't look at Kydd, who suddenly remembered that Cockburn had left his home and family as a midshipman, a future officer, but had yet to make the big step. It would not be a glorious homecoming, without anything to show for his years away, neither promotion nor prize money.

Impulsively, Kydd tried to reach out. "Ye'll be welcome t' come visit the Kydds in Guildford, Tam. We've a rare old —"

"That's kind in you, Tom, but in Spithead I've a mind to petition for transfer to a frigate, if at all possible."

There were far better chances for promotion and prizes in a frigate rather than part of a fleet, but Kydd knew that his chances among all the others clamoring for the same thing were not good. He stayed for a space, then said, "Best o' luck in that, m' friend," and went forward. He didn't want his elation to be spoiled.

Captain Dwyer paced grimly up and down the quarterdeck. "What is the meaning of that damned Irish pennant?" he snarled at the boatswain, pointing angrily up at a light line tapping playfully high up on the after edge of the main topgallant sail. Welby snapped at the mate-of-the-watch and a duty topman swung into the shrouds and scrambled aloft. It would not do to be laggardly when Dwyer was so clearly in a foul mood.

Dwyer stopped his pacing, and glared at

Binney. "I have it in mind to press some good hands, replace our prize crew." These would now be in captivity — the lieutenant would in due course be exchanged, but the seamen had nothing but endless years of incarceration ahead, their captors knowing that trained seamen were far more valuable than any soldier to England.

"Sir."

"We haul in one of your fat merchantmen — there, like that one," he said, gesturing ahead at a large and deep-laden vessel anxiously crowding on all sail to get past the dangers always to be faced at the mouth of the Channel.

"Inward bound, sir."

"Yes!" Dwyer snapped. "You don't agree?"

Binney was clearly uneasy at his position. "Well, sir, this one could've been on passage six months, a year or more. Who knows what hazards and pains he's been through? And now, in sight of home, if we then —"

"A damnation on your niceties, sir!" Dwyer's face was pale with anger. "We're at war, it may have escaped your notice. Where else do you propose I get men? The quota? Debtor's jail?" His glare subsided a little, but his tone remained hard. "You will recollect, our people have been away from England all of two years — are they then to be pitied? No, sir!"

He thrust his hands behind his back and snapped, "Mr. Binney, I desire you to ready a boarding party to press a dozen hands from that merchantman." He saw the look on Binney's face and gave a hard smile. "And I'll not be satisfied with less, damn it!"

Kydd sat in the sternsheets of the boat with Binney. Six marines were also crowded into the small space, clutching their muskets and staring out woodenly. The bluff-bowed launch met the short, steep waves on her bow, occasionally sending spray aft.

Kydd looked at Binney: pale-faced and thin-lipped, he was clearly out of sorts. If this was because they would soon be pressing men, Kydd sympathized with his reservations: he had been a pressed man himself. But cruel and inhumane though it might be, the fleet had to be manned at a time when England herself stood in such peril. These merchant seamen had chosen to take the higher pay and quiet life while the navy stood guard over them. Now was the chance for some of them to play a real part.

The merchant ship had been brought to with a gun, but she affected not to understand and stood on. It had taken dangerous jockeying for the big ship-of-the-line to draw abreast and to windward. This stole the wind from her and at the same time brought her close enough to be within hail. There had been an undignified exchange and another shot ahead of her bowsprit before the vessel had reluctantly gone aback.

The launch bobbed and jibbed alongside. A rope ladder was finally thrown down and they boarded; the marines were sent up first, and Kydd followed. Heaving himself over the bulwarks, he was confronted by a tight circle of hostile faces. Under the guns of a ship-of-the-line and the stolid line of marines there was no trouble expected, but he watched warily until the boarding party was all on deck.

Binney introduced himself formally. "Your papers, if you please, Captain," he added politely.

"Cap'n Heppel, barque *Highlander* of Bristol. From Callao, bound f'r London." He wore an old-fashioned long coat and tricorne, and his tone was frosty as he reluctantly produced the papers. Binney inspected them carefully. Pressing men from ships of the wrong flag could flare up into an international incident with unfortunate consequences for the officer responsible.

Kydd looked around. A ship always had a domestic individuality that meant everything to a sailor, her little ways at sea, her comfortable smells, the tiny compromises of living. This one had sailed continuously for six months or more; her ropes were hairy with use and her canvas sea-darkened to gray. There was evidence of careful repair of sea hurts and hard hours of endurance in some ocean storm far out to sea.

Binney handed back the papers. "In the name of the King, I ask you will muster your crew, Captain," he said uncomfortably. "We mean to have a dozen good hands from you."

"A dozen!" The owners of a merchant ship always kept crew to a bare minimum, and so many taken would mean grim and exhausting labor to work the ship for those left.

"Yes, sir. My captain will not allow me to return without them." Binney was discomfited, but stood by his orders, patiently waiting for a response.

"It's an outrage, sir!" Heppel spluttered and moved to confront Binney. Kydd stepped up quietly beside his officer and the marines fingered their muskets. There was nothing this captain could do: under the law the ship could be stripped of all but the mates and apprentices.

"All hands on deck," Heppel flung over his shoulder.

Kydd counted the sailors as they emerged from the hatches — just nineteen. It was impossible to work even a two-watch system with only these. There were more. He looked at Binney, who seemed to have come to the same conclusion. "Come, come, sir, the sooner we have them, the sooner we shall leave."

The nineteen were a ragged bunch, their sea gear worn and threadbare from thousands of miles of long voyaging, their bodies hardened and browned. They gazed back warily, stoically.

"Sir, ye want me t' go below, rouse 'em out?" Kydd asked loudly. "I know about th' hidey-holes an' all the tricks."

Binney appeared to be considering Kydd's words. The best seamen were obviously concealed below, and his hesitation implied that if the navy men were led a merry dance then their officer might vindictively press more than his dozen. He let it hang until more appeared resentfully from below decks, shuffling into the group abaft the mainmast.

Kydd's thoughts stole away to his own ocean voyaging. These men had lived closely together, through dangers and hardships that, over the months at sea, would have forged deep respect and friendships the like of which a landlubber would never know — and now it would be ended, broken.

Stepping forward, Binney addressed them. "Now, my men, is there any among you who wish to serve England in the King's Service? As a volunteer, you are naturally entitled to the full bounty."

This was a threat as much as a promise. Unless they volunteered, they would be pressed, and then they would neither get a bounty nor would see much liberty ashore.

Three moved forward. Kydd guessed the others did not join them because of the belief that if they were later caught deserting, volunteers would be treated more harshly as having accepted money; the others could plead, with some justification, that they had been forced against their will.

"Come on, lads, *Achilles* is only bound f'r Spithead an' a docking. Y're volunteers, an' there could be liberty t' spend y'r bounty. Good place f'r a spree, Portsmouth Point."

Another moved over. The rest shuffled sullenly together.

"So. This means eight pressed men. Now who's it to be?" Binney was not to be put off by the stony hostility he met, and pointed to one likely looking young able seaman.

"Apprentice!" snapped Heppel.

"Y'r protection, if y' please," Kydd said heavily, holding out his hand for the paper. A weak explanation for the absence of papers died at Kydd's uncompromising stare.

The rest were quickly gathered in: There were several prime seamen who could look forward to a petty officer's berth if they showed willing, but one had Kydd's eyes narrowing — a sea lawyer, if he wasn't mistaken, probably a navy deserter who would give a purser's name," a false name, to the muster-book and would likely be the focus of discontents on the lower deck.

"Get y'r dunnage then," Kydd told the new-pressed hands. They went below to fetch their sea chests and ditty bag of small treasures, all they had to show for their endless months at sea.

Binney signaled to *Achilles*. The cutter would take the chests and sea gear to their new home. "Thank you, Captain," he said courteously. "We'll be on our way now."

Heppel said nothing, but his fists bunched.

"Ah — ye'd be makin' up the pay, Cap'n?" Kydd asked quietly. It would suit some captains conveniently to forget wages for pressed long-voyage men and pocket the sum; it was the least Kydd could do to insure they were not robbed.

"Haven't the coin," Heppel said truculently.

"Then we'll accept a note against the owners," Binney responded smoothly, and folded his arms to wait.

The press catch mollified Dwyer — they were all seamen and would not take long to become effective in their posts. *Achilles* got under way and, with the brisk north-easterly, stood out into the Channel for the long board to Spithead.

On the quarterdeck the atmosphere improved and Dwyer could be seen chatting amicably to the midshipmen. He turned leisurely to the officer-of-the-watch. "Should you sight a fisherman, we'll take some fish for the people."

"A pilchard boat, sir," the officer-of-the-watch reported later. The boat bobbed and dipped in the steep mid-Channel waves. Faces turned to watch the big warship approach and come aback as she drifted down on the fishing boat.

"A Frenchy, sir."

"The fish tastes the same, does it not?" Dwyer asked. It was an unwritten custom not to interfere with the fisheries, for among other things fishermen could be sources of intelligence. "Pass the word for Mr. Eastman."

The master was a Jerseyman and knew the Brittany language like a native. "Tell 'em we'd be interested in a few baskets of pilchards if the price is right, if you please."

The transaction was soon completed. It was more profitable to tranship a catch at sea and continue fishing. The master leaned over the rail, gossiping amiably as baskets of fish were swayed inboard. He straightened abruptly. A few tense sentences were exchanged and then he strode rapidly over to Dwyer and whispered something urgently to him. Conversations died away as curious faces turned toward them.

Eastman returned quickly to the ship's side and spoke to the old fisherman again. Then he returned to Dwyer, his face grave. Dwyer hesitated and the two went below, leaving an upper deck seething with rumor.

"Mr. Kydd! Mr. Kydd, ahoy — lay aft, if you please." Binney's hail cut through Kydd's speculations about the situation with the boatswain and he went aft to the helm, touching his hat to the lieutenant.

"We are to attend the captain in his cabin," Binney said shortly, turning on his heel. Kydd followed into the cabin spaces. Strangely, the marine sentry had moved from his accustomed place at the door to the captain's day cabin and had taken position farther forward. Binney knocked and, at the brisk "Enter," tucked his hat under his arm and opened the door. In the spacious cabin Dwyer and the master stood waiting.

"I have your word of Kydd's reliability," Dwyer said curtly, looking at Binney.

"Why, yes, sir, he is —"

"Very well." Dwyer looked disturbed, even hunted. "What I have to say, you will swear not to divulge to a soul aboard this ship." He looked first at Kydd, then Binney.

"Sir." Wary and tense, Binney spoke for both of them.

Dwyer's eyes flicked once more to Kydd. Then he said, "The fisherman has sure knowledge of a danger to the realm that in all my experience I can say has never before threatened these islands." He took a deep breath. "The fleet at Spithead has refused duty and is now in a state of open mutiny. There is a red flag over every ship and they have set at defiance both the Admiralty and the Crown." He wiped his brow wearily. "The fisherman cannot be expected to know details, but he swears all this is true."

Kydd went cold. The navy — the well-loved and sure shield of the nation — infected with mad revolution, Jacobin plots? It was a world turned upside down.

"By God's good grace, we have been spared blundering into the situation, but we have to know more."

"The Plymouth squadron, sir?" The forward base was nearest the main French naval strength at Brest.

"He's not sure, but thinks they may have gone over to their brethren." Dwyer looked at the master.

"Near as I c'd make out, sir."

Dwyer paused. "I cannot risk this ship being overrun by mutineers. This is why I have sent for you, Mr. Binney. I understand you come from these parts?"

"Yes, sir. Our estate is in south Devon,

some small ways east of Plymouth."

"Good. I desire you to land at a point on the coast with Plymouth near at hand, such that within a day you may enter the port in a discreet manner and make contact with the true authority, then to withdraw and report back to me. Now, do you know how this may safely be done?"

Binney hesitated for a moment. Desperate mutineers would make short work of him if he was caught.

He requested a chart. It was the standard approach to Plymouth, and he quickly found his place. "Sir, to the east."

"Wembury?"

"No, sir, that has an army garrison. Farther to the east, past the Mewstones," Binney said, bringing to mind the sea mark of unusual conical rocks to the southeast of the port. "Along the coast four or five miles. If I land here —" he indicated a small river estuary "— I'm out of sight on all sides, out in the country. I strike north about two hours and reach Ivybridge. This is on the highway and the posting house for the last change of horses before Plymouth, and there I can ride the Exeter stage into Plymouth."

"This seems a good plan. Well done, Mr. Binney."

Eastman took a closer look at the chart. "Hmmm, the Yealm and then the river Erme. Suggest you take the four-oared gig in, under sail."

"That will do — it's sand, and I'd be satisfied to reach as far up as Holbeton."

"Kydd, boat's crew. This is you and . . . ?"

"Poynter, sir, gunner's mate. An' one other. Let me think on it, sir."

Dwyer appeared satisfied. "So we'll raise the coast at dawn, send the boat away, and hope to have you back before dark?"

"Aye-aye, sir," said Binney quietly.

"Then I don't have to remind you all that if this terrible news gets abroad . . ."

In the chill of early dawn, *Achilles* stood in for the river Erme. The gray, formless land firmed and revealed its rugged character. It was strange to be so close to a perilous shore from which a big ship would normally keep well clear. Sails were backed and within minutes the gig had touched water. Binney and Kydd, with Poynter and a seaman, boarded and set the lug foresail and mizzen to bellying life.

As *Achilles* got under way to assume position out to sea, the gig headed inshore. It was clear that Binney knew where he was. The small river estuary ending in a wide flat sprawl of sandy channels met the sea between a pair of bluffs. Binney took the biggest channel, following its sinuous course upstream, past dark woods, some isolated dwellings, steep pastoral idylls and at one point wispy effluvia of a lime kiln.

It was dreamlike in the early morning to be passing from the vastness and power of the open sea to the enfolding quiet so close to the depths of the lovely English countryside, the farmland, grazing animals, orchards — and in a ship's boat. The smell of wildflowers, cows, cut hay and sun-warmed soil turned Kydd's mind irresistibly to memories of his youth and past summers in Guildford. It was difficult to reconcile where they were to the actuality of what they were doing.

"Damn," muttered Binney; the boat had touched sand. Poynter poled off with the boat hook. The wind localized, becoming fluky and light; the sails were doused and oars shipped. Later the sand turned to flecked silt and then to dark mud, and it was at this point that Binney put the tiller over and brought their inland voyage to an end.

"Yarnink Nowle," Binney announced, coming up to a decaying timber landing place. It took Kydd some moments to realize that the words meant the place, not an order. It was a quiet wood down to the water's edge; a rough path headed steeply up out of sight into it. "Kydd, with me, you men stay with the boat."

Kydd climbed over the gunwale and for the first time since Gibraltar had the good earth under his feet. They trudged up the steep, sinuous path, Binney leading and dressed in nondescript coat and breeches, while Kydd followed in as non-sea rig as he had been able to find.

They left the wood to cross deep green fields with curious sheep, and Kydd looked at Binney, worried. "The crew'll hear of th' mutiny fr'm the folks hereabouts."

Binney flashed a grin. "Not here they won't. They know the navy and the press-gang in this part o' the world — they'll keep well away." Kydd thought of the hard-faced Poynter, and grinned back.

They crossed another field, ignoring a gaping milkmaid, and arrived at the back of a thatched-roof farmhouse. A dog barked once, then approached to nuzzle at Binney; a leather-gaitered yeoman appeared at the noise and stopped in surprise at seeing Binney. "Well, whot be doing yer, Maister Binney?"

Binney smiled. "Is Jarge going for the post this morning?"

"Eys, 'ee be saddlin' up thikky donkey."

Binney glanced triumphantly at Kydd. "Nothing changes in the country — we'll be riding to Ivybridge."

Sitting on the end of the farm trap with legs dangling as it ground bumpily over the country track, Binney was youthfully spirited, nervous tension working with pleasure at the unexpected return to his roots.

It was not far to Ivybridge. They passed two tiny villages on the well-worn road to the north and suddenly reached a crossroads. They dropped to the road from the trap, dusting down, and let the mystified farmer continue on his way.

Binney took a deep breath. "The London Inn — over by the river. The Exeter mail should be along by ten." A soft whispering on the morning breeze strengthened until they reached its cause, the Erme River, a crystal clear boisterous rushing over moss-green rocks.

The beauty and settled loveliness of the tiny hamlet reached out to Kydd; it seemed to belong to another world, one without blood and war, without the unthinkable threat of a fleet mutiny. His mind shied at the very notion — could it be, perhaps, just one of those endless wartime rumors?

They tramped up the road beside the river toward a remarkably pretty humped bridge, set among a profusion of oaks and chestnut and dappled with sunlight. On the left were some well-kept and dignified mansions; he glimpsed the name "Corinthia" on one and wondered who could have had the fortune to live there in such a place of peace and beauty.

They reached the London Inn on the other side of the dusty Plymouth turnpike; a smithy was already in industrious activity beside it, and ostlers readied horses in the post stables.

"Mr. Kydd, I'd be obliged should you wait for me here," Binney said, his tone low and serious. "If I do not return before evening, you are to return to *Achilles* and tell the captain."

"Aye-aye, sir," Kydd acknowledged. Without his naval officer's uniform Binney looked absurdly young for such a risky enterprise and all traces of his earlier animation were now gone. They remained standing awkwardly together under the gaudy inn sign, the occasional passerby curious at the presence of such a pair so out of keeping with Ivybridge.

The coach finally came wheeling down the turnpike, and stopped with a brave crashing of hooves and jingling of harness; snorting, sweaty horses were led out of their traces and fresh ones backed in, the horsey smell pungent in Kydd's nostrils.

Binney climbed inside the coach, his grave face gazing out of the window. With bellows from the driver, the whip was laid on and the coach jerked into motion. Kydd had an urge to wave, but at the last instant made a sketchy naval salute. The coach clattered over the bridge and was gone.

Kydd stood irresolute. It was hard to remain idle while others faced perils — it was not the navy way. He let the morning sun warm him, then sat on the bench outside the inn and felt the tensions seep away as he listened, with eyes closed, to the cheep and trill of country birds, the rustling of breezes in the hayfield close by, myriad imperceptible rustic sounds.

His thoughts tumbled along: only hours before he had been at sea, now in longed-for England — but in such circumstances! Where was Renzi? Should he do something? Restless, he opened his eyes and got to his feet. It was getting toward noon and he was hungry. Perhaps he should take a meal.

In the dark interior of the inn, all glinting brass and pewter, there was only one other, reading a newspaper in the corner. Kydd left him to it and settled in a high-backed bench, relishing the rich sickliness of ale on sawdust.

"Bliddy blackguards!"

As there was no one else in the room, Kydd leaned around. "I beg y'r pardon?" he asked mildly.

"Thikky mut'neers, o' course," the red-faced man said, shaking the newspaper for emphasis. His appearance suggested landed folk. Kydd caught the "mutineers" through the round Devon accent and tensed. There was now no question of rumor, it was actuality. "They'm maakin' fresh demands, tiz maize."

"Demands?"

"Eys zertainly, where've 'ee bin th' last couple o' weeks?" the man asked suspiciously.

"Out o' the country," Kydd said quickly. "C'n I take a quick look, friend?"

The man paused, then passed the paper across. "Leave it yee when you be vanished, I'll zee 'ee dreckly avter."

Kydd snatched up the paper, the *Times* of London. The front page was all advertisements — "A patent Oeconomic machine . . ." and "Marylebone Cricket Club, Anniversary Dinner . . ." Impatiently he turned the page. He wanted to see with his own eyes words that would tell him the navy was in revolution. ". . . the Jacobin papers have turned all their speculations . . . to the meeting at Portsmouth . . ." ". . . notwithstanding all the idle and ignorant reports detailed in the Morning Papers of the day of the discontents at Portsmouth having been rapidly adjusted, we are sorry to say that no such good news has been received . . ." Kydd could hardly believe his eyes. ". . . the conduct of the seamen . . . is reprehensible in the extreme . . ." ". . . Is any man sanguine as to think that Mr. Fox could retrieve the general anarchy that threatens us?"

He stared at the report. This was worse than he had feared, almost beyond credibility. Kydd sat back in dismay. A farmer entered, looking in Kydd's direction with a friendly grin, but Kydd could not talk: he turned his back on the man and read on. ". . . correspondence between the Board of Admiralty and Deputation of Seamen . . ." The Admiralty reduced to treating with mutineers — it was unbelievable.

He rose, feeling an urgent need to get

outside into the bright sunlight. He found the bench, all thoughts of a meal dispelled, and read the report again. There was a deal of breathless comment on the audacity of the sailors, their conduct and a sinister "The success of the enemy in corrupting our brave Tars is truly formidable. What have we to expect, if we are not true to ourselves at this dreadful moment, when we are betrayed on every side?"

He turned to the next page. It was in tiny print, and began: "The Petition, or rather Remonstrance, of the sailors of Lord BRIDPORT's fleet, is now before the Public, and we most sincerely wish that it was not our duty to publish it." Underneath was column after column of the verbatim demands of the mutineers, apparently printed under duress by the *Times*. Reluctantly, he continued to read.

THE HUMBLE PETITION — of the SEAMEN and MARINES on Board His Majesty's Ships, in Behalf of Themselves.
Humbly sheweth — That the Petitioners, relying on the candor and justice of your Honorable House, make bold to lay their grievances before you, hoping, that when you reflect on them,

you will please to give redress, as far as your wisdom will deem necessary. . . .

Kydd scanned ahead. A central issue emerged: a number of grievances specified not as a demand but a careful "laying before their Lordships with a hope of redress."

Slowly he folded the newspaper. This was no sudden rising of seamen, this must be organized, deadly. Who or what was at the bottom of it all?

"Sir, it is as we feared. Plymouth is now in the hands of the mutineers, and the ships have gone over, every one." Binney was tired and distracted, but respectful before his captain, Kydd at his side. He had returned close-mouthed and abrupt, leaving Poynter and the seaman wondering.

"Mr. Binney, did you make your duty to the admiral's office?" Dwyer snapped. It was a crucial matter for him. His own conduct in the immediate future could well be examined later, but if there were orders . . .

"I was unable, sir, but I do have this." Binney fumbled inside his coat and handed over a document.

Dwyer took it quickly. "Ah, this is the admiral's seal. Well done, Mr. Binney." He tore open the paper and scanned the few words in haste. "Thank God — here we have conclusive proof and assurance that the North Sea fleet and the Nore did not join the mutiny, and these are our orders to proceed there with all dispatch."

Achilles leaned to the wind and, through a strangely deserted Channel, beat eastward. The Start, Portland Race and a distant Isle of Wight passed abeam, all treasured sights for a deep-sea mariner inward bound; Beachy Head loomed up, and past it was the anchorage of the Downs, protected to seaward by the Goodwin Sands. Home — after such adventures as most could only dream of. At the North Foreland they tacked about and ran into the estuary of the Thames, the sea highway to London, the keys to the kingdom.

And the Nore. Soon after the low-lying marshy island of Sheppey spread across their course they came upon the unmistakable sight of a forest of black masts: the fleet anchorage of the Great Nore.

Kydd saw them — it was not the first time for it was here those years ago, at the outset of the war, that he had first stepped on the deck of a man-o'-war. With a stab, he remembered that he had been a pressed man then, miserable, homesick and bitter, but now . . . A reluctant smile acknowledged the thought that he had indeed returned home — to his original starting point.

But the Nore was not a home to one of England's great battle fleets, it was a base for shelter, storing and repair, and an assembling point for the Baltic convoys, a working-up area for new vessels from the Chatham and Deptford shipyards and a receiving and exchange point for the continuous flow of unfortunates from the press-gang tenders and quota transports. It was a place of coming and going, of transience and waiting.

In winter a northerly could bring a biting, raw wind for weeks on end, the only solace ashore the drab, isolated garrison town of Sheerness, a bleak place at the northerly tip of Sheppey. The town's sole reason for existence was the dockyard and garrison fort. The rest of the island was a place of marshes, decaying cliffs and scattered sheep pasture, an effective quarantine from England proper.

Taking no chances, *Achilles* passed down the line of ships at anchor. No red flags, no mutinous cheering, only the grave naval courtesies of a ship rejoining the fleet. Under dull skies the 64 found her berth and the great bower anchors tumbled into the muddy gray where the Thames met the North Sea, and she composed herself for rest.

Chapter 6

"This is Mr. Evan Nepean, my lord. He will furnish you with as complete an account as you'd wish and, dare I say it, more succinct in the particulars." As a politician and not a seaman, the First Lord of the Admiralty was happy to turn over an explanation of the calamitous events at Spithead to the secretary; he knew the sea cant of the sailors in mutiny and would field the more delicate matters capably.

"Very well, then," said Lord Stanhope, easing himself wearily into one of the carved seats around the board table. "Not the details, if you please, just the salient facts." Stanhope had made an urgent return from Sweden at the news of the outbreak and was plainly exhausted. But his discreet journeyings abroad had earned him the ear of William Pitt, and it would be folly to underestimate his power.

Nepean moved around the table the better to access the hanging maps above the fireplace. He pulled down one of Great Britain. "As you will appreciate, sir, our concentrations of force for the defense of the kingdom are the Channel fleet here at Portsmouth to be directed against the French in Brest, and at Plymouth we find our advanced squadron. At Yarmouth we have the North Sea fleet, which looks directly into the Netherlands and the Baltic, and near there we have the Nore anchorage and the dockyard at Sheerness to victual and maintain them.

"For some weeks prior to mid-April, discontent became apparent at Spithead, and on the fifteenth of April last this resulted in open mutiny; the seamen refused duty and the fleet was unable to proceed to sea. They are in such a state at this time, and unhappily have been joined in their mutiny by the Plymouth squadron."

"Is the situation stable?"

"It appears so at the moment, my lord," Nepean said carefully. "The mutinous seamen are keeping good order and discipline, and await a resolution. However, I am not sanguine this will continue — in an unfortunate excess of zeal, blood was shed and the seamen are affronted."

Stanhope pondered. "So as we speak, in essence, the approaches to these islands are entirely defenseless."

"The men talk of sailing to meet the French if they make a sally, my lord, and please note that — praise be — the Nore and North Sea squadron are left to us, they did not mutiny."

"Pray, why do they persist in their mutiny?"

Nepean shot a glance at Earl Spencer — his was the responsibility for some kind of resolution — but the First Lord continued to regard him gravely, so he continued: "My lord, they have a number of grievances which they demand find redress before they'll consent to any kind of return to duty."

"And these are?"

"The level of wages, of course, provisions served at short weight, no vegetables in port, that kind of thing."

Stanhope looked up with a cynical smile. "And?"

"Er, liberty in port and some oversight with the sick and wounded — and your lordship will no doubt recall that a couple of years ago the army were rewarded with an increase."

Frowning, Stanhope turned to Spencer.

"It seems little enough. Can we not . . ."

"With the government's position the weaker for Lord Moira's unfortunate interference, any attempt on revenues will upset a delicate situation — we have suspended gold payments at the Bank of England, we are in dire need of every penny to buy off the Austrians, our last ally in all of Europe. Need I go further?"

"Our entire standing in foreign chancelleries is threatened, sir. Do you propose to allow the situation to continue indefinitely?"

"No, my lord," Spencer said heavily. "We have compounded with the mutinous rascals for a substantial improvement in their pay, we have even secured a free pardon for this whole parcel of traitors, but still they will not yield." He wiped his forehead wearily. "They will not listen to Parliament, sir."

Nepean broke in: "This is true, sir," he said smoothly, "but we have secured the services of Earl Howe to intercede for us with the sailors. He is to coach to Portsmouth shortly, with plenary powers."

"Earl Howe?"

"Whom the sailors call 'Black Dick.' He led them to victory in the action of the Glorious First of June, and they trust him like a father." A wintry smile appeared. "It is our last resource. If he does not succeed . . ."

Kydd stood in the foretop as one of the last rituals of the transition from live sea creature to one tethered and submissive was enacted. The sails were furled into a pristine harbor stow, the bunt taken over the yard into a graceful "pig's ear" and plaited bunt gaskets passed to his satisfaction.

He found himself looking up to take in the somber brown cliffs and bleak seacoast of Sheppey over the mile or so of scurrying drab sea. Emotions of times past returned sharp and poignant. A great deal had happened since he had left home . . .

"Clap on more sail, if y' please, Mr. Cantlie!" Kydd threw at the inboard seaman on the footropes. The sailor stared up resentfully but did as he was told. "Lay in," Kydd ordered, when the furling was complete. The men came in off the yard and assembled in the foretop, but as they did so the piercing wail of calls from the boatswain's mates cut through. "*Haaaands* to muster! Clear lower deck — all hands lay aft!"

It appeared that Captain Dwyer would

address his ship's company before going ashore to pay his respects to the admiral. It was unusual — minds would be set on the joyous sprees to be had ashore, and a bracing talk more properly belonged to an outward-bound voyage.

Kydd took up his position, facing inward midway between the officers aft on the poop deck and the men crowding the main-deck forward, feet astride in an uncompromising brace.

"*Still!*" the master-at-arms roared. Muttering among the mass of men died away quickly, and the captain stepped forward to the poop-deck rail. "Men of the *Achilles!*" he began, then paused, surveying them grimly. The last shuffling of feet subsided. Something was in the wind. "I have to tell you now the gravest news, which affects us all. I am talking about nothing less than the very safety of this kingdom and the survival of these islands."

He had total attention; some sailors had jumped into the lower rigging to hear him better. "It is a stroke of war that the enemy have been able to achieve by cunning, treachery, and inciting our honest tars to treason."

Puzzled looks were exchanged. This was nothing like a hearty call to arms.

Dwyer glanced at the stony-faced marine lieutenant, then continued: "The news I will give may well come from others who do not have the true facts, which is why I am telling you now, so you have no reason to believe them."

Suspicious looks appeared, eyes narrowed.

"It is my sad duty to have to inform you that your fellow seamen of the Channel fleet at Spithead have mutinied." The suspicion turned to shock. "In fact, the mutineers, led we believe by French agents, have joined together to hold Old England to ransom with a list of impossible demands that they have had the gall to inflict on Parliament this past week."

An appalled silence was followed by a rising hubbub. *"Silence!"* screamed the master-at-arms. His voice cracked with tension, and the marines fingered their muskets. The noise lessened, but did not fade entirely.

"The fate of these blackguardly rogues you may guess. England will not forgive easily those who have so perfidiously betrayed their mother country, be assured." His voice rose strongly. "But do not *you* be gulled by free-talking scoundrels into thoughtless acts of treason, crimes for which only a halter at the yardarm is the answer. Your duty is plain before you — to your ship and His Majesty, no other!

"Mr. Hawley," he called to the first lieutenant. "Three cheers for His Majesty!"

Hawley took off his hat and called loudly, "M' lads, an huzzah for King George: hip, hip . . ."

The cheers were distracted and uncertain, however, and Dwyer's face creased into a frown. "Three more for our ship!" he ordered. These cheers were somewhat louder, but to Kydd's ears they sounded mechanical and lacking in spirit. The captain waited for them to die, then continued evenly, "I'm going ashore now. Mr. Hawley will prepare your liberty tickets while we see about your pay. Carry on, please."

Achilles's ship's company went to their noon grog in a ferment of anticipation. The talk of pay was promises only, but liberty ashore in an English port, however barren, after so long in foreign parts would be sweet indeed. The more thoughtful reflected on the danger to the realm of the British fleet in a state of insurrection. Individual ships had mutinied before, the most prominent the *Bounty* less than ten years earlier, but this was a planned wholesale rising — who or what could be behind it?

At six bells the captain went ashore with all ceremony to make his number with the port admiral, Vice Admiral Buckner, and the ship settled to harbor routine. In the main this consisted of a controlled bedlam, a mix of those happy souls making ready to step ashore to taste the dubious delights of Sheerness and others whose duties kept them aboard.

The arrival of a big ship was always a gratifying sight to those shoreside, and it was not long before *Achilles* became the focus of a host of small craft coming around Garrison Point. Kydd sighed. He knew what was coming and, as mate-of-the-watch to Lieutenant Binney, he would have most to do with it. Binney was on call below. Alone on the quarterdeck, Kydd watched as the hordes converged. He had made all the dispositions he could — boarding nettings were rigged below the line of the gunports, as much to deter desertion as unwanted visitors; gear had been triced up to allow more deck space, the guns run out to broaden the width of gundecks; and canvas screens rigged on the lower deck.

"Here they come, the saucy cuntkins!"

piped a midshipman in glee.

"Clap a stopper on it, young 'un!" Kydd growled. "M' duty to Mr. Binney, an' they'll be alongside presently."

Binney came up just as the first boats arrived at the side steps. "One at a time, and they're to be searched," he said, in a bored tone. Men lined the side, chuckling at their prospects. Kydd motioned at random to one of the boats. It responded with alacrity and the woman at the oars made a dextrous alongside. She hoisted a basket of goods to her head and, grabbing the manrope, easily mounted the side, leaving a companion to lie off on her oars. "An' the best o' the day ter yez." She bobbed familiarly at the lieutenant. Chubby, and of invincible cheeriness, she submitted to the cursory search with practiced ease, then pushed through the gathering sailors to set up position forward for her hot breads, pies and oranges. Others came aboard, some with trinkets, several with ingenious portable workbenches for tailoring, cobbling and leatherwork, and still more with cashboxes ready to take a seaman's pay ticket and change it — at ruinous discount — into hard cash.

More crowded aboard. The master-at-arms and ship's corporals were hard put to keep up with the stream. The hubbub grew, and Kydd stepped back for the sanctity of the quarterdeck just as the master-at-arms thrust an arm under a fat woman's dress.

"*That* f'r yer cat's piss, m' lovely!" he snarled triumphantly. The squeal of indignation faded into the embarrassment of discovery as a knife cut into a concealed bladder and cheap gin flooded into the scuppers.

"Heave her gear overside," Binney ordered, and to mingled shouts of protest and derision her tray of gewgaws sailed into the sea. The gin was destined for sale below decks and Kydd suspected from the growing merriment that other sources had already found their way there.

"Sweethearts 'n' wives, sir?" Kydd asked Binney.

"Cap'n's orders are very clear," Binney replied, with a frown. "Wives only, no pockey jades to corrupt our brave tars." The master-at-arms raised his eyebrows but said nothing. Binney turned and left the deck to Kydd. The officers would now retreat to their wardroom and cabin spaces, and in time-honored fashion the ship would be turned over to the men and their wives of the day.

"They shows their lines," ordered Kydd. There would be some genuine wives; the rest would carry unimpeachable marriage lines, obtainable for a small fee ashore. But this fiction served to demonstrate to an increasingly prim public ashore that HMS *Achilles* was taking its responsibility seriously concerning the traffic in women's bodies.

He walked to the side and beckoned the waiting outer circle of watermen's boats. They bent to their oars with a will, the bulwarks lined with sailors lewdly urging them on. It was as much to reduce numbers aboard as anything, but as practical senior of the watch he had the dubious honor of selecting those allowed to entertain *Achilles* men. The invading crowd swarmed aboard, modesty cast aside as the women clambered over the bulwarks. It was hard on the watermen. Those whose passengers were rejected must return them ashore, a good mile or more and not a sixpence in it for their trouble.

The lucky ones pranced about on the pristine decks. A fiddle started on the foredeck and an impromptu dance began about the foremast. Feminine laughter tinkled, roars of ribaldry surged — the stern man-o'-war lines of *Achilles* melted into a comfortable acquiescence at the invasion. Real wives were easy to spot. Often with awed children, they bore lovingly prepared bundles and a look of utter disdain, and while they crossed the bulwarks as expertly as their rivals, they were generally swept up in a big hug by a waiting seaman. Some were told "Forrard on the gundeck, m' dear" from a gruff master-at-arms. Their spouses being on duty, there they would find a space between a pair of cannons, made suitably private with a canvas screen, the declared territory of a married couple.

It was nearly six bells; when eight sounded and the evening drew in, Cockburn would relieve Kydd, and he could retreat to the gunroom. The midshipman's berth was, however, only too near and it would be a noisy night.

Cockburn came on deck early. Harbor watches were a trial for him, the necessary relaxation of discipline and boisterous behavior of the seamen hard on his straitlaced Scottish soul.

"What cheer, Tam? Need t' step ashore? Cap'n wants t' get a demand on the dockyard delivered b' hand f'r a new wash-deck pump. Ship's business, o' course, gets you off the ship f'r an hour."

"In Sheerness?" Cockburn retorted

scornfully. Kydd was looking forward to getting ashore and seeing something of the local color, but Cockburn remained glum. "Join me in a turn around below-decks afore I hand over the watch," he said to the young man, trying to draw him out of himself. "Younker, stand by on the quarter-deck," he threw at the bored duty midshipman. The rest of the watch were together around the mizzenmast swapping yarns, a token number compared to the full half of the ship's company closed up at sea.

They strode off forward, along the gangways each side of the boat space. "Clear 'em off forrard," Kydd said, to a duty petty officer following, who duly noted in his notebook that the wizened crone and the young child selling cheap jewelry on a frayed velvet cloth should be moved forward to clear the gangways. The foredeck was alive with cheerful noise. Traders, expert in wheedling, had set out their portable tables and were reluctantly parting with gimcrack brass telescopes, scarlet neckcloths, clay pipes and other knick-knacks that were five times their price ashore.

By the cathead another basket of fresh bread was being hauled up from a boat.

Teamed with a paper pat of farmhouse butter and a draft from a stone cask of ale, it was selling fast to hungry seamen. A cobbler industriously tapped his last, producing before their very eyes a pair of the long-quartered shoes favored by seamen going ashore, and a tailor's arms flew as a smart blue jacket with white seams and silver buttons appeared. All appeared shipshape forward, and Kydd grunted in satisfaction. Beyond the broad netting, the bare bowsprit speared ahead to the rest of the ships at anchor.

Cockburn indicated the old three-decker battleship moored farther inshore. "*She*'ll never see open water again." Stripped of her topmasts and running rigging, her timbers were dark with age and neglect; her old-fashioned stern gallery showed little evidence of gold leaf, and green weed was noticeable at her waterline.

"Aye, *Sandwich* — she's th' receiving ship only," Kydd answered. Too old for any other work, she acted as a floating prison for pressed men and others.

"Do you know then who's the captain of the sixty-four over there?" Cockburn asked.

"*Director*? No, Tam, you tell me!"

"None else than your Cap'n 'Breadfruit'

Bligh, these five years avenged of his mutiny." He paused impressively.

Kydd did not reply. In his eyes Bligh should have been better known for his great feat of seamanship in bringing his men through a heroic open-boat voyage without the loss of a single one. He turned abruptly and clattered down the ladder. Sitting cross-legged on the fore-hatch gratings, a fiddler sawed away, his time being gaily marked by a capering ship's boy with a tambourine weaving in and out of the whirling pairs of sailors and their lasses. Some of the women wore ribbons, which the men took and threaded into their own jackets and hats. Groups gathered near the foremast playing dice, perched on mess tubs; others tried to read or write letters. The whole was a babble of conviviality and careless gaiety.

Kydd looked about. There was drink, mainly dark Kent beer but not hard spirits. So far there was no sign of real drunkenness — that would come later, no doubt. Groups of men, probably from other ships, were in snug conversation at mess tables farther aft. Ship visiting was a humane custom of the service, and even if liberty ashore was stopped, acquaintances with former shipmates could be pleasantly renewed. But as he moved toward them, the talk stopped and the men turned warily to face him. "Lofty." He nodded to Webb, a carpenter's mate.

The man looked at him, then the others. "Tom," he said carefully.

"Nunky," Kydd greeted an older able seaman.

There was the same caginess. "Yes, mate?"

The seamen looked at him steadily. The visitors were clearly long-service and showed no emotion. Kydd shrugged and moved down the fore-hatchway to the gundeck, the lower of the two lines of guns, and to the screened-off areas for the married men along the sides of the deck between each pair of cannon. There was an air of an unexpected domesticity, ladies gossiping together on benches along the midline of the deck, brats scampering about. A dash of color of a bunch of flowers and the swirl of dresses added an unreality to the familiar warlike neatness of the gundeck. Kydd answered the cheery hails of some with a wave, a doff of his hat to others, and passed aft, happy there would be no trouble there.

A final canvas screen stretched the whole width of the deck. Kydd lifted it and ducked beneath. In the way of sailors, girls they had taken up with in this port before became "wives" again for their stay. But in deference to real wives they were not accorded the same status or privacies. In hammocks, under hastily borrowed sailcloth between the guns, the men consorted with their women, rough humor easing embarrassment.

Kydd moved on, eyes steadily amidships, alert for the trouble that could easily flare in these circumstances. Then down the hatchway to the orlop — the lowest deck of all. In its secretive darkness anything might happen. He kept to the wings, a walkway around the periphery, hearing the grunts and cries from within the cable tiers. It was a harsh situation, but Kydd could see no alternative; he would not be one to judge. On deck again he was passed a note by a signal messenger. "Fr'm offa bumboat, Mr. Kydd." It was addressed to the officer-of-the-watch. Kydd opened it. It was in an unpracticed but firm round hand:

Dere Sir,
I humblie pray thet yuo will bee so kind as too allow my dere bruther, Edward Malkin, be set ashor on libbertie. Whyle he was at see, his muther dyed an I

must aqaynt him of itt. Iff yuo find it in yor harte to lett him on shoar to the atached adress he will sware to repare back on bord tomorow afor cok-crow.

Yor servent, sir
Kitty Malkin
Queen Street
Sheerness

Kydd's heart sank. There had not been so many deaths on *Achilles*'s commission, but Ned Malkin's had been one, a lonely end somewhere in the night after a fall from a yardarm into an uncaring sea. His pay had stopped from that hour; Kydd hoped that the family were not dependent on it.

The captain had not yet returned with the admiral's sanction to liberty, and no one could go ashore, except on ship's business. He stared across the gray sea to the ugly sprawl of Sheerness at the tip of the island. The least he could do while he was delivering the dockyard demand was call and gently extinguish false hopes. As he gazed at the land, he imagined a forlorn soul looking out across the stretch of water, silently rehearsing the words of grief she would have to impart. Folding the paper and sliding it into his coat, he said,

"Tam, you have th' ship. L'tenant Binney is in the wardroom. I'm takin' a boat to the dockyard."

As he watched the modest ramparts of the garrison fort rise above gray mudflats, the low marshy land stretching away on Sheppey island as well as across the other side of the Medway, the isolation of the place settled about Kydd. Even when they rounded the point and opened up a view into the dockyard, the bleakness of Sheerness affected his spirits.

The dockyard itself was concentrated at the Thames-ward tip of Sheppey, the usual features easily apparent — a ship under construction on the stocks, a cluster of hulks farther along and countless smoky buildings of all sizes and shapes. An indistinct clamor of activity drifted across the water as the cutter went about and headed into a mud dock. The last of the tide had left the stone steps slippery with weed, and Kydd stepped carefully ashore, finding himself to one side of a building slip. His experience in a Caribbean dockyard did not include new ships and he looked up at the towering ribbed skeleton with interest.

Directly ahead, across the dusty road, were the dockyard offices. These had seen many a naval demand and Kydd was dealt with quickly. He was soon out again in the scent of fresh-planed timber and smithy fumes. He gathered his thoughts. The dockyard was not big. He would find where the Malkin family lived fairly quickly, then get it over with. While still in the boat he had seen a huddle of houses just outside the gates, and guessed that this would be where most lived.

It was not far — between the saw pits and clangor of the smith's workshop, past more graving docks, one holding a small frigate with cruel wounds of war, and then to the ordnance buildings with its gun wharf adjacent. Finally, there was the extensive mast pond and, out from it, half a dozen sizable hulks close to each other. The gates of the dockyard were manned by sentries, but they merely looked at him with a bored expression. A master's mate would never be asked for a liberty ticket. "D' ye know where I c'n find Queen Street?" he asked.

One man scratched his jaw. "Doan think I know that 'un," he said, after a pause. "This 'ere is Blue Town, yer knows," he said, gesturing to the mean streets and ramshackle dwellings that crowded close after the drab burial ground. "Ye c'n get anythin' yer wants there," he said, eying Kydd curiously.

Kydd started off down the rutted street, which passed along the boundary of the garrison. A crazy web of little alleys intersected it and a stench of sewerage and decay was on the air. Blue Town was not the kind of area to be graced with street signs. The barefooted urchins were no help, and his shoes spattered mud over his coat. As the settlement thinned into marshland, Kydd saw the road wind away across the marshes into a scatter of far-off buildings he assumed was Sheerness town. It was time to return; he had tried. He trudged back, irritated. At the gate, the sentry stopped him. "Oi remember, naow. What yer wants is Queen Street on th' Breakers."

The other sentry tut-tutted wisely. "Shoulda known." At Kydd's look he added hastily, "That's all them 'ulks a-floatin' out there — proper town they has on 'em, streets an' all."

There were prison hulks in Portsmouth for prisoners of war and the assembling of convicts for the miserable voyage to Botany Bay, but Kydd had never heard of ships being used as formal accommodation. On looking closer he was impressed:

built over with roofs, chimneys everywhere and commodious bridges between them, in the evening light they were a curious species of goblin rookeries, neat and well cared for.

He mounted the first bridge out to a two-decker; the whole upper deck was built over, all guns had been removed and a row of "houses" lined the sides of the "street." Each house had tubs of plants, white-painted pebbles, picked-out window frames, and in front of him was a scarlet and green street sign: George Street. A cheery soul told him that Queen Street was in the next vessel, and Kydd passed across, daring a peep into one window where places were being laid for an evening meal in a room as snug as any to be seen on dry land.

The message gave no street number, but there were painted name-boards on each door. Kydd found one marked "Malkin" and knocked. The door squeaked open and a young woman appeared, in a pinafore and mob cap. "Oh!" she said faintly, at Kydd's uniform. Her blue eyes had a softness that was most fetching.

"Er, Thomas Kydd, master's mate o' *Achilles*," he said gently. "An' you must be Miss Kitty Malkin?"

Her hand flew to her mouth. "Yes, I am, sir," she said. "It's about Edward!" she blurted. "He's in trouble, isn't he, an' can't get ashore?" The eyes looked at Kydd appealingly. "It's been a long time, sir, to be away . . ."

"C'n I speak to y'r father, if y' please?"

Something about his manner alarmed her. "Whatever has t' be said to m' father can be said to me, sir."

Kydd hesitated.

"Then please t' step inside, sir." Kitty opened the door wide to allow Kydd to enter. It was a tiny but neat and pleasing front room, rugs on the floor, sideboard displaying treasured china and some bold portraits on the wall; Kydd thought he could recognize Ned Malkin in one set about with crossed flags and mermaids. A polished table was half set for an evening meal — there was only one place.

"Pray be seated, sir," she said, her eyes never leaving his. The two cozy chairs were close to each other and Kydd sat uncomfortably. "It's kind in you to come visit," she said. Her hands were in her lap, decorous and under control.

"Ned — a taut hand," he began.

"Is he in y'r watch, sir?" she asked. It was odd to hear a woman familiar with sea terms.

"No, but I've seen him in the tops in a blow, right good seaman . . ." Kydd tailed off.

She picked up on his hesitation. Her face went tight. "Somethin's happened to Ned, hasn't it?" She sat bolt upright, her hands twisting. "I c'n see it in your face, Mr. Kydd."

Kydd mumbled something, but she cut it short. "Y' must tell me — please."

"I'm grieved t' have to tell ye, Miss Kitty, but Ned's no more."

Her face whitened in shock. "H-how did it happen? Fever? But he was always so strong, Ned . . ."

"It was a tumble fr'm a yardarm at night." There was no need to go into details; the utter darkness, everything done by feel up in the surging rigging, the hand going out and clutching a false hold and a lurch into nothing until the shock of the sea. Then, seeing the ship's lights fade into the night and the lonely horror of realizing that, no matter how hard the struggle, the end must surely come — minutes or long hours.

"Wh-when?"

"Jus' two nights afore we made soundings," he said. No more than a week or so ago, Ned Malkin could be seen on the mess-deck enjoying his grog and a laugh, spinning a yarn on a night watch . . .

For a long while she stared at him, then her face sagged. She glanced just once at the picture on the wall. "Thank you f'r coming, sir — many wouldn't," she said, in a small voice.

The moment hung, stretching out in a tense silence that seemed to go on forever. Faint sounds penetrated from the outside. Kydd cleared his throat, and made to rise. "Ah, must return on board," he muttered. She rose as well, but came between him and the door.

"Can I offer you refreshment, er, some tea?" There was pleading in her eyes, and Kydd knew he couldn't leave her to her grief just then.

"Oh, a dish o' tea would be mos' welcome, Miss Kitty."

She didn't move, however. Her white face was fixed on his. "Since Mama died, m' father went back t' Bristol to work for his brother." He wondered why she was telling him. "An' here I work in the dockyard — I sew y'r flags 'n' bunting, y' see. I like it, being near th' ships and sea — to see Ned sail away t' his adventures . . ." Her eyes suddenly brimmed, then the tears came, hot and choking, tearing at Kydd's composure.

He stood, but found himself reaching for her, pulling her close, patting her and murmuring meaningless phrases; he understood now the single place at table. She was on her own — and asking for human comfort.

Night had fallen, and Kydd could see lights on other vessels through the curtained gunport. Her arm was still over his chest as they lay precariously together on the small bedstead. Kitty's fine blond hair tumbled over his shoulder; her female form discernible under the coverlet.

She murmured something indistinct, turning to Kydd and reaching for him. He responded gently, wondering at the dreamlike transition from comforting to caring, to intimacies of the heart and then the body. So instinctive had it been that there was no need for modesty as she rose, pulling her gown around her and trimming the small light. She turned to face him. "I'd take it kindly, Thomas, if you'd tell me more about Ned an' *Achilles*," she said.

"A moment, Kitty, if y' please." Kydd swung out, retrieving his shirt and trousers, needing their dignity. "*Achilles* is a ship-of-the-line —"

"A sixty-four."

"But not a big 'un, so we gets to see parts o' the world the fleets never do."

"Ned says . . . said, that *Achilles* was bigger 'n' any frigate, could take on anything that swims outside th' thumpers in a fleet."

"That's in the right of it, but it means we get more convoy duty than any, 'cos o' that." He stopped. "Er, Kitty, d'ye think y' could get some scran alongside?" he asked sheepishly. He had not eaten since the morning.

"O' course, m' dear," she said brightly, then paused. "As long as ye're back aboard b' daybreak, you'll be safe 'n' snug here." There was only the slightest inflection of a question.

"Aye, that I will, thank ye."

When Kydd went aboard *Achilles* the next morning it was drizzling with a cutting northeaster. Liberty for all had been granted the previous evening, so there was no need to explain his absence, although Binney regarded him quizzically as he reported. He hunched in his oilskins as the rain drummed, watching a bedraggled and sullen group of sailors bring down a topmast from aloft. Normally a seamanlike evolution, now it was an awkward and sloppy display from a fuddled crew. The refined tones of the first lieutenant through his speaking trumpet crackled with irritability, but a hastily applied hitch on rain-slick timber might slip — then the spar would spear down and there would be death in the morning.

After a false start, the fore topmast lay safely on deck, and Kydd was able to dismiss the wet men. He stayed on the deserted foredeck; although the women had been sent ashore the mess-decks were just as noisy and he needed solitude for a while, thinking of what had passed.

There was no question: Kitty understood — they both did — that what had happened was spontaneous, impetuous, even, and nothing could be implied in the situation.

His eyes focused on a boat approaching in the drizzle. Most bumboats were huddled into the ship's side under their tarpaulins, but this one was a naval longboat, four oars and a couple of seamen passengers aft. Probably more ship-visiting, but Kydd was uneasy: these were not jovial shipmates but a sober, purposeful crew. They came aboard, quietly removing their hats and reporting to the officer-of-the-watch before moving quickly below. That this was shortly before the noon dinner — and issue of grog — was probably not of consequence, but with the main battle fleet in open mutiny in Spithead, nothing was above suspicion.

As usual, at the meal, he made it his duty to take a turn around the mess tables, available, but listening, alert for trouble. The fife had played "Nancy Dawson" with its cheery *tumpity-tump* on a drum for the issue of grog, the sailors had welcomed the arrival of rum-darkened mess kids, and the high point of the day began. But there was something amiss — a jarring note; Kydd couldn't sense what it was. He saw Farnall, the educated quota man, whom he sensed would always be on the fringes of trouble. Kydd walked over to his table — the same wary silence, the faces following him. He passed by, his easy "What cheer?" to Lofty Webb only brought a frightened swiveling of eyes.

He reached the end of the mess-deck. Out of the corner of his eye Kydd saw movement, and turned. Farnall's table sat motionless, looking at him. A piece of paper slowly fluttered to the deck. No one moved. Talk died at nearby tables. He picked up the paper. It was badly printed and well creased, but it began boldly: "Brother Tars! Who hath given all for the cause of yr countrys freedom! Now is the time . . ." Kydd's eyes lifted slowly, a red flush building. "Whose is this?" he said thickly. The mutinous tract must have been brought aboard from someone in touch with the Spithead mutineers.

Not a man stirred. They met his eyes steadily, neither flinching nor wavering, yet possession of a seditious document was sufficient evidence of treasonable intent whatever the circumstance. Then it dawned upon him: they had *wanted* him to read it. Cold anger replaced his uncertainty. "Y' heard y'r captain — take notice o' this jabberknowl an' ye'll be dancin' at the yardarm afore y' knows it." In the sea service, mutiny was the one unforgivable crime, a swift court-martial and death a sure end for the offender. To see shipmates stark and still at the end of a rope for a moment's foolishness would be heartbreaking.

He glared at them, and met nothing but a stony gaze. His duty was plain and explicit: he should seize the culprit and haul him aft for just punishment. But which one was it? He hesitated. He went to rip up the paper but something stopped him and he stuffed it lamely into his waistcoat.

"Ye're all under m' eye fr'm this hour. That's you, Nunky, an' Lofty — you too, Farnall, 'n' don't think t' practice y'r sea lawyer ways aboard *Achilles*. We're true man-o'-war's men in this barky." He had the satisfaction of seeing Jewell's eyes flicker and a quick look of appeal from Webb to Farnall.

Kydd stalked away in the tense silence, hearing the low, urgent rumble of talk behind him. His mind cooled. It was clear that agents of the Spithead mutineers were at work aboard *Achilles*. He must bring this to the quarterdeck; but curiosity made him head first for the master's sea cabin, which he knew was empty as Eastman was ashore. Guiltily, he drew out the paper to read.

He scanned quickly past the wordy patriotic protestations, snorting at the references to victims of tyranny and oppression and laws of humanity. It went on to claim the support of Charles Fox — Kydd's father had a sympathy for the radical, he remembered, but Kydd had minimal interest in politics. That was a task for the gentlemen of the land, not him.

He read further — pampered knaves in

power at Westminster, His Majesty ill advised by them . . . The substance of what the mutiny was said to be about was much the same as he had read in the *Times*. But what had his eyes returning time and again was one ringing sentence: "In all humanity is it a wrong to ask for bread and an honest wage, that it is a crime that must be paid for at the yardarm?" He could think of no easy answer, and fell back weakly on the reply that if it was the law of the land then that was how it must be.

Carefully he folded the tract. His head told him to take the poisonous scrap aft immediately, but his heart urged him to settle things in his own mind first. He hesitated. The rain had stopped and he stepped out on deck among a general resumption of noisy quarreling and laughing humanity. It was hard to think anything through under conditions like this. If only Renzi was on hand the whole question could be logically teased out to its only possible conclusion . . . But Renzi was part of the past. Now he must make his own judgments.

He roused himself. In his place what would Renzi have done? Discuss it logically. With whom? Not Cockburn, he was an officer-in-waiting, and had no way of knowing the strengths and good sense to be found before the mast — his answer would be short and implacable. The master? A long-service man of the sea with only a few years before his well-earned retirement ashore. Then who?

"So nice in you, m' love, to call, but if you're going t' stay f'r supper, then I must send for some vittles." Kydd settled back in the chair, cradling his china mug of porter — it had on it a colorful pair of handsome sailors each side of crossed flags and "Success to the Formidables, and damnation to the French!" in gold lettering beneath.

She had been pleased to see him, that was clear; pleasure and guilt in equal measure came to him at her warm embrace. In an awkward, masculine way he sensed that a woman could accept a situation for what it was without the need for logical justification.

He drew out the tract, holding it gingerly. "This'n was found on the mess-decks earlier." She took it with a questioning glance, and read slowly with a frown of concentration, her lips moving as she spelled out the words. As their import became clear, her brow lightened.

"Someone is takin' the sailor's part at last," she said happily. "I know about th' vittles an' such, Ned told me, so I know it's true what they say."

"Kitty, m'dear, what you are holdin' is an incitement t' mutiny an' treasonable — it c'n cost a man his neck." She stared at him uncertainly. "It's m' duty to hale aft any I fin' with this. An' then it's a court-martial an' the rope . . ."

She looked at him, incredulous. "Ye're tellin' me that *you*'d see a man choked off f'r this?" she said, shaking the grubby paper at him.

Kydd shifted uncomfortably. "It's m' duty, as I said." He could have mentioned the Articles of War and their savage view of sedition and treasonable writings, but it seemed beside the point.

Her look hardened. "I don't need t' remind you, *Mr. Thomas Kydd,* what it's like t' go before th' mast in the navy. So when some gullion says as how it is, where's y' great crime? Tell me!"

"Don't ask me that, Kitty, it's not f'r me to say," Kydd said, in a low voice. "All I know is, the fleet's in open mutiny at Spithead, an' if the French sail —"

"Then they'll sail 'n' fight, they've promised that," she said scornfully.

Kydd looked at her with a frown. "Kitty, ye know a lot about this."

"Aye!" she said defiantly. "There's those who think t' make the journey all the way fr'm Portsmouth t' the Nore just to let their brother Jack Tars know what's happening."

"They're here, now?"

"Cruise along t' the Chequers Inn one night, and could be ye'd hear somethin' will get you thinking." Her face was uncompromising in its conviction, and in it he saw an unspoken rebuke for his lack of involvement.

Before he could speak, she thrust another paper at him, printed as a broadsheet but somewhat smudged. "It's a petition, asking f'r redress. Sent t' Black Dick Howe three months ago, an' it was not th' first. Read it!"

Before he had covered the preliminaries she was on the offensive. "Provisions at sixteen ounces to th' pound! Common liberty t' go about y'r pleasures ashore! T' be paid while you're lyin' wounded in th' service of y' country!" She sniffed loudly. "Stap me, but doesn't this sound like what th' meanest grass-comber on the land c'n lay claim to without he goes t' hazard his life?"

This was not what he had come to see

her for. He longed for the cool, balanced assessment he knew he would get from Renzi; her passionate sincerity on behalf of his shipmates made him feel ashamed. Stiffly, he returned the paper. "I have m' duty, is all," he said.

"Duty!" she spat. "Aye — I'll tell you about duty!" She faced him like a virago, her eyes afire. "An' it's to y'r shipmates — they who share th' hazards o' the sea with ye, who're there by y'r side when y' face the enemy! Not what some scrovy smell-smock in th' Admiralty tells ye."

She held him with her eyes, then her head fell. When it rose again there was a glitter of tears. "Please go," she said, in a low voice. "I've some grievin' to do."

There was no answer he could find to what she was saying. "I thank ye for the refreshments." He picked up his hat and, without looking at her, made his way to the door.

"Thomas!" she called. "You're a good man. But soon it'll be time t' choose." Her eyes held his with a terrible intensity. "Y' can never steer two courses at th' same time. When it's time, I pray t' God you take the right one."

The Nore anchorage spread out over a

mile of sea, a breathtaking display of sea power, but Kydd was not seeing it as they rounded the point. He couldn't return the bibulous chatting of the boatswain of *Director*, and pretended to stare out over the anchorage.

It had to be faced. The terrible uprising at Spithead had cast its shadow as far as the Nore and soon he would have to choose. In his heart he knew that he could never condemn a shipmate for wanting full measures from the purser. The alternative, however, ran against all he had ever felt for the navy.

On board *Achilles* there was unaccustomed quiet. An evening on the foredeck without dancing, grog and laughter was unsettling. Kydd could see men there, in the usual social groups, but there was none of the jovial camaraderie or careless noise, they were talking quietly together.

Below in the gunroom there was a pall of foreboding. The gunner and carpenter had left their cabins forward looking for company and now sat cradling their glasses, gloom etched on their faces. Kydd pulled down a book, but the light of the rush dips was so bad he gave up and gazed moodily at Cockburn, who was as usual scratching out a piece of poetry and oblivious to all else.

"Himself not back aboard, then," offered Mr. Lane, the gunner. No one was inclined to reply. The captain's erratic movements in the last several days needed little explanation.

The sharp-nosed surgeon's mate gave a thin smile. "We takes any more o' the doxies an' we'll have the other half o' the crew under Venus's spell."

"What d' you care, Snipes? Ye takes y'r silver off 'em either way," snapped the gunner, many of whose mates would be owing some of their meager pay to the surgeon's mate for venereal treatment.

The smile vanished. Morice, the carpenter, stirred and looked significantly at the two subdued midshipmen at the end of the table boning their best shoes. Without a word, Kydd reached for a fork and, blank-faced, jammed it into a well-worn cleft in a deck beam. The midshipmen looked up, and quietly left. Morice leaned forward. "I've heard as how we got Spithead men aboard," he said quietly.

"Aye." The gunner would be more in touch than the carpenter with the main body of sailors and their concerns. "Can't stop 'em coming aboard to see their mates in course."

"I bin in a real 'nough mutiny once," Morice muttered. "Ain't something y' forgets too easy."

Lane glanced at him with interest, and Cockburn stopped his scribbling and looked up.

"Yair, *Culloden* in th' year 'ninety-four." Morice, aware of the attention he was getting, became animated. "That's right, Troubridge was our cap'n, an' a right taut hand was he. A fine seventy-four she was, Slade built an' a fair sailer —"

A polite cough from Lane steadied him, and he went on, "Ship lyin' in Spithead, they thinks t' send us t' sea short on vittles. Ship's company doesn't like this idea, they just in fr'm a cruise an' all, 'n' starts talkin' wry. Then one o' the quartermaster's mates — forget 'is tally t' my shame — we calls him Cocoa Jack on account of him being touched b' the sun, fine, hard-weather kind o' man . . ."

The carpenter's expression grew troubled at the memory, and his voice changed when he resumed: "Yeah, fine sort o' seaman. Well, he sees we ain't the stores aboard 'll let us sail, an' gets to speakin' with the men. Right reasonable he was, says Cap'n Troubridge would see 'em right if they shows firm." He looked around the table gravely. "He says as if they weren't t' take the barky to sea until she was stored proper, it was only their right. Gets half a dozen of his mates an' goes about th' ship organizin'. S' next mornin' they all stands fast when it's 'hands t' unmoor ship' — jus' that, willin' t' do any duty but unmoor, they was."

"Well, where did you stand in this?" Kydd asked.

Morice's eyes flicked once at him, and he continued, "An' the cap'n listens, calm as y' like. Lets Cocoa Jack have his say, nods 'n' says, 'Fair enough,' or some such. 'Yes,' he says, when they asks f'r a pardon if they goes back t' duty."

"Did they get one?"

"Sure they did, and fr'm the cap'n's own mouth in front of the whole company."

Kydd let out his breath. "So all square and a-taunto then," he said.

"Not quite," Morice said, in an odd manner. "Hands turn to, but quick as a flash, when they wasn't expectin' it, Troubridge has 'em all clapped in iron garters, an' before they knows it they're in a court-martial in the flagship f'r mutiny." He paused significantly. "They claims pardon — but funny thing, mates, th' court couldn't find any evidence o' one, no *written* pardon." Another pause. "So five on 'em, includin' Cocoa Jack, gets taken out 'n' hung on the fore yardarm afore the whole fleet."

While he drained his pot noisily the others exchanged glances. Letting the atmosphere darken, Lane waited and then growled, "I was in *Windsor Castle* previous t' this'n, left before they has *their* mut'ny." He looked for attention. "Now that was a downright copper-bottomed, double-barreled swinger of a mut'ny.

"Remember it's a bigger ship, ninety-eight she was, a stronger crew, and they has the admiral an' all on board. An' it's just the same year as yours, mate, but out in th' Med. Can't swear t' the details, 'cos I'd left b' then, but I heard it all fr'm mates later. Now, ye'll find this a tough yarn, but it's true enough — in the flagship an' all, so hear this. They mutinies because they don't like the admiral, the cap'n, the first l'tenant *an'* the bo'sun, and demands they all gets changed!"

There was a shocked silence, until Morice chuckled. "Yeah, heard o' that one," he said, to the chagrin of Lane who was clearly winding up to a climax.

"Well, what's t' do then?" Kydd demanded.

Lane finished resentfully, "No court-martial — barring the cap'n only, I should say, an' the cap', first luff an' not forgettin' the bo'sun, all gets turned out o' their ship, just as they says."

"That's all?"

"Is all," confirmed Lane, " 'ceptin' they gets a pardon, every one."

The surprised grunts that this received were quickly replaced by a thoughtful quiet. Cockburn soberly interjected: "This is different. At Spithead it's not just one ship but the whole fleet. The Admiralty will never forgive them — there'll be corpses at every yardarm for months."

"I saw in th' *Times* the mutineers are talkin' to Parliament, even got 'em to print their demands in th' paper. It's already past the Admiralty — wouldn't be surprised if Billy Pitt himself ain't involved," Kydd said.

"Good Lord! I didn't know that." Cockburn appeared shaken by the news. "If that's so then this — well, it's never gone so far before. Anything can happen."

Lane's face tightened. "O' course, you knows what this means f'r us . . ."

"It's about to start here," said Cockburn.

The gunner gave a hard smile. "No, mate. What it means is that Parlyment has t' finish this quick — that means they'll be askin' us an' the North Sea fleet t' sail around to Spithead an' settle it wi' broadsides."

"No!" Kydd gasped.

"C'n you think else?" Lane growled.

"Could be. Supposin' it's like y'r *Windsor Castle* an' they agree t' do something. Then it's all settled, we don't need t' sail."

"You're both forgetting the other possibility," Cockburn said heavily.

"Oh?"

"That the Spithead mutiny spreads here to the Nore."

A wash of foreboding shook Kydd. Out there in the night, unknown dark forces were tearing at the settled orderliness of his world, upheavals every bit as threatening as the despised revolution of the French.

"Need t' get me head down," muttered Morice. "Are ye —" The little group froze. From forward came a low rumble, more felt than heard. It grew louder — and now came from the upper deck just above. It came nearer, louder, ominous and mind-freezing. It seemed to be coming straight for them, thunderous and unstoppable.

Then, abruptly, the noise ceased and another rumble from forward began its fearful journey toward them. Unconsciously, the surgeon's mate gripped his throat and, wide-eyed, they all stared upward. The gunner and carpenter spoke together: "Rough music!"

This was a rough and ready but effective way for seamen to let the quarterdeck know of serious discontent. In the blackness of night on deck, a twenty-four-pounder cannonball from the ready-use shot garlands would be rolled along the deck aft, the culprit impossible to detect.

It was nearly upon them — whatever storm it was that lay ahead.

They were waiting for him at the fore jeer bitts, hanking down after re-reeving a foreyard clew-line block, making a show of it in the process. Standing in deliberate, staged groups, eyes darted between them.

Kydd saw the signs and tensed. "Ah, Mr. Kydd," Jewell said carefully, inspecting critically the coil of line in his hand as though looking for imperfections.

"Aye, Nunky," Kydd replied, just as carefully. The others stopped what little work they were doing and watched.

"Well, Tom, mate, we're puzzled ter

know what course we're on, these things we hear."

"What things, Nunky? The catblash y'r hearing about —"

"The actions at Spithead, he means, of course."

Kydd turned to Farnall, sizing him up. "And what've y' heard that troubles ye so much?" He was not surprised that Farnall was there.

"As much as you, I would say," Farnall said evenly.

Kydd colored. "A set o' mumpin' villains, led like sheep t' play their country false, the sad dogs."

Farnall raised an eyebrow. "Sad dogs? Not as who would call the brave victors of Saint Vincent, just these three months gone."

Pent-up feeling boiled in Kydd and, knocking Jewell aside, he confronted Farnall. "You an' y'r sea lawyer ways, cully, these 'r seamen ye're talkin' of, fine men ye'd be proud t' have alongside you out on the yard, gale in y' teeth — what d' ye know o' this, y' haymakin' lubber?"

Jewell spoke from behind. "Now, Mr. Kydd, he's no sailor yet, but haul off a mort on 'im, he's tryin'."

Breathing deeply, Kydd was taken unawares by the depth of his anger: Farnall was only an unwitting representative of the rabid forces of the outside world that were tearing apart his share of it. "Aye, well, if ye runs athwart m' hawse again . . ."

"Understood, Mr. Kydd," said Farnall, with a slight smile.

Kydd looked around and glowered; the group drifted apart and left under his glare, but Boddy remained, fiddling with a rope's end.

"Will?" Kydd would trust his life with someone like Boddy. He was incapable of deceit or trickery and was the best hand on a sail with a palm and needle, the sailmaker included.

"Tom, yer knows what's in th' wind, don' need me ter tell yez."

Kydd didn't speak for a space, then he said, "I c'n guess. There's those who're stirrin' up mischief f'r their own reasons, an' a lot o' good men are goin' to the yardarm 'cos of them."

Boddy let the rope drop. "Farnall, he admires on Wilkes — yer dad probably told yer, 'Wilkes 'n' Liberty!' an' all that."

"I don't hold wi' politics at sea," Kydd said firmly. "An' don't I recollect Wilkes is agin the Frenchy revolution?"

"Aye, that may be so," Boddy said uncomfortably, "but Farnall, he's askin' some questions I'm vexed ter answer."

"Will, ye shouldn't be tellin' me this," Kydd muttered.

Boddy looked up earnestly. "Like we sent in petitions 'n' letters an' that — how many, yer can't count — so th' Admiralty *must* know what it's like. They've got ter! So if nothin' happens, what does it mean?"

He paused, waiting for Kydd to respond. When he didn't, Boddy said, "There's only one answer, Tom." He took a deep breath. "They don't care! We're away out of it at sea, why do they haveta care?"

"Will, you're telling me that ye're going t' trouble th' Lords o' the Admiralty on account of a piece o' reasty meat, Nipcheese gives y' short measure —"

"Tom, ye knows it's worse'n that. When I was a lad, first went ter sea, it were better'n now. So I asks ye, how much longer do we have ter take it — how long, mate?"

"Will, y're talkin' wry, I c'n see that —"

"Spithead, they're doin' the right thing as I sees it. No fightin', no disrespeck, just quiet-like, askin' their country ter play square with 'em, tryin' —"

"Hold y'r tongue!" Kydd said harshly.

Boddy stopped, but gazed at him

steadily, and continued softly, "Some says as it could be soon when a man has t' find it in himself ter stand tall f'r what's right. How's about you, Mr. Kydd?"

Kydd felt his control slipping. Boddy knew that he had overstepped — but was it deliberate, an attempt to discover his sympathies, mark him for elimination in a general uprising, or was it a friend and shipmate trying to share his turmoil?

Kydd turned away. In what he had said Boddy was guilty of incitement to mutiny; if Kydd did not witness against him he was just as guilty. But he could not — and realized that a milestone had been passed.

He did not sleep well: as an eight-year-old he had been badly shaken when his mother had returned from a London convulsed by mob rioting, Lord Gordon's ill-advised protest lurching out of control. She had been in a state of near panic at the breakdown of authority, the drunken rampages and casual violence. Her terror had planted a primordial fear in Kydd of the dissolution of order, a reflexive hatred of revolutionaries, and in the darkness he had woken from terrifying dreams of chaos and his shipmates turned to ravening devils.

Glad when morning came, he sat down

to breakfast in the gunroom. The others ate in silence, the navy way, until Cockburn pushed back his plate and muttered, "I have a feeling in m' bowels, Tom."

"Oh?" Kydd answered cautiously. This was not like Cockburn at all.

"Last night there was no play with the shot-rolling. It was still, too quiet by half. Have you heard anything from your people?"

"I heard 'em talkin' but nothin' I c'n put my finger on," he lied.

"All it needs is some hothead." Cockburn stared morosely at the mess table.

Kydd's dream still cast a spell and he was claustrophobic. "Going topsides," he said, but as he got to his feet, the gunroom servant passed a message across. There was no mistaking the bold hand and original spelling, and a smile broke through. This had obviously been brought aboard by a returning libertyman.

"The sweet Dulcinea calls?" Cockburn asked dryly. It was no secret in the gunroom that Kydd's dark good looks were an unfailing attraction to females.

He broke the wafer.

It wood greeve me if we are not to be

291

frends any moor and I wood take it kindly in yuo if you could come visit for tea with me.

Yoor devoted
Kitty

His day brightened; he could probably contrive another visit that afternoon — after his experience in an Antiguan dock-yard he was good at cozening in the right quarters. Stepping lightly, he arrived on deck; it was a clear dawn, promising reliable weather for the loosing and drying of the headsails.

The duty watch of the hands appeared; the afterguard part-of-ship rigged the wash-deck hose and the morning routine started. Kydd could pace quietly one side of the quarterdeck until the petty officer was satisfied with clean decks and then he could collect the hands.

He tried to catch a glimpse of their temper. He knew all the signs — the vicious movements of frustration, the languid motions of uncaring indolence — but today was different. There was a studied blankness in what they were doing; they worked steadily, methodically, with little of the back chat usual in a tedious job. It was unsettling. His musing was interrupted by the approach of a duty midshipman. "Mr. Kydd, ol' Heavie Hawley wants to see you now."

Kydd's heart gave a jump. With the captain ashore, the first lieutenant was in command, and for some reason wanted his presence immediately. He stalled: "An' I don't understan' y'r message, y' swab — say again."

"First l'tenant asks that you attend him in his cabin, should you be at liberty to do so at this time."

"I shall be happy t' attend shortly," Kydd replied guardedly, and the reefer scuttled off.

It could be anything, but with increasing apprehension he remembered his talk with Boddy. If anyone had overheard, or had seen that it had not been followed by instant action to take the matter aft, he was in serious trouble. Removing his worn round hat, he hurried down to the wardroom and the officers' cabins. The polished dark red of the first lieutenant's cabin door looked ominous. He knocked.

"Come in." Hawley's aristocratic tones were uncompromising, whomever he addressed. He was at his desk, writing. He looked up, then carefully replaced his quill in the holder and swiveled around. "Ah,

Mr. Kydd." His eyes narrowed. "I've asked you here on a matter of some seriousness."

"Er, aye, sir."

"Some in the service would regard it more lightly than I, but I would not have it in question, sir, other than that I would rather put my duty, as asked of me, ahead of anything I hold dear in this world. Is that clear?"

"Aye-aye, sir."

He picked up a paper. "*This* is duty! It is from the King himself." He paused as if struck by sudden doubt, then recovered. "Shall I read it to you?"

"If y' please, sir." It was probably his commission: Kydd had never seen an officer's commission, the instrument that made them, under the King's Majesty, of almost sacred power aboard a man-o'-war. He had heard that it contained the most awful strictures regarding allegiance and duty, and he was probably going to read them to Kydd before striking his blow.

"Very well." His lips moved soundlessly as he scanned down to the right spot:

" 'The Queen's House, the 10th day of May, 1797.

" 'The Earl of Spencer, to avoid any delay in my waiting . . .' er, and so forth '. . . that a fitting reception for the newly wed Princess Royal and His Serene Highness the Prince of Württemburg be made ready preparatory to their embarkation in *San Fiorenzo* for their honeymoon. Also attending will be Colonel Gwynn, Lord Cathcart and the Clerk of the Green Cloth and two others. I desire orders be given . . .' more detail '. . . by return rider.'

"There! What did you think of that? From His Majesty, Mr. Kydd."

"I — er, I don' know what t' think, sir. Er, the honor!"

Clearly pleased with the effect, Hawley unbent a little. "Means we are required to mount an assembly of sorts for the Princess Royal and party prior to their boarding *San Fiorenzo*. I've spoken to Lieutenant Binney, who will be involved in the entertainments, and Mr. Eastman will be looking into the refreshments. Of course, Captain Dwyer will have returned from the court-martial by then."

Fighting the tide of relief, Kydd tried to make sense of it. To be meeting royalty was not to be taken calmly, and it would be something to bring up casually at mess for years to come. "Sir, what —"

"In the nature of these things, it is possible that the party may be delayed or *San Fiorenzo* is obliged to take an earlier tide, in which case the whole occasion will have to be abandoned."

"What is my duty, if y' please?"

"Ah, yes. You will understand that a royal retinue is accustomed to an order of civilized conduct above that normally to be found in a ship of war. Your, er, origins make you uniquely qualified for this duty."

"Sir?"

"You will insure that the ship's company as far as possible is kept out of sight, away from the gaze of this party, that those unavoidably on duty are strictly enjoined to abjure curses, froward behavior and unseemly displays, and that silence is kept below. You may employ any expression of discipline you see fit."

Despite his relief, Kydd felt a dull resentment. What were his men, that they must be herded away from the gaze of others, they with whom he had shared so many dangers by sea and malice of the enemy? "Aye-aye, sir," he said softly.

"So we —" Hawley broke off with a frown. From the deck above sounded the thump of many feet, ending suddenly, just as if the cry of "all hands on deck" had sounded.

He stared at Kydd. "Did you —" Distantly there came the unmistakable clamor of cheers, a crescendo of sound that echoed, then was taken up and multiplied from all around them.

"Good heavens! You don't suppose —" Seizing his cocked hat, Hawley strode out on deck, closely followed by Kydd. It seemed the entire ship's company of *Achilles* was cheering in the lower rigging, a deafening noise.

Around the anchorage in the other ships it was the same. In the flagship *Sandwich* the rigging was black with frantically waving seamen, the urgent *tan-tara* of a trumpet sounding above the disorder, the crack of a signal gun on her fo'c'sle adding point to the moment.

"You, sir," Hawley shouted, at a bemused midshipman. "What the devil is going on?"

Before he could answer, a crowd of seamen moved purposefully toward him on the quarterdeck, ignoring the others in the shrouds cheering hoarsely. Kydd's stomach tightened. He knew what was afoot.

They didn't hesitate. Kydd saw Farnall conspicuously in front, Boddy and Jewell, some of his own forward gun crews, others, all with the same expression of grim resolution. They were not armed: they didn't need to be.

"Sir," said Eli Coxall gravely to the first lieutenant. "I'll trouble ye for the keys t' the magazine."

Shocked, Hawley stared at him. The cheering in the rigging stopped, and men dropped to the deck, coming aft to watch. Kydd stood paralyzed: a mutiny was now taking place.

"Now, sir, if you please!" Farnall's voice held a ring of authority, a quota man turned mutineer, and it goaded Kydd into anger. He clenched his fists and pushed toward him. "Do ye know what ye've done, man?" he blazed. "All y'r shipmates, headin' for a yardarm —"

The big bulk of Nelms, a seaman Kydd knew more for his strength than judgment, shoved beside Farnall. "Now, yer can't talk ter Mr. Farnall like that, Mr. Kydd."

Kydd sensed the presence of others behind him, and looked unbelieving at Coxall, Boddy and others he knew. They stared back at him gravely.

"This is open mutiny, you men," Hawley began nervously, "but should you return to your duty, then —"

"We have charge o' the ship," Coxall said

firmly. It was a well-organized coup that was all but over.

Binney's voice came from behind. "Sir, do you —"

Hawley recovered. "No, Mr. Binney, I do not believe hasty actions will answer. These scoundrels are out of their wits at the moment, but they do have the ship." He turned to Coxall. "Very well. You shall have the keys. What is it you plan to do with the vessel? Turn it over to the French?"

"Oh, no, sir." Only Farnall showed an expression of triumph; Coxall's voice continued level and controlled. "We're with our brethren in Spithead, sir, in their just actions. I'd be obliged were ye to conform t' our directions."

Kydd held his breath. It was as if the heavens had collapsed on them all, and he dreaded what was to come.

"And these are?" Hawley hissed.

"Well, sir, we has the good conduct o' the fleet well at heart, so if we gets y'r word you'll not move against us, why, y' has the freedom o' the ship, you an' y' officers. We're not goin' t' sail, we're stayin' at moorin's till we've bin a-righted." Kydd was struck by Coxall's dignity in the appalling danger he stood in: he was now undeniably marked out, in public, as a ringleader.

"My word?"

"Aye, sir, the word of a king's officer."

Hawley was clearly troubled. It was deadly certain that the gravest consequences would follow, whatever happened, and his every act — or omission — would be mercilessly scrutinized. What was not at question was that if word was given, it would be kept.

The crowd grew quiet, all eyes on the first lieutenant.

"I, er, give my word."

There was a rustle of feeling, muttered words and feet shuffling.

"Thank ye, sir," Coxall said. "Then ye also have the word o' the delegates at the Nore that y' shan't be touched." Hawley began to speak, but Coxall cut him off. "Sir, the business o' the ship goes on, but we do not stir one inch t' sea."

"Very well." Hawley had little choice — in barely three minutes he had gone from command of a ship-of-the-line to an irrelevancy.

A scuffle of movement and raised voices came from the fore-hatchway. A knot of men appeared, propelling the boatswain aft, his hands roughly tied.

"We gives 'im medicine as 'll cure his gripin'!" crowed Cantlie, dancing from foot to foot in front of the detested Welby. "Go reeve a yard rope, mates!"

From the main hatch the boatswain jerked into view, hatless and with blood trickling from his nose, a jeering crowd of seamen frog-marching him aft. "Here's one t' do a little dance fer us!"

It was met by a willing roar, but Coxall cut in forcefully. "Hold hard, y' clinkin' fools! Remember, we got rules, we worked it out."

"Rules be buggered!" an older fo'c'sle hand slurred. "I gotta argyment wi' first luff needs settlin' now!" Hawley, pale-faced, tensed.

Coxall spoke quietly, over his shoulder: "Podger?" Nelms's beefy arm caught the troublemaker across the face, throwing him to the deck. "I said, mates, we got rules," Coxall said heavily. He turned to Boddy. "Will, these two are t' be turned out o' the ship *now*. C'n yer clear away the larb'd cutter?"

A seaman with drawn cutlass came on deck and reported to him. It seemed that the marines were powerless, their arms under control and all resistance impossible.

Coxall raised his voice to a practiced roar and addressed the confused and silent mass of men. "Committee meets in the st'b'd bay now. Anyone wants t' lay a complaint agin an officer c'n do it there." He glanced around briefly, then led his party out of sight below.

Chapter 7

Mutiny! A word to chill the bowels. *Achilles* was now in the hands of mutineers, every one of whom would probably swing for it, condemned by their own actions. Kydd paced cautiously; men gave way to him as a master's mate just as they had before. There were sailors in the waist at work clearing the waterways at the ship's side, others sat on the main hatch, picking oakum. Forward a group was seeing to the loosing and drying of headsails. A few stood about forlornly, confused, rudderless.

It was hardly credible: here was a great ship in open insurrection and shipboard routines went on largely as they did every day. Binney paced by on the opposite side of the deck; seamen touched their hats and continued, neither abashed nor aggressive.

Impulsively, Kydd clattered down the hatchway to the main deck and made his way to the ship's bay, the clear area in the bluff bow forward of the riding bitts. There was a canvas screen rigged across, with one corner laced up, a seaman wearing a cutlass at ease there, on watch. "I have a question f'r the delegates," Kydd told the man.

He smiled briefly. "Aye, an' I'm sure ye have," he said, and peered inside. He straightened and held back the corner flap. "Ask yer questions, then," he said, looking directly at Kydd.

Farnall sat at a table, Boddy on his right. Others were on benches and sea chests, about a dozen in all. They were discussing something in low, urgent tones, while Farnall shuffled a clutch of papers. Boddy wore a frown and looked uneasy.

"What cheer, Tom?" This came from Jewell, who was with others to the side. Boddy looked up and nodded. Others stopped their talk and looked at him.

"Nunky, Will," Kydd acknowledged.

"And to what do we owe this honor?" Farnall asked.

Kydd folded his arms. "I came t' see if there's anyone c'n explain t' me this ragabash caper."

There were growls from some, but one called "Tell 'im, Mr. Farnall."

Farnall rose to his feet. Gripping the lapels of his waistcoat he turned to Kydd, but before he could speak, Kydd interrupted forcefully: "No, I want t' hear it from a reg'lar-built sailorman, not a land-toggie who doesn't know his arse from his elbow about sailoring."

Farnall's face grew tight, but he sat down. Boddy stood up and hurried over to Kydd, taking him by the elbow and leaving the bay. "Tom, it'll do yez no good to get up Farnall's nose. He's a delegate now, an' he's got friends."

They emerged together on deck — the spring sunshine out of keeping with the dire events taking place. Kydd glanced up wistfully at the innocent blue sky. "What has you planned f'r *Achilles*, Will?" he asked.

Boddy paused. "Fer an answer, ye needs ter know what's happened altogether, like." He pursed his lips. "We feels they has a right steer on things in Spithead, Tom. They's standin' f'r hard things that should've bin done an age back. What we're doin' is giving 'em our backin', 'cos they need it. What we done is, we have two delegates f'r each ship, an' a committee o' twelve. We decides things b' votes an' that, Farnall knows all about this. An' we hold wi' discipline,

Tom. We won't have any as is half slued around the decks, not when we're so close t' the wind like this'n."

"Who's y'r delegates?" Kydd asked.

"Coxall 'n' Farnall, but we got some good men in th' committee. We already have rules o' conduct: no liquor aboard wi'out it's declared, respects to officers, ship is kept ready f'r sea — an' this is because we swear 'ut if the Mongseers sail on England, we're ready ter do our dooty."

Kydd looked squarely at Boddy. "Will, who's it behind this all — who organized it?" If there was the barest whiff of French treachery he would have all his doubts resolved, his duty clear.

"Why, we're follering Spithead, is all, nothin' more."

"No Frenchies at the bottom of it, a-tall?"

"No, mate. If they noo that the whole navy of Great Britain was hook down an' goin' nowhere, they'd soon be crowdin' sail for England. They ain't, so there's no plot. They don't even know."

"But there's someone takin' charge?"

"O' course — someone has ter. *Sandwich*, she's the Parlyment ship, the committee o' the fleet meets there. We has a president o' the delegates, name o' Dick Parker. We'll see 'im soon, wouldn't wonder." Boddy looked shrewdly at Kydd. "Look, Tom, it's started, cuffin, an' mark my words, we're goin' to stand fast. Now why doesn't ye come in wi' us? There's many a soul looks up ter you, would take —"

Kydd's harsh reply stilled Boddy's words, but the latter's eyes held reproach, sadness, which touched Kydd. Boddy glanced at him once, then turned and went below.

Kydd paced restlessly. If the likes of Will Boddy had seen it necessary to hazard their lives to stand for what they believed needed righting . . .

It had to be admitted, the mutiny had been conducted on the strictest lines. The committee was even preparing articles of conduct for preserving good order and naval discipline in the face of the absence of authority, an amazing thing, given the circumstances. But most astonishing was the mere fact that the complexity of daily life — the taking aboard of stores to meet the needs of seven hundred men, the deployment of skilled hands to maintain the miles of cordage and sea-racked timbers, the scaling of cannon bores — was continued as before.

The noon meal was a cheerless affair in the gunroom; the midshipmen were subdued, the senior hands edgy, Cockburn introspective. It was made more so by the waves of jollity gusting from the sailors on the gundeck relishing being in relaxed discipline.

Glad to return on deck and get away from Cockburn's moodiness, Kydd kept out of the way of the sailors at the gangway waiting to board the boats to take them ashore. Liberty tickets were being issued on a generous scale. These were of the usual form to protect them from the press-gang and prove them not deserters, but they were signed by a delegate, not an officer.

A shout from the waist caught Kydd's attention. Someone called out, "An' if I'm not wrong that longboat comin' under our stern now is 'imself come t' visit."

Men ran to the ship's side to catch a glimpse of the president. The boat curved widely, the men at the oars pulling lustily in a play of enthusiasm. In the sternsheets was a dark-featured man sitting bolt upright, looking neither to left nor right; he did not acknowledge the surging cheers.

The boat hooked on, and the passenger, wearing a stylish beaver hat and a blue coat with half-boots, came down the boat. He clambered up the side, and there was a scramble among the men at the top, a cry of "Side!" A hurrying boatswain's mate arrived and, with appropriate ceremony, President of the Delegates Richard Parker was piped aboard HMS *Achilles*. Kydd held back at the parody, but was drawn in fascination to the scene.

Parker carried himself well and looked around with studied composure, his dark eyes intelligent and expressive. He doffed his hat to Hawley, who had come on deck but did not speak with him; he went forward, and stood on the fore gratings, folding his arms, waiting for the men to come to him.

Sailors gathered around, their talking dying away. "Brother Tars," he began, fixing with his eyes first one man, then another. "Your waiting is over. Your long wait for justice, rights and true respect — is over." His voice was educated, assured and direct, but somewhat thin against the breeze and shipboard noises. "We have joined our brothers in Spithead, as they asked us, and even while we celebrate, there are dispatched our representatives to

Yarmouth, to the North Sea squadron, to beseech them also to join us. When they do, with Plymouth now aroused, the entire navy of Great Britain will be arisen in our cause."

Kydd listened, unwilling to leave. The North Sea squadron! This was news indeed: the last battle squadron left to Britain, the one strategically sited to confront the Dutch and the entrance to the Baltic, if it mutinied then . . .

"This will make His Majesty's perverse ministers sit up. It will show that we are steadfast, we mean to win entire recognition of our grievances — and as long as we stand together and united, we cannot fail." Parker's eyes shone, as though he was personally touched by the moment.

Scattered cheers rose up, but there were as many troubled and uncertain faces.

"We are His Majesty's most loyal and dutiful subjects. Our intentions are noble, our motions virtuous. Why then do we, victims of a barbarous tyranny, have to clamor for justice? I will tell you! King George is surrounded by corrupt and treacherous advisers, but now they have been brought low, the scoundrels, by common seamen. By us!"

Despite himself, Kydd was transfixed by

the scene. Here was the man who had pulled together seamen from a dozen ships in common cause — so many hard men, tough seamen who had met the enemy in battle and prevailed: they were not a rabble to be swayed by wild words. They were being asked to risk their necks for others, and would not easily have been convinced.

Parker's voice rose. "While we stand steadfast, they must treat with us, and our claims are just and few. As I speak, in London there are meetings of the lords and nobles, the ministers and secretaries — and they are meeting because they have to! No longer can they ignore us. And all because we stood up for our rights, without flinching."

Kydd saw men around beginning to look thoughtful, others becoming animated.

"Fellow seamen, let's give it three hearty cheers — and I invite any who will to step ashore this afternoon and lift a pot with me to the King, and confusion to his false friends."

Coxall stepped forward with a grim smile. "An' it's three cheers 'n' a tiger!" he roared. This time the exultation was full-hearted, and there was an air of savage joy as Parker stepped down to make his way back to the boat.

Achilles's boats were soon putting off full of libertymen keen to taste the sweets of success in a ran-tan ashore.

Kydd gazed around the anchorage. *Sandwich* swung serenely to her buoy, but her decks were alive with activity, her boats similarly employed. Inshore of *Achilles* was *Director*, Bligh's ship. Kydd wondered what had happened to him: this was the second mutiny he had suffered. Astonishingly, the ships showed little sign of the breathtaking events taking place, all men-o'-war at the Nore were flying their flags and pennants as though nothing had happened.

Kydd had not been turned out of the ship, like some of the officers, but he found his estrangement from the seamen irksome. But if they were enjoying a spree ashore, he saw no reason not to step off himself — if only on ship's business. He had a seaman in his division in sick quarters ashore somewhere. He would visit, and perhaps call on Kitty. He found himself a place in the cutter, enduring jovial taunts from sailors who had no doubt where he was headed.

They rounded the point and ran the boat alongside. The dockyard was in uproar. Sailors and their women were everywhere. Along with grog cans some bore rough banners — "Success to our cause!" "Billy Pitt to be damn'd!"

Dockyard artisans left their workshops and joined the glorious merrymaking, and here and there Kydd saw the red coats of soldiery; it seemed the garrison was taking sides.

A brass band led by a swaggering sailor with a huge Union Flag came around the corner in a wash of raucous sound, scattering urchins and drawing crowds. It headed toward the fort on the point and Kydd was carried forward in the press. The militia was formed up, but the procession swirled around them, and while officers and sergeants tried to march the soldiers off, laughing sailors walked along with them, joking and urging.

Kydd found himself caught up in the carnival-like mood. He took off his blue master's mate coat, swinging it over his arm in the warm spring sunshine before wholeheartedly joining in the chorus of "Britons Strike Home."

He resisted the urge to join fully in the roistering, feeling a certain conscience about the sick man he had come to see, and took the road to Blue Town, passing the hulks and on through Red Barrier Gate, which was unmanned.

Blue Town had taken the mutineers to its heart. The shantytown, with its maze of mean alleyways, taverns and bawdyhouses rocked with good cheer. Seamen came and went raucously and more processions brought people spilling out onto the street to shout defiance and condemnation.

Kydd set off the quarter mile over the marshes for Mile Town, a rather more substantial community with roads, stone houses and even shops for the quality. As he entered the settlement, he saw that there was a quite different mood — the few sailors who had strayed this far were neither feted nor cheered, shops were shuttered and in the streets only a few frightened souls were abroad.

The temporary sick quarters were in a large hostelry, the Old Swan, which was near the tollgate for the London turnpike. Kydd turned down the path and walked through the open door, but the darkstained desk just inside was deserted.

He walked farther — it was odd, no orderlies or surgeons about. Suddenly, noise erupted from a nearby room, and before Kydd could enter a black-coated medical man rushed past. "Hey — stop!" he called, in bewilderment, after the figure, who didn't look back, vanishing down the road in a swirl of coattails. Not knowing what to expect, Kydd went into the room.

"Ye'll swing fer this, mate, never fear," a bulky seaman shouted, at a cringing figure on his knees.

"N-no, spare me, I beg!"

Another, watching with his arms folded, broke into harsh laughter. "Spare ye? What good t' the world is a squiddy ol' ferret like you?"

It was a sick room. Men lay in their cots around the walls, enduring. One got to his elbow. "Leave off, mates! Safferey, 'e's honest enough fer a sawbones." He caught sight of Kydd standing at the doorway. "Poor looby, thinks th' delegates are comin' to top 'im personally." The surgeon was desperately frightened, trembling uncontrollably. "Said they were here ter check on conditions, an' if they weren't up to snuff, they'd do 'im."

"Shut yer face, Jack," one of the delegates growled. "O' course, we're in mutiny, an' today the whole o' the fleet is out 'n' no one's ter stop us gettin' our revenge — are you?"

"Time t' let him go," Kydd said, helping the shattered man to his feet. Wild-eyed, Safferey tore free and ran into a side room, slamming the door behind him.

The thick-set delegate's face hardened. Kydd snapped, "Y'r president, Mr. Parker, what does he think o' yez topping it the tyrant over th' poor bast'd? Thinks y' doing a fine job as delegates, does he?"

The two delegates looked at each other, muttered something inaudible and left.

A muffled clang sounded from the side room, then a sliding crash. Kydd strode over and threw open the door. In the dim light he saw the form of the surgeon on the floor, flopping like a landed fish. The reek of blood was thick and unmistakable as it spread out beneath the dying man, clutching at his throat.

The mutiny had drawn its first blood.

"Take a pull on't," Kitty urged, the thick aroma of rum eddying up from the glass.

Kydd had been shaken by the incident, not so much by the blood, which after his years at sea had lost its power to dismay, but by the almost casual way the gods had given notice that there would be a price to pay for the boldness of the seamen in committing to their cause.

Paradoxically, now, he was drawn to them — their courage in standing for their rights against their whole world, their restraint and steadfast loyalty to the Crown, their determination to sustain the ways of the navy. It would need firm control to insure that hotheads didn't take over; but if they never left sight of their objectives, they must stand a good chance of a hearing at the highest levels.

"Thank ye, Kitty," he said.

Her face clouded for a moment. "An' that was a rummer I had saved f'r Ned, poor lamb."

The snug room was warmly welcoming to his senses, and he smiled at Kitty. "It's a rare sight in the dockyard."

"Yes, an' it's not the place f'r a respect'ble woman," she said, with feeling.

"Ye should be pleased with y'r sailors, that they've stood up f'r their rights."

She looked away. "Aye." Then, turning to Kydd with a smile, she said, "Let's not talk o' that, me darlin', we could be havin' words. Look, we're puttin' on a glee tomorrow on Queen Street. Would y' like to come?"

"With you? As long as I c'n get ashore, Kitty, m' love."

She moved up to him, her eyes soft. "Come, Tom, I've a fine rabbit pie needs attention. An' after . . ."

Coxall waited until Kydd sent his men forward and was on his own. "If I could 'ave a word, Tom."

"Eli?" he said guardedly.

"Well, Tom, ye knows I ain't as who should say a taut hand wi' the words."

"Er, yes, mate?"

"An' I have t' write out these rules o' conduc', which are agreed b' the committee. They has to get sent t' *Sandwich* fer approval." He looked awkwardly at the deck. "Heard ye was a right good word grinder an' would take it kindly in yez if you could give me a steer on this."

"What about Farnall? He was a forger, y' knows."

"He's over in *Sandwich* wi' Dick Parker."

"Eli, y' knows I'm not in with ye."

"I understands, Tom, but we ain't in the word-grubbin' line a-tall, it's a fathom too deep for me an' all."

"I'll bear a fist on y' hard words, but — y' writes it out fair y'selves afterwards, mind."

"Right, Tom," said Coxall.

The other delegates moved over respectfully, giving Kydd ample room on the sea-chest bench. He picked up the draft and read the scratchy writing.

"What's this'n?" he asked, at the first tortuous sentence.

"Er, this is ter say we only wants what's agreed b' everyone, no argyments after."

"So we has this word for it, and it's 'unanimous,'" Kydd said. "We say, 'To secure all points, we must be unanimous.'" He reached for a fresh paper, made a heading, and entered the article.

"Thanks, Tom."

"An' this one: 'We turns out o' the ship all officers what come it the hard horse.' You may not say this, cuffin, they'd think you a parcel o' shabs." He considered for a space. "Should you like 'All unsuitable officers to be sent ashore' in its place?"

"Yes, if y' please." They dealt with the remaining articles in turn, and when it was finished, he handed back the sheet. "Now ye get them copied fair, an' *Achilles* is not let down a-tall."

A seaman in shore-going rig hovered nearby. "Why, Bill, mate, are y' ready, then?" Coxall asked.

"Yeah, Eli," the seaman said. He had his hat off, held in front of him, but Kydd could make out *Achilles* picked out in gold on a ribbon around it.

"Then here's y' money." It was five

pounds, all in silver and copper. The man accepted gingerly.

Coxall turned back to Kydd. "We're sendin' delegates t' Spithead, tellin' 'em we've made a risin' in support. Bill and th' others are goin' t' bring back some strat'gy an' things fr'm the brothers there. On yer way, cully."

Coxall found no problem in confiding in Kydd. "They're doin' right well in Spithead. Had a yatter wi' the admiral, an' th' Admiralty even gave our tally o' grievances to the gov'ment." He allowed a smile to spread. "All we gotta do is follow what they done."

Despite all that was going on, Kydd never tired of the vista. Even after several days the estuary of the Thames was, in its ever-changing panorama, a fascinating sight, the sea highway to the busiest port in the world. Sail could be seen converging on the river from every direction; big Indiamen, the oak-bark-tanned sails of coasters, bluff-bowed colliers from the north, plain and dowdy Baltic traders, all in competition for a place to allow them to catch the tide up the sweeping bends of the Thames to the Pool of London.

Kydd knew it took real seamanship: the

entrance to London was probably the most difficult of any port. The outlying sand-banks — the Gunfleet, Shipwash, the Sunk — were intricate shoals that the local coasters and the pilots alone knew; only the careful buoyage of Trinity House made transit possible for the larger vessels. The ebbing tide would reveal the bones of many a wreck if ever a lesson were needed.

The fleet anchorage of the Great Nore was to one side of the shipping channels, safely guarded by these outer hazards, but in its turn acting as the key to the kingdom, safeguarding the priceless tor-rent of trade goods and produce in and out of London.

In the calm sea, the anchorage was a-swarm with boats, under sail and going ashore, or with oars while visiting each other. Some outbound merchantmen tacked toward the scene, curious to see the notorious fleet in mutiny, but kept their dis-tance.

Reluctantly, Kydd went below to see the master; no matter that the world was in an uproar, charts still needed correcting, ac-counts inspected. But Eastman was not in his cabin. He made to leave, but was stopped by Coxall. Five others were with him.

"Beggin' y'r pardon, mate, but Mr. Parker begs leave t' make y'r acquaintance."

Every ship had its smell, its character, and *Sandwich* did not prove an exception. Approaching from leeward, Kydd was surprised at its acrid staleness and reek of neglect and decay.

They hooked on at the main-chains, Kydd gazed up at the 90-gun ship-of-the-line with interest; this vessel had started life nearly forty years before, in the wonderful year of victories, and had gone on to see service in most parts of the world. But she had ended up as a receiving ship for the Nore, little more than a hulk that would never again sail the open sea. She was now where the press-gang and quota men were held before they were assigned to the ships of the fleet.

The old-fashioned elaborate gilded scrollwork around her bows and stern was faded and peeling, her sides darkened with neglect, but nevertheless she was the flagship of Vice Admiral Buckner, commander-in-chief of the Nore, now humiliatingly turned out of his ship and ashore.

Kydd grabbed the worn manrope and

went up the side. He was curious to take a measure of the man who had brought his shipmates to such peril. Stepping aboard, he was met by two seamen. "T' see Mr. Parker," he said.

"Aye, we know," one said, "an' he's waitin' for ye now."

The ship was crowded. Men lay about the deck, barely stirring in attitudes of boredom; others padded around in not much more than rags. As well as the usual gloom of between-decks there was a reek of rot and musty odors of human effluvia.

They thrust through, making their way aft, and into the cabin spaces. "One t' see th' president," called his escort. A seaman with a cutlass came out, and motioned Kydd inside.

It was the admiral's day cabin, with red carpets, hangings and small touches of domesticity. Kydd had never entered one before, but he was not going to be overawed. "Th' admiral's cabin suits ye?" he said to Parker, who had risen from a polished table to meet him.

Parker stopped, a slight smile on his face. "It's the only quiet place in the ship, Mr. Kydd," he said pleasantly. "Please sit yourself down, my friend."

Kydd bristled. He would be no friend to

this man, but he thought better of challenging him openly at this stage. He found a carved chair with a gold seat and sat in it — sideways, with no pretense at politeness.

"It's kind in you to visit, Mr. Kydd. I know you don't subscribe to the validity of our actions, so I particularly wanted to thank you for the handsome way you helped the delegates aboard your ship."

"They're no taut hand as ye might say at words," Kydd said carefully. This Parker was no fool: he was educated and sharp.

"I should introduce myself — Richard Parker, for the nonce president of delegates, but sometime officer in His Britannic Majesty's Sea Service. My shipmates are happy to call me Dick."

"Officer?" Kydd said, incredulous.

"Indeed, but sadly cast up as a foremast hand after a court-martial as unjust as any you may have heard." Parker's voice was soft, but he had a trick of seizing attention for himself rather than the mere offering of conversation.

"Are ye a pressed man?" Kydd asked, wanting time.

"No, for the sake of my dear ones, I sold my body as a quota man back to the navy.

You may believe I am no stranger to hardship."

The dark, finely drawn features with their hint of nervous delicacy were compelling, bearing on Kydd's composure. "Do y' know what ye've done to my men, Mr. Delegate President?" he said, with rising heat. "Y've put their heads in a noose, every one!"

"Do you think so? I rather think not." He leaned across the table and held Kydd with his intensity. "Shall I tell you why?"

"I'd be happy t' know why not."

"Then I'll tell you — but please be so good as to hear me out first." He eased back slightly, his gaze still locked on Kydd's. "The facts first. You know that our pay is just the same as in the time of King Charles? A hundred and fifty years — and now in this year of 'ninety-seven an able seaman gets less than a common plowman. Do you dispute this?"

Kydd said nothing.

"And talking of pay, when we're lying wounded of a great battle, don't they say we're not fit to haul and draw, so therefore not worthy of wages?"

"Yes, but —"

"Our victuals. Are we not cheated out of our very nourishment, that the purser's pound is not sixteen ounces but fourteen? I could go on with other sore complaints, but can you say I am wrong? Do I lie in what I say?"

"Aye, this is true, but it's always been so."

"And getting worse. You've seen this ship for yourself — the navy is falling into a pit of ruin, Tom, and there's no help for it. And because you've got uncommon good sense, I'll tell you why.

"Has it crossed your mind, there's been petitions from sailors going up to the Admiralty crying out with grievances in numbers you can't count, and for years now? Yet not once have we had a reply — not once! Now, I've been on the quarterdeck, I know for a cast-iron fact these *do* get carried on to London. *But they never get there!* How do I know? Because if they did, then we'd be heard and we'd get redress."

He let it sink in, then continued: "You see, Tom, they're not meant to arrive. There are, up in London, a parcel of the deepest dyed rogues who have ever been, a secret and furtive conspiracy who have placemen everywhere, and live by battening on those who can't fight back — I mean the common seaman, who is away at sea and never allowed ashore to speak."

Kydd frowned. There was nothing he could think of that said this was impossible.

"You doubt? I've thought long and hard of why it is that wherever we go in the sea service we always come on those who have a comfortable berth and leech on the poor sailor. Have you seen them in the dockyards? Such corruption, and all unchallenged! The victualers, sending casks of rotten meat, the merchants buying up condemned biscuit and selling it back at a price — how can they cheat so openly? It's because they're protected by this conspiracy, who in return receive a slice of the proceeds . . ." He sat motionless, the intensity of his expression discomfiting Kydd.

"Now, Tom, whatever you think, this is the *only* logical reason for it being everywhere at the same time, *and* never being in danger of prosecution. My friend, if you can find another explanation that fits every fact — any other at all — I'd be thankful to hear it."

Kydd looked away. It fitted the facts only too well, and he'd heard rumors of a conspiracy at the top. Was Fox right, that Pitt himself was as corrupt as any, that . . .

"Ah, well, I have t' say, I've never really thought about it before, er, Dick. Ye'll pardon m' straight talkin', but c'n you tell me why *you* want t' be the one to — to —"

Parker stood up abruptly. "Humanity, Tom, common humanity. How can I stand by and see my fellow creatures used so cruelly, to see them in their simple ways oppressed by these bloodsuckers, their dearly won means torn from them, degraded to less than beasts of the field?" He turned to Kydd, his eyes gleaming. "I have advantages in education and experience of the quarterdeck, and they have done me the honor of electing me their representative — I will not betray their trust."

Moving like a cat, he sat down and faced Kydd again with the same intense gaze. "Those brave men at Spithead, they gave the example, showed what can be done — we cannot let them down, Tom! They saw the injustices, and stood bravely against them. How can we let them stand alone? Are we so craven that we stand aside and take what others win by peril of their necks?"

"You ask 'em to go t' the yardarm —"

"No!" Parker said emphatically. "I do not! Consider — the fleet at Spithead, Plymouth and now the Nore — all are now united, resolute. Does the Admiralty hang the whole fleet? Does it cause the army to march against the navy? Of course not. *As long as we stand united* we are untouched, preserved. If we hang back — but we did not, we kept the faith. And besides . . ." he left the words dangling, relishing the effect ". . . we now have word from Spithead — we have an offer. And it is for a full and complete Royal Pardon *after* we have had our grievances addressed."

It was incredible: the mutiny had won — or was winning — an unprecedented concession that recognized . . .

"Now is the time! It is the one and only chance we will ever have of achieving anything! If we miss this chance . . ." His forehead was beaded with sweat. "At Spithead they know only their daily rations and liberty. They strive for more bread in port instead of flour; more liberty ashore; vegetables with their meat — this is fine, but we can see further. We know of the rats gnawing at the vitals of the navy, and we're going to expose them, force them into the daylight. We have to be sure the whole world sees them for what they are and howl for their extermination."

Kydd was excited, appalled and exhilarated by turns. It all made sense, and here was one who was prepared to risk his very life for the sake of the men, his shipmates.

And, above all, had the intelligence and resolve to do something about it. "And if th' French sail?"

"Ah, you see, they won't. At Spithead it was voted that, no matter what, if the French moved against England, then the fleet will instantly return to duty and sail against the enemy. They know this, so at this moment they lie in their harbors, unmoved."

Kydd took a deep breath. "Then ye're still loyal — t' King 'n' country, I mean."

"We are, Tom," Parker said seriously. "What could be more loyal than ridding His Majesty of such base villains — these scum?"

He rose unexpectedly and crossed to a cabinet. "I want you to drink a toast with me, Tom." He busied himself pouring. "To success for our brave tars — standing against the whole world!"

Kydd took the glass suspiciously. "Don't worry, this is not the admiral's, it's common grog only," Parker said, with a smile.

"Aye. Well, here's t' our brave Jack Tars!" Kydd drank heartily.

Parker moved to a chair to one side. "Tom. Let me be straight with you," he began. "Your common foremast jack is not

330

best placed to see the whole of matters. He is brave and honest, but without guile. His nature makes him the prey of others, he has not the penetration to see he is being practiced upon. What I am saying is that there are many who do not see the urgency, the dire necessity of our actions at this time, and hesitate. This is a folly, and puts at great hazard all those who have seen their duty to their shipmates and acted."

He refilled Kydd's glass. "We need men to declare their devotion to their shipmates, to end their hesitation, men that are fine and strong, men when others look upon to set them a course to steer. Tom, we need *you* to stand with us. To give us your —"

"No!" Kydd slammed down his glass, suddenly icy cold. "Parker, I believe in what ye're doing, but this is not th' way — it can't be!" He turned to go, flinging open the door.

"Kydd!" called Parker from behind him. "Just think on this. If you really care about your men, *do* something, but otherwise go away — and then try to live with yourself."

Kydd left, Parker's words echoing in his ears, again confronting the dank, crowded decks, the misery in the faces of the men, the air of hopelessness and despair.

Only one thing kept hammering at his senses: he could no longer walk away.

"You've been aboard *Sandwich*," said Cockburn flatly. "You're not such a fool, Tom, that you don't know the penalty for treasonous association, consorting with mutineers. Just for the sake of curiosity, you'd let it be seen . . ." Something in Kydd's face made Cockburn tail off.

"I know what I did."

Kydd left the gunroom and moodily made the upper deck. His mind was in a spin of indecision as he paced along slowly. Abreast the mainmast he stopped. A young sailor was working by the side of the immense complexity of ropes belayed to their pins that girdled the mast. Spread out on a canvas in front of him were blocks and yarns, fid and knife.

Seeing Kydd stop, he scrambled to his feet. "Oh, Mr. Kydd, I'm ter strap th' spanker sheet block 'ere fer the cap'n o' the mizzentop."

"Carry on, younker. But what's this I see? You mean t' work a common short splice, an' it's t' be seen b' the quarterdeck?" Kydd hid a grin at the lad's worried look. "Well, sure enough, we usually use a short splice, an' for our sheet block we turn the tail to a selvagee — but this is upon the quarterdeck, an' *Achilles* is a crack man-o'-war. No, lad, we doesn't use an ugly short splice. Instead we graft the rope, make it fine 'n' smooth around the block, then other ships go green 'cos we've got such a prime crew who know their deep-water seamanship."

"But, Mr. Kydd, please, I don't know yer grafting."

"It's easy enough — look, I'll show ye." Kydd picked up the strap and shook the strands free, then intertwined and brought them together, very tightly. "Now work a stopper each side, if y' please." The lad eagerly complied. "Now we c'n open out y' strands, and make some knittles — just like as if y' was doin' some pointin'." Kydd's strong fingers plying the knife made short work of producing a splay of fine lines above and below the join. His coat constricted his movements so he took it off and threw it over the bitts. "An' now y'r ready to graft. Lay half y' knittles on the upper part . . ."

It was calming to the soul, this simple exercise of his sea skills: it helped to bring perspective and focus to his horizons — and, above all, a deep satisfaction. "An' mark well, we snake our turns at the seizing — both ends o' course." It wasn't such a bad job, even though it was now a long time since he had last strapped a block. He watched the lad admiring the smooth continuity of the rope lying in the score of the block and hid a grin at the thought of the captain of the mizzentop's reaction when he went to check the young sailor's work.

He put his coat back on and resumed his pace, but did not get far. A midshipman pulled at his sleeve and beckoned furtively, motioning him over to a quiet part of the deck. "What is it, y' scrub?" he growled.

"Psst — Mr. Hawley passes the word, he wants to see all officers an' warrant officers in the cap'n's cabin," he whispered.

"*What?*"

"Please don't shout, Mr. Kydd. It's to be secret, like."

"I've called you here for reasons you no doubt can guess," Hawley whispered. The sentry had been moved forward and the quarterdeck above cleared with a ruse; there was little chance of being overheard.

"This despicable mutiny has gone on for long enough. I had hoped the mutineers would by now have turned to fighting among themselves — they usually do, the blaggardly villains. No, this is too well organized. We must do something."

There was a murmur of noncommittal grunts. Kydd felt his color rising.

"What do you suggest?" Binney said carefully.

Hawley took out a lace handkerchief and sniffed. "The ship is unharmed — so far," he said. "I don't propose that she be left in the charge of that drunken crew for longer than I can help." He leaned forward. "I'm setting up communication with the shore. This will enable us to plan a move against the knaves with the aid of the army garrison —"

"Sir!" Kydd interrupted, his voice thick with anger. "You gave your word!"

"I'll thank you, sir, to keep your voice down, dammit!" Hawley hissed. "As to my word, do you believe it counts when pledged to mutineers — felons condemned by their own acts?"

"You gave y'r word not to move against them while y' had freedom of th' ship," Kydd repeated dully.

"I choose to ignore the implication in view of your — background, Mr. Kydd. Have a care for your future, sir."

Kydd stared at the deck, cold rage only just under control.

"I shall continue. When I get word from the shore that the soldiers are prepared, we take steps to secure their entry to the vessel, probably by night through the stern gallery. Now, each of you will be given tasks that are designed to distract the —" He stopped with a frown. "Good God, Mr. Kydd, what is it now?"

Breathing raggedly, Kydd blundered out of the cabin. He stormed out on to the main deck, feeling the wary eyes of seamen on him. A realization rose in his gorge, choking and blinding. If he was going to do something that meant anything for his shipmates — and be able to live with himself later — then it was not going to be by throwing in his lot with those who wanted to turn the sky black with the corpses of his friends.

Kydd wheeled and marched off forward, scattering men in his wake. At the starboard bay, he stopped before the startled committee, panting with emotion. "M' friends! I'm in wi' ye. What d' y' like me t' do?"

He emerged shortly from the fore-hatch, defiant and watchful. By now the news was around the ship and he knew eyes every-where would be on him. The seamen seemed to take it all in their stride, grin-ning and waving at him. He went farther aft. The master was by the mizzenmast, hands on hips, staring down at him. He reached the gangways and passed by the boat spaces. Binney was on the opposite gangway and caught sight of him; he turned, hurried aft and disappeared.

He reached the quarterdeck but Cockburn pushed in front of him, barring his way. "The quarterdeck is not the place for you any more, Kydd," he said stiffly.

"I've got ev'ry right," he snarled and, thrusting Cockburn contemptuously aside, he stalked onto the quarterdeck. All those who were aft froze.

Hawley strode out, and placed himself squarely in front of Kydd. He jammed on his gold-laced cocked hat at an aggressive angle and glowered at Kydd. "You've just ten seconds to save your neck. Make your obedience and —"

"Sir," said Kydd, touching his forehead. His gaze locked with Hawley's, not moving for a full ten seconds. Then he deliberately turned forward. "You men at th' forebrace bitts," he threw, in a hard bellow. "Pass the word f'r the delegates."

He turned slowly and waited until Coxall hastily made his appearance, Farnall close behind with a dozen men.

"I lay a complaint. Against this officer." Kydd's fierce stare held Hawley rigid. "He means t' break his solemn word, an' move against you — us!" There was an awed shuffling behind Kydd. "I demand he be turned out o' th' ship, an unsuitable officer."

There was hesitation for a fraction of a second: the incredible enormity of what he had done pressed in relentlessly on Kydd, the knowledge that the moment could never be put back into its bottle, but in his exaltation that he had done right he would dare anything.

"Get y'r gear, sir. One chest is all," Coxall said firmly. Two seamen moved forward and stood to each side of the officer, much the same as they would for a man to be led to the gratings for lashes.

"He's turned ashore — away larb'd cutter, Joe."

Shocked, Hawley turned to confront Kydd. "I shall see you dance at the yardarm if it's the last thing I do on earth."

Coxall said evenly, "Now then, sir, no sense in makin' it worse'n it is."

It was like waking yet still being in a

dream. Kydd moved about the decks, passing familiar things, trying to bring his mind to reality, yet all the while recalling Hawley in the receding boat, staring back at him.

Cockburn ignored him. The gunroom was full of tension, and it was impossible to remain, so Kydd slung his hammock forward. Some regarded him with wonder and curiosity, as though he were a condemned man walking among them.

The master waited until there was no one near and came up to Kydd, removing his hat. "It's a brave thing ye're doing, Mr. Kydd, an' I need to say as how I admires it in you." His hands twisted the hat and he finished lamely, "If it weren't f'r m' pension coming ver' soon — which I needs for m' wife and her sister livin' with us — I'd be there alongside ye an' all."

In a half-world Kydd waited for word from the delegates — they said they needed to contact the president. He paced up and down, the exaltation ebbing little by little.

Then word came. "Fr'm Mr. Parker. He wants yer to go aboard *Sandwich* — an' help 'im personal, like. C'n we bear a hand wi' yer dunnage, mate?"

Parker was waiting for Kydd at the entry port; his handshake was crisp and strong. "A sincere welcome to you, my friend," he said. "Be so good as to join me at a morsel for dinner — we've a lot to discuss."

As Kydd sat down at the table, Parker's eyes glowed. "Tom, it's very good to see you here. It was my heartfelt prayer." Kydd beamed. "But might I ask why're you in the rig of a foremast hand? Where are your breeches, your blue coat?"

"O' course, I wanted to show unity with our tars. Tell me, Dick, how goes things?"

Parker pushed back his plate with a smile, hooked his waistcoat with his thumbs and tilted back his chair. "Success is very near, Tom, be assured of that." He jumped to his feet. "Come with me."

They went out onto the sweeping curve of the admiral's stern walk. Before them was the entire anchorage of the Nore, dozens of ships of all descriptions, each tranquil and still.

"There! You see? Every one is owing allegiance to the great cause we have set in train. Each one like a link in a chain binding to the next, so we have an unbroken bond uniting us all. And see them — ships-of-the-line, frigates, even fire ships — all with but one mind."

"A rousin' fine sight," Kydd agreed. The very presence of the fleet before him was a calm assertion of the rightness of their course, a comforting vision of thousands of like-minded seamen ready to hazard all for what they believed. He lingered, savoring the grand vista of men-o'-war about him, then rejoined Parker inside.

He was sitting at the admiral's secretary's working desk, rummaging and assembling papers. "So! To work, then. Now, what are we going to do with you, Mr. Thomas Kydd? *Achilles* already has her delegates, and *Sandwich* is the Parliament ship for the fleet. No, I fancy your talents can command a higher position. You seem to have a practicality rooted in intelligence that I have seen rarely, and a loyal heart. However —" He pondered, then looked up, vexed. "The delegates can be a disputatious and difficult crew at times and, I'm grieved to say, not always motivated by reasons of selflessness. In you I perceive a purity of purpose and a noble soul, and if only it were in my power to raise you high — but this is not possible. We are agreed to be an assembly of equals, and as president I — I can only be the voice of my people. I'm sorry, Tom."

"Don't ye concern y'self f'r me, Dick. I'll bear a fist with anythin' I can. Never did want t' top it the bigwig, anyway. But y' must find somethin' I c'n do — y' must have a clinkin' great pile o' things t' do?"

Parker's face eased. "Well, now, since you offer — you've no idea how much *detail* such a venture as ours commands, yet to neglect it is folly, leading inevitably to calamity and ruin. Consider this. We are many thousand, here together. How are we to be fed and watered without there are arrangements of supply? And if we vote on regulations of conduct, how are these to be given out to the fleet, unless they are written out fifty times? Do accept to be my aide at least, I beg, and take these duties from my hands."

"Aye," Kydd said firmly, "I will." This was something he could do that had clear value. He would find men who could read and write, set them up at their tasks, and he himself could be available to Parker as needed.

"My very sincere thanks, Tom." He held out his hand. "I'll remember this day."

The papers were loosely organized: minutes of meetings, rough drafts of proclamations, messages from delegates — it needed pulling together. Kydd put a proposal to Parker: "C'n I find two good men t' stand by me, an' a private cabin?" He would need somewhere his papers would be safe.

"Of course. The admiral's dining cabin will not be entertaining this age — the table will serve well, and we may meet around it. I have in mind two who can assist. Both have their letters and are not friends to the bottle."

Kydd gathered his resources; he sent his assistants to secure boxes for the papers, then set about sorting and reading them. Parker had a fine, imaginative flair for words, with ringing phrases and legal-sounding threats. It appeared, though, Kydd had to conclude, that his inclination was more toward the florid than the detailed.

At one point a well-built, fine-looking seaman entered the big cabin. "William Davis, cap'n of *Sandwich*," he rumbled, with a hard-jawed grin. "Do I see Tom Kydd, come fr'm the Caribbee?"

"Aye," Kydd said.

"Quartermaster's mate in *Artemis* as was, goin' aroun' the world? Gets turned over inta — what, some sail-o'-the-line?"

"*Trajan.*"

"An' ends up in a squiddy cutter, saves 'em all after a spell in a boat?"

"Th' same."

"Then tip us yer daddle, cully," he said warmly, holding out his hand. "Thoroughbred seaman like you is who I wants now under m' lee while we're in shoal waters like this'n."

Kydd was grateful for the uncomplicated trust: Davis appeared the very best kind of blue-water seaman and he knew he had a friend in whatever lay ahead. "Tell me, Bill, d'ye know much about Dick Parker?"

Davis sat down, his seaman's gear — knife, marline-spike, fox yarns around his neck — incongruous reflected in the deep mahogany of the table. "Well, it's true about 'im bein' an officer, was a reefer in *Mediator* fer the American war, then shipped in *Assurance* — but the poor bugger ran up agin Bully Richards who does 'im fer contempt. Court-martial an' he's disrated 'n' turned afore the mast. Few years later, an' he gets ill an' goes ashore. Dunno what 'appened next, 'cos he ends up in clink fer debt, buys his way out b' volunteerin' fer the quota. Don't know much else — he's eddicated, you c'n tell that, comes fr'm Exeter, but wife in the north somewheres. But don't y' ask 'im too much about that, he's struck on 'er, very close they is."

Kydd worked through the afternoon; at five bells Parker returned. He was buoyed up as he greeted Kydd. "If you'd wish it, there's room in the boat for another when I make my visits. It'll be a chance to see something of our achievement."

Kydd decided papers and lists, however important, could wait. It was about time he knew something of the greater arena.

Before, the barge, a thirty-two-footer finished in green, scarlet and gilt and under fourteen oars, was to be seen conveying captains and admirals. Now it was crowded and noisy with oarsmen, two men arguing over a giant Union Flag, a seaman's band with trumpets, flutes and drums led by the ship's fiddler, and general revelers. Many wore ribbons threaded through their hats, some the popular band of blue with "Success to the Delegates" in gold. There was no sign of liquor that Kydd could detect.

Davis took the tiller, Parker and Kydd with him in the sternsheets. "Where to, Dick?" Davis shouted, above the din.

"*Director* — then *Inflexible*, of course, we'll see."

"Yair. Let go, forrard!" he roared at the

bowman. "Give way together, m' lads!"

The boat surged away from *Sandwich* and the band struck up immediately. They approached *Director*: her ship's company, drawn by the merriment, lined her decks. Some mounted the rigging, and cheers sounded, rolling around the anchorage. Parker rose and waved, more cheers came. He looked down at Kydd, flushed and distracted, but there was no mistaking the elation in his face.

They went about under *Director*'s stern, the racket of the band echoing back from the formidable lines of the 64, then shaped course for *Inflexible*. As they approached the big ship-of-the-line, there was the flat thud of a gun and smoke eddied away from the fo'c'sle.

"A salute to th' president," said Kydd.

Parker acknowledged him with a smile. "The Inflexibles are our most ardent," he shouted, in Kydd's ear.

Again the decks were lined, and cheers rang out. When Parker rose, this time he shook both fists in the air, bringing a storm of raucous applause. He repeated his success at the next ship, the frigate *Proserpine*, which promptly erupted in volleys of cheers. "I believe this calls for a libation of sorts," Parker said happily. "Bear up for the dockyard steps, Bill."

Just as soon as the boat came alongside, the men scrambled ashore and formed up into a parade, as the band took up a rowdy thumping. The huge flag was proudly held high and taken to the front of the procession.

"Do come with me, Tom. My place is at the fore, and you should share the honors." Without waiting for a reply, he strode up to the head and bowed to the assembling crowd. Kydd followed, and eased into line behind Parker, who turned and pulled him abreast of himself.

"Delegates, advance!" shouted Parker. The drums thudded twice rapidly, and the colorful procession stepped off gaily to the tune of "Rule Britannia." It attracted a noisy, adoring crowd that brought apprentices running, women leaving their work and small boys capering alongside.

As the column swung away down the road, Parker waved affably at the spectators, bowing to some, blowing kisses at the ladies. At first Kydd could only manage a stiff wave, but after a laughing girl threw rose blossoms over him, he joined in with gusto.

Around the corner and through Red Barrier Gate. Thumping lustily, the band brought the first of the Blue Town people running. Cries of "Huzzah to the delegates — and be damned to Billy Pitt!" were heard. Beribboned sailors already ashore added to the uproar.

A larger crowd waited at a timbered building — a tavern with a sign hanging, the Chequers. The band played a hurried final flourish and spilled inside. "With me, Tom," Parker called. Kydd found himself at a dark-stained table in the smoky interior.

Davis arrived, his large frame wedging in the high-backed seat. "Tom, me ol' cock, what c'n I get you?"

Parker intervened. "Kydd's with me, Bill, and I'll be having my usual. Tom?"

"Oh, a stout pint o' the right sort'll do," replied Kydd, happily. Parker's tipple turned out to be dog's nose, the splicings being a liberal dash of gin in the beer. The blue haze thickened in the tavern in due proportion to the noise and soon it was a merry throng that celebrated together.

A seaman bawled for attention near the door. "Dick Parker, *ahoooy!*"

Parker lurched to his feet. "Who wants him?" he returned loudly.

"Why, yer speechifyin' — when are yer comin', Admiral?"

"I've said not t' call me that," Parker grumbled.

"Aye-aye, Yer Majesty."

In front of the Chequers a space had been cleared and several boxes pushed together formed a stage, already bedecked with flags and boughs of greenery. A few chairs were in precarious position atop the boxes.

A roar went up when Parker appeared. He stood to acknowledge the cheers, then jammed his beaver hat at a rakish angle and mounted the stage. Beaming, he held up his hands for silence, and the crowd subsided, while more ran up to catch the occasion.

"Friends! Brothers!" he began, his face flushed. "How dare their lordships presume to try the patience of the British tar, to deny him his rights, to ignore his courage and resource? I will tell you something that even these false ministers, these *traitors*, cannot conceive of — the true value of a British seaman!" He paused, and looked into the crowd. "Ah, there he is!" he cried. "Brother Tom Kydd, new-won to the cause. Come up here beside me, Tom!"

There was a warm roar of welcome. "Tom here was a master's mate in *Achilles*, but that didn't stop him standing for what he believed. The first lieutenant hales him to the quarterdeck and calls him to account — but Tom Kydd here, he tells him to sling his hook! So it's Heave-ho Hawley in the boat and turned ashore, mates, all because Tom didn't flinch when the time came. How can m' lords of the Admiralty prevail when we've got the likes of him in with us? Let's hear it for Brother Kydd, friends!"

Chapter 8

At dawn the soft gray coastline of England appeared far ahead. After the tedium of a Baltic convoy, complicated by an outbreak of ship fever in the fo'c'sle, it was a welcome sight. But Renzi had mixed feelings: it was now just a few months before his term of exile was over. Then he must make his peace with his family, and resume his life on the land. It would be hard to leave the sea. The gentle lift and surge of a deck had its own compelling sensuality and the life perspective to be gained from numberless foreign horizons was precious — but there was no going back. Before the year was out it would be finished, all over.

As he paced back along the gangway, a depression settled, one that was never far away these days. There would be no interesting exotic finale to his last months. They were to spend a couple of days in

Sheerness, repair and victual, then *Glorious* was to rejoin the North Sea fleet in Yarmouth, resuming its watch over the Dutch in the Texel, a powerful fleet now loyal to the French and which, sooner or later, would have to be dealt with.

The low coastline ahead hardened to a deep blue, then acquired features: dark splotches, pale blurs. There was sail in all directions, converging to the south, a river of commerce, for here was the entrance to the Thames and the port of London.

Renzi sighed heavily, and started pacing the other way. *Glorious* was not a happy ship. The captain was unimaginative and set in his ways, remote from his men, and the first lieutenant was a bully. The ship's company was a collection of individuals, not a team, and petty tyrannies flourished.

They joined the flow of vessels into the Thames, the master watchful and alert for the lookouts' hail as another buoy was sighted. Then the dark forest of masts that was the Great Nore came into sight, reassuring in its powerful presence at the entrance to the capital.

Signals fluttered up from *Glorious*'s quarterdeck. The mass of fifty-four ships of the Baltic Trade astern were now released and broke into an undignified straggle as they jockeyed for position for the beat upriver to the docks.

"*Haaaands* to moor ship!"

They closed with the fleet. Saluting guns were loaded, but as *Sandwich* was not flying her admiral's flag they were not needed. *Glorious* glided in, her anchors tumbled down to the muddy seabed, her sails were furled and she prepared for storing.

Finished with the veering crew at the hatchway, Renzi regained the deck to find the officer-of-the-watch, but his curiosity was taken by three boats making for *Glorious*. A giant Union Flag was in one, and from another what sounded like "Rule Britannia" was being pounded out by a scratch band.

"Hail them, if you please," ordered Murray, the officer-of-the-watch. Aboard *Glorious*, sailors crowded to the deck edge, astonished by the display. The lead boat shaped course to come alongside; it was then plain there were no officers aboard.

"Damme an' I know what's afoot, m'lads," Renzi heard the flabbergasted boatswain say.

"Lay off, the boat!" warned Murray, sensing something wrong. The boat took no notice and hooked on at the main-chains. Seamen nimbly mounted *Glorious*'s side.

"What in God's name —"

The lead seaman, a bulky sailor with cutlass and two pistols, came easily over the bulwarks; another two were not far behind. Murray stalked down from the quarterdeck. "Did you not hear my order? Why the devil did you —"

Bringing a paper out of his waistcoat, the first seaman announced, "Sir, I'm commanded by th' president of the delegates of th' whole fleet of His Majesty's navy in the river Medway and the buoy of the Nore ter give you this'n."

"What nonsense is this?" said Murray aghast.

The captain appeared from below. "Mr. Murray, why are these men in arms?"

The boarders smiled grimly. "An' as of this minute, Cap'n, you're released fr'm duty. You're desired ter yield up yer ship to th' committee."

Gobbling with anger, the captain opened his mouth to speak.

"No, sir, we'll take none o' yer pratin'. Take a squiz there." The seaman indicated *Director*, lying barely a hundred yards abeam, and *Inflexible*, fine on the bow. "These're all risen, they is, every one. An' if I signal, well, there's more'n a hundred guns'll answer." As if on cue, gunports opened all down the sides of the ships-of-the-line.

At the threat there was little that could be done. The mutineer went to the ship's side and hailed the waiting boats. "Right, lads, let's get ter work."

After securing the ship, the mutineers set up a committee in the starboard bay, holding court on the unfortunates against whom complaints had been laid. First the officers: most of them were deemed "unsuitable" and given fifteen minutes to be clear of the ship. One boatswain's mate was taken below in irons to be dealt with later, and a sergeant of marines was given a ducking. Liberty tickets were freely given under the hand of the committee.

Renzi watched the proceedings with interest, for without doubt it would be talked of for years to come. But then the new-elected delegates called him below, and he was asked to give a statement of position, and abruptly told, "Fer a foremast jack yer've got a wry way o' talkin', cuffin. I thinks fer y' own sake, better ye're ashore 'n' out of it."

In the boat on the way to Sheerness, Renzi's eyes lifted as he took in the unmistakable bulk of *Achilles*. The boat's crew cheered as they passed, and were answered with a full-throated roar from the ship. Renzi wondered if Kydd was aboard, or had been turned ashore, perhaps after an intemperate but loyal outburst. Whatever the case, probably within the day he would be seeing his friend once more.

He glanced at the boat's crew. They were in high spirits and full of what they would do ashore. In their way, these men were as close to the paradigm of Natural Man as it was possible to find: the suborning elements of civilization were necessarily denied to them — he would never find such stout beliefs and open character in the elegant, blasé world that awaited him.

The dockyard was in a state of feverish chaos and open disorder. People were all about but the gaunt ribs of new ships were not thronged with shipwrights and their sidesmen, the sawpits were deserted and the smithy silent.

Renzi was able to share a handcart for his sea chest with one of the lieutenants at the price of pushing the creaking relic. The lieutenant was eager to be quit of Sheerness and saw no reason why he should not return to his family until the whole disgraceful episode was over.

They quickly crossed the marshes and left the noisy revelry of Blue Town behind. The lieutenant waited for a coach in the small hotel at the start of the London turnpike, but Renzi was not sure what to do. He had no plans after being so recently turned out of his ship; it would need some thinking about but, given the tumult and isolated nature of Sheppey, it was unlikely he would stay either.

The lugubrious landlord took a deal of gloomy pleasure in telling them of developments at Spithead as current rumor had it. Such events did not greatly surprise Renzi. The wonder in his mind was that the seamen had not acted earlier, given the criminal neglect of their circumstances. That the mutiny was brilliantly organized, widespread and effective was the surprising element. Could it be the work of Jacobin agents? However, with Robespierre executed there was a more skeptical cast to the power struggle now ensuing that probably didn't include such a hot desire to export their revolution — but without a doubt the French would be mad not to seize the opportunity to act against England. It was as grave a state of affairs as he had known, and the government would be well advised to act rapidly and decisively against the mutineers.

He had to speak to Kydd — that much was clear. Leaving his sea chest, he walked back through the apprehensive inhabitants of Mile Town to the carnival atmosphere in Blue Town. Outside one of the larger timbered hostelries in the high street a crowd was gathered, applauding two rabble-rousers. Renzi winced even though, at the distance, he couldn't hear the words, but the exultant roars that punctuated the speech did not leave much doubt over the nature of the harangue. He had to pass by to reach the dockyard in his mission to find Kydd, and glanced over the back of the crowd at the speakers. One was a dark, intense individual who appeared almost messianic in his zeal. The other was Kydd.

Rigid with surprise, Renzi stared at his friend while the other man declaimed against His Majesty's treasonable ministers. A sailor whooped his approval next to him. "Who are these gentlemen?" Renzi asked him.

"Why, that's the president o' the delegates, Dick Parker, is he. Th' admiral we calls 'im on account he berths in th' admiral's quarters in *Sandwich*."

"And the other?"

"Ah, that there's Tom Kydd, mate off

Achilles. Right ol' fire-eater he, faced down t' th' first luff an' got him turned off 'is ship an' then got in wi' Dick Parker ter be his sec'tary, he havin' an education an' all."

Struck dumb with astonishment, Renzi stayed until the speeches had run their course, then pushed into the crowd. "Tom!" he called, unable to get through the jovial mob. "Ahoy there, shipmate!"

Finally it penetrated. Kydd looked up from his conversation with a pretty woman. "Nicholas!" he shouted, above the hullabaloo. "Make a lane there, y' lubbers!"

Kydd was back in simple seaman's rig, white duck trousers, waistcoat and short blue jacket, and was flushed with the occasion. "Hey, now! Nicholas, well met, m' fine frien'."

"An' this is Kitty, Kitty Malkin. She's walkin' out wi' me, lives on the hulks in as snug a home as any I've seen. Look, let's away fr'm here 'n' talk."

Kitty flashed Renzi a shrewd look. "Pleased t' make y'r acquaintance, sir." She turned to Kydd and patted his arm. "Do go wi' y'r friend, dear, I have some shoppin' to do."

Renzi fell into step with Kydd. They found the road across the marshes relatively peaceful, and slowly walked together. "Such a happenin' the world's never seen." Kydd chuckled. "Dare t' say that in Parliament they're rare put to think what t' do."

"Er, yes, I'm sure that is the case," Renzi said. "But do you not think that Mr. Pitt — under pressure as he is — would not in any wise tolerate a new mutiny just as the old one is at a crisis?"

Kydd's face darkened. "That's not th' question. It is, do we stan' with our brothers in Spithead, or do we shamefully leave 'em t' the hazard all alone?"

"Of course, dear fellow, I quite see that — an expression of support is *demanded* at this time." He allowed the moment to cool, then continued, "You are assisting Mr. Parker . . . ?"

"I am," said Kydd, "but not in a big way, o' course. He's got a mort o' work t' do, bringin' all th' ships together f'r the cause, some as are bein' fractious an' ill disciplined." He looked at Renzi directly. "Dick Parker is a great man, Nicholas. A real headpiece on him. He's given himself t' the cause of his shipmates, an' that makes him a right good hand by me."

Renzi hesitated. "This is open mutiny — you stand in peril of your life."

Kydd smiled. "Not really, Nicholas. Y'

see, we have it fr'm Spithead that there'll be a pardon for ev'ryone after it's all settled."

"And this is declared in writing? From Parliament — or the King? This requires an Act of Parliament at the least."

"Damn you, Nicholas, why do ye always see the gloomy side o' things? We're goin' t' stand tall 'n' demand that we be heard, an' won't move until we get our justice."

"For the sake of friendship, I have to say again — it is no flogging matter, you are in mutiny. This is a capital crime!"

"We'll have th' pardon!"

"You *think* you'll have the pardon!"

Kydd squared up to Renzi. "You're sayin' as I shouldn't stand f'r what I know's right. How's that f'r y'r talk o' principle an' moral right as y' used to tell?"

Renzi could see Kydd was incensed: there was no way to reach him. "I do not dispute the rightness of your cause, only the way in which you pursue it," he replied quickly.

"Tell me how else we should, seein' as how f'r the first time we're gettin' the whole fleet to rise at th' same time? You say we have t' drop ev'rything now, just when we're a whisker away fr'm success?" Kydd snorted. "Somethin' has happened t' you, Nicholas. Y' go around wi' the blue devils all the while, an' now when y' shipmates need y'r help an' understandin' then y' go cold 'n' condemn 'em. I recommend y' sort out whatever ails ye an' think about things. I have t' go — things t' do."

Renzi trudged back to the little public house in Mile Town. It was madness, of course. The government would not survive the crisis of a second mutiny and would not, could not, let it succeed.

A small note sent later in the day to *Sandwich* inviting Kydd for a supper together was returned promptly with an inability scrawled on the back. The noise and laughter of Blue Town echoed across the marsh, and Renzi needed to get away. Possibly there was a pardon on offer — unlikely, yet not impossible. But if not, there would be grim scenes soon.

He decided to join the other shipless exiles in the coach to Rochester, where they would wait out the inevitable in the more agreeable surroundings of the ancient town.

Kydd had regretted his manner even before he returned to *Sandwich* but he didn't want to see Renzi just now. He realized that it was due to the excitement of the hour, the exalted state of achieving so much against the world's antagonism and the extraordinary festive air, all being thrown down in the dust by his friend. There might have been some truth in what Renzi said, but he was not privy to the kind of information that Parker had relayed to Kydd from Spithead.

There was movement in the anchorage as he returned to *Sandwich*. A smart eighteen-pounder frigate had unwittingly moored at the head of the Nore, just having sailed leisurely down-river. "*San Fiorenzo*," Kydd was told. He remembered that this was the frigate assigned to take the royal couple on their honeymoon.

Back aboard, Kydd looked at the ship. "Has she declared f'r us?" he asked.

"No signs yet, mate." Coxall lowered his glass and gave it to Kydd.

"Give 'em three good 'uns, lads," Kydd said. Men leaped into the rigging and obeyed heartily, but through the glass he could see no sign of yard-ropes being reeved on the frigate, and there was no cheering. "They'll come to it when they hears," Kydd said.

The bulk of *Inflexible* under topsails slid around the point, on her way to the Great Nore. From another direction came a pair of boats headed for *San Fiorenzo*. Kydd lifted his glass again. "The delegates, lads. They'll put 'em straight."

There was activity on her deck, but nothing could be made out for sure until figures went down her side again and the boats put off. By this time *Inflexible* had drawn close, slipping past on the tide. A massed roar of cheers broke out, but the frigate remained silent. Another volley of cheers brought no response. The battleship did not vary her course, but as she drew abreast of the frigate, a sudden puff erupted from her fo'c'sle, and the sullen thud of a nine-pound gun echoed.

"Be buggered!" The shot had gone close under the frigate's bowsprit, whipping ropes apart and tearing into the sea less than a hundred yards beyond. In one stroke the mutiny had changed its character. Kydd whipped down the telescope. "Dick's below?" he snapped, but didn't wait for an answer and plunged down the malodorous decks to the cabins aft. He burst in on Parker without ceremony. "*Inflexible* jus' fired on *San Fi*!" he shouted.

"I know," said Parker mildly.

"Y' know? Dick — do y' know what they did? They fired on a King's ship! That's worse'n mutiny, that's treason!"

"Tom, I know the Inflexibles are warm for the cause, they may have overstepped, but look there. *San Fiorenzo* is reeving yard-ropes and cheering as well as we."

Kydd looked past Parker through the open ornamental stern lights at the ship, now manning yards and cheering.

Parker leaned back. "You see? They are now free to express their loyalty to a cause that before they could not. I will not hide it from you — when we rose, we had the advantage of surprise for success. In this way the rising was bloodless, direct. We no longer have this luxury. A ship may be in a tyranny, the seamen unable to throw off the trammels, but if then a superior argument is brought to bear, they are released to stand for their beliefs, and equally bloodless. You see?"

"But with guns?"

"Just so." Parker sighed and steepled his fingers. "There is no escaping the imperatives of cold reason, my friend. You will agree that our cause is just, pure in motivation, the higher matter?"

"O' course."

"And for this task we must set to, heart and hand, until it is finished?"

"Aye."

"Then we have the choice. Either we

bow to the forces who oppose us, and allow them to carry off in despotism the very souls we are striving to serve, or we righteously show our determination, and make it possible for them to spring free of their shackles."

Kydd looked away, searching for objections. "Ye're in th' right of it, as usual, Dick," he came back. "If we don't show firm, then it's t' betray y'r shipmates, an' that I'll never do."

"It may be," Parker added softly, "that we could be forced into some even more difficult choices before we prevail."

The day had turned to bright sunshine, and ashore families were enjoying picnics on the grassy slopes of the old fort. Boats crisscrossed the anchorage, ship-visiting, going to parades ashore, bringing delegates to *Sandwich*.

Parker greeted Kydd warmly. "If you please, my friend, we have a Parliament committee in the Great Cabin, and I would be happy for you to attend, in the character of a scribe or some such."

Parker clearly relished his role. As the delegates arrived he was punctilious as to seating and precedence based on size of ship, and greeted each with grave politeness or hearty welcome according to temper. Kydd sat at the other end of the table, preparing to take minutes in the best way he could. Farnall was there, representing *Achilles*, and looked down the table at him several times, but did not speak.

The rumpled, middle-aged John Hulme reported *Director* quiet with Captain Bligh still aboard and in his cabin, the mutineer captain of *Proserpine* complained of short stores and Davis of *Sandwich* dryly told the committee of one Thomas McCann. He had apparently been sent ashore sick, complained loudly of the lazaretto beer and returned to *Sandwich*; when his messmates sent him to another ship's sick quarters he had said he was afraid of the ship's butcher — he had helped duck the man the day before.

Daily details dealt with, Parker turned to the more congenial task of further codifying the regulations. This was not particularly to the liking of most, who were visibly bored, but Parker and Farnall obviously enjoyed the cut and thrust of debate, the points of order, seconding of motions and the like. Kydd industriously covered the exchanges, but did not bother with the explanations demanded by baffled sailors.

Parker's expression hardened. "While

Mr. Kydd prepares a fair transcript of the regulations for copying, it is my sad duty to have to tell you that James Watt, in flagrant contravention of our regulations for conduct, was taken in drink in the orlop. Now I don't have to tell you that if there is a general breakdown in discipline then —"

"Flog the bugger!" Hulme was in no doubt.

Parker looked pained. "First we must have a trial, at which —"

"Fuck me, we'll be 'ere all day. I vote we flogs 'im an' done wi' it. Who says 'aye'?"

"You can't just —"

"Aye!"

The forceful shout drowned Parker, who looked around darkly. "How will —"

"I'll do it m'self, the useless skulker! Anythin' else, mates?" There being no further business, the meeting adjourned.

Kydd arrived at the Chequers, weary from his unaccustomed writing, just as the sunny afternoon was giving way to a warm dusk. He found Parker in fine form, the center of a crush of seamen. Kydd smiled, letting his friend do what he did best, and settled at a distance. "Shant o' y'r best," he threw at the potboy. He was looking forward to visiting Kitty; she would be finished with her work at sundown. The beer arrived, dark and foaming, and he took a grateful pull.

He looked idly about. There were few he knew — one or two Achilles, a Sandwich or three. The Chequers was known as the rendezvous of the delegates, and Kydd could think of many who would be too apprehensive to enter. The buzz of talk and Parker's high voice droned on, and Kydd started to nod off. A noise outside did not register, and a young seaman burst into the room shouting: "It's true, I swear it! It's all over, mates, an' we got what we want!" The room broke into a babble of excitement.

"Gangway, yer mundungo-built beggar! Let's see what it's all about."

The crowd about Parker deserted him instantly and surrounded the ecstatic sailor. "Spithead — they got it all settled! They gets pay 'n' all — an' a full pardon, damn me eyes! Black Dick Howe 'imself signed the paper."

A rising elation swept away Kydd's weariness.

"Where did you hear this?" Parker called, above the uproar. If it was true, and it was a victory, their own mutiny had lost its purpose.

"I got it straight fr'm th' telegraph office. They just got word fr'm Spithead, an' the Admiralty sends it on t' here." By a miracle of the clacking shutters spaced out between Sheerness and the roof of the Admiralty in London, apparently word of the settlement had been relayed to them over the long miles.

"Clap a stopper on yer jabber, Joe, let's hear it all."

The young sailor paused. "Well, t' tell the truth, Mr. Wells it was tol' me. He works f'r Admiral Buckner."

The room grew quiet. "So it could be a rumor, like?" someone piped up.

"No, can't be!" the sailor said scornfully. "He showed me th' signal 'n' said I was t' find Mr. Parker an' tell him."

The room fell silent as the enormity of the event sank in. Kydd glanced over to Parker, who was shaking his head slowly, a weary smile on his face. "What's t' do, Dick?" he said.

Parker didn't answer at first, then looked about the room, catching the eye of this one and that.

"Yair, what next, then, Dick?" came a call.

Levering himself to his feet, Parker stood before them. His hands grasped the lapels of his coat. "Brothers," he began softly, "can I ask you one question? Just the one! And if you can answer it to satisfaction, then I'll sit down again and be silent."

Uncertain smiles showed, men glanced at one another.

"This I ask, then. If you were in power — at the highest — and your entire fleet was in the hands of those who have embarrassed you with the exposing of your perfidy, and you are desperate, would it not be a rattling good plan to win back control by a very simple contrivance? You tell the Nore that the Spithead matter is resolved, and to Spithead you say that the Nore is reconciled. In this way, you get both to return to duty, and having dropped their defenses you are then at liberty to seek whatever vengeance . . ." The words hung in the silence. "Then, this I ask, shipmates, is this an impossible plan?"

"Be damned! They wouldn't —"

"The slivey fucksters! Once they got us t' sea —"

"They lied at th' *Culloden* trials. My mate —"

The room broke into angry shouts, but Parker held up his arms for order. "I say then, we hold fast. We keep the faith. Only when we have *proof* — solid evidence —

will we even begin to consider the situation." He sat down to shouts and gusts of applause, accepting a large glass as he did so. But when Kydd next saw him, he was looking distracted.

"Why, Tom, m' darlin'!" Kitty laughed. "Such a surprise!" She kissed him soundly. Then she gazed at him earnestly, and hugged him tight. "Do take care of y'rself, m' dear Tom," she whispered. "In m' bones, I have a dreadful feelin' this is all goin' to end wi' blood an' weepin' — there's been nothin' like it this age." She let her arms drop, but when she looked up again, a smile adorned her face. "Dick Parker, y' knows him now. What's he like — I mean, as a man?"

Kydd laughed. "Well, he's a swell cove, right enough, his beaver hat 'n' all. But a great one f'r thinkin' and planning. None o' this would've happened but f'r him, an' I'm proud t' call him m' friend. An' has a wife in Leith, who he's very partial of," he added.

They laughed together, but it died quickly and she looked him in the eyes again. "Tom, there's somethin' on y'r mind."

"Just worries — 't would oblige me if we

could talk a while, Kitty."

She caught something in his voice. "We will, love. But not here — jus' wait for me to fetch m' bonnet an' we'll take a walk."

Arm in arm, they stood on Minster Hill, looking down on Sheerness and the dockyard. At this distance, a couple of miles away, they were close enough for details, but removed from the noise and distraction. The walk had cleared Kydd's mind, and the sparkling air was invigorating.

"I jus' feel — well, it's such a — an awful thing that I did, Kitty," he muttered. "Here am I, master's mate, an' I turned an officer out of his own ship. It has t' be said, I'm a mutineer."

She looked at him shrewdly. "It's a big thing ye did, Tom, that's f'r sure. But that's not all, is it?"

"No." In a low voice he went on. "It's my particular frien', a shipmate o' mine since I was pressed. We — we had many a rare time together, been aroun' the world b' Cape Horn, been at hazard wi' the enemy so many times I can't count." He stared at the cold hard line of the sea horizon. "We had hard words together, Kitty. He doesn't see that sometimes ye've got to — to follow y'r heart an' do what y' need to.

Nicholas is a taut hand at logic, 'n' it's hard to keep with him at times. Says that th' gov'ment won't stand a second mutiny, an' will be down on us like thunder, an' we're going at it the wrong way — don't say what the right way is."

Kitty squeezed his arm. "I knows how ye feels, but there's sailors not born yet who'll bless ye."

"They say th' telegraph has news o' Spithead, that th' mutiny is over."

"I heard that. What d' you think?"

"Dick Parker thinks it's lies 'n' treachery by th' Admiralty, that they want t' get us back under discipline an' take revenge."

"I asked what you think, Tom."

Kydd looked down at the disorderly revelry around Blue Town, and nearer, the streets of Mile Town clear of honest folk. Out at sea clustered the ships at the Great Nore, a broad cordon of open water around them. "Fine view," he said, taking it all in. "Gives ye a perspective, as y' might say." He turned to Kitty. "What do I think? We wait 'n' see. Dick's right, we don't give up an inch until we c'n see proper proof, real things th' government can't deny after. We stand fast, m' love."

As days passed, the rumpus ashore subsided, as much from satiation as from a shortage of means to continue, and the men stayed aboard. The people of Sheerness began to appear on the streets, believing that Spithead was on the point of settlement and that the Nore would soon follow.

But without proof, the Nore did not drop its guard. Routines were maintained, watch was kept. Parker held apart. A lonely figure, he rose regularly at dawn and paced slowly along the decks, his face remote and troubled.

Kydd became increasingly impatient. With the Royal Navy idle in port and a government set to defiance, a resolution must come soon. At the back of his mind, but as menacing as a caged beast, was the question: Would the rumored pardon be general enough to cover each and every one, no matter what their actions?

He returned to his work. The business of victualing was in actuality no real difficulty. The pursers were in the main detested and had been sent ashore but their stewards were quite capable of making out demands on stores, which although signed by delegates were duly honored by the dockyard.

Even the press-gang was accommodated.

New-pressed hands were processed in the usual way aboard *Sandwich*: the seamen and able-bodied were sent out to the fleet, the quota men and broken-down sailors kept aboard.

Kydd lifted his pen. It was all very necessary, but quill driving was no work for a seaman. His eyes glazed, but then a round of shouting and cheers broke in.

"Dick!" called McCarthy, one of the delegates sent to Spithead to get the true lay.

Parker emerged from an inner cabin. Kydd was puzzled that he did not appear more enthusiastic.

More men crowded in. "We done it! 'S all over!" Their elation was unrestrained. "Got th' pardon an' all, the lot! Th' fuckin' telegraph was right, Black Dick did it f'r us!"

The deck above resounded with the thump of feet as the news spread. A wave of relief spread over Kydd, until he remembered the pardon — the wording would be critical.

"Have you any proof with you?" Parker said edgily.

McCarthy lifted a seabag and emptied a pile of printed matter on the desk, some still smeared with printer's ink. "An' we have one th't Black Dick hisself clapped his scratch on." Evidently pleased with himself, he added, "S' now I goes below an' I lays claim ter a week's grog."

Parker sifted quickly through the papers, and straightened. "It does seem we have something, I believe," he said, but the intensity of his expression did not relax. "The Parliament committee meets here in this cabin this afternoon."

"No, it don't!" chortled a seaman. "We meets at th' Chequers, an' after, we kicks up a bobs-a-dyin' as will have 'em talkin' fer ever."

"Meetin' comes ter order!" bawled Davis, a broad grin belying his ferocity. Red faces and loud talk around the table showed that perhaps the celebration had been a little early in starting.

Parker had the papers in a neat pile before him, and waited with impatience. The meeting settled down and, with a frosty look to each side, he began: "You elected me president of the delegates because you trusted me to see through the knavish tricks of the Admiralty. I have to tell you today, I mean to honor that trust." He picked up a paper. "This," he said, dangling it as though it were soiled, "is what they intend for us. It's all here, and plain to any who have any schooling in law whatsoever. They've been forced to agree on certain points, only by the steadfast courage of our brothers in Spithead, but it's trickery."

"Why so?" came a shout.

Parker smiled wolfishly. "For anything to have any meaning, a rise in wages, a full pardon, everything, it has to have the force of Parliament, evidence to the world that for a surety things are to be changed. This means an Act of Parliament! Now, if you inspect this document carefully, you will see that the instrument they choose to promulgate these *concessions* is an order in council, which as you may recollect retains its force for only a year and a day. So, at the end of this time?"

An angry muttering swelled. "Show us th' paper!" snarled Hulme, the delegate from *Director*, who had no patience with his more moderate colleagues. Parker ignored him, and placed it neatly out of sight under the pile.

"But the worst is to come." He paused dramatically. "I'm speaking of the pardon." Kydd went cold. "Our precious pardon! Without this to protect us, then everyone here seated today stands to dance at the yardarm within the month. Agreed?"

His words were met with a stony silence. "Very well. See here . . ." he tapped a column in a printed broadsheet " '. . . George R' — that's the King — 'Whereas, upon the representation of our Lords-commissioners of our Admiralty, respecting the proceedings of the seamen . . .' It goes on, but we are interested in one thing only — the date. This pardon is dated the eleventh of May. Therefore, it cannot possibly cover any actions *after* that date — and our rising *was*. We're not covered in any whit by this pardon. It's a scrap of paper only, and we must prepare for —"

His words were drowned in a breaking wave of anger. Men used to the open sea were quite unfitted for pettifogging wordplay. Some turned on the committee, preferring to believe that this was a slip of the pen that could easily be altered later, others cursed the stupidity that had led them this far.

"Still!" Davis roared. "Shut yer noise, y' mumpin' lubbers, 'n' listen!"

The meeting, now cold sober, turned once more to Parker. "So. You will ask me why they do this. It's simple, and so predictable. Have you not noticed? In Spithead they have Admiral Howe to meet the delegates personally. The First Lord,

Earl Spencer, he sees fit to make the journey all the way from London to treat with them, and in the end, according to Brother McCarthy, the admiral then has a rousing good dinner with them, foremast jacks and all, there in the governor's mansion.

"Now, shipmates, you don't need me telling you, nothing like that has happened to us. No! And why? Because — now, don't take this amiss, I should have thought of it before — the government are deeply embarrassed by a successful mutiny. Therefore they pay it off to get it over with, and then they can turn all their attention to us. What does this mean? Again, it doesn't need too much thinking to see that without a pardon, just as soon as we return to duty, they're free to hang the lot of us. Friends, we're nothing else but political *scapegoats* for Spithead."

In the uneasy quiet came a lone call. "So what's t' do then, Mr. President?"

"Just to get things on the record, is there any of you wants to trust the pardon and give himself up, hoping that I'm wrong? No? Then please write that down, Mr. Kydd. We're still all as determined as we always were."

Parker leaned forward intently. "Now

this is what I say. You and I both know the only reason the government listens to us is that we hold the biggest hand of all — the keys to the kingdom, the fleet at the Nore. And a bit of thought says that, in truth, we have 'em at our mercy, or they wouldn't let us stay at liberty like this. So — seeing what can be achieved at Spithead, why don't we go further, do better than them?

"First, we make sure we get a special pardon of our own." Rumbles around the table indicated that his point was well taken. "Then we make our own demands, good tough ones that finish the job that's just started. This way we save our necks, and at the same time earn the hearty cheers of all our fellow tars from this day."

There was a stunned silence. Parker sat down and waited. After a minimum of discussion, John Blake of *Inflexible* spoke for all. "We're in. Now, let's be started. What about them demands?"

The delegates started with a first article that Kydd noted down as: "Article 1. That every indulgence granted to the fleet at Portsmouth, be granted to His Majesty's subjects serving in the fleet at the Nore, and places adjacent."

That was never in dispute, but matters of liberty ashore, arrears of pay and prize money and so many others that presented themselves would not be so easily disposed of. By the dog-watches they had only two articles settled, and it was then that a message arrived from Admiral Buckner, addressed directly to the delegates.

Parker opened it. "Ah — at last!" He laughed. "Here, mates, our first official communication. And it says, *ta-tum, ta-tum,* 'I wish to visit *Sandwich* to notify His Majesty's pardon upon the terms expressed in their lordships' direction. . . .' Be damned! It means they're coming to negotiate at last. Tom, let's work a polite reply, saying something like, 'Being sensible of the honor . . .' and all that, and we'll be happy to meet him next morning, and, um, escort him in a procession of grace through the fleet to *Sandwich*, and so on. That's what they did for Black Dick Howe in Spithead — we can't do less. But we've got to work on these demands, get 'em written fair to present to him tomorrow."

The meeting continued through the night, men of stalwart beliefs but plain thinking grappling with the formulation of intent into words, the consequences of the effect on meaning of word choice, the sheer effort of rendering thought onto the page. In the morning there was a demand of eight articles ready for negotiation.

The deputation went ashore at two, after taking the precaution of a restorative nap in the forenoon. They landed at the dock-yard steps, where a curious crowd waited for the singular sight of what rumor promised would be common seamen making terms with a vice admiral in his own flag-ship.

"Rare day!" Kydd murmured to Parker, as they formed up on the quayside.

Parker seemed preoccupied, but he lifted his chin high and, with a bearing of no-bility and resolve, told Tom, "Today we make our mark forever upon the annals of this fair country." The moment was clouded a little by squabbles among befud-dled sailors in the onlookers, spurring them on with impossible suggestions.

Preceded by a large flag the deputation wended through the dockyard to the com-missioner's house, a square and forbidding mansion with smoke-blackened bricks, many white-edged windows and a large black polished front door. The whole seemed in defiant repose, like a castle with its drawbridge up.

The deputation quietened, and looked to

their president and head of deputation. Parker hammered the big brass knocker three times. Immediate movement behind the door suggested that their arrival was not unexpected. It opened and a gold-laced servant appeared.

"The president and delegates of the fleet of the Nore. We are here to be heard by Admiral Buckner," Parker said loudly. The servant withdrew quickly, firmly closing the door.

The door catch rattled, and into view stepped Admiral Buckner. He was in full uniform and sword, gold lace on blue, but appeared curiously shrunken, an old man. Kydd knew he'd been a lieutenant at Quiberon Bay and with Rodney at his smashing victory in the Caribbean.

Hats flew off as naval discipline reasserted itself with marks of respect due a flag officer. Parker lifted his beaver cap, but did not remove it. "Sir, we have come to escort you on a procession of honor to HMS *Sandwich*."

"Thank you, er . . . ?" His voice was dry and whispery.

"Richard Parker, president of the delegates."

"Then, Mr. Parker, shall we proceed? I have with me a plenary letter from their lordships that gives me authority to notify His Majesty's full pardon to you all."

Parker reached inside his waistcoat, and withdrew papers bound with a red ribbon. "Yes, sir, but you may wish to read these in the boat before we sit down together."

"Wh-what are they?" Buckner said, taking them.

"Why, sir, this is the substance of our negotiating. Be free to read them now, if you wish."

Buckner untied the ribbon. His hands trembled as he read. "I — I cannot! No, no, sir — this is impossible!"

Parker frowned. "Sir, I cannot see that these articles in any way —"

"No! You do not know what you are asking. I cannot do it — I have no authority. I cannot discuss anything, you understand."

"You can't discuss anything?" asked Parker, with barely concealed scorn. "Then, sir, who can?"

"Er, it is for their lordships to —"

"Then that is where we must address these grievances."

The old admiral stared at Parker in horror. "Common seamen? I mean — not an officer? It would be most improper, sir."

The papers dropped from Buckner's fingers. He stooped hastily to pick them up again, straightening painfully.

Parker folded his arms and stared back. "Then, sir, we are at a stand. You cannot treat with us, and the ear of the Admiralty is stopped to us."

Murmurs arose from the rest of the deputation. "We'll give 'em to Ol' Knobbs 'imself, then."

"The King! You — you must not! Recollect yourselves, I beg you!"

Parker held up his arms. "Hold, you men, we're pleased to grant Admiral Buckner a period of reflection on this matter. May we see you at nine tomorrow, sir?"

Soon after dawn, the sloop *Firefly* approached from the north under all sail. She went about under the lee of *Sandwich*, her boat in the water before she had lost all way. It stroked swiftly to *Sandwich* with five passengers.

Parker lost no time in introducing them to Kydd. "These are delegates from the North Sea fleet, Tom," he said, satisfaction rich in his voice. "This is our man from the *Leopard*, and this is the delegate from *Agamemnon*." Kydd shook hands; the men looked hard and capable. "Come from

Yarmouth to let us know what they think of our eight articles," Parker continued.

"We like 'em main well, Mr. Parker," the older delegate said, looking curiously around him. "It's right good in yer to set us straight about their tricksy lordships, an' I can say we're with ye."

Later, in the capacious cabin, Parker exulted, "Damn me eyes, but this is rare good news!"

Kydd was scratching away at a letter but stopped immediately.

"Tom, it means that in one go we've doubled our numbers. With the North Sea fleet, they dare not act against us now, and we *will* be heard." Parker stared raptly into space.

Kydd picked up on the relief he sensed behind the jubilation. "Y' mean they've been foxed, the rogues. Found a tartar athwart their hawse, did they?"

Parker's worry lines had fallen away. He laughed softly. "Yes, let's see what they think of that."

"Th' admiral will be aboard presently," Kydd reminded him.

"Oh? Ah, yes. Well, now, I do believe it would be a good thing were we to establish our respective positions in a more, er, imaginative way. *Sandwich* will not await his personage in the usual way, no. Instead he will wait on myself, president of the delegates. So, Tom, we'll absent ourselves, and return after himself is on board. We'll besides set the Parliament to debating our articles while we're gone, keep 'em out of mischief."

"Dick — he's a flag officer!" This ran against all the habits of respect and obedience Kydd had imbibed since his early days in the navy. "An' *Sandwich* is his own flagship we turned him out of."

"All the sweeter!" Parker laughed.

Admiral Buckner, the captain of *Sandwich* and another officer took boat and arrived at *Sandwich* at nine. They came aboard without ceremony and were told that the delegates were in session and could not be disturbed.

Buckner paced slowly around the deck of his former flagship. After half an hour, Hulme told him truculently that he would be handed the demands after discussions were concluded. The three officers continued standing about the decks.

At eleven the delegates emerged in a body from the Great Cabin. "You said we waits fer Mr. Parker!" one whispered fiercely.

"An' where's he at, then?" Hulme said, with contempt. "Skiving off, so he's not seen t' do th' dirty work? We does th' job ourselves."

Hulme carried the documents in a signal pouch, and pushed forward to the front of the group. In a previous existence an admiral in gold-laced cocked hat and silk stockings standing with his officers on his own quarterdeck would hardly notice a common seaman. Hulme seemed determined not to be affected. He removed his hat elaborately with a mock bow, and took out the papers.

"Admiral, this 'ere is th' final word o' the delegates." He looked around at his consorts grandly. "An' I'm ter tell ye, we don't give up the charge o' this ship, or any other, until these conditions are done." Passing across the sheets of paper, he added, "As our brother seamen at Spithead wuz honored b' the personal presence o' th' Board of Admiralty, then we got a right t' expect 'em to come t' Sheerness 'n' see us. Which we insists on."

He backed into the group again. Davis came forward and, in a quiet voice, said, "Sir, we means no disrespect t' you or y' flag, but we will be heard."

Buckner passed the papers behind him

without looking at them. His lips set in a tight line, but his voice was thin and weak. "Do you understand that I have no authority to concede on any point?"

Muttered discontent rose to shouts. "Why did yer come, then?" It was McCarthy. "Keep an eye t' wind'd, Admiral, we c'n easily set yez ashore like we did before."

Davis looked around and glared.

"You may," said Buckner, quavering in his indignation, "but I also have my instructions, which are that I may not even *discuss* any points you might bring forward."

So engrossed were the seamen with the drama on the quarterdeck that they did not notice Parker appear from the main-hatchway. He strode quickly to the admiral and, without ceremony, deftly detached him from the confrontation.

Kydd followed and stormed over to the delegates. "What the blazes are ye about, y' swabs? Couldn't y' wait f'r Dick?"

Hulme scowled. "What's ter wait, cock? We done the talkin', we done the votin', admiral lies to, waitin' fer a steer — where's Parker?" His lip curled contemptuously. "Not as 'oo should say, a real copper-bottomed pres-i-dent!"

The admiral and Parker returned. Buckner faced the delegates. "Ahem. I have your er, articles, and I shall send these by special rider to the Admiralty this very hour, together with my recommendation for their early attention. But this I have to tell you, I am not sanguine as to their reception." His face sagged in fatigue, and his voice was barely above a sigh. "But I beg you once more, do you please accept His Majesty's gracious pardon and return to duty."

McCarthy sidled around until he was behind Parker. He leaned forward and whispered hoarsely, "Why don' ye settle him?" There was a scandalized pause until it was evident that no one was going to notice the provocation.

Parker crossed to the main-hatchway, gesturing unmistakably. "Thank you for your visit, sir, we will not delay you further. Mr. Davis!"

As soon as the admiral was clear of the ship, Parker turned on McCarthy. "You lubberly knave! Do you think to destroy our reputation? Damned rogue!"

"Scrag the bastard!" Hulme shouted, and a dozen seamen threw themselves at McCarthy. Held by others, a halter was fashioned from a running bowline, and he was dragged forward along the deck.

Terrified, clawing at the tightening noose, McCarthy gurgled, "What've I done, mates? What're yer doin'?"

"Let him go!" Parker shouted, but it had no effect. Stepping forward Kydd bawled at the leaders of the horseplay, but they obviously wanted their sport. Something snapped. He threw himself at the men, taking blows and giving them. Others joined in until the master-at-arms and boatswain's mates intervened.

"We gives him a trial first — a court-martial," Kydd snarled. They frog-marched McCarthy below to the Great Cabin and lashed him struggling in a chair.

"Court comes ter order," growled Davis. "Stands accused o' sedition."

Parker arrived, breathless. "You can't do this!"

"Guilty!" spat Hulme, who had taken a punch that had bloodied his nose.

"What are you about? This man —"

"Who votes fer guilty?" More seamen crowded into the cabin. "Is there any who'll speak fer Charles McCarthy?" No one offered.

"It's m' sad dooty to pass sentence on yez, McCarthy. Are ye prepared?" The rope was produced again — but the sentence turned out to be one of transportation.

"Take him away!" He was thrown in a boat, turned out of his ship.

Kydd watched, brooding, but Parker was clearly nettled. "At times I despair of the quality of these men's devotion to the cause we all share."

The following day was sulky, gray and cool. Drizzle hung in slowly moving curtains over the Nore.

The morning wore on, but there was no word. Then a rumor came from ashore; it seemed extraordinary, but Admiral Buckner had been seen wandering about the dockyard, stopping any sailor he could find and urging him to persuade the delegates to submit; the Admiralty would never agree to terms.

"It seems apparent to me," Parker said, "that the cowardly knave has had his answer from their lordships, and is frightened to tell us." His assessment seemed reasonable, and Davis went ashore to seek out the old man and find the truth.

The mutineer captain of *Sandwich* returned within the hour.

"So that's it," Parker said, sitting suddenly. Davis remained standing, his arms folded. "Did he give any hope of a parley?"

Davis shook his head. "Nope. My feelin' is that he's got a cast-iron 'no' fr'm their fuckin' lordships, an' is too yeller t' tell us ter our faces."

Parker stared at the table, his face gray. "This I don't understand. At Spithead they talked with the delegates, the board came down to listen, they agreed their demands. Why don't they do the same for us? Why are we treated like lepers, criminals?" His voice tailed off in dismay.

"So what d' we do, then, Dick?" Kydd asked gently.

"Do?" With rising anger Davis pushed forward and said forcefully, "We got a pardon not worth a brass razoo, no hope o' gettin' our gripes heard, an' now no clear ways ahead."

Parker raised his head. "Possibly it might now be time —"

"Ain't no way we c'n backwater on this'n," Davis broke in. "Our necks 're in a noose soon 's we give it in. I reckon there's only one course t' steer. We show we means what we says. An' goes at it hard, like."

"That's what we do, no doubt about it. It's the only way we're going t' get them to see we're not f'r turnin'," Kydd agreed vigorously.

Parker gave a ghost of a smile.

Sailors began landing in numbers, each with a red cockade in his hat. The processions started again but there was no festive mood, no hilarity. Instead, it was a march of grim-faced seamen preceded by a huge red flag, damp and streaming in the oppressive drizzle.

Townsfolk watched apprehensively, sensing the mood of anger and frustration. Some called encouragement but for most it was a disturbing, frightening sight — jolly Jack Tar in an ugly mood.

Aboard *Sandwich* a meeting was called. Parker, pale-faced but resolute, addressed the Parliament. "We need to step up our vigilance, keep a strong hand in our discipline." The assembled delegates waited. "I have here a list of proposed regulations that we —"

"Enough of yer soddin' regulations! Let's 'ave some action, blast yer eyes!"

"The chair recognizes Brother Blake, *Inflexible*," said Parker warily.

"Are we sittin' around here while they waits us out? Be buggered we are! Look, I heard there's soldiers on th' march fr'm Chatham, comin' over King's Ferry now. So how about some regulations fer that, Mr. President?"

The news caused a buzz of dismay, but the fire-breathing Blake stood up and challenged, "Strike Admiral Buckner's pennant, an' hoist the Bloody Flag fr'm the masthead instead. Every fuckin' man-o'-war t' do the same and be damned t' any who stand in th' way of justice an' our rights!"

In the animated discussion that followed, Parker rapped on the table. "It's more serious than that. If they are moving troops against us, when we have always been peaceable, we are betrayed, brothers. And we can do only one of two things. Surrender without a pardon, or resist. I leave it to this meeting to decide."

Kydd laid down his quill while argument raged. Soldiers, sent to Sheerness Fort no doubt. Did this mean a deliberate act of encirclement or was it something more innocent? Whatever the reason, Parker was right: their alternatives were few. Their only chance now was a show of strength to persuade the Admiralty that negotiation was in their own best interest. He raised his voice stoutly over the din. "We take steps t' secure the fleet."

"An' what's that supposed ter mean?" Blake stared at him suspiciously. Kydd was not a delegate and had no right to speak, but he was given a hearing.

"All ships t' shift moorings t' the Great Nore, ground tackle down so's we're in a defensive circle, that sort o' thing. Then f'r sure they can't come close without we c'n greet 'em with a broadside. They'll never try that, so we'll be safe 'n' snug."

"Um, intelligent," Parker mused. "They can't accuse us of an offensive action, no provocation, but by this we render ourselves quite beyond their power to harm us."

"What about th' standin' force o' gunboats?" Hulme had made little contribution so far, but this idea was good. Sheerness as a naval port had its local defenses, and these included a small squadron of gunboats.

"We helps ourselves, in course," said Blake warmly. "An' then we has th' buggers around us t' see off any cuttin' out tricks b' boats."

"Er, it sounds a useful move, I'll admit," said Parker doubtfully. "We must suppose that if we leave them, they may well be used against us. Very well, we make our plans."

One by one the men-o'-war of the Nore

took up their positions; concentrated in a double crescent, their combined broadsides were a fearsome threat. Every vessel in Sheerness that could sail was brought out to join the fleet. Some were fearful of the way things were shaping, and a certain amount of coercion, sometimes forceful, was employed.

The column of soldiers made their appearance on the Queenborough road — two full regiments — but they turned out to be militia, and succumbed quickly to the antics of the seamen ashore, who ran alongside taunting or striking up patriotic songs. The soldiers straggled into their barracks in disarray.

In the dockyard the sailors found allies among the shipwrights. In sympathy with the wronged seamen, they resolved never to take any vessel for repair unless it was flying a red flag at main. Blue Town loyally urged on the sailors they had taken to their hearts, and when a flotilla of armed boats from the fleet swept around the point they were roundly cheered.

Eight gunboats were boarded and carried, with most crews joining the mutineers. Without delay, they set out to join the fleet.

"Should be comin' in sight any minute,"

said Kydd to Parker, clamping his telescope against a shroud.

"And I'd never have considered Blake the man to do it," Parker said.

Kydd looked out over the low-lying fortifications. "He's a short-fused beggar, I know, but he's the kind o' man y'd like next to you in a boardin'." He saw the masts. "Here they come, thanks be."

The gunboats drew abreast of Garrison Point. Then came a jet of smoke and the thud of a gun. The next vessel passed; it also fired. And the next took its turn. There was no mistaking this time: an untidy scatter of black fragments leaped skyward. "Jesus!" shouted Kydd. "They're bombardin' the fort!"

Chapter 9

"Kind in you, Dundas — my own shed a wheel this morning, most aggravatin'."

The secretary of state for war did not appear particularly communicative, staring out of his carriage window at the sunset traffic on the Thames as they passed over Westminster Bridge.

"Billy Pitt must be hell-bent on some adventure, callin' a cabinet meeting at such a notice," Windham, leader of the Commons, offered.

"He has much to consairn him." The burr of a lowland Scot had not entirely left the secretary, but Windham knew that, of all men, Dundas was closest to the beleaguered prime minister. "Know it for a fact that Lord Moira is tappin' his friends with a view to bringing him and his gov'ment down — wants Northumberland as premier an' Fox to be a minister."

"Fox! The wily beggar — you know he waited on the King?"

"Aye, he did, and His Knobbs saw him, would you credit it? Didn't say a word to him, I'm told."

The carriage clattered off the bridge at New Palace Yard, passing the twin flambeaux at its entrance crackling in the gathering dusk. It swung right into Parliament Street with a loud creaking of leather springs, then slowed and came to a stop.

Dundas thumped on the roof with his stick. "Dammit, man, we have to be in —"

A caped coachman leaned down. "The mobility, sir," he said heavily. Dundas leaned out of the window. A straggling, noisy crowd was astride the road: some of them bore crude banners, others were supporting an effigy.

"Drive on!" Dundas snapped, and withdrew inside. He hefted his stick — it was capped with a heavy silver embossing. Windham loosened his sword, a paltry spadroon. Neither man spoke as the coachman urged the carriage forward with cracking whip.

"No war! Down with Pitt!" came angry shouts.

Dundas leaned out of the window again. "Don't stop!" he roared. The driver plied his whip, but the horses were now shying at the ugly crowd ahead, flicking their heads to the side, eyes bulging white.

The mob fell back sullenly before the charging carriage, with its scarlet and green coat of arms, but as it plunged among them, some beat at the sides, screaming. A stone shattered a window to the front, then another. More blows drummed on the side of the carriage as it thundered through the mob.

The horses whinnied in terror, but the impetus now was to get away, and in a terrified clatter of hooves the wildly swaying carriage was through to the safety of the White Hall precinct with its redcoat guard.

"Thank you, gentlemen, for your prompt attendance — you will find your celerity is amply justified by events." Pitt rubbed his eyes in weariness, staring at the new Corinthian columns as though they were on the point of dissolving.

They filed in: Grenville, the stern and principled foreign minister; the Duke of Portland, home secretary; the secretary of state for war and the war minister, still pale from their experience in the carriage. The big oval table was bare except for a small sheaf of papers and a glass of port before the prime minister.

"Do be seated. A muzzler, Henry? I heard you were accosted by the mob."

"If you please, Prime Minister."

"Good. Now, this is the essence." Pitt's pale, noble face was slashed with lines of strain.

Windham wondered how any single person could take the whole weight of this utterly new kind of war, let alone keep aloof from the fierce political brawling in the Commons every day.

"The situation abroad is critical." Taking up his port Pitt gestured to Grenville to continue.

"Indeed. Since Rivoli the Austrians have lost heart. I now find they are parleying secretly with General Buonaparte for peace, their price Venice — which, of course, is now in his gift. We've been thrown out of the Mediterranean, not a ship farther in than Gib, and we find that the French by autumn will be in occupation of the left bank of the Rhine. This is something that last happened a thousand years ago." Grenville stopped, and looked grimly about the table. "In short, we've not a single friend left. The coalition is finished."

Pitt put down his glass with extreme

care. "The whole business of war has put an intolerable stress on our resources. The national debt frightens me, and I won't hide it from you, gentlemen, that unless a miracle occurs or we can think of a radical new way of taxing, we shall be bankrupted."

The Home Secretary muttered indistinctly; the others stared grimly.

"You will ask what more can happen — then I shall tell you. If our standing abroad is so sadly diminished, our domestic is worse. Those bad harvests leave us with precious little to show for four years of war, we are balanced on a knife edge of economics, but our precious trade, the lifeblood of our islands, this is to be guarded with all we have. And we nearly lost it all to those mutinous wretches at Spithead. Fortunately, they've been appeased, and Dundas tells me the Channel fleet is now back at sea again. A damn near thing, gentlemen, for a run-on. 'Change would ruin us in every chancellery in Europe."

His eyes glazed, and he made a visible effort to recruit his strength. "Now, it seems, we have a new mutiny, this time at the Nore. I was assured — the Admiralty were confident — this would blow over just as soon as we'd acceded in the

Spithead case. But now, far from returning to duty, they're making new demands and saying our general pardon doesn't cover them. The admiral in those parts — that useless ninny — says that guns have been fired at a King's ship, and the Sheerness fort has been bombarded.

"My friends, this is a far more serious matter altogether. Grenville has unimpeachable intelligence that the Dutch are preparing a major fleet challenge from the Texel at the goading of the French. If they succeed by our ships useless at their moorings, then they can within hours secure the Channel for a massed landing. If they get wind of this mutiny it will be all up with us, I fear."

He finished his port in one and set down his glass. "I — we cannot withstand a second mutiny and consequent concessions. This administration would certainly fall. Added to which, each hour the mutineers are free to strut about is encouragement to every crackpot radical in the land. As we talk, Sheerness is *en fête* for their mutinous heroes, and the garrison is now considered unreliable. What we are faced with must be accounted the worst crisis I have ever encountered.

"So, I want suggestions, plans, strategies,

anything, but this rising must be stopped — now! Charmed or crushed, it has to be over speedily and the ringleaders punished, visibly. I trust I'll have your strongest recommendation for action.

"Oh, and quite incidentally, I have the Lord Chancellor's ruling on the applicability of the King's Pardon to the Nore. It is that the mutineers were right in the essentials, their offenses are indeed *not* within the purview of the Spithead pardon."

"Th' poxy, slivey, cuntbitten shicers!" Hulme would not be consoled.

"An' so say we all," Kydd agreed, with feeling. "Dick, I owns y' was right. I'd never have thought 'em shabs enough f'r that grass-combin' move. If we'd accepted th' pardon we could all be — Well, we didn't." It was a low blow, a cold-blooded act of policy. "We stands fast," Kydd said sturdily.

"Yes, Tom, the only thing we can do." Parker seemed to find strength in Kydd's words, and raised his voice: "Do you all listen! We know where we stand now. There's no going back, lads. We either win or die.

"The ancient Romans carried a bundle

of sticks to show to all that one stick might be taken and easily broken, yet all taken together you may not break them. And when Benjamin Franklin put pen to the Declaration of Independence, he swore that 'now, indeed, we must all hang together, or, most assuredly, we shall all hang separately.'

"Now, there are some — we may hazard who — are, as one might say, lacking in zeal. There are some who would let others risk all to win for them while they keep in with the authority. Still more are thinking to desert their shipmates. These are a danger and peril to all of us. We have to take steps to prevent them loosening our unity — by any means. If necessary, by compulsion!

"Joe, I want you and your mate to spend your hours visiting each ship. See yard-ropes are rove and the Bloody Flag flies high and free! All hands to wear a red ribbon in his hat in token of our struggle.

"Cap'n Davis, every morning at sunrise, the men of *Sandwich* are to clear lower deck and give three rousing cheers. And you entertain on board every Thames pilot you can find — they shall not remain at large and free to navigate any foolish expedition the government thinks to send against us.

"There is a special service awaiting Brother Hulme. Word has been passed to us that in the Thames beyond Tilbury, at Long Reach, lies *Lancaster* sixty-four and others. We mean to set them free to drop down-river to join our company. You may use any measures to secure the ships against those who would wish to maintain their tyranny.

"And to all you brave hearts, it is now time to take courage. Let none doubt that we are resolved — at the cannon's mouth, if need be — to stay true to our cause."

There was a breathless silence in the Great Cabin, then Blake scrambled to his feet. "An' it's three times three fer our Pres-i-dent Parker! Let's hear it, y' shabs!" The cheers echoed deafeningly while Parker sat, red with pleasure, eyes sparkling.

"An' then we toasted like good 'uns damnation to their lordships 'n' Pitt 'n' his scurvy crew!" Kydd laughed.

Kitty did not join in. "Thomas — please! Ye have to know, people are afraid. They know y' don' have the pardon an' they're worried f'r what ye'll do now. An' some of y' sailors are takin' boats 'n' landin' in Whitstable 'n' Faversham t' kick up a bobbery. Honest folks 'r' now takin' *agin* you, m' love."

Kydd's heart softened at the genuine worry in Kitty's face. "M' dear Kitty," he said softly, holding her tight, "it'll all be over soon — we're united, see, and they has t' treat wi' us. An' the first thing we asks afore we talks is a right full pardon fr'm the King."

She dropped her eyes and, in a muffled voice, said, "I know you, Thomas. You'll be true t' the end, th' last one t' yield, an' then they'll take y' up as a ringleader, an' then — an' then . . ." She turned away and wept.

A cold wave stole over Kydd. Women often had a second sight denied to men. "Come, now, Kitty, that's a fine carry-on f'r a man t' take away. Mark my words, lass, I'll wager their lordships 'll be down here, and a-treatin' with us, like they did in Spithead, in only a day or so," he said strongly. But the chill feeling stayed.

"Did he, by God!" Parker heard the seaman out, his face darkening. "Is he not aware who is the power in this anchorage? Does he think to top it the mandarin in our presence? Pass the word for Bill Davis, if you please, Tom, we're going ashore to set straight our Admiral Buckner."

The barge glided in to the steps, and the president of the delegates and his staff stepped ashore. They strode directly across to the fort gate, ignoring the sentry, and went straight to the commissioner's house. "Mr. Parker, president o' the delegates, t'see the Admiral," Kydd told the flag lieutenant at the door.

"He is not to be disturbed," the officer replied, his face tight.

"He'll see Mr. Parker now," Kydd said, moving closer.

"Impossible. He's hearing charges at this moment."

Parker stiffened. "Why do you think we're here, sir?" He moved closer.

"Very well. I will tell the Admiral."

Parker did not wait. Following the lieutenant into the room, he stood, feet astride, surveying the occupants. "Captain Hartwell," he acknowledged to the dockyard commissioner. "Captain Cunningham," he added, seeing the captain of *Clyde* to one side. They glowered back at him.

"Yes, what is it, Mr. Parker?" Admiral Buckner asked, obviously embarrassed.

"You have two marines in your custody, I understand, Admiral," Parker snapped. "Please to yield their persons to me."

"I don't understand, Mr. Parker. These men were taken up in the town drunk and riotous, and as they are members of the Fleet it is of course my duty to detain them."

"That, sir, is precisely why I am here," said Parker, in hard tones.

"Sir?" Buckner's voice was weak and unsure.

Parker paced forward. "Sir, your flag no longer flies and your authority is now gone. These are then my prisoners and will be disciplined by the Fleet."

The old admiral's face sagged. "Mr. Parker, my flag is struck, it is true, but, sir, consider my feelings."

Around the room there were expressions of astonishment at this display of emotion from so senior a personage.

"I have feelings too, Admiral Buckner, and I do consider yours. I'm sorry to say it, but it's not in my power to change things."

There was an appalled silence. Then a chair crashed to the floor as Captain Cunningham leaped to his feet and drew his sword. Kydd lunged across and seized his arm, smashing his wrist down on the chair back. The sword clattered to the floor.

"You bloody dog!" Cunningham shouted. "I'll run ye through, you base-born rogue! God rot your bones for a vile mutineer an' blackguard!"

Parker looked at the captain with contempt. "Have a care, sir. The men are not delicate in the matter of chastisement, should I put it to them." He turned again to Buckner. "Admiral, we have not had an answer respecting the Board of Admiralty's attendance on us. We will talk to no other, this is our solemn resolution."

Buckner's reply was hastened aboard *Sandwich* by early afternoon.

"Worthless, I knew it." Parker dropped the letter to the table. "We can't waste time talking to that feeble loon. We bring their lordships to account directly. A letter; be so good as to agree its wording . . .

To the Lords Commissioners for executing the Office of Lord High Admiral of Great Britain and Ireland &c.

I am commanded by the Delegates of the Whole Fleet assembled in council, on board His Majesty's Ship *Sandwich*, to inform your lordships, that they have received your letter at the hands of Admiral Buckner, which informs them that it is not your intention of coming to Sheerness, the same has been communicated to His Majesty's ships and vessels lying here, and the determination of the whole is, that they will not come to any accommodation until you appear at the Nore, and redress our grievances.

Richard Parker, President
By order of the Committee of
Delegates of the Whole Fleet

"There, that should start proceedings," Parker said, with satisfaction.

Kydd went below to the starboard bay as soon as he heard of the return of Hulme. Rumor had it that it had been quite an adventure to reach *Lancaster*.

"Damme, but they wuz shyin' hot shot at us fr'm Tilbury fort, mates. Think on it! Two longboats an' a pinnace, they thinks it's the Dutch comin' up the river agen." Hulme was grimed with powder smoke, looking tired but determined to tell his tale. "We touches at Gravesend fer a spell, but after th' guns, the folk ashore think

413

we're some kind o' pirates or somethin' and has at us wi' what they c'n find. We offs ter Long Reach, but th' Admiralty has smoked what we're about an' sends a rider ter warn off th'captain — Wells, 'is name. But, we're up th' side 'n' on the quarter-deck in a brace o' shakes. Bit of a mill, then Cap'n Wells, he legs it out o' the stern lights an' is away."

"Hey, now, did they come across then?" Kydd wanted to know.

"That they did! An' ter prove it, here's yer new cap'n of *Lancaster*, Cap'n James Wilson."

"Well met, cuffin!" Kydd was glad to shake his hand.

Hulme wiped at the powder smoke on his face and finished his story: "We gets balls aroun' our ears goin' up, we entertains 'em wi' muskets goin' down — 's only fair dos."

At this Kydd winced: such would not endear them to the townsfolk. Still, the Bloody Flag was now floating proudly high above, not much more than a dozen miles from White Hall itself.

At six bells came extraordinary news. Busy with his endless work transcribing and requisitioning, Kydd heard a sudden eruption of excitement on the decks above that swelled and spread. He potted his quill, and collided with Davis at the door. "Tom, mate, better go topsides handy like, there's somethin' you better hear."

The whole ship's company, animated and noisy, appeared to be on the upper deck. The focus was Parker, who stood abreast the mainmast holding a paper. When he saw Kydd he flourished it in the air vigorously. "Tom!" His face was wreathed with a seraphic smile. "My dear friend! At last." He drew Kydd aside. "History," he said quietly but proudly. He passed across the paper and watched for reaction.

"Why, this is tremendous! It's — well, tremendous!" Here was the final consequence of all they had done, the pinnacle of their striving: a historic achievement. The First Lord of the Admiralty had agreed to come to Sheerness, together with the august Board of Admiralty, there no doubt to add plenary weight to decisions on the eight articles. And with him he would be bringing a King's Pardon.

The news spread ashore. One by one, the red flags and crimson banners disappeared, and the Union Flag of Old England was welcomed back; people walked freely, shops reopened and Blue Town took on all the old jollity of a fleet in port.

Kitty took the news with huge relief, dabbing her eyes. "Leave it t' us, m' dear — jus' make sure y' have the main deck rigged so."

Thus it was that at dusk the main deck of *Sandwich* was squared away fore and aft, lanthorns were placed above each gun and every piece of bunting that could be found was hung and draped in a brave display of color. Seamen, their women on their arms, came aboard from every ship in the anchorage. The larboard side of the main deck was draped with ensigns of all the friends of England, especially at the center, opposite the mainmast. There it was expected that President of the Delegates Parker would speak.

Between the guns on the starboard side of the deck, tables were tastefully laid with festive fare and the main gratings were spread with jugs and baskets. An enthusiastic band scraped away forward — "Britons Strike Home!" and "Rule Britannia" particular favorites. These were interspersed with hornpipes and spontaneous dancing.

A storm of applause greeted Parker as he

moved forward to take his place. It went on and on, and Kydd could see the emotion of the moment tugging at him.

He spoke fine words: the triumph of right, true brotherhood, loyal hearts. When he finished, William Davis, mutineer captain of *Sandwich*, stepped forward, and, in an unaffected, manly voice, sang:

Old Neptune made haste,
  to the Nore he did come,
To waken his sons who had slept far too long.
They heard him, 'tis true,
  the lion boldly roused
Their brethren at Spithead their cause
  did espouse;
Each swore to the King forever to be true
But one and all tyrants would strive
  to subdue . . .

But Kydd knew the best was to come. From the fore-hatchway tripped a line of women in gala array, dresses swirling, ribbons whirling, to form a line of chorus. The girl who took position in the front was his Kitty.

She blew him a kiss, assumed a roguish pout and, dancing bawdily, began the age-old ditty of the sailor's Poll:

Don't you see the ships a-coming?
Don't you see them in full sail?
Don't you see the ships a-coming
With the prizes at their tail!
Oh! my little rolling sailor,
Oh! my little rolling he;
I do love a jolly sailor,
Blithe and merry might he be!

To general merriment and the mortification of the soldiers who had accepted invitations, Kitty launched into the second verse:

Sailors, they get all the money,
Soldiers they get none but brass;
I do love a jolly sailor,
Soldiers they may kiss my arse!
Oh! my little rolling sailor,
Oh! my little rolling he;
I do love a jolly sailor,
Soldiers may be damned for me!

A lump formed in Kydd's throat; this was what it was to be among the fellowship of the sea, the precious warmth of shared dangers and ocean mysteries, pride in fine sea skills and a handsome ship — there was no other life conceivable.

With this nightmare over and a Royal

Pardon, he could take back his rank and place in the navy — perhaps with Kitty . . .

"Lord Spencer, you know General Grey." In Pitt's cabinet rooms the First Lord of the Admiralty bowed politely to the senior field officer commanding land forces in the south.

"Mr. Pitt is unavoidably delayed, I fear, First Lord." Windham took Spencer's cloak and ushered him to a seat next to Grey.

"Not surprised," murmured the Duke of Portland. "Fox did promise that he would make this the speech of his life against his government. An' I saw Sheridan in his cups as usual — he'll be there to stir it along, you can be sure."

The table buzzed with desultory conversation until the door flew open and Pitt entered, his face even paler than usual. "My apologies, gentlemen."

"Er, how went it, William?" Dundas could be forgiven the familiarity.

"Crushed. Obliteration. We shall see little of Fox and the opposition from now forward."

"The votes?"

"I didn't stay for the division." Pitt seemed energized by the recent clash, and picked up his papers. "This mutiny. We must act. That is why I have called you to this place. Developments. My lord?"

Spencer took up the thread. "Er, we received an impertinent demand from the chief mutineer that my own good self — and my board! — should take carriage for Sheerness to wait on *them*, for God's sake. They have ceased speaking through their admiral and say they will not listen unless they hear it from us."

"That's as may be, sir. I would have thought it more to the point that not a great deal above a dozen miles from this room we have anchored a ship-of-the-line of five dozen guns flying the red flag with perfect impunity." He glanced at Grey and went on acidly, "And how boatloads of armed mutineers were able to pull past the hottest fire from Tilbury fort to get at these upstream ships without a scratch escapes me. The noise of the guns alone caused panic and terror in east London, last seen under De Ruyter."

The general glowered. Pitt ignored him and pressed on: "No, gentlemen, these are desperate men. They're also clever. They insure their force is undiminished by deploying force to prevent the loyalists regaining control. They show no desire for reconciliation and are no doubt ready to do anything."

Pitt broke off to cough wretchedly into a handkerchief. The table waited watchfully while he gulped some port, then resumed hoarsely, "And we got ominous news this morning. Every available Thames pilot has been rounded up and is being held prisoner by the mutineers! I need not remind the landlubbers among us that the shoals of the estuary are among the worst in the civilized world — the implications of this move are therefore quite clear: the mutineers are holding their ships in readiness to deliver them up across the Channel to the Netherlands perhaps, or even France."

"They wouldn't dare!" Spencer said, aghast.

Pitt spared him a withering look and continued: "I have summoned the House to an all-night sitting this night — following our meeting," he added significantly. "I'm exercised as to what I shall tell them . . ."

Unexpectedly, it was Grey who spoke first. "Harrumph. May I take it, sir, that we must end this farce at once? Precipitate, right? Then you've only the one choice. Close with the buggers and finish 'em now, and be damned to the caterwauling of the press."

"And just what is it you propose, General?" Pitt said silkily.

"Like this." He would get a fair hearing — his first combat was with Wolfe on the plains above Quebec nearly forty years before. "We act with resolution and dispatch. We have infantry at Gravesend, reinforced by artillery from Woolwich. They combine with the Tilbury artillery across the water to cover the approaches to London. The Warwicks are at Chelmsford, they move down to mass around the crossing at Purfleet. I can do more, but I need m' adjutant and maps. Now, sir, how reliable is your North Sea fleet? Hey?"

"Admiral Duncan sees no reason to doubt other than they will do their duty when called upon, sir," said Spencer, frostily.

"Then this is what happens. You an' your board take coach to Sheerness. Let 'em know you're coming, calm 'em down. When you're there talkin' your North Sea ships sweep in from seaward an' take 'em, while I get together what troops I can an' go in from the land. Hey?"

Spencer wiped his forehead. "Are you seriously proposing that we resolve this matter in a public battle between our own ships right outside our own capital?"

"I do! If necessary. They, of course, may well desire to capitulate on seein' our force."

Pitt leaned forward. "I like it. Any objections?" He looked about the table.

"Sir, if you'll forgive —"

"Mr. Windham?"

"The country at large may well laud your decisive action. But do you not feel that the more, er, clamorous of the radicals may object?"

"Pah! The saintly and ancient Tom Paine himself is in France this minute, lecturing the Jacobins on the conduct of their revolution, he's a broken reed. Godwin is lying low for the sake of his wife, Mary Wollstonecraft, Cobbett is safely away in America writing some damn-awful paper called the *Porcupine* or some such — and Fox, well, after today he's vowed to leave the Commons forever, if we can believe it.

"But I take your point. Let's leave it like this. We stay our hand, offer them their pardon. If they then accept and return to duty, well and good. If not, they suffer the full consequence of their acts.

"Very well! General, please begin your

deployments without delay. This has to end for them."

"How do I appear, my friend? Fit for the great day, in full feather?" Parker had taken extra care with his appearance, laying aside his cherished beaver hat in favor of a pristine seaman's round hat, his customary boots polished and smart.

"It'll do, Dick," Kydd said.

"My greatest day, in truth," Parker said, face aglow. He continued, as if to himself, "It will be a hard struggle. The hardest will be not to lose countenance before the person of the First Lord, and jeopardize the quality of the negotiations."

"You won't — he it will be who has the harder, o' course. President o' the delegates is a high enough office."

Parker pulled a fob watch from his waistcoat. "I do believe that our time is come. Be so good as to advise the delegates and muster the boat's crew."

Kydd had also taken care with his appearance. It would definitely be the first and, very probably, the last time that he would catch sight of the ultimate head of the navy, the legendary First Lord of the Admiralty.

"They shall have constituted their board

by now," Parker said, in the boat. The other delegates were subdued, but defiantly wore their red ribbons. Many more followed in boats behind, determined to be present at the historic occasion. They stepped out on the wharf, marched resolutely to the commissioner's residence, and assembled in the foreyard. The vast flag of Admiralty, only flown by the Lord High Admiral of England, floated from the central staff of the mansion.

Kydd held his breath. This was the moment for which they had put themselves in the shadow of the noose.

With every eye on him, Parker walked up to the black door and knocked. It was immediately opened by Admiral Buckner.

"Sir," Parker said, with the utmost gravity, "I understand that the First Lord is present within."

"He is." There was tension in Buckner's voice.

"And the board?"

"They are." Something about Buckner's manner made Kydd uneasy.

"We should like to know if these are the same lords who have been at Portsmouth."

"They are."

Parker stepped back a pace. "Then, sir, we respectfully request their lordships to come aboard the *Sandwich* and settle the business."

There was a rustle of anticipation in the delegates behind him. They would finally get a glimpse of the shadowy figures with whom they had been locked in a clash of wills, but there was not a single movement.

"Sir?" prodded Parker.

Buckner stood irresolute. He said something in a voice so low it was inaudible.

"I beg your pardon, sir?"

"I said, their lordships will not do that."

"Will not do that? Please be clear, sir."

"Er, excuse me." Buckner withdrew into the house. Rumbling of speech could be heard, then he reemerged. "His lordship insists he will see you only for the purpose of declaring that you accept the King's Pardon and return to duty."

Parker drew a deep breath. "Then pray sir, how will our grievances be taken under consideration, if the First Lord will not hear them?"

Again Buckner wavered. "I — please, pardon." He again disappeared inside.

The seaman next to Kydd shifted his position and muttered, "Shy bastard, 'is lordship, don't want t' be seen talkin' to our faces."

Buckner came out, visibly agitated.

"Lord Spencer reminds you that all of your grievances have been redressed. No discussion can possibly take place with their lordships."

"Sir, you are a man of sense. This is no way to conduct negotiations between —"

"If you accept His Majesty's most gracious pardon you will be allowed to declare it personally to their lordships. Their lordships will then pronounce to you the pardon in the King's name."

"Then —"

Buckner straightened his stoop and looked Parker directly in the eye. "That is all."

For a long moment Parker stared doggedly ahead, then wheeled around and pushed his way through the crowd. "Wh- where 're we going, Dick?" someone asked.

"To perdition, shipmate!" he replied hoarsely.

Kydd hurried to keep up. "Th' Chequers?"

"*Sandwich!*"

The admiral's Great Cabin filled rapidly. Anyone not a delegate was unceremoniously ejected. "Gangway! Clear th' house, y' lubbers." Blake's husky bellow was unmistakable.

"They won't listen, Tom," Parker said, in stricken tones, as they pushed their way to the front. "They really don't want to talk to us."

Kydd was alarmed by Parker's ashen pallor. Whatever he had seen in Buckner's face had seriously unmanned him. "Do take a roun' turn, Dick. Y'r people are relyin' on you," he said urgently. "Look, we've just the same force now we always had. Nothing's changed." He tried desperately to reach him. "An' their precious lordships, did they come t' Sheerness jus' to tell us of the pardon? They're expectin' a fight of it."

"The pardon? Perhaps we should, after all, accept it."

"Dick!" said Kydd, in quiet anguish. "Don't fail us now. We have them here, they're waitin' for us. F'r Christ's sake, stay by us!"

"What's goin' on?" came a catcall. "Why aren't we layin' it into 'em?"

"Dick!" Kydd could say no more.

Davis loudly called the meeting to order as Parker made a visible effort to compose himself. Shortly into the heated debate that followed Parker was summoned away. He returned promptly, carrying a bundle of papers. "Here it is, brothers. This, then, is the position their lordships hold. It was given to me by our old captain himself."

He stood behind his chair and held up a document. He broke the seal, read the contents, but did not speak. He swayed, and when he looked up his face held a deep anguish.

"Well, what'd it say?" came a call.

"Er, matters have reached a certain, shall we say, impasse." Parker looked again at the document as if needing confirmation of grave news.

"Blast yer eyes, then give us a look," Blake said, reaching across.

"No," said Parker oddly, holding the paper protectively to his chest.

"What does it say, Dick?" Kydd asked firmly. The meeting would have to know sooner or later.

"It says — it tries to drive a wedge into our unity, to appeal —"

"What does it say, fer God's sake?"

Parker sat down heavily, holding the paper close. "It says — it says that all those who wish to accept the King's Pardon must do so before noon tomorrow. After that time, their lordships will strike their flag and return to London, leaving those still in a state of mutiny to their fate."

Some sat stunned, others looked visibly

relieved, more still were angry and disbelieving. "Those scurvy shabs!" Hulme spat contemptuously. "Why don't they give us the same as they served out to 'em at Spithead? What's wrong wi' we that they won't talk man t' man like they did before?"

A rumble of agreement turned into a roar. "Shipmates! Brothers!" Parker tried to get their attention, but his voice was drowned in the fury. Eventually he got a hearing. "It's my duty to tell you, much as it pains me — yet I must say it as I see it — it is my unhappy conclusion that their lordships have no intention whatsoever of negotiating with us. For whatever reason, they are turning their backs on us and our complaints. I do not understand why," he added heavily. "They are obstinate and heedless of our cries, and I fear are implacable. Therefore it is my sad duty to recommend that we accept the pardon and — and give up our venture."

"You what?" shouted Blake. "Give it away! Nothin's changed. C'n I remind our president, we still hold all the cards! We're a fleet o' near five hundred guns — no one's goin' to go up against us. We calls their bluff, mates."

Parker rummaged around and slapped a

thick wedge of papers. "These are printed copies of the pardon for distribution around the fleet. What will the common sailors think? That this is their chance, and you will deny them?"

Hulme leaned over. "They don't have ter know," he snarled.

"Yeah," said Blake. "We's the true elected delegates, we speak fer them, an' we decides what ter do. What are we about, th't we do their fuckin' lordships' work for 'em? Burn the lot, I say, an' stand steadfast!"

Davis intervened: "Y' know what this means — the noos is goin' ter get out anyway, an' that says there's goin' to be them what are now ready t' give it in. What'll we do then, half our strength goes?"

"We p'suades 'em ter stay," said Blake, with a grim smile.

A vote was taken, but too late in the evening to bear to their lordships. A substantial majority was for continuing with their action. They broke up noisily and the Parliament of delegates returned to their ships, leaving Parker, Kydd and Davis alone in the Great Cabin.

"What d' we do, then?" Davis asked, reflecting the doubts of those who had voted against continuing the action. "Ask pardon?"

Parker's gray face lifted. "I was elected by the men to be their president. You may seek pardon, that is your decision. For myself, I will do my duty by my shipmates, as they trusted me to do, and convey their determinations to the Admiralty as needed."

Cast down after the exaltation of the morning, Parker's misery was intense, Kydd realized, but the nobility of character that had impelled him originally was still as strong as ever.

"No, mate," Davis said. "I'll be stayin'."

Kydd was too. "If ye're standin' by the men, Dick, then what kind o' gullion is it wants t' skin out now? I'll be with ye."

The day of the ultimatum was raw and gray. Kydd had spent a hard, sleepless night, the noises of the old ship around him now sounding ominous. He pulled on oilskins and ventured to the upper decks. To his surprise, he saw a party of seamen charging the guns, loading and running them out, then covering their gunlocks with a lead apron.

"Cheerly, lads, don't wan' t' make mistakes, now do we?" It was Hulme. What crack-brained scheme was this?

"What's this'n, John?" Kydd asked carefully. The rain pattered insistently on his oilskins.

Hulme looked at him. "Tell me, Kydd, honest now. Are you loyal? *We* all is."

Taken aback, Kydd could only reply, "As much as th' next, I reckon."

"Stan' clear, then, cully."

Sandwich snubbed sulkily at her moorings, the wind's blast uneven. Under her guns there was no enemy, no ship closer than the humble *Pylades*. A forward gun went off, a sullen, subdued thud. Another fired, the smoke rolling downwind. In the distance *Inflexible* began firing. It was so unreal, in keeping with his imaginings of the night. Kydd shook himself. "A salute?" he asked dully.

Hulme grinned and pointed up. At the mainmast head the Bloody Flag streamed out, wet and dull. But at the fore, and in all the other ships, the Royal Standard fluttered, its striking colors unaffected by the rain.

"King's Birthday?"

"No, mate, Restoration Day." The day nearly one and a half centuries ago when the second King Charles had been restored to his throne after Cromwell's mutiny.

"Shows 'em we're still loyal, like."

It was still four hours to the expiry of the ultimatum — four hours to come to a different conclusion and accept the King's Pardon, to resume his sea life, put it all behind him. But if he did, how would he get away to present himself? Stand up and tell them that Thomas Kydd wanted to save his skin? Steal off in a boat, in disguise so none would recognize who was creeping off?

He tried to crush the bleak thoughts, and went below in search of Parker, the water streaming off his foul-weather gear. The wind had freshened, gusting in, and was quickly kicking up a sea; the lurching and tugging of the ship added seasickness to the misery of the press-gang victims.

Below, an ill-tempered meeting was still in progress; Parker was sitting motionless, not intervening. He did not notice Kydd, who quietly left.

As the morning wore on, the weather got worse and the old ship-of-the-line leaked. Water dripped and ran from waterways above, penetrating decks below. The result was sodden hammocks and the fetid smell of wet bodies.

The hours turned to minutes, and then it was noon.

Ironically, the seas were so much in motion that it was impossible for boats; even the gunboats sought shelter around the point. But the seamen were resolved. All votes had been taken, all arguments exhausted. It only needed the President of the Delegates to close, lock and bar the last gate, to inform their lordships formally of the sense of the Parliament.

"They could see we're meanin' what we say an' come round," Kydd said hopefully, to the lonely figure of Parker at his quill.

Parker raised a troubled face. "I don't think it possible, my dear friend." He sanded the sheet and passed it to Kydd. "This is the form of words voted by the delegates."

Kydd read it aloud. " 'My Lords, we had the honor to receive your lordships' proclamation (for we did not conceive it to be his Majesty's). . . . How could your Lordships think to frighten us as old women in the Country frighten Children with such stories as the Wolf and Raw head & bloody bones or as the Pope wished to terrify . . .' "

"They can't send this!"

"It gets worse."

" 'Shall we now be induced from a few Paltry threats to forsake our Glorious plan

& lick your lordships feet for Pardon & Grace, when we see ourselves in possession of 13 sail of as noble Ships as any in His Majesty's service, and Men not inferior to any in the Kingdom? . . .' "

Kydd went cold. This would push the whole into unknown regions, it was a bitter, provocative taunt — but his heart was with the reckless courage and defiant spirit that were all the seamen had left.

"I have to send it. This is their feeling."

"Yes. I see," Kydd murmured.

In the afternoon, the Bloody Flag fluttered down in *Clyde* and a white one appeared. Kydd and Parker watched in silence as the same happened in *San Fiorenzo*. But then the masts of *Inflexible*, anchored between, changed their aspect: she had a spring to her cable and heaved around so the wavering vessels faced two lines of guns apiece. The red flag slowly ascended again.

By early evening, the seas had moderated. The gunboats sailed out to the fleet again as the president of the delegates made ready to go ashore. *Niger* was seen without her red flag; cannon fire was heard again in the anchorage, but in vain. The frigate slipped away.

Parker and the delegates entered the boats and pulled ashore through squally weather. Soaked but defiant, the men marched once more to the commissioner's house.

"Here is our response, sir," Parker said, handing the letter to Admiral Buckner. "I shall return for your reply."

He turned and retired from the scene with dignity. There was brave and fool-hardy talk at the Chequers, but Parker sat apart.

At six, they filed out for the quarter-mile walk to where the flag of the Lord High Admiral of England still flew. The people of Blue Town lined their way, but in the rain there were only thin, scattered cheers. Most remained somber and quiet, watching the seamen as if they were going to meet their fate.

Buckner emerged promptly, but his head was held high and he kept his distance.

"Good evening, sir," Parker said. "May I know if their lordships have an answer to our letter?"

"They have not! There will *be* no answer. Are you here to make your submission?"

Parker kept his silence.

"You may still, through their lordships' grace, accept the King's Pardon. But if you fire again on a king's ship, then every man will be excluded from the pardon," the admiral added hastily.

Not deigning to reply, Parker gave a low bow, and left.

"The kippers, if you please. They are particularly succulent, I find." Renzi's lodgings in Rochester were small, but quiet. His words caused the merchant gentleman opposite to lower his newspaper and fix him with a warning glare: conversation at breakfast was of course entirely ill-mannered.

Renzi inclined his head and picked up his own *Rochester Morning Post*. He quickly opened it to the news; with the big naval-construction dockyard of Chatham close by and Sheerness but a dozen miles farther out, it was to be expected that coverage of the recent shocking events at the Nore would be extensive.

He particularly wanted news on the much talked-about visit by the lords of the Admiralty, with their promises of pardon, but what he saw was far worse. It seemed that after intolerable insults from the mutinous seamen, their lordships had washed their hands of the matter and taken themselves and their pardon back to London.

The editorial wondered acidly whether this meant that readers could now, all restraint gone, expect a descent by hordes of drunken seamen.

Renzi slowly laid down the newspaper. This was the worst news possible. For some reason the mutineers had rejected their last hope; they had nowhere else to go. Pitt would never forgive them now, not after the inevitable spectacle of the army or the loyal remnant of the navy ending the mutiny in a welter of ignominious bloodshed.

He couldn't face breakfast with the knowledge that his dearest friend was now beyond mercy, the pardon withdrawn. He left the lodging, striding fiercely in a rage of hopelessness, past the curious medieval streets and shops, up steep cobbled roads.

Logic said that there were only two courses: that Kydd could be miraculously saved, or that Renzi should resign himself to his friend's fate and spare himself the hurt. The former was for all practical purposes impossible, the latter he could not face.

That left the ludicrous prospect of trying to find a miracle. The path turned into a grassy lane down to the river crossing, and the soft and ancient gray stone of a

Norman castle. His hand reached out to touch its timeless strength, willing an inspiration, but none came.

All Renzi knew was that he had to do something, *try* something . . . He came to a resolution: he would go to London.

The coach was uncomfortable and smelly, but he made the capital and the White Hart Inn well before dark. Restless and brooding, he left his bag at the inn and braved the streets. London was the same riotous mix of noise and squalor, carriages and drays, horses and hawkers, exquisites and flower girls. Instinctively he turned into Castle Street and south past the Royal Mews — time was pressing, and it could all come to a conclusion very soon.

He trudged through the chaos of Charing Cross, then entered the broad avenue of White Hall. Past the Treasury was Downing Street, where he knew behind the bland frontage of Number Ten the prime minister was probably in cabinet, certainly taking swift and savage measures.

Renzi stopped and looked despondently down the street. His father had powerful connections in Parliament, a rotten borough and friends aplenty, but he knew he could be baying at the moon for all the help they would give him now.

He retraced his steps. This was the seat of power, the center of empire. Rulers of strange lands around the globe, the King himself, but not one could he think to approach.

On past Horseguards he continued, and then to the Admiralty itself. Staring at the smoke-grimed columns, the stream of officers and bewigged civilians coming and going, he cudgeled his brain but could think of nothing that might break the iron logic of the situation: Kydd was a mutineer who had publicly declared for the insurrection — there could be no reasoning with this.

Black thoughts came. Would Kydd want to see Renzi at the gallows for his execution, or brave it out alone? Was there any service he could do for him, such as insure his corpse was not taken down for dissection?

The lamplighters came out as the dusk drew in, and Renzi's mind ached. As he waited for a grossly overloaded wagon to cajole and threaten its way around Charing Cross, he concluded that there was no possible answer he could find. Perhaps there was someone who could tell him of one — but who, in his whole experience, would know both naval imperatives and political expediencies?

From somewhere within his febrile brain came memories of a quite different time and place: the sun-blessed waters of the Caribbean, a hurricane, and a fearful open-boat voyage. It was a slim chance, but he had no other: he would seek out Lord Stanhope, whose life and mission he and Kydd had secured together.

Stanhope would never stoop to using his standing with the government for such a cause, but he could give Renzi valuable inside knowledge of the wheels of power, perhaps an insight into how . . . But Stanhope was beyond reach for a mere mortal. Dejection returned as Renzi thought through the impossibility of gaining access to a senior government figure in a wartime crisis.

Then another flood of recollection: a crude palm hut on a Caribbean beach, an injured Stanhope and a promise exacted from Renzi that if Stanhope were not to survive, he should at all costs transmit his intelligence to a Mr. Congalton, at the Foreign Office.

Renzi hurried back to the White Hart. The landlord provided writing materials, and in his tiny room he set to. It was the height of gall, but nothing could stop him now. The form of the letter was unimportant: it was simply a request for a hearing, through Congalton to Stanhope, shamelessly implying a matter of discreet intelligence.

He folded the letter and plunged out into the night, scorning the offer of a link boy. Without a long coat and sword he would not be worth the attention of robbers. The Foreign Office was well used to late-night messages passed by questionable figures, and he slipped away well satisfied.

A reply arrived even while he was at an early breakfast — "Hatchards, 173 Piccadilly, at 10 a.m." He forced his brain to an icy calm while he rehearsed what he intended to say, and in good time he made the most of his attire, clapped on a borrowed hat and appeared at the appointed place.

It turned out to be a bookseller recently opened for business, well placed in a quality district and just down from Debrett's. No stranger to books, Renzi eyed the packed shelves with avarice. Bold titles on political economy and contemporary analysis tempted, as well as tracts by serious thinkers and pamphlets by parliamentary names. Engrossed, he missed the activity around the carriage that drew up outside.

"You would oblige me by the use of your back room, Mr. Hatchard."

Renzi wheeled around. It was Stanhope, the lines in his face a little deeper, the expression more flinty. Renzi bowed and was favored by a brief smile.

"If you please, sir." An assistant took Stanhope's cloak, then led the party up a broad spiral staircase to a comfortable upper room at the rear, where they were ushered to the high-backed chairs before the fire.

"Coffee, my lord?"

"Thank you, John, that would be welcome. Renzi?" The interval, as the assistant served, allowed time for Renzi to compose himself.

"A long time, my lord," Renzi said, his heart hammering. There was now no one else in the room. The chandelier threw a bright, pleasing light over several reading desks arranged to one side.

"You have not asked me here on a matter of intelligence," Stanhope said shortly, his voice just loud enough to be heard.

"Er, no, my lord," Renzi said. He knew enough of Stanhope to refrain from dissimulation: it would help nobody to delay.

"Then . . . ?"

Renzi took a deep breath. "Your advice is solicited, sir, in a matter which touches me deeply."

"Go on."

"A very dear friend has been unfortunate enough to be caught up in the recent mutiny, and I am concerned how to extricate him."

"The Nore?"

"Just so."

"Therefore he has chosen not to avail himself of the King's gracious pardon?"

"It would seem that is the case."

Expressionless, Stanhope steepled his fingers and said, "You realize, of course, I can have no influence on the course of this unhappy affair once it has reached its climax. It is completely within the jurisdiction of the Admiralty courts, his only hope of mercy lying in the King's express forgiveness. I rather suggest that in the circumstances of the King's known hostility to the mutineers' actions this will not be a likely prospect. I advise you, Renzi, to resign yourself. Your friend unhappily has nothing but the gallows to reflect upon."

"Nothing?"

"I think I made myself clear?" Stanhope frowned.

"Yes, my lord, but —"

"There is no hope, either at law or in the machinations of politics — no one would be fool enough to put himself forward in the cause of a mutinous seaman at these times, no one."

"I understand, my lord," Renzi said quietly. He paused, then continued softly, "Sir, the man is Thomas Kydd, whom you remember perhaps from the Caribbean."

Stanhope looked up sharply. "You may believe I am grieved to hear it."

"He has taken the plight of his seamen brothers to heart. Sir, he has the ardor of youth compelling him to rash acts, but still has the love of his country foremost."

Staring into the fire, Stanhope said nothing.

"His would be a great loss to the sea profession, but a greater one to myself."

Still no response. Then a stirring. "Mr. Renzi," Stanhope said, his voice sad and gentle, "there is nothing I crave more than to be of service to this young man, nothing. But my eminence is as nothing compared to the forces he has caused to be raised against him. I am in truth powerless."

Renzi felt hope die. This was the end for his friend. He looked at the floor through misted eyes.

There was a discreet cough. "I said that there was nothing I could do. This is certain. But if the Admiralty found that they had good reason to spare him, even to pardon his crimes . . ."

"Sir, Kydd could never find it in him to inform on, to delate upon his shipmates. This is an impossible course." Renzi's head dropped again.

"Then there is one final action that may answer."

"My lord?"

"You will forgive the elliptical speech — my conscience is a hard master, as I know is yours." He considered carefully. "I can conceive of a circumstance that would have the same effect, result in the same happy conclusion. This will require an act of — of imagination by one devoted to the subject's well-being, yet at the same time be kept from his knowledge at all costs. Renzi, I am speaking of —"

"I conceive I penetrate your meaning, sir. Am I to understand you mean this, er, associate to establish a proxy connection to —"

"Precisely."

It was a chance; it was also uncertain and dangerous, but it was a chance — if he had the will and necessary guile.

In the stillness steps could be heard coming up the stairs. An austere man in gray entered with books for the reading desk. "Frederick, dear fellow!"

"Ah, the country burns and you are at your Grecian odes, William. Might I present Mr. Renzi, visiting London. Renzi, this is Baron Grenville, Mr. Pitt's foreign minister."

"Sir." Renzi managed an elegant leg, noticing Grenville's polite curiosity. He guessed that few of Stanhope's mysterious acquaintances would merit an introduction.

"I understand you have further business, Renzi, I won't detain you."

The coach left from the Blue Boar's Head at two; he had time. At the Fleet market at Holbourn he found a well-used and capacious periwig, and an old-fashioned lace-edged frock coat of the kind more likely to be seen on supercargoes in an East Indiaman; these he bundled into a bag with a pair of pattens — clogs to raise the shoes clear of mud.

A spectacle shop on Cheapside provided

an old silver pair of smoked glasses, like those needed by persons with weak eyes. A heavy faux-silver-headed cane and a large body-purse completed his outfitting.

After a weary and impatient journey he was finally in Rochester. Firmly locking the door to his room, he tried on his gear. It would do, but much hung on its effectiveness.

Wig powder — he loathed it for the inevitable dusty droppings on his high coat collar, but it was essential for appearances. His face was too healthy, tanned and weather-touched; ladies' face powder would subdue it to an indoor appearance. There was nothing more he could do that night so he took a modest supper and went to bed.

He couldn't sleep. It was a perilous undertaking, and Stanhope had all but declared that he would be on his own. If he failed — if he was discovered, then . . .

Too hot in the strange bed, he threw off a blanket. In theory it *could* just work, but it would mean personal peril, patience and, at the right time, Kydd doing exactly — to the letter — what was asked of him.

At the Nore the weather had not improved. Rainy, gusty, and raw off the North

449

Sea, it was Sheerness at its bleakest.

As usual, Kydd's first morning task was to assemble the day's victualing requisitions. He relied on the other ships to render their lists of requirements: sides of beef, lemon juice, small beer in the cask, dried pease and, this being harbor routine, bread. When the requirements had all been consolidated, he would send these ashore.

That duty done, he went to see Parker, who was finishing a letter. "Good day, Tom, we have to call an assembly of the Parliament, you'll agree. Then it's my intent to tour the fleet and speak to the men. I'll wait until we've the stores under hatches, though."

It would be a critical meeting. If their united front broke under the strain of competing loyalties it would be a merciless end for them all — but if they held staunch there was still a chance.

On deck they waited for the boats to thrash out to them. In these racing seas they would be making heavy weather of it, but Kydd had told the other ships to insure they were not short of provisions for just this eventuality — he knew the dockyard hoys would put discretion before the bellies of sailors when it came to filthy weather.

The wind whipped at Kydd's oilskins, sending a shiver down his backbone. How was it that Sheerness weather had a quality that made the town seem the rawest, most desolate spot in the kingdom?

"I spy our cutter," Parker said, in some puzzlement, pointing to where a boat with the distinctive old-fashioned lug mizzen projected over the transom made its laborsome way toward them. The crews were there to supervise the loading of the hoys, and for some reason were returning early.

The petty officer in charge came up the side quickly. "We bin flammed, Mr. Parker. The shonky bastards, they've stopped vittlin'."

"What — gave ye no stores? None at all?" Kydd couldn't understand it.

"None!"

Parker looked at Kydd. "I fear, Tom, you and I must get ashore and see what's afoot. Fetch your papers."

The victualing storekeeper was not helpful. It was a matter of authority, and for that they had to see a clerk of the check. They trudged across the dockyard, aware of the changed atmosphere. No longer the cheerful processions and hands waved in comradeship. Now it was in a sullen, hostile mood.

"You see?" The clerk's finger stabbed at the requisition form. "The signature. We have no authority to issue against this." It was Parker's signature.

"And why not? You have before."

"You needs an orficer ter clap 'is scratch to these."

"An' since when did we have t' do this?" Kydd snarled.

"Steady, Tom," Parker muttered.

"This's not th' business of a mutineer," the clerk said contemptuously.

"You — you fawney 'longshore bugger, what d' you know about it?" Kydd seized the man's none-too-clean coat and forced him to his knees. "Why don't y' let us have our vittles?"

"H-help! M-murder! Help!" The clerk's eyes rolled. Passing dockyard workers stopped. A few moved warily toward Kydd.

"Let him go, the bastard!" hissed Parker.

Kydd dropped his hands and stepped back.

The man dusted himself down ostentatiously. "Yair, well. Since y' must know, we have orders," he said, aggrieved but triumphant. "An' the orders are fr'm the Admiralty, an' they say no vittles t' any ship what wears th' Bloody Flag."

A sizable group of dockyard tradesmen gathered at the commotion. "T' hell wi' the black mutineers!" shouted one. "In th' oggin wi' 'em!" yelled another.

Kydd bunched his fists. "First man wants t' have his toplights doused, I c'n oblige ye."

"Let's be back aboard, Tom," Parker said. "It's as I thought. They're going to starve us out."

Even before they arrived back on the ship they caught sight of the 38-gun frigate *Espion* slowly turning, her slipped cables splashing into the water. Too quick for the mutineer vessels to bring their guns to bear, she went in with the tide and disappeared around the point.

In somber mood, Parker and Kydd rejoined the Parliament in the Great Cabin.

"Reports," Parker ordered.

Davis, looking cast down and ill, opened. "We now has *Espion* an' *Niger* in th' dockyard wi'out the red flag. I have m' doubts on *Clyde* and *San Fi* as well. They wants out, we know. Th' fleet is restless, they don' know what ter do, an' when they gets noos of th' stoppin' of vittles . . ."

"Brother Bellamee?"

This fo'c'sleman, a shrunken gnome of a sailor, spent his time ashore, listening and observing. He waited until it was quiet. "Shipmates, th' sojers, they're on th' march, hundreds on 'em, an' all marchin' this way. They got this Gen'ral Grey with 'em, an' he's a tartar. Got 'em all stirred up, settin' guns across the river to th' north, an' I heard he has clouds more of 'em all over in th' country —"

"Thank you, Mr. Bellamee."

"— an' he's goin' ter put two whole reggyments inter the fort. Dunno where they'll kip down, mates. Word is, we can't go ashore anymore, 'less we has a pass an' a flag o' truce."

The mood became black. It didn't take much imagination to picture a country in arms against them, relentlessly closing in.

"I was in Mile Town, mates, an' there was a sight." Kydd had never heard MacLaurin of *Director* speak before. "See, all the folks think we's goin' to riot or somethin' fer they're all in a pelt, women 'n' children an' all, a-leavin' town, carts 'n' coaches — anythin' to get away."

Parker shot to his feet. "My God," he choked, "what are we doing?" His anguished cry cut through the murmurs of comment. Astonished, all eyes turned to him. His head dropped to his hands.

"What's wi' him?" Hulme demanded.

Blake's eyes narrowed. "Could be he's a-gettin' shy, mates!" Growls of discontent arose — there were many who still distrusted Parker's educated tones. "We doesn't have ter have the same president all th' time, y' knows."

It brought all the talking abruptly to a stop.

"I votes we has an election."

In the first possible coach, a villainous unsprung monster of a previous age, Renzi headed away from Rochester. Time was critical. The coach wound through fields and marshland, across the Swale at King's Ferry and on to the island of Sheppey. Then it was an atrocious journey over compacted, flint-shot chalk roads to his destination — the ancient town of Queenborough, just two miles south from the dockyard but unnoticed since Queen Anne's day.

There was only one inn, the decrepit Shippe. With much of the population on the move away, there was no questioning of the eccentric merchant with the fusty wig who chose to take rooms just at that time.

"I'm an abstemious man," Renzi told the

landlord. "It's my way to take the air regularly." He was particularly pleased with his affected high voice, and he had taken the precaution, for local consumption, of laying out a reason for his presence — he was a merchant hoping to do business with the dockyard, waiting out the tiresome mutiny at a safe distance.

The oyster fishermen at the tiny landing hard were curious, but satisfied by Renzi's tale of gathering sketches for a painting, and for a generous hand of coins agreed to show him many wonderful views, the events of the Nore permitting. They had no fear of the press-gang for the oyster fishers of Queenborough carried protections whose rights dated back to the third King Edward.

Renzi strolled along the single bridle path that led to Sheerness. Behind his smoked glasses, his eyes darted around — angles, lines of sight, cover. The undulating marsh grass was possible, but not easy.

The road ended at the intersection with that of Blue Town on the way out of the dockyard. He turned left — his business was with the authorities. A stream of people were leaving: old women, fearful men with family possessions on carts,

stolid tradesmen at the back of drays —
and in the other direction troops of soldiers were on their way to the garrison.

Renzi clutched his bag to him as though
in alarm, and shuffled toward Red Barrier
Gate. This was now manned with a sergeant and four.

"I've been asked to attend upon the captain," Renzi squeaked. The sentry gave
him a hard look, then let him through.
Renzi passed the hulks, then the public
wharf, which was perilously crowded by
those begging a passage on the next
Chatham boat.

The entrance to the fort was also well
guarded. A mustached sergeant was
doubtful about his stated mission and
compromised by providing an escort. They
set off for the commissioner's house, the
seat of operations.

At the door, Renzi instantly changed his
demeanor; now he was in turn wordly and
discreet, knowing and calculating. He
bowed to the flag lieutenant. "Sir, I desire
audience with Captain Hartwell at your
earliest convenience. I may have information . . ."

Chapter 10

"No hard feelin's, Mr. Parker," said Hulme, after the vote.

"None that a mort more trust wouldn't cure," Parker said stiffly, reassuming his seat. The interruption, however, had allowed him to regain countenance, and he leaned forward in the old, confident way. "It's clear that the soldiers are deploying to deny us the shore," he said crisply. "They have reinforced the garrison, and we've had reports from *Pylades* that there are parties of militia splashing about in the mud the other side of the Thames."

It brought laughter. If the intention was to surround them with troops, then there would be a lot more cursing, mud-soaked soldiers floundering about in the marshlands.

"But we have to face it," Parker continued. "Ashore we're in danger anyway — they could cut us off and have us in irons in no time. We're much safer snug on board in our fleet."

"Damme," rumbled Blake, "an' I was gettin' ter like th' marchin' up an' down wi' our red flag in front of th' ladies."

Parker's rejoinder was cut off by a piercing hail. "Deck *hooooo!* Ships — men-o'-war, ships-o'-the-line — standin' toward!"

There was a general scramble for the deck. The lookout in the maintop threw out an arm to the open sea to the northeast. On the horizon was a fleet — no motley collection of vessels, but a first-class squadron of ships-of-the-line in battle order. It was upon them. There was no more time to debate, to rationalize the fighting of fellow seamen — a decision had to be made.

"They're flyin' the red flag!"

"The North Sea squadron! They've come across, joining! Two, five, six — eight of their ship-o'-the-line! It's — it's marvelous!" Parker skipped about the deck in joy. "Don't you see? We've lost three or four frigates and smaller, but now we've got eight — eight — of the line more."

"Doubles our force," Kydd said. "At last, th' shabs came across."

"An' I'm Joe Fearon, *Leopard,* an' this is Bill Wallis o' *Standard* — we come t' say we signed y' eight articles an' we mean to abide by 'em t' death."

Kydd responded warily. These were hard men and would need careful handling.

"Thank you," said Parker. "There are many —"

"An' we've brought a few of our own, like," Fearon said flatly.

"Oh, may we hear them?"

"Right. Fer the first we has this. Court-martials on seamen ter be made o' fore-mast hands, not grunters."

"Yes, well —"

"Fer the second, we want prize-money three-fifths forrard, two-fifths aft."

There was no use in opposing: they had to hear it out. All told, there were four articles, which had to be voted upon. Then it was insisted that they be taken ashore and presented to the Admiral.

"I do this from duty, Tom, not by choice. You stay here, my friend."

Kydd's spirits were low as he saw him off in the rain. They had doubled their force, but the Admiralty was not moving an iota toward meeting *any* of their grievances. Where was it all leading?

When Parker returned, the fleet was in joyous mood, with singing and dancing on deck in the clear moonlit evening. But his face was deeply lined. Buckner had refused even to accept the articles, and the fear and chaos ashore were worse. Now it was open hostility.

Early the next day the seamen's Parliament met.

"Brother Kydd, how d' we stan' in the matter o' vittles?" Hulme opened.

Kydd had estimates. Dry stores and those in cask could possibly be shared out among the ships that were running short, but there was already hardship. The difficult part was the usual problem of finding wood and water. Cooking salt beef needed a good deal of both, and all had been held back.

"We c'n hold out f'r another week or so. Then it's two upon four f'r another —"

"Those fuckin' toads! It's insultin' to us. Th' Admiral here commands thirteen o' the line — that's nigh-on what Old Jarvey had at Saint Vincent." Hulme scowled.

Parker sat quite still.

"Why we has t' sit here, takin' all they

wants ter dish out . . ." Hulme finished morosely.

Parker's face animated suddenly. "Perhaps we don't."

"Ah, how so?" Blake drawled, clearly reluctant for yet another of Parker's schemes.

But Parker was energized and would not be stopped. "Think of it, brothers, we could, with one stroke, win free of these shackles and at the same time force their lordships to accept our terms."

Conversations stopped around the table. "Go on, then, cully, let's hear yez," Fearon, of *Leopard* in the North Sea squadron, said.

Parker waited until he had complete attention. "We have all the means we need to call their lordship's bluff. If they don't want to come to us and talk — we'll force 'em."

Hulme sneered. "Yair, you'll —"

"We throw a blockade on London."

There was an appalled silence, then everyone spoke at once. Parker leaned back in his chair, a smile playing, while he waited for quiet. "Indeed. We have the power to clamp our hold on the richest trade gateway in the land. No one would dare touch us while we stop every merchantman, arrest everything that sails.

Trade comes to a standstill, the mills of industry stop for want of materials, companies fail for want of exports — the City collapses, the government falls."

"No!" Kydd burst out. "This is madness! T' bring y'r country to its knees? We can't sink s' low we'd do this t' England."

"It would work." Parker's reply was flat and final.

Renzi returned to Queenborough along the bridle path, his mind preternaturally alert in a cold race of logic and action. The rhythm of walking helped focus his thoughts, and he settled to the task: to review and test the rationalizations that had brought him to this.

At base, the principle of deception, his pose as a merchant, with an interest in an early resolution to the mutiny who was prepared to use agents of commercial intelligence to that end, was successful; Hartwell had been covetous of a clearly first-grade reliable source in place of the usual illiterate ramblings from disaffected sailors. The harder part was to make the intelligence convincing, without jeopardizing either Kydd or doing violence to his conscience.

His ground rules were settled. First, the

overriding objective was the saving of Kydd, but only in so far as it did not require betrayal of his country. The next was more difficult: he would transmit nothing that could not be concluded by any intelligent observer for themselves, a hard thing to make convincing. And, finally, no names of individuals would go forward.

They seemed sound, and Renzi lightened. For the immediate future he must acquire intelligence to establish his credentials. He had already found a suitable observation post. There was an elbow in the seawall going away from the fort, which obscured him both from the fort and the mile houses.

He slid down the wall into the marsh grasses at the water's edge and watched the fleet's movements through a small brass telescope. If he was caught with the instrument he could well be taken up as a French spy, but there was no other way.

But he had to get closer. "Good day to you, gentlemen," he greeted the oyster fishermen. "Do you think today is a good day for seeing the sights?" He fumbled absentmindedly for some shillings, squinting at the silver.

"But o' course it be," the nearest said. "Where'd ye like t' go?"

"Oh, do you think we might go past the, er, fleet in mutiny?" he asked breathlessly.

The fishermen grinned. "Thought ye might. Why, o' course, they don't worry th' likes of us."

The oyster smack was a gaff-rigged cutter, decked in with hatches and reeking of shellfish. Renzi sat doubtfully on one side, then allowed himself to slide down the deck with a cry of alarm when the boat took the wind, and had to be hauled up to windward by an amused deckhand.

They rounded Garrison Point and shaped course toward the end of the fleet. Renzi sat openmouthed, apparently admiring the formidable display of naval might, but his eyes were moving furiously behind his dark glasses. All yards were crossed, topmasts a-taunt, the ships in an impregnable double-crescent formation.

His eyes strayed to the biggest; there, in *Sandwich*, Kydd would be now with Parker and the Parliament, probably discussing some grave move. "Could we go a bit closer, do you think?" he asked, only just remembering his high voice.

The two crew exchanged doubtful looks, but closed with the nearest two-decker. "Jem — over yonder!" one said urgently. It was a naval pinnace emerging from around the stern of the ship and foaming toward them.

Tiller hard over, the smack went about, but only to end in the path of another. A musket was wielded in the boat astern, a puff of white appeared and a ball slapped through their mainsail. "Give over, Jem, they'll do us, mate!"

The pinnace came up quickly once their sails were doused. "What're yez doin' here, then?" Renzi thought he recognized a boatswain's mate and shrank. No mercy would be shown an officer's spy.

The older crew member spoke up. "Well, mates, y' know us t' be honest oyster fishers, fr'm Queenboro'. An' this is a merchant cove wants t' do business wi' the dockyard, once things 'r' settled, like."

"A merchant?"

"An' wants t' see the fleet, tell 'is frien's all about it."

Renzi quaked in fear at the rough sailors.

The boatswain's mate grinned wickedly. "If he's a merchant, he'd be smart t' shift 'is cargoes a mort sharpish — we're goin' t' be puttin' a stopper in this 'ere bottle," he said, grandly encompassing the estuary.

"Yer what?" one of the fishermen asked.

"A blockade," he said proudly. "We got the ships, we got the guns. After we finished, nothin' swims 'less we say so!"

In the sleepy quiet of late night, hooves crashed on the cobbles at the back of 10 Downing Street. The messenger slid down the flanks of his panting horse, grabbed an Admiralty pouch from the saddlebag and sprinted up the stairs.

A little later, the prime minister of Great Britain, in his nightgown, was reading the urgent dispatch. "Good God above!" he said, slowly lifting his eyes from the page. "Merciful heavens! Toby! Toby, here this instant, you rogue!" The majordomo tumbled out onto the landing, blinking. "The cabinet — all of 'em, a meeting this hour!"

As the man hurried off, Pitt went to the empty cabinet room and sat, staring. His servant came with his long coat, which he draped over his shoulders, and later a small carafe of port.

He was granted minutes of thought only before a confused babble began at the door, getting louder. They filed in, shocked into silence by Pitt's unkempt, wild appearance. He nodded a greeting to the most eminent, and raised the dispatch. "This news is the worst I have ever received in this entire war." He paused, fixing his gaze on everyone present. "I will tell you. In brief, it is that the mutiny at the Nore has exploded in our faces."

He glared contemptuously at General Grey as he continued. "There were those who thought that left to itself, cut off from the land, the mutiny would in some way wither and die. The same assured us that we should have nothing more to do with them. Now they've called our bluff. We have it from an unusually reliable source in the Medway that the mutineers will deploy their recently augmented fleet to instigate a total blockade on the capital."

He paused grimly. "Why I have called you here is obvious. The solution, however, is not. General Grey?"

"Prime Minister, I — I don't know what I c'n say, sir. We've got 'em boxed in, troops on the northern shore, defense in depth on the banks of the Thames, but, sir, I beg to point out, we are up agin a fleet of ships, not an army."

"So, no further suggestions?"

"I regret, no, sir. We're helpless."

Pitt sighed. "Lord Spencer? Can you offer us hope of a way out?"

"Prime Minister, there are no ships of force closer than the Downs and the rump of Duncan's North Sea fleet. Together, they are easily outnumbered by the mutineer fleet, and even if we suppose that the seamen will fire on their brothers, I cannot be sanguine with respect to the outcome. The sight of our brave Jack Tars destroying each other . . ."

Pitt's eyes half closed. "Then I take it that our combined wisdom has been defeated by a mutinous rabble? Is there nothing that can be done before they fall upon our lifeblood?" His words lashed into the silence.

Spencer muttered, "I fear not, Prime Minister."

"How long can they hold out? Have we stopped all victuals reaching them?"

Spencer sighed audibly. "Sir, it is of no effect. If they are going to bail up the river, then they will have all the provisions in the world there for the taking."

"Have they broken out, rioted, loosed violence in some way?"

"No, sir, they have always comported themselves, er, honorably."

"Pity. It would stir the people against them. Gentlemen — friends, we are at a stand. If this catastrophe is allowed to take place I would offer short odds that with the total loss of revenue and credibility this government would fall within a week, and the country would be lost in disorder and rebellion within the month.

"This is now a war — a war of an increasingly personal nature, I'm sorry to say. The mutineers have a malignant genius conducting their affairs, one who seems to sense our motions and moves his forces accordingly."

"Richard Parker," murmured Spencer.

"Just so. My conviction, however, is that his origins preclude the notion that he is acting alone. I believe that he is secretly funded and directed by Jacobins."

There was murmuring around the table, but Pitt went on scornfully. "This is neither here nor there. They expect to make their move in the next day or two, and just what are we going to do about it?"

Nobody spoke, so Pitt carried on: "We do nothing. Nothing! Any half-baked move would make us look fools, lose our moral standing as well as our reputations. If they carry out their threat then we suffer. But we let the world know that any mutiny without a cause must have the French at the bottom of it. This is our only hope. That they lose the support of the people, turn them against these knaves. Already they will earn the hatred of common folk for the ruination they will do to honest trade. That it is at the bidding of a Jacobin master will be hard to take.

"Evil must cast out evil. I will insure the newspapers receive plenty of fuel for their fulminations. Meanwhile, I want to clamp a complete hold on their fleet — they are neither to receive nor send any communications other than through channels controlled by us. We smuggle newspapers and tracts to the common seamen so they'll have no doubt what odium the people of England now hold them in and drive wedges between them and their leaders. Tomorrow I shall introduce bills to the Commons concerning sedition and treason that will treat mutiny with the severity it deserves, and mark out as treasonable any who aid a mutineer."

Pitt took a long pull at his port. "This is a fight to the finish. Victory can only go to he who is still standing at the end."

"Ye mustn't do this thing — I beg of ye, don't!" Even as he spoke, Kydd knew that his words were merely a useless echo in his own ears.

"You are asking me to surrender our only real chance? To throw away all we've done so far? You're a sad dog at times, Tom. Now we have real power! Pitt can't stand his taxation revenue stopping or go against the City merchants, it's obvious. Nothing stands in our way now."

"Dick, till now, we've played it square, kept discipline, and all we c'n be accused of is *not* doing somethin'. Now we're guttin' the trade o' these islands — don't y' think that we'll lose any feelin' for us we had before?"

"Feeling?" Parker said scornfully. "Do we take feelings into account? Damn it, we're nearly there! Now if you feel qualmish about putting a halter around Billy Pitt's neck then kindly keep it to yourself. And if you have nothing further to add, then leave me alone, I have work to do. This will bring their lordships here at the run, and I'm going to consolidate our grievances and articles into one, to hand over to them when they get here." He lowered his head and returned to his writing.

Kydd's anger rose. "An' if this doesn't bring their lordships, what then? Sail aroun' t' Portsmouth an' give the Channel fleet a pepperin'? Fire on y'r —"

Parker looked up, his face venomous. "This is my concern, not yours. I'm president, not you! If you don't like the way we're proceeding, with democratic votes, then you'd better run."

★ ★ ★

Kydd sat in the deserted foretop, his back to the mast, staring out over the Nore. There had been so little time to stop and consider. He had been carried along by events and was as powerless to affect them as a leaf in a fast stream. The ever-spreading consequences of their actions, the multiplying dire possibilities, the implications for all he held loyal and true, was it too late to turn away?

It had begun with the noblest of motives, and this had held him to the cause. But this had not changed: what had were the stakes. Now it was the mutineers against the world on a numbing scale. Parker placed final victory for the mutiny against distress to the country as a whole, and this was something Kydd could not accept.

But could he desert, and betray the trust and reliance of his shipmates, especially if at this point they might be winning? He knew he could not.

He had respected Parker, even admired his knowledge and learning, but there were troubling flaws in his character. And his influence as president over the more hot-tempered men showed a worrying lack of common leadership. In effect, the belligerents were

473

taking control. If they sparked off some sort of confrontation, it would most certainly end quickly and bloodily. He could not have this on his conscience, no matter what the outcome.

This, then, was what it came down to: he would not desert, he would remain — not so much in devotion to the cause but to do what he could to restrain the hotheads. Resolved, he swung over the edge of the foretop and regained the deck.

"Mr. Kydd, we bin lookin' fer you," Hulme called, catching sight of him. "Plannin' fer the blockade in the bays — chop, chop!"

The bays forward on the main deck, both sides, could hold more men than the Great Cabin, the better to hear the detailed planning. Kydd took up position to one side and noticed Parker looking at him suspiciously.

"Our Great Plan," Parker announced, once they had all settled. "A complete blockade of the Thames."

It did not take long to go over the main items. The blockade was to consist of battleships spaced at half-mile intervals anchored right across the channel, lying to their anchors in the tide; this would insure that any vessel passing through would take a full broadside on both sides from a ship-of-the-line — effectively, utter destruction. Each side of the line would be patrolled by a frigate and ship sloop. An anchoring ground on both sides of the Thames was designed as a holding area for the arrested ships.

"This will be your authority," Parker said, holding up a paper. "Warrant of detention, signed by the committee."

More details, then the meeting broke up in noisy cheerfulness. It was a daring stroke, and action instead of the boredom of waiting. Some were uneasy. Perhaps this would set government and Admiralty implacably against them, with avenging to be wrought afterward, no matter the result.

But Thomas Jepson, the lively fiddler of *Sandwich*, put the sailors' feelings best: "We gets what we ask, or all London 'll be in an uproar Sat'day night."

The next morning Kydd joined Parker on the fo'c'sle head. Standing in the desultory rain, arms folded and looking out over the gray expanse of the Thames estuary, the President of the Delegates affected not to notice him.

"Goin' well, then," Kydd said.

Parker glanced once at him. "You're with us."

"Aye."

"Made peace with your conscience?"

"I know what I have t' do."

Unbending, Parker pointed to the battleships. "I should suppose they'll kedge and warp across."

"Wi' this useful easterly an' on the ebb? They'd be lubbers if they don't cast t' larb'd an' make a board across t' their place, lettin' go the stream anchor . . ." He tailed off, aware that he was contradicting Parker.

"You'd never make a politician, but always a damn fine seaman, Tom." Parker laughed.

They both looked out at the scene. Without officers, and with the minimum of fuss, the big ships-of-the-line took up their moorings and, under topsails and fore-'n'-aft canvas, leaned to the wind to find their allotted places. Within hours, they were in position, and the sea highway to the capital was securely closed.

"This is what I want to see," said Parker. It was the several picket craft sailing to intercept merchantmen, working together with the patrolling frigates to shepherd them to a holding anchorage. One by one merchant captains found themselves joining a growing number of vessels crowding the mudflat.

As the numbers swelled, Parker grew more somber. "To see it happen, to know it is my work — it gives me no pleasure, if you'll believe me. Did I do right? Or have I brought down forces of vengeance that will undo our precious cause?"

Three sailors deserting from *Lion* were brought to the gangway. The committee decided on two dozen lashes to be applied immediately. But by night disaffected seamen could take boats and reach the Essex mudflats, the remote marshlands of eastern Sheppey or the Isle of Grain, and disappear.

HMS *Maria* was a victualer from Deptford. She was laden with stores and provisions for Jervis — newly created Earl St. Vincent — and his fleet still at Lisbon. Given the Admiralty's non-supply to their own fleet, the committee deemed it proper that the stores should rightfully go to where they were most needed. Kydd was soon entering this accession of stores in open declaration and making out disbursement lists.

The *Inflexible* men took more direct

means. Several boats were taken ashore where sheep were seized from terrified farmers and carried bleating out to sea. Others relieved a fishing smack of its catch.

Days passed. Newspapers told of fear and disorder, chaos on the trading floors, hunts for Jacobin spies. Editorials were full of rage at the mutineers. Still there was no word of a peace mission.

Parker toured the ships to raise spirits. Some, like *Montagu*, *Director* and *Inflexible*, turned on him, demanding yet more acts against the silent Admiralty, while others begged a resolution before their world disintegrated.

"We cannot cravenly surrender now," Parker said softly. "They'll crucify us for what we've done." He smiled wanly. "Do you know, Tom, there are now proclamations posted in Sheerness that accuse me of 'divers acts of mutiny, treason and rebellion' and promising five hundred pounds for my apprehension? How long before we all have our fame published so far and wide?"

Kydd saw Parker's despondent look. "They *must* yield! It c'n only be a matter of time, Dick." Parker didn't reply.

The breakthrough came just after dawn.

The lookouts in the maintop of *Sandwich* hailed the deck. "Deck *hooooo!* Ships — men-o'-war, ships-o'-the-line — standin' toward!"

Eager eyes identified the remainder of the North Sea squadron; *Agamemnon*, previously Nelson's own famed ship-of-the-line; *Ardent*, of equal force; *Leopard* and *Isis*, 50-gun ships. They all flew the Bloody Flag at the main.

"Now! Now we have it! Dare I say it?" Parker said, exulting in the moment. "We have a fleet, such a fleet that is the biggest in England!" The tension of the days fell away, men manned the shrouds and cheered themselves hoarse.

"With this force," Parker said, his eyes bright and staring, "I can do anything. I've more power than any admiral — I can descend on whole countries and make them quiver. There's nothing I can't do. Think of it!"

The Parliament of the Delegates was called instantly; the agenda, final determination. Discussion raged — but there was really only one issue; how to wrest attention and redress for their grievances.

Parker let the arguments roll on, then stood up tall and proud. "There is only one course now left to us, brothers. I'm

479

speaking of the King." He got complete attention. "As I detailed to this Parliament at the beginning of this affair, it is my contention that the King is surrounded by ministers and advisers who are evil, self-seeking and avaricious. Now we have the power to cut through those who have until now insured that we are never heard, and approach His Majesty directly." He paused and smiled. "I therefore ask this committee for a form of wording of a loyal address to His Majesty, detailing our grievances. Thank you, brother seamen."

There was general polite applause then discussion began again, but not for long. "Loyal address be buggered!" Blake snapped. "We tells 'im what we want, an' that's all."

There were hearty roars, then Hulme put in harshly, "An' that sharp 'n' quick, too. We gives 'im a time."

The idea took root and Blake shouted, "One day is all, lads."

"Give 'im time — two days," said Hulme.

"Right. We dates it fer next morning, Toosday, eight o' the clock, an' he has until eight on Thursday t' give us our reply," Fearon said, nudging Kydd to note it down.

"We needs some time t' get it to the palace," Davis intervened.

"Then we adds six hours t' that," Fearon dictated.

Kydd wrote as if in a dream. To demand things of a king! They had reached the end of their hold on reality.

Parker stood up. "Find the captain of *Monmouth*, if you please, Brother Davis. He's the Earl of Northesk and has the ear of the King. He is to be alongside ready for my letter to His Majesty within two hours."

The cabinet waited in respectful silence for Pitt to begin. His strained face was sufficient warning that his news would not be in any wise good. Finally he raised his eyes, his voice unnaturally soft. "By Admiralty telegraph I have received the most appalling news." He broke off to cough harshly into his handkerchief. "This morning at dawn the remainder of the North Sea fleet went over to the mutineers."

Spencer went white.

"So there is no mistaking the situation. I will go over the main points. At the moment there is at our most vulnerable point a battle fleet fully armed and manned by desperate men, larger by far than even Jervis and Nelson had at Saint Vincent. With the final rising there is now no chance whatsoever that any force can be brought to bear to end this situation.

"We have endured this blockade as long as we can. Our losses are catastrophic and there are no more reserves. And now Captain the Earl of Northesk has brought the final disgrace, an ultimatum addressed to the King himself. I will attend His Majesty after this meeting."

He paused, choosing his words. "The mutineer chief now has a number of possibilities, all of which are deadly to this country. He can sail wherever he wishes, and menace whoever he will. He is untouchable. He may wish to use this power to threaten us, and by that I include the promise to deliver his fleet to the enemies of this country, France, the Dutch, any. I need hardly say that, in that event, England is certain of defeat. I confess before you now that I can no longer see any further act of significance that can have any effect on the outcome of this miserable affair."

"There's still Trinity House, Prime Minister," Spencer stuttered.

"Yes, my lord, you'll spare me the details

of my worthy and salty old gentlemen's valiant endeavors, please. But in the main, just what are their chances?"

"They have started at the northern limits, around the Swin, but there is difficulty . . ."

"Quite so. I understand," Pitt said wearily. "Putting that aside, we have to face reality, gentlemen. And that is, we have tried and we have lost. There is now no further course left. Except one. Grenville, it is with the deepest reluctance imaginable, but I have decided that the time has come to approach the French and treat for peace."

Renzi returned to the Shippe Inn, tired and dismayed after his early-morning walk. Despite his warnings, nothing had been done to prevent the blockade. It had been days, and the entrance to the Thames was now a chaos of jammed shipping, the wealth of England wasting away on the mudflats. It could only be a short while before the nation collapsed into anarchy.

The oystermen grinned a welcome; his liking for a daily trip to the Nore was a profitable sideline. The smack put out from the Queenborough jetty, went smartly about and beat out to the anchorage.

Renzi sat bolt upright. To his shock there

were now additional ships, big ones, settling to their moorings at the Great Nore. With them how many more thousands of sailors had swelled the numbers of mutineers? It was a fantastic, unreal thing that was unfolding, unparalleled in history.

As he let the fishermen circle the anchored warships he counted and memorized. It was a difficult and brain-racking chore to come up with small gems of intelligence gleaned from his observations yet which obeyed the principles he held. But it was vital if Kydd was going to have any chance to escape his fate.

The smack returned, Renzi careful to rhapsodize on the quality of the sunlight on cliffs, seagulls and sails. With as much patience as he could muster, he allowed the oystermen to fuss him ashore, brush him down and set him on his way.

The situation was now a matter of the greatest urgency. He wandered about the village and, when sure he was out of sight, stepped rapidly along the path to the dockyard. The amiable sentry passed him through and Hartwell came immediately. "Sir," said Renzi abruptly, "I advise most strongly that tonight is the best — your only chance."

"Do I understand you to mean —"

"You do. Trinity House! Pray lose no time, sir. I need not remind you of what hangs on this night."

He left immediately, and on the way to Queenborough he kept looking over his shoulder. Before he was halfway, to his immense satisfaction, the telegraph on its stilts above the dockyard clashed into life, the shutters opening and closing mechanically with their mysterious code.

The afternoon passed at an interminable pace, giving ample time for reflection. The stark fact was that he had chosen a course of action that contradicted the principles he had arrived at. He could alert the mutineers and nullify the action, but this he had coldly and logically decided was a matter touching on the safety of the realm, and it must remain.

Now it had to be. Renzi knew that the attention of the mutineers would be on celebrating the arrival of their powerful new brothers; this would be the only time that the daring operation planned by the Elder Brothers of Trinity House had even the slimmest of chances.

It was, besides, a source of some satisfaction that Hartwell had trusted him enough to divulge the plot and consult him on the timing. His strategy was working.

At last, sunset. He waited for a further hour, then made his way in the dark to the jetty.

"Why, sir, you haven't a grego," an oysterman said kindly. "Ye surely needs one on th' water at this time o' night."

Renzi accepted the fishy-smelling surcoat and boarded the smack by the light of one dim lanthorn. "How exciting!" he made himself say. "What kind of creatures are abroad at this hour, I can hardly conceive!"

Under easy sail to the night airs, the smack put out into the Swale. The moon came and went behind ragged clouds, and Renzi scanned the night tensely.

A splash nearby startled him. "Don' never mind him, sir. Jus' a fish out on a frolic."

They met the Medway and paid off to starboard. Still no sign. Then he caught a sudden blackening of the wan glitter of moon on sea. "What's that?" he asked quickly.

"That? Oh, jus' the *Trinity Yacht*, sir. Don' rightly know why she's abroad now, don't usually."

Renzi settled back with relief. It was happening. His part was now finished.

From seaward, the approaches to

London beckoned with lights in a confusion of beguiling sea paths — hundreds of golden pinpricks ashore and afloat, the larger navigation beacons and the Nore light-vessel.

The Thames met the sea in a maze of sandbanks that stretched out to sea for miles, each one marked with the wrecks of countless unfortunate vessels that had strayed from the deep-water channels. No sailing master in his right senses would attempt to enter or leave without thankful reference to the buoys and lights set and maintained by the brethren of the Corporation of Trinity House, whose ceaseless work continued even in wartime.

On this night, Trinity House began a different task. To the seamarks of the Whiting, Rough and Gunfleet to the north, Girdler, Shivering Sand and Pan in the center, and the Blacktail, Mouse and Sheers, their vessels converged under the command of Captain Philip Bromfield.

The *Trinity Yacht*, purpose-built for buoy lifting and heavy cable work, slipped through the night to her first rendezvous. She was fitted with a massive capstan and particular cathead to starboard. Her decking was of Danzig deal for laying out buoy and ground tackle, but her captain did not rig for buoy lifting. Instead, the buoy was hove short and the night's quiet was broken by the sound of men wielding axes and hammers, smashing into carefully crafted staves, wrecking tightly caulked seams. Then the buoy was let go, to disappear into the black depths.

One by one the seaward buoys that the buoy warden of Trinity House had dedicated his life to preserve were sunk without a trace. The work continued through the night, as quietly as possible, as they approached the Nore and the mutinous fleet.

By morning it was complete, carried off during the only night when there was any chance of success — a daring feat that so easily could have gone wrong. To seaward not a buoy or beacon remained: the Nore fleet was trapped, unable to get out across lethal sandbanks now lying concealed under an innocent sea.

Kydd found Parker forward, right in the eyes of the ship, alone. He was gazing out across the smooth, unblemished sea to the hard gray line of the horizon, his face a picture of grief.

"Why? Why do they force my hand in this way?" Parker mouthed.

Kydd mumbled something, but his own

mind was in a chaos of feeling. Just hours ago they were dictating terms to the King himself, now they were trapped in their own impregnable lair. He could see nothing but the blackness of defeat ahead. Their mighty fleet was impotent — they would rot in place until . . . Kydd forced himself to the present. "What was that ye said, Dick?"

Parker turned to him with an intense expression of noble suffering. "My friend, by their stubbornness, stupidity and malice they have forced me into the position where there is only the final sanction, the last move in the game. They insult us to think we would carry the fleet over to the enemy, for they've shown by their actions last night that this is their concern. Very well, this is barred to us. But this we can do. I have ten thousand men and a thousand guns at my command. At the expiry of our ultimatum, if the King is led by false advice to deny us our right, then we sail, upriver, to the capital. There we shall demand our due, and if not we shall with broadsides reduce the City to utter ruin."

"Yer mad bastard, ye've lost y'r mind!" shouted the *Lancaster* delegate.

"Damn yer blood, c'n ye think of a

better?" snarled Hulme.

Kydd put down his pen. In the violent discussions nothing was being decided. "Mates, do we have t' fire on London t' get our way? Is this the only thing t' do?"

"Shut yer face, Kydd, you ain't a delegate," snapped Blake.

Hulme added, "An' yeah, if it saves our necks, cully."

"I don' like this a-tall," MacLaurin, delegate of *Lancaster*, said. "Can't be right, firin' on our own, like that. There's kitlings 'n' all ashore, like t' stop a ball. I tell yer, we —"

Kydd was nauseous, his head ready to burst. He excused himself, went to the captain's sea cabin and pulled out the victualing list. Some ships were running far short of proper rations.

"*Director* needs six tons o' water b' sundown, Mr. Kydd." It was the dour purser's steward of the ship; he had asked before, but Kydd had been caught up with the endless arguments in the Great Cabin.

"Ye can't have any now," Kydd snapped.

"I asked ye yesterday forenoon, Mr. Kydd."

"Goddamn it t' hell! Listen, the water hoy won't come 'cos the dockyard maties want t' slit our throats, *Proserpine*'s waterin' party was all took b' the soldiers, an' *Leopard* thinks now a good time t' find her water foul 'n' wants more fr'm the fleet."

"I said, *Director* needs 'er water," the purser's steward repeated obstinately.

Blind rage surged up. "You come here pratin' on y'r problems — y' fuckin' shaney prick, you — you — Get out! *Out!*"

The man left soundlessly, leaving Kydd to hold his head in his hands.

How long could he hold on? Pulled apart by his loyalty to the navy and that to his shipmates, in a maelstrom of half-belief in the wickedness of the highest in the land, he had now to come to terms with the prospect, if the mutineers voted it, of doom and destruction to the heart of his country.

He threw himself out of the suffocating closeness of the cabin, needing the open sky and air. At the main shrouds he stopped, breathing heavily. He grabbed one of the great black ropes, wanting to feel in his hands its thickness, its seaman-like simplicity. He looked up at the towering maintop: its stark, uncompromising outline was urgent with warlike strength, yet in its form there was also grace and beauty for those who knew the sea.

Not long afterward red flags descended

on three of the smaller ships and were re-placed by white. Fighting could be seen on the decks of one, and the red flag ascended once more, but the other two slipped away around the point to the dockyard, and safety.

Parker came on deck. "They're deserting their shipmates!" he called loudly. "Damn them to hell, don't we say, men?" There were weak cheers and cursing from those in earshot. But Kydd could see he was pale and shaking.

"There goes *Leopard*, the bloody dogs!" someone called excitedly.

Fearon, delegate to the *Leopard*, raised his fists. "I know the gib-faced shab 'ut did that. When I get aboard . . ."

The bigger 50-gun ship slid away with the tide. Others in the fleet opened fire on her but she made her escape. Then it was the turn of *Repulse* — but her furtive set-ting of sails had been spotted by the alerted fleet and guns started to go off.

"Captain Davis, call away my barge," shouted Parker. "I'm going to send those beggars to the devil by my own hand, see if I don't!" The boat put off, and pulled madly for *Director*.

Repulse's sails caught the wind and she heeled, gathering way. Parker scrambled up the side of *Director* and could be seen arguing with her gun crews — they had not opened up on *Repulse* as she slipped away — but then *Repulse* suddenly slewed and stopped, hard aground.

Parker flew into his boat again, and stood in the sternsheets wildly urging on its crew as it made for *Monmouth*, the closest to the stranded ship. He swarmed up the side and ran to her fo'c'sle. An indistinct scrimmage could be seen around a nine-pounder. Then it fired — and again.

Kydd watched in misery as *Monmouth* and other ships poured fire on *Repulse*. All the high-minded sacrifice, hard work and dedication, the loyalty and trust, now crumbling into vicious fighting.

Hundreds of Sheerness folk lined the foreshore to watch as the mutineers' guns thundered, the stink of powder smoke drifting in over them. They would have something to tell their grandchildren, Kydd thought blackly.

Miraculously, *Repulse* seemed unscathed through the storm of fire. Then Kydd understood why. Savage splashes and spouts rose all around the ship, none on target, an appalling standard of gunnery — the gunners were firing wide.

The masts of *Repulse* changed their aspect as the ship floated free with the tide. She spread more canvas, eased off and away.

The night passed interminably. The ultimatum would expire at two in the afternoon. Would they then go to the capstans, bend on sail and set course for London? By this time tomorrow the biggest city in the world might be a smoking ruin — an impossible, choking thought.

Kydd couldn't sleep. He went on deck: the lights of the fleet were all around, the three-quarter moon showing the row guards pulling slowly around the periphery of the anchorage. His eyes turned to other lights glimmering on shore. In the nightmare of the past few days he had not had time to think of Kitty. What would she be feeling now? Would she think badly of him? Had she already fled into the country?

His breast burned and, as he looked up at the stars, a terrible howl escaped into the night.

In the morning Parker appeared. There were dark rings around his eyes. "Good day to you, Tom," he said quietly. "My deliberations are done. And they are that we cannot do this thing. I am preparing a petition asking only that we receive pardon. We send this to the Admiralty today."

An hour later, Captain Knight of *Montagu* arrived in a boat. He carried the King's reply. In the plainest words possible King George comprehensively condemned the actions of the mutineers and utterly refused to entertain any further communication.

Captain Knight carried back Parker's petition by return.

When the news emerged, there was outrage at Parker's betrayal. *Director* and *Belliqueux* shifted moorings to the bow of *Sandwich* to put her under their guns, and the wait resumed. At noon the fleet began to prepare for sea — sail bent on ready for loosing, lines faked out for running, topmen at their posts.

"Is the signal gun charged?" Parker hailed.

"Ye're not goin' ahead with it?" Kydd's voice broke with anguish.

"I am their president, they have voted for it, I will do my duty," he said woodenly, turning away to consult his fob watch. "It is now two. You may fire, if you please."

The six-pounder cracked spitefully, and from all around the fleet came acknowledging gunfire. Capstans were manned, topmen lay out on the yard ready to loose sail. It was their final throw.

But a noise was heard, a swelling roar of voices, that welled up from the farthest reaches of all the ships. Fierce arguments, louder rejoinders, fighting — but not a capstan turned or a ship moved.

The seamen had decided: the mutiny was over.

They had fired on the King's ships, stood as a deadly threat to the government of the day and repudiated the King's Pardon. There would be no limit to the Admiralty's vengeance. It left Kydd numb, in a floating state between nightmare and reality, but also with a paradoxical sense of relief that all the striving, doubt and uncertainty were now resolved forever.

He stood on the fo'c'sle with Parker, watching boats full of soldiers heading for any ship flying a white flag. The first made for them.

"It's finished f'r us, Dick," Kydd said, in a low voice, "but we face it when it comes."

Parker crossed to the ship's side and gripped a line. "History reached out and touched me, Tom. Did I fail? Was it all in vain?"

Kydd could find no words to reply. He noticed the white of Parker's knuckles and saw that he was only just in control.

"Any with a shred of humanity could not stand by and see those men groan under the burden of their miseries. I could not!" He turned to Kydd, eyes bright. "So you might say I am the victim — of the tenderest human emotion."

He resumed his dogged stare at the approaching boats. "They could only ever see us as a mortal threat, never as sailors with true cause for complaint. At any time they could have remedied our situation and claimed our loyalty, but they never did. Instead they bitterly opposed everything we put forward. They offered redress and pardon at Spithead, but to us nothing."

He heaved a deep breath. "I was the one that the illiterate, base-born seamen turned to when they needed a leader — they elected me to achieve their goals, but . . . It grieves me to say it, my friend, but the material I had at my command was not of the stuff from which is wrought the pure impulse of a glorious cause. They were fractious, hot-tempered, impatient and of ignoble motives. In short, Tom, my friend, I was betrayed."

The approaching boat came alongside,

and the unbending Admiral the Lord Keith came aboard.

"Which one of you is Richard Parker?"

The president of the delegates walked toward him. "I am."

"Then I arrest you in the King's name. Provost corporal, do your duty."

Parker smiled briefly.

"That will do. I'll be back for the others. Get him ashore."

Kydd watched Parker move to the ship's side. He turned once toward him, then disappeared.

The boat returned, and Kydd was ordered aboard with others for the journey ashore. A numb state of resignation insulated him from events, but when they approached the small dockyard wharf his heart nearly failed him. Nothing had prepared him for the degradation, the baying crowd, the noise and the shame. Hoots of derision, small boys playing out a hanging, the hisses of cold hatred — and Kitty, her face distorted and tear-streaked.

Flanked by soldiers who kept the crowds at a safe distance, the seamen shuffled off, shackled in pairs with clumsy manacles. They were taken to the fort, searched at the guardhouse and then on toward the garrison chapel. Under the chapel were the cells; dark, dank and terrifying. And there Kydd waited for his fate.

Renzi watched Kydd, with the others, stumble out of sight into the fort. He forced his mind to rationality: Kydd's incarceration in the fastness of the garrison with two regiments of soldiers in the guard was unfortunate for his plan. He would, in probability, be moved like Parker to the security of Maidstone Jail until the court-martial. This would be at night, and without warning.

The whole plan hinged on communicating with Kydd, passing on the vital message — and, of course, Kydd playing his part without question. But if he could not even make contact?

Condemned men — and Kydd was as good as condemned — had a certain unique position, and it was permitted that they could be visited by loved ones; no one would question a woman's privilege in this regard.

"O' course, you'd be meanin' Kitty Malkin. She's over on t' next one, Queen Street."

She didn't answer the door, but Renzi

saw inside through the curtained window that there was a light. He knocked and waited, feeling conspicuous. Eventually the door opened, and a rumpled and tear-stained Kitty appeared.

"I hesitate to intrude at this sad time, Miss Malkin, but do you remember me?"

She looked at him without interest. "No, sir, I do not."

"I am the particular friend of Thomas Kydd." Her eyes flared but she said nothing. "Please, don't be alarmed. I come to you to see if you will do him a service. A particular service, which may be the means of saving him from an untimely end."

"Why did ye not save him afore now, may I be s' blunt as to remark it?"

"A long story, er, Kitty. It is a simple enough thing — a message needs to be passed to him, that is all. You may be sure there is no danger or inconvenience to you —"

"You know I will! Who *are* you, sir?"

"I am Nicholas Renzi, and my friendship with Thomas begins with his very first ship. Please believe that since then we have been through much together."

"What do ye want me t' do, Mr. Renzi?"

Outside the Great Cabin of HMS *Neptune*,

anchored off Greenhithe, the first batch for trial sprawled listlessly in leg irons. Among them was Thomas Kydd, mutineer.

The numbness was still there but the misery had reached ever-increasing depths. The shame he was bringing on his family — his father would be trying to hold up his head in Guildford town, and his sister, Cecilia, would hear and her hero worship of Kydd would die, her own situation with a noble family perhaps threatened.

He tried to move position. The clanking irons drew irritation from the other prisoners and a glare from the deputy provost marshal. The nightmare days before the end had left him exhausted and ill; lack of sleep was now sapping his will to live.

The interminable waiting, being prevented from talking — his mind tried to escape to other realms and hallucination was never far away. Bright, vivid imagery crowded into his thoughts: fierce, exhilarating seas so real he could taste the salt spray, the bloodlust of a gundeck in action with its death and exultation — and the many sights of great beauty and peace he had seen as a deep-sea mariner. It faded, as it always did, into the gray pit of desolation that was now his lot.

The door to the Great Cabin opened. He looked up; it was Parker. He stood there, white-faced. "It's death," he said, with no emotion.

The provost marshal came with the irons, clamped them brutally to his legs. "Mark this, you damned one-eyed bugger," Parker said venomously, "when you put on the halter, I'll give you such a kick as will send your soul to hell."

Davis saw Parker being dragged away, and murmured, "If they serve me th' same way, I'd ask ter die with him."

There was indistinct movement inside the Great Cabin, and a lieutenant emerged. "Court is adjourned. It will meet to-morrow," he informed the provost marshal.

They were brought to their feet and taken down to confinement in the gloom and mustiness of the orlop. There, they were placed in bilboes, a long bar with sliding leg irons; it would be a dozen hours or more before they could hope to be released.

Kydd tried to lie, but his legs twisted awkwardly. Four marine sentries watched, their expressions impossible to make out in the dimness of the two lanthorns. Some of the prisoners talked quietly; most lay motionless.

Some had visitors; a dissenter chaplain led prayer for a Scots boatswain's mate and a disreputable legal gentleman escorted by a lieutenant attempted to question one prisoner, but left quickly. Fearon's mother came, but was so overcome she had to be attended by the surgeon.

The screaming and weeping tore at Kydd and he struggled to stay rational. Then a young woman, brought by the marine lieutenant, appeared before him. It was Kitty.

"Tom, m' darlin' man, t' see you here!" she said piteously, her hands writhing together.

"Kitty, m' dear," said Kydd, his mind scrabbling to keep a hold on reality. "Y' shouldn't be here — why, it's a long way from —"

"Tom, oh, Tom," she wept, and clung awkwardly to him. The marine lieutenant looked away politely. Kydd could just get his arms around her, and held her while she sobbed.

She pulled away, dabbing her eyes, then leaned forward to whisper. Next to Kydd, Davis pushed at Hulme and they leaned away so as not to overhear the endearments. "Tom, m' love, listen to me," she whispered urgently. "Are ye listening?"

"Aye, Kitty," he said.

She kissed him quickly. "Then mark what I have t' say, on y' life, Thomas. On y' very life, I said!"

He mumbled, she kissed him again. "This is what ye must say th' very instant y' steps into the court. Don't ask any questions — just say it. For my sake, darlin'. Are y' ready?"

Davis appeared at the door, unbowed, and said, with a laugh, "Aye, well, death o' course, I never doubted it." His irons were clamped on and he shambled off to the condemned cell. They were accelerating the pace.

"Bring in the prisoner Thomas Paine Kydd." A plunging fear seized him, but only for a second. His future was ordained; there was no mercy through those doors, he would leave as a condemned felon. He would therefore face his fate without flinching.

Light patterned prettily through the mullions of the sternlights in the Great Cabin. The room was filled with figures in blue and gold lace, grim faces.

"You may stand there." An officer indicated with a sword.

"You are Thomas Paine Kydd?"

"I am, sir."

"You stand charged, that —"

"I claim Cap'n Hartwell t' speak f'r me." He heard his voice, weak but firm.

"You'll have your chance later, my man. Now, on the twelfth day of May 1797, you did —"

"Sir! I claim Cap'n Hartwell —"

"Silence! Silence in court! If you do not keep silence, I will see you gagged, sir!"

"Oh, yes. Ah, er, I do believe we have a rather nice point here." Kydd's eyes focused on the speaker. "Might I crave the court's indulgence, sir, and ask the court be cleared?"

"Do you indeed, Cap'n Hartwell? At this stage to be toppin' it the lawyer, dammit!"

"Sir, I have to insist."

The president of the court glowered. Then, seeing Hartwell's quiet obstinacy, he agreed. "Clear the court — prisoner can go to the officers' waiting room, but keep a damn close eye on the villain, sir."

There was a general shuffling about the court. All save the sitting captains and president left the room. Kydd was taken under close escort to the admiral's sleeping quarters, temporarily a waiting room.

"Now, sir, what is this infernal matter that it must so inconvenience the court?"

Hartwell spoke in a low voice, but forcefully. "Sir, this Kydd is one of the most courageous young men I have known. His loyalty to Crown and country was such that he deliberately sought out the friendship of Parker and the so-called Parliament and, in appalling danger, passed us vital intelligence — warning about the blockade and the best chance for Trinity House to play their part is only some of it. Sir, we can do no more than sympathize with his terrible ordeal, and instantly set him free with a full pardon."

Rumbles of approval came from around the table, but the president remained unmoved. "How do ye know it was this man? Did you go out t' the ship an' ask for him?"

"Sir, a good question, if I may remark. It was in fact through the loyal services of a Queenborough merchant that the information was passed."

"I shall want t' see the merchant identify this man. Is he at hand?"

"He is on deck at this moment, sir."

"Pray find him — an' make haste if you please, Captain."

"Sir, this is the merchant in question. He wishes to resume trading at Sheerness shortly and therefore begs for your discretion in the article of naming. He will answer to 'Mr. X'."

"Harrumph! Well, Mr. X, we will bring in a prisoner. You will identify him as your informant, and if it is, you will declare to the court, 'This is the man,' or 'This is not the man,' accordingly."

"I understand," said Renzi, his high voice raising eyebrows.

"Bring in the prisoner."

Kydd returned and stood facing the court, swaying slightly.

"This *is* the man," Renzi said.

"Very well. Remove the prisoner." When Kydd had been led out, he resumed. "You are asking me to believe that you boarded a ship in active mutiny to interview this Kydd?"

"*No,* sir, I wouldn't *dare!* Those were desperate men —"

"Quite. Then, if I may ask . . ."

"I secured the offices of his — his paramour, if you will excuse the indelicacy, sir. She it was who regularly passed between, utterly without suspicion."

"Then it only needs the young lady to be produced to identify both parties and th' link is complete. Is she . . . ?"

"She is nearby, sir. I'll ask her to attend immediately."

★ ★ ★

Kydd entered the court for the second time. "Kitty!"

"This 's the man, so please y', sir," she said, avoiding Kydd's eye.

The prisoner was taken away.

"And this man, do you know him?"

"Yes, sir, I do indeed."

"Then the court thanks you, m' dear, for your assistance." The president waited for them both to leave, then sat back.

"I find the identity proved and, in the light of what we have heard, find the man Kydd exonerated of all culpability. Are there any to gainsay? Then I rule that the prisoner receive a full and general pardon. This ruling is made in camera without prejudice to the prerogatives of the court and, for the protection of the individual concerned, is entered without record. These proceedings will not be discussed outside this court now or at any future date. Bring in the prisoner.

"Thomas Paine Kydd, this court finds that, for reasons not for record, you have been exonerated of culpability in the matter of the charges brought against you, and that the gracious pardon of His Majesty be deemed to extend to you. You are hereby freed. You may go."

Utterly confused, mind a-swim, Kydd had to be helped to the door. It opened, and there were Hulme, Fearon and the others looking up at him. "P-pardoned," he said hoarsely, and the irons were struck off.

Chapter 11

"For pity's sake, tell me!" Kydd pleaded. Snuggled deep into Kitty's bed, he was still feeling woozy after a deep sleep and the draft she had slipped into his negus.

She fussed at his coverings and replied, with a sigh, "I've told ye before, m' dear, not until Mr. Renzi comes. I promised him he'll be th' one t' tell you." Lowering her voice she added wistfully, "You are s' lucky, Tom, t' have such a friend as will do this f'r you."

As consciousness returned, the past galloped back to crowd his thoughts, bringing with it all the desperate feelings of the last few weeks. He had to know why he had been spared, if only to be sure that he wouldn't in some way find himself back there again.

He dressed and looked out of the gunport window at the ships at anchor in

Sheerness and farther away, still where they had fled after escaping the mutineer fleet. The sight of them brought back dark memories that tugged at his sanity — but for now he let the enfolding warmth of Kitty's caring soothe his soul.

Kydd sat in the armchair staring at the miniature of Ned Malkin, the simple patriotic Toby jugs and souvenirs of far voyaging, and let his thoughts drift. A knock at the door shattered his reverie. Renzi entered diffidently, his hat in his hands. "My dear fellow."

"Nicholas." Kydd was unsure how to treat a friend he'd last seen when on a riotous procession and who apparently had contrived to spare him the gallows.

"I pray I find you in good health?"

"With Kitty t' care f'r me, how can I not be?"

Renzi found another chair, and sat delicately on it. "I'm wondering if you might be up to a little —"

"Why am I pardoned?" Kydd demanded hotly.

"Shall we —"

"I need t' know now, damn you, Nicholas. I have t' think, sort it out."

They climbed silently up the hill to Minster and from the top looked out across gray, wanly sparkling sea and dreary saltmarsh. Kydd sought out the *Sandwich*, the largest black ship in the Medway, nearly lost among scores of other craft. Then his eyes focused on the desolate scatter of dockyard buildings at the end of the island and, next to it, the huddle of hulks that was Kitty's home.

They sat down on a grassy ridge. Kydd was first to speak. "Then tell me, Nicholas."

Renzi plucked a grass stem. "I remember, years ago it was, in a place very far from here." Kydd waited impatiently. "The Great South Sea it was, on an island to which I was, er, particularly fond," Renzi continued, "and there you had the gall to thwack me on the calabash, so to speak, rendering it impossible for me to continue there. And, might I remind you, you have never once since begged pardon for the presumption."

"God preserve me! Nicholas, be damned t' the history, this is m' life we're about." Kydd snorted, then added, "Aye, I do remember, but I recollects as well, *while* we're discussin' it, that if I hadn't you'd be cannibal scran b' now."

"My point precisely." Renzi smiled back, waiting.

Kydd kept his silence.

"We each of us have our principles, some dearly held, some of which are of the loftiest motivation, some mere rank superstition. I rather believe that in both our cases principles were informed by the purest of motives, but were not necessarily grounded in strict practicality. My position is that I have merely redressed the balance, perhaps achieved a measure of revenge."

"Nicholas, I have to know! What did ye do, tell me, that th' court thinks to pardon me so quick, like?"

"Oh, nothing but the judicious exercise of family patronage, the shameful deployment of interest among the highest on your behalf. Do you know, I met Grenville, the foreign minister, in Hatchards the other day? Delightful fellow, much attached to Grecian odes."

"Spare me y' politics, Nicholas," Kydd threw at him. "Do y' really mean t' stand there 'n' tell me it's by corruption that I'm delivered?"

"It was my decision to use any power within my reach to preserve for the service a high-principled and gifted seaman. I do apologize if I offended," Renzi said, with the utmost politeness. "And, of course, the deed is now in the past, all done," he added. "No prospect of winding back the clock."

Kydd's eyes burned. He raised a fist. "God damn ye for a bloody dog, Renzi. I have t' live with this now."

"Just so."

"I was in insurrection agin my king an' country."

"This is true. You have also been given the chance to atone — I'd hazard your loyalty to the sea service from now on will be a caution to us all."

"You cold-blooded bastard! There are men I know over there in chokey waitin' t' be led out t' the fore yardarm, an' all you can do —"

"Mr. Kydd! At some point you will put all this behind you, and step out to your future. It may be a week, a year or even half your remaining days, but it will come. The rational thing is to accept it, and make it earlier, rather than filling your days with regrets. Which will it be for you?"

Kydd lowered his head, and tried to cool his anger. Renzi's words made sense: there was nothing at all he could do about his situation other than humbly accept his fortune and move on.

"Shall we rejoin Kitty?" Renzi said gently. "I have been promised a mutton pie, which I lust for."

Kydd sat for a little longer, then lifted his head. "Yes." He stood facing the far-off men-o'-war. "It's all over, then, Nicholas," he said thickly. His eyes glistened.

"All over, my dear friend."

They walked together down the hill.

"Nicholas," Kydd began hesitantly, "y'r decision t' return to y' family. May I know —"

"My position is unaltered."

"Welcome aboard, Mr. Kydd. You're in Mr. Monckton's watch, he'll be expectin' you." The master of HMS *Triumph* shook Kydd's hand and escorted him below. A considerate Hartwell had insured that he would rejoin the fleet as a master's mate in a new ship, a well-tried 74-gun vessel in for minor repair.

Monckton looked at him keenly. "I heard you were caught up in the late mutiny."

Kydd tensed, then said carefully, "Aye, sir, I was." He returned the curious gaze steadily.

Monckton did not pursue the matter, and went on to outline Kydd's duties and battle quarters. He looked at Kydd again, then added, "And everyone knows of your splendid open-boat voyage. I'm sure you'll be a credit to *Triumph*, Mr. Kydd."

The ship was due to return to station at Yarmouth, but first she joined others in taking position in the Medway, at Blackstakes. Kydd knew what was happening — *Sandwich* was moored midstream, ships of the fleet around her. On the banks of the river spectator stands were erected; at Queenborough and the public landing place at Sheerness small craft were sculling about, kept in their place by naval guardboats.

Troops filed out of the fort and along the foreshore. With fixed bayonets they faced seaward in a double line toward *Sandwich*. The crowd surged behind them, chattering excitedly, and boats started heading for the big three-decker.

At nine, the frigate *Espion* fired a fo'c'sle gun. A yellow flag broke at her masthead, the fleet signal for capital punishment. *Sandwich* obediently hoisted a yellow flag in turn.

Kydd watched with an expression of stone, but his soul wept.

Just a few hundred yards away a temporary platform had been built on the starboard cathead, a scaffold — the prominence would give a crowd-pleasing view.

"Clear lower deck! *Haaaands* to muster, t' witness punishment!" The boatswain's mates of HMS *Triumph* stalked about below until the whole ship's company was on deck, many in the rigging, the fighting tops and even out along the yards.

Kydd stood between the officers and the seamen, and moved to the ship's side. In *Sandwich* the men had similarly been called on deck, with marines in solid ranks forward and aft.

A rustle of sighs arose at the sight of a figure entirely in black emerging on deck from the main hatchway, flanked with an escort. It was too far away to distinguish features, but Kydd knew who it was.

Parker paused. His face could be seen looking about as if in amazement at the scene. Over on the Isle of Grain women jostled each other for the best view of the spectacle and men stood on the seafront with telescopes trained.

The distant prisoner knelt for a few moments before a chaplain on the quarterdeck. When he arose, his hands were bound and he passed down the length of the vessel to the fo'c'sle, then to the cathead under the fore yardarm.

An interchange occurred; was Parker being allowed to speak? It seemed he was, and he turned aft to address his old ship-mates. The provost marshal approached with the halter, which would be bent to the yard-rope, but there was some difficulty, and the presiding boatswain's mate was needed to secure the halter above. The provost marshal put a handkerchief into Parker's hands, and he stumbled up to the scaffold. The officer pulled a hood over Parker's head, then stepped down.

Parker stood alone. A party of seamen was ranged down the deck with the yard-rope fall ready to pull. The signal to haul would be a fo'c'sle gun, their cue apparently Parker's handkerchief.

In that endless moment Kydd struggled for control, the edge of madness very near.

Without warning Parker jumped into space. Taken by surprise, the gun then fired, and the sailors ran away with the hanging rope, jerking Parker's body up. It contorted once, then hung stark. A handkerchief fluttered gently to the water.

Kydd bit his lip. Even to the last Parker had thought of the seamen: he had effectively hanged himself to spare them the guilt.

The next day five vessels at the Great Nore flew the Blue Peter; *Triumph* was one.

The North Sea squadron would be whole again, and at sea.

Of all the memories Sheerness would hold, there was one that shone like a beacon for Kydd. He secured an understanding permission to go ashore for a few hours before the ship sailed, and stepped out for the hulks.

"Kitty, how do I find ye?" He hugged her close.

"Come in, Tom, darlin'," she said, but her voice was tired, subdued.

Kydd entered the familiar room and sat in the armchair. Kitty went to fetch him an ale. "I'm master's mate in *Triumph* seventy-four," he called to her. "She's gettin' on in years but a good 'un — Cap'n Essington."

She didn't reply, but returned with his tankard. He looked at her while he drank. "We're North Sea squadron," he explained. "C'n expect to fall back on Sheerness t' vittle 'n' repair, ye know."

"Yes, Tom," she said, then unexpectedly kissed him before sitting down opposite.

Kydd looked at her fondly. "Kitty, I've been thinkin', maybe you 'n' me should —"

"No, Tom." She looked him in the eyes. "I've been thinkin', too, m' love." She looked away. "I told ye I was fey, didn't I?"

"Y' did, Kitty."

She leaned forward. "Tom Kydd, in y'r stars it's sayin' that y're going t' be a great man — truly!"

"Ah, I don' reckon on that kind o' thing, Kitty," Kydd said, pink with embarrassment.

"You will be, m' love, mark my words." The light died in her eyes. "An' when that day comes, you'll have a lady who'll be by y'r side an' part o' your world."

"Aye, but —"

"Tom, y' know little of the female sex. Do y' think I'd want t' be there, among all them lords 'n' their ladies, knowin' they were gigglin' behind y'r back at this jumped-up seamstress o' buntin'? Havin' the fat ol' ladies liftin' their noses 'cos I don't know manners? Have you all th' time apologizin' for your wife? No, dear Tom, I don' want that. 'Sides, I couldn't stand th' life — I'm free t' do what I want now." She came over and held his hand. "Next week, I'm leavin' Sheerness. What wi' Ned 'n' all, there's too many memories here. I'm off t' my father in Bristol."

"Kitty, I'll write, let me —"

"No, love. It's better t' say our good-bye now. I remember Ned once said, 'A ship's like a woman. To think kindly of her, y' have t' leave her while y'r still in love.' That's us, Tom."

Triumph put to sea, her destination in no doubt. She would be part of Admiral Duncan's vital North Sea squadron, there to prevent the powerful Dutch fleet emerging from the Texel anchorage. If they did — if the Channel was theirs for just hours — the French could at last begin the conquest of England.

It was at some cost to ships and men: beating up and down the coast of Holland, the French-occupied Batavian Republic, was hard, dangerous work. The land was low and fringed with invisible sandbanks, a fearful danger for ships who had to keep in with the land, deep-sea ships whose keels brushed shoals while the Dutch vessels, designed with shallow draft, could sail down the coast and away.

But it was also a priceless school for seamen. With prevailing winds in the west, the coast was a perpetual lee shore threatening shipwreck to any caught close in by stormy winds. And as the warm airs of summer were replaced by the cool blusters of autumn and the chill hammering of early winter, it needed all the seamanship the Royal Navy had at its command to stay on station off the Texel.

Kydd hardened, as much as by conflicts within as by the ceaseless work of keeping the seas. The mutiny of two months ago was now receding into the past, but he had still not put it truly behind him. He accepted the precious gift of reprieve, however achieved: life itself. But so many had paid the price: the gentle Coxall, the fiery Hulme, the fine seaman Davis, Joe Fearon, Charles McCarthy, Farnall, others. The Inflexibles, led by Blake, had stolen a fishing smack and gone to an unknown fate in France.

It could have been worse. Vengeance had been tempered, and of the ten thousand men involved, only four hundred had faced a court, and less than thirty had met their end at a yardarm.

To say farewell to Kitty had brought pain and loneliness, and with Renzi about to return to his previous life, there was now not a soul he could say was truly his friend, someone who would know him, forgive his oddities as he would theirs in the human transactions that were friendship. His reticence about speaking of recent events had stifled social conversation, and a burning need to be hard on himself had extended to others, further isolating him. He withdrew into himself, his spirit shriveling.

Days, weeks, months, the same ships that had been in open mutiny were now at sea so continuously that the first symptoms of scurvy appeared. Sails frayed, ropes stranded, timbers failed, and still they remained on station. By October signals from the flagship showed that even the doughty Duncan was prepared to return to Yarmouth to revictual and repair.

The storm-battered fleet anchored, but there would be no rest. Duncan had said, "I shall not set foot out of my ship . . ." It would be a foolhardy captain indeed who found he had business ashore. Storing ship, caulking gaping seams, bending on winter canvas — there was no rest for any.

Then, early one morning in the teeth of a northwesterly blow, the *Black Joke*, an armed lugger, appeared from out of the sea fret to seaward of Yarmouth sands. Signal flags whipped furiously to leeward; a small gun cracked out to give emphasis to them, the smoke snatched away in the stiff wind. "Glory be!" said *Triumph*'s officer-of-the-watch peering through his telescope. "An' I do believe the Dutch are out!"

By noon the North Sea squadron had secured for sea, and without a minute lost, Duncan's fleet put out into the white-streaked waters under a dark, brooding sky with every piece of canvas that could draw set on straining spars.

The wind, however, was astern; the fleet streamed toward Holland in an exhilarating and terrifying charge. The next day they raised land, the Texel, the ancient home of the Dutch fleet, low, sprawling and foreboding under gray skies.

The Dutch were not there, but Duncan's scouts were. Their dogged tracking of the enemy fleet enabled them to inform Duncan that indeed the Dutch were at sea — and heading southward. The British fleet wheeled to follow, keeping the shore in sight under their lee all the time. Now at last there was a chance that the enemy could be brought to bay. If they caught up, then without doubt there would be a major battle, a formal clash of fleets that would enter history. The stakes could hardly be higher: if they lost the day then the way would be clear for enemy troops to make a landing on the shores of England.

It would be Kydd's first major fleet action. He almost looked forward to the fight: a purging by combat of all the devils that haunted his soul. But would ex-mutineers fight? Under Lieutenant Monckton, Kydd was in charge of the center main-deck twenty-four-pounders, and to his certain knowledge there were five in the gun crews he had seen parading under the red flag, including both quarter-gunners.

At nightfall hopes faded. They had not overhauled the enemy — they could be anywhere, or have changed course to the north and open sea. The fleet shortened sail for the night, standing off the coast.

Dawn came with driving rain, clearing to blustery squalls that sent men aloft to take in sail. While they were fisting the wet canvas, *Circe* frigate hove in sight, a signal hoist and a gun to leeward bringing every man on deck.

Kydd hastened to the quarterdeck to hear developments. The signal lieutenant had his glass up, his midshipman beside him with the signal book. "Enemy in sight, sir!" he said, following the frigate. "Three leagues to the sou'east."

The news spread, and from all parts of the ship roars of satisfaction and ribaldry arose, but Captain Essington waited grimly.

"Enemy course north, sir."

"Ah! That's what I want to hear. They've heard we're at sea and are turned back for home. How far from the Texel?"

"Er, the town yonder must be Kamperduin, so that makes the Texel fifteen miles distant, sir."

"Umm. De Winter has to form up. If we can bring him to action before noon, we have a chance." The quarterdeck became animated, high spirits breaking through, but Essington did not join in. "Do you bear in mind, gentlemen, the Dutch are an old and proud race. They have bested us once before in the last age, and we can be sure they will consult their honor again today. Their admiral is of the first rank, and their ships are not worn by stress of weather. They are of equal numbers and they are fighting for their hearth and home in their own seas. Today will be hard won for the victor. Enough talk! Clear for action, if you please."

The boatswain piped the order and the ship was plunged into instant activity. The boatswain's party went to the tops. Their task was to sway up and rig chain slings to restrain hundred-foot yards from plunging down if their tie blocks were shot away, with quarter slings on the lower yards.

Along the decks topsail sheets were stoppered properly, preventer braces led along and a netting spread between main and mizzen to catch wreckage falling from above.

The galley fire was put out, its cinders placed in tubs amidships ready for scattering over pooling blood, and hammocks were hoisted into the tops to form protective barricades against enemy muskets.

Below, in the gloomy orlop, the surgeon and his mates readied the cockpit. Who could guess how many men would be carried in agony and fear below?

Kydd had little time to think about an unknown future. His quarters were the big twenty-four-pounders along the main deck, and specifically those aft of center. Standing near the main-hatch gratings he watched his gun captains make ready their pieces: the implements of gunnery — the handspike, sponge, crow — could be relied on to be in place; what was more important were the details.

He knew what to look for. The match tubs next to each gun for use in case of misfire would be useless without slow-burning match ready alight and drawing. The gunners' pouch of each gun captain must contain tools and spare flints for the gunlock, and quill ignition tubes checked that the tallow cap had been removed.

The sound of a grindstone came from forward: pikes, cutlasses and tomahawks were getting a fine edge. A cook's mate carried a scuttled butt of water to place on the centerline for thirsty gun crews. It was well spiked with vinegar to slow their drinking.

Activity slowed, the ship was cleared fore and aft. It now only required the enemy to appear and the ship would beat to quarters. During the wait, biscuit and cheese were issued, and a double tot of rum to all hands. It was nearly time . . .

The enemy fleet was sighted at nine, sail upon sail startlingly pale against the dark gray clouds, occupying half the horizon. Beyond lay the flat terrain of Holland. Men came up from the gundeck to catch a glimpse of the enemy; once in action they would not see them again until they closed and grappled.

At half past, de Winter formed his line of battle. On the quarterdeck Kydd heard the officers' conversation. The taut enemy line was heading to the north — the Dutch, still apparently hoping to reach safe harbor, were sailing close to the land.

Duncan's strategy was simple: braving the massed broadsides of the enemy he would without delay throw his fleet at their line in two groups, one to larboard under himself to take the Dutch van, the other to starboard under his vice admiral, Onslow, to fall on their rear. *Triumph* would go with Duncan.

More signal flags soared up on the flagship, but Kydd never found out what they were for the urgent thunder of a drum sent the ship to quarters. With an iron resolution, he clattered down the main hatchway past the marine drummer madly rattling out "Hearts of Oak." Of one thing he was certain: he would do his duty to the limit.

Touching his hat to Monckton, he verified the presence of the young midshipman and three men standing by the centerline grating, then turned his attention to the guns. If they fought both sides at once they would be shorthanded; some gun numbers would have to cross the deck to work the opposite gun.

He stepped up on the grating while the wash-deck hose swashed across the deck. A seaman followed, scattering sand to give grip to the feet. Powder monkeys brought up the first cartridges in their long wooden salt boxes, and he watched as the quarter-gunner settled ear pads on the young lads. Gun-crews made do with their bandannas, tying them tightly around their heads.

Kydd took his broad crossbelt, settling it to take the weight of his cutlass, which, as a boarder, he would wear for the rest of the battle. When the order came, he would seize a brace of pistols from the arms chest and lead the second wave of boarders.

He paced slowly along, checking and re-checking. The middle of a battle was not a good time to be finding missing spares. Tucked in along the sides of the main-hatch, beside the ready-use shot lining it, were ranged spare breeching, complete training tackles, gun lashings, all becketed up neatly.

As he walked, he saw the gun crews looking at him, eyes flashing. They would be forced to stand idle for all of the time it took to reach the enemy, their own guns unable to bear, while the Dutch could concentrate their whole fire unopposed. After their line was reached it would be another story. As they passed through they would blast a storm of balls down the length of an enemy ship from each side.

But first they had to reach them. *Triumph* was as ready as forethought and devotion to the sea crafts could make her. Now the fortune of war and the courage of her men would decide the day.

The enemy began to fire just after midday, the thunder of their guns loud on the inactive gundeck. Kydd joined the gun crews leaning out of their ports to see. The whole line of the enemy ahead was nearly obscured in gunsmoke, the sea between torn by shot. To starboard Vice Admiral Onslow's division was diverging, his flagship, *Monarch*, in the lead of a straggling group. Duncan must be anxious to start the fight, thought Kydd, that he did not form line of battle.

He crossed to the other side of the deck. As he did, the first cannon strikes thudded home. These were longer-range shots and taken on the ricochet; closer in they would crush and splinter. Out of the gunports Kydd saw their own flagship, Duncan's *Venerable*, streaming out ahead, her blue ensign defiantly aloft, others coming up on her flank.

The sea hissed past a few feet below. They were running large, directly to leeward in the stiff wind — their time to fight would not be long delayed. Kydd pulled himself inboard. A sudden crash sounded somewhere forward. Something hissed past him, striking a deck beam then angling down to a gun, which it hit with a musical clang.

Then came the welcome smash of their own carronades on the deck above. Kydd dared a quick last look out of a port and saw, in a single flash ahead, *Venerable* bearing down on the big Dutch flagship, and at the same time the Dutch next astern courageously closing the gap to prevent *Venerable* passing through and breaking the line. He pulled in and took post, conscious that his duty was to make sure Lieutenant Monckton's orders were carried out — whatever the circumstances.

"Point your guns!" The enemy were very near now. Gun captains scrambled to sight down their pieces, signaling for handspikes to muscle the heavy guns around to train on target, then tracking it, waiting with gun lanyard extended for the word to fire.

So close. Smashing strikes and cries of injured men were general now, the moments seeming to last forever. But then it died away and the sea outside shadowed suddenly. It was the enemy line.

"Fire!" came the order. In a rippled broadside from forward the twenty-four-pounders crashed out in a vengeful smash straight at the unprotected stern of the unknown Dutch ship — thirty-seven heavy iron balls at point-blank velocity in a merciless splintering path of destruction right down the length of the ship. The noise was overwhelming, going on and on as they passed through.

Kydd bent his knees to see. Through the smoke he caught sight of an ornate stern gallery riven into gap-toothed ugliness. Wreckage rained down and turned the sea white with splashes. He wheeled around, still bent, and briefly glimpsed, through the opposite side, the tangled bowsprit of another ship.

Crews flung themselves at their guns: sponging, the lethal gray cartridge and wad, then the deadly iron ball. Kydd felt the deck sway over to starboard and realized they must be coming around to lock into their opponent. He yelled hoarsely at the crews. Doubling the rate of fire was as good as doubling the number of guns, and once around they would be facing an equal broadside from their opponent.

It came early, before they were fully around — and at ten-yards range the effect was lethal. The iron shot tore through the sides of *Triumph*, the balls rampaging the whole width of the gundeck before smashing through the far side, tearing and shattering. The deck trembled as more balls struck below.

Monckton raised his speaking trumpet and was thrown violently along the deck. He did not move. Kydd ran to his body; there was no mark on it, but a red rash was spreading on the side of his face. He put his hand inside the officer's coat and felt for the heart: it still beat.

"Bear a hand!" he roared at the men hovering around. They dragged Monckton to the centerline gratings and laid him out on his back. He had been knocked unconscious by the close passage of a round shot. If he recovered he would want to be at his post, but for now Kydd must perform his duty.

A midshipman arrived from forward, wide-eyed, his hand convulsively gripping the hilt of his dirk. "Get back to y'r post," Kydd told him. "Orders are th' same."

Kydd turned to the gun crews. There was no need for interference; the men worked like demons, their gun captains throwing a glance his way, then getting on with it.

A messenger raced down from the quarterdeck and skidded to a stop at the sight of Monckton's body. Kydd stepped up. "I'm in charge. What's y'r message?" The order was clear: each gun was to fire alternately at maximum depression or elevation. This would send their shot down to the enemy's keel or up through her unprotected decks, a terrifying ordeal for an opponent. Kydd ran along the guns, tasking off the gun captains.

The hull of the enemy ship loomed through the gunports in the thinning smoke; dull black, with signs of cannon strike everywhere and jerking activity at her gunports. Their own guns crashed out. *Triumph*'s gun crews worked savagely, needing no goading. Smoke swirled thickly back into the gundeck, obscuring everything. A mounting warrior's bloodlust set Kydd's heart aflame for victory.

There was no pretense at aiming; fire was general. "Double shotting!" Kydd bellowed. As the two balls diverged at the muzzle, aim would be affected but the damage would be broadened and doubled. "Smash it in 'em, lads!" he bawled. Yet in the wildness of the battle Kydd felt a serenity, the calm of a dedicated ferocity that he knew would take him through anything.

High screams close by — a young powder monkey with his lower body soaked in blood, pulling himself helplessly away on his elbows. Kydd motioned to an opposite gun crew to carry the lad below.

A wrecked gun, its barrel askew and carriage in pieces, its crew in a moaning, bloody heap, was being cleared of its dead, tumbled out of the gunport to the sea below.

Then, unbelievably, a messenger appeared, shrilling urgently, "Cease firing!" The crews, working like automatons, checked their fire and subsided into a trembling stillness. Kydd ran to the side and looked out. Roiling gunsmoke still hid much of the enemy, but there was an unnatural quiet aboard their adversary. Confused shouting from behind caused Kydd to turn around — but then came cheering, and maniac roars of jubilation. The enemy had struck!

It was ironic, thought Renzi, that when he had been reassigned to another ship at the last minute it had been this one, *Tenacious*, and within weeks of his final retirement from the sea he was headed into his second major fleet action in a year.

He knew Kydd had been shipped in *Triumph*, and there she was, the other side of Duncan's *Venerable*. He hoped that the lottery of war would spare his friend, whom he had not seen since their farewell in Sheerness — but this was going to be no stately fight against unwilling Spanish allies.

The Dutch were rightly proud of their maritime past, yet at the same time would be fearing the submergence of their national identity following their defeat and occupation by the French. If they could rise victorious over a field of war on their own, this would be preserved. It would be a sanguinary conflict indeed.

Renzi's post was at the quarterdeck nine-pounder battery. He would see what was developing, a mercy compared to the hell of a gundeck below, but he would be a target for enemy musketry. At least if he survived he could retire to the estate with as unique a claim to fame as any in the county set, he mused.

The enemy opened fire. It would be a hard thing to achieve, a breaking of the line, but *Venerable* led the division nobly, her signal for close action seemingly nailed in place. The fire got hotter. A ball slammed through a file of marines and left bloody corpses in its wake. Twice Renzi staggered at the vicious slap of wind from a near miss.

He forced his mind to float free, calmly observing his actions and freeing his thoughts of a vortex of anxiety — it was the only rational course.

Venerable was close to starboard, clearly heading for the enemy flagship. *Tenacious* kept faithful station on her, and when they were closer Renzi could see she was going around the stern of de Winter's ship to deliver a crushing, raking fire — but her next astern bravely closed the gap and *Venerable* had to bear away to round her instead.

Tenacious, a humble 64, found herself alone in taking on the big Dutch flagship. As she swung to bring her own broadside to bear, the space between the two filled with acrid powder smoke and a devastating storm of shot. The enemy were not, like the French, aiming for rigging and spars to disable the ship. Instead they were smashing their shot home directly into the hull of their opponent in a brutal prizefight.

There were no broadsides now; both ships at less than a hundred yards' range pounded to the limits of endurance. The air was torn by the whir of chain-shot, the heavy slam of thirty-two-pound balls, the vicious wasplike hum of bullets — the whole against the continuous noise of guns and shattered timbers and the dry reek of gunpowder smoke.

Men struck by balls were blown into

pieces like sides of beef in a butcher's shop or were disemboweled in an instant; those hit by splinters shrieked in agony as they were skewered. Renzi saw a midshipman, then the signal lieutenant drop in their tracks, and over at a disabled nine-pounder a corpse exuded blood that made tracks on the deck as the ship rolled and heaved.

The captain dropped to his knees with a bloody graze on his head, then crumpled to the deck; a midshipman started weeping, the pain from a crushed foot overcoming his young attempt at bravery. Renzi paced along the deck, watching his nine-pounder crews throwing everything into a frenzied cycle of violence, and ferociously excluded the logical probability that his own survival was in doubt.

He turned, and started to pace back the other side. Something like a horse's kick from behind threw one of his legs from under him. He fell to the deck. There was no immediate pain, and he scrabbled about trying to locate the source of a growing numbness, then noted spreading blood on the scrubbed deck. He sat up, trying to rise, but then the hot pain began and he flopped down again.

"Get yez below, mate," said an out-of-breath gun captain, who lifted his arms. In shock, Renzi fell back while another took his feet in an awkward carry-and-drag to the blood-smeared hatchway. They bumped him down the ladder and staggered around to lower him down the next.

On the orlop it was a scene from hell. The entire deck was carpeted in wounded, an operating table contrived from midshipmen's chests in the center. But the surgeon was not there; he with his loblolly boys could only move about the stream of wounded, as they came down, trying their best to ease their suffering.

Renzi was placed on an old piece of canvas, which was rapidly soaked with blood from his wound. He lay light-headed in the infernal gloom, listening to groans and cries. But there were also cheers of encouragement and bravery from some of those who would soon face the knife and saw. The back of his leg throbbed with increasing pain and he wondered abstractly if he would lose it.

A lanthorn bobbed nearer. It was the surgeon and his helper. In the navy way men were seen in the strict order they were carried below, no matter the severity of their wounds. Renzi waited for his turn, hearing the noise and shaking of the gundeck in action above.

The surgeon in his black smock, stiff with bloodstains, turned to him. His eyes were glazed. "Where is the wound, if you please?" he said, kneeling beside Renzi.

Renzi tried to turn over but could not. The two loblolly boys — older men no longer suitable for work on deck — rotated him. He felt the surgeon's hands rip away clothing and tensed for the knife, but after a pause and cursory poke the surgeon straightened. "You're lucky, my man. Superficial tissue loss but we'll need to staunch the blood." He probed the area. Renzi could feel the man's breath around the wound. "Yes, fit for duty in weeks. You know what to do," he told the loblollies; then he was gone.

The excruciating pain of a vinegar solution on the raw flesh brought tears to his eyes, but relief was unfolding in a tide of emotion — he would not suffer under the saw. A dressing, a tourniquet; additional pain came from the biting cord. Then the indignity of being dragged to a farther corner to recover — or die.

Somewhere outside the battle's fury continued; the fabric of *Tenacious* shuddered with savage blows. On deck it would be chaos, but the cruel logic of war meant that duty must be done and the battle fought irrespective of the hideous scenes.

Renzi rolled to his side in discomfort. Then he noticed the glint of gold lace being carried down the hatchway. It was the first lieutenant, his head lolling ominously to one side. The quarterdeck was being cleared fast.

Possession of their prize — *Wassenaar* — released *Triumph* for hotter work. Passing *Venerable* and *Tenacious* she rounded into the enemy line again, laying herself bow to bow with a yellow-sided man-o'-war.

Her guns opened again with a thunderous broadside, which was answered with equal venom by their opponent — but having practiced over long weeks at sea the English guns spoke faster and truer. Kydd, below, drove on his men with bellows of encouragement as the side of their opponent bulked just yards away.

But *Triumph* was coming under fire from another quarter. A previously untouched Dutch ship had approached and opened up on her opposite side. Kydd was taken by surprise at the sudden irruption of cannon fire — but almost immediately the sea was lit by a flash, and a sullen boom rolled over the waves.

The enemy fire slackened and stopped.

A ruddy glow tinged the sea. Fire! Kydd stooped to look out, and saw, only a few hundred yards off, the attacking warship lit by a spreading blaze near the base of the mainmast. Something must have touched off powder on deck, and if the flames reached tarred rigging and sails she would turn into a fire ship, a danger to friend and foe on the crowded sea.

Kydd turned back to his task and saw that the yellow-streaked ship's angle away had changed and, after another exchange of fire, she could be seen gathering way: she was fleeing! *Triumph* continued on to wear around; she was keeping clear from the burning ship and falling back to support the hard-pressed *Venerable*. Kydd set about squaring up.

In the lull a midshipman messenger hurried down the ladder to Kydd. "Captain desires your report, if y' please."

Kydd tried to keep his mind calm as he emerged on deck. *Triumph* was cut about grievously, wreckage strewn about, ropes trailing from aloft, blood smears on the deck. This was his first sight of the open battlefield. While he hurried aft, his eyes took in the vastness of the scene: ships in every direction at every angle, boats in the water, cannon splashes around ships still under fire, an immense pall of smoke over the whole area.

"You, er, Kydd?" The captain was obviously in pain, his arm in an improvised sling, his face blackened and red.

"Sir."

"Lieutenant Monckton?"

"Regret he's still unconscious, sir. I have him on th' gratings 'midships so if he comes to . . ."

"Quite right. And the guns?"

"Number seven larb'd dismounted, number nine larb'd has a blown vent bushing. Lost a truck off number six stb'd, but the crew is managin'. Er, we lost six men on number seven, an' there's a total of — let me see — thirteen been taken below." Kydd added, "We c'n still give ye a full broadside less two t' larb'd, an' all to starb'd, but could be pressed t' fight both sides. But, sir, we're in fine spirits, don't worry of us."

Captain Essington nodded slowly, looking closely at Kydd.

"Sir, may I know — f'r the others — how's the day?"

Essington smiled grimly. "You see there," he pointed to the south, "the starb'd division has taken all five of their opponents and are bearing up to join us.

And there," he indicated the ships they were steering for locked together in the throes of combat, "that is their flagship, and she has lost all her masts, and fights three of our ships. I rather fancy she will strike soon — and the day will then be won."

Kydd touched his hat and went below. Monckton was still unconscious, breathing heavily, so Kydd tried to make him comfortable and turned back to the task of clearing away the debris of battle.

A swelling roar of cheers sounded on deck followed by a shout at the ladderway. "She's struck! The Dutchy admiral threw it in!" The cheers were instantly taken up on the gundeck by Kydd's men, smoke-grimed, bloody, but victorious — and in that moment all the emotional tensions of recent events melted away for Kydd. He punched the air with rediscovered pride.

The deck heeled once more, staying at an angle. They were wearing around to the north again, seeking new opponents. Kydd leaned from a gunport; two or three vessels could be seen away to the north, but the guns of all those nearer were silent. The background rumble and thunder of heavy guns was no longer there.

The battle was over.

It was hard, having to work at the pumps, repair the shot-torn rigging, and sluice the decks of blood smears and endless smoke stains without the urgency of battle. But it was very necessary, for if the Dutch had any reinforcements they might descend on the weary, battered English and quickly reverse the verdict of the day.

Lines of battle dissolved. Beaten ships, now the prizes of war, bent on sail and set course for England while the men-o'-war lay together, working repairs for the voyage home.

"Mr. Kydd — passing the word for Mr. Kydd!" He looked up. "T' attend the captain," the messenger said importantly, "in his quarters."

Monckton was recovering in his cabin, the guns had spoken faithfully. He should not have any cause for worry.

The captain's door was open, a stream of people entering and leaving while he and his clerk sat behind a desk of papers.

"Kydd, sir?"

A flustered, battle-worn Essington looked up briefly. The redness in his face had turned to a bruising, and he had not yet changed his clothes. "Go to *Monarch*, they're expecting you."

"Sir?"

"Now, if you please, sir," said Essington irritably.

"Aye-aye, sir," Kydd said hastily, wondering what his mission could be.

The boat joined others crisscrossing between other ships. Close to he could see that the sea was speckled with pieces of wreckage, some as big as spars, some smaller unidentifiable fragments. His eyes lifted to the loose cluster of men-o'-war ahead, every one showing where they had endured.

Monarch was the flagship of Onslow, vice admiral of the other division. Kydd went up the pockmarked side of the big 74 and, touching his hat, reported.

The officer looked at him curiously. "Come with me." He was escorted to the admiral's Great Cabin. "Mr. Kydd, master's mate, *Triumph*, sir."

Onslow put down his pen and came around his desk. The splendid blue and gold, the stars and epaulettes — all the grandeur of naval circumstance — brought to Kydd a surge of guilt and apprehension.

"Ah, Mr. Kydd." He looked appraisingly at Kydd, who stuttered something about his tattered, smoke-grimed appearance. "Nonsense, my boy. All in th' line of duty. Well, now, you must be feelin' proud enough that your captain speaks s' highly of ye."

"Sir?" To his knowledge there was no reason that Essington could have even to mention his existence to such an august being.

Onslow's eyebrows rose. "You don't know why ye're here?" He chuckled quietly. "Then I'll tell you. Since Admiral Duncan is entertainin' the Dutch admiral, he's left certain jobs to me. An' one of 'em is this. In the course o' such a day, sadly there's some ships have suffered more than others. Your captain was one o' those asked to spare a suitable man t' fill vacancies in these. He seems t' think you're suitable, so by the powers vested in me by the flag officer-in-command, I order that, as of this moment, ye're to be known as Lieutenant Kydd."

"S-sir, I — I —"

It was staggering — it was marvelous! It was frightening! It was —

"Unusual name, that — Kydd. Don' come from Guildford, b' any chance?"

"Sir —" He couldn't speak. Feeling his face redden with pleasure, the broadest of smiles bursting out, he finally spluttered, "Aye, sir."

"Related t' the Kydds who opened the navy school not so long past?"

"M-my father, sir," he said, in a near delirium of emotion.

"A fine school f'r Guildford. Like t' pay my respects to y'r father at some time."

Speechless, Kydd accepted the precious letter of commission and turned to go.

"And, Lieutenant, might I have the honor of takin' your hand? It gives me a rare pleasure to know that Guildford can still produce fightin' seamen. Ah — do ye not wish t' know which ship?"

"Sir?" Any ship that swam would do.

"*Tenacious* sixty-four. Good fortune to ye, Mr. Kydd."

His heart full, Kydd tried to concentrate in the boat on its way to the battle-worn *Tenacious*. But he was a lieutenant! An officer! A — gentleman! His universe spun as he attempted to readjust his worldview; strictly, his father should touch his forelock to him, his mother curtsy when introduced — and what would they say in Guildford?

But what about Renzi, supposing they ever met again? Would he accept him as a gentleman? Would they . . .

His seabag and chest lay between his

legs. When he had returned to *Triumph* to fetch them, Essington had cut short his thanks. "We were signaled for a suitable man. Do you wish to dispute my choice, sir? I know something of your history. Pray you will live up to your step — and the best of luck, Mr. Kydd."

This was absolute evidence for Kydd that the Admiralty held nothing against him over his support for the seamen; there could be no doubt now, no more feelings of guilt, betrayal or ambivalence. Now he was a naval officer, with all the rights and privileges. It was altogether incredible.

Tenacious loomed. "Boat ahoy!" came the distant cry.

"Aye-aye!" their bowman roared. Kydd started — but then, of course, *he* was the naval officer they carried! A long sigh came from the depths of his being.

The boat hooked on, and Kydd sprang for the handropes. Impatiently he mounted the side, passing by an openmouthed boatswain's mate at the entry-port. Embarrassed, he retraced his steps down and across to the entry port. He entered the carved portal, the silver call pealing out to all concerned that a naval officer was boarding *Tenacious*.

"Sway aboard my dunnage, younker," he

told a duty midshipman.

"Aye," the youngster said.

"What was that?" Kydd snapped.

"Er, aye-aye, sir," the midshipman corrected himself, stiffening and touching his hat.

"Very well." Kydd remembered too late that he still wore his master's mate plain coat, and grinned at the discomfited lad. There would be time to find a uniform later. "Where's the captain?" he asked.

"Dead," the boy said. "So's the first and third lootenant. We're getting replacements, o' course," he confided, then added a hasty, "er, sir."

Kydd went up the main hatchway to the upper deck, marveling at the ruin on all sides. There were overturned guns, beaten-in bulwarks, broken spars hanging from aloft — and a tattered figure hobbling about, using a broken rammer as a make-shift crutch.

He stopped, staring keenly. It was — it couldn't be — Renzi? "Nicholas! You're — you're wounded!"

"I fear so, old fellow. It is but an inconvenience, the doctor assures me that I shall be made whole in some weeks." A warm smile stole over his face. "Thomas! You have survived our day of trial!" He held out his hand. Kydd gripped it, the events of the day threatening to unman him.

The midshipman appeared. "Shall I stow your gear in the third's cabin for now, sir?"

"Please."

He turned back to Renzi, but the cat was out the bag. "You — you have been —"

"I have," said Kydd, in the purest happiness. "Ye have t' call me sir, now, Nicholas."

"Oh. I'm afraid that's not possible."

"Er, may I know why not?"

Renzi looked down for a moment, and when he looked up again, Kydd could see he was struggling for control. "Because, Thomas, you will be grieved to hear that as senior master's mate, I also have been elevated to the quarterdeck. And, given recent promotions, you will be fifth, and I the fourth, so it will be you who are obliged to render the honorifics to me."

Their heartfelt laughter brought grins from the others on deck.

Kydd had just one question. "Nicholas, does this mean that — y'r intent, you know, t' leave the sea . . . ?"

A half-smile showed briefly. "It rather appears, dear fellow, that I may have to revisit that decision . . ."

Author's Note

Some people have asked me how much my books are based on my own life. In a way how could they be? The protagonist and I are separated by two hundred years and a revolution in technology, and I chose the sea while he had little choice; but as I got into the series I realized that Tom Kydd and I do share much.

We both deeply relate to the sea's magic, its potency and vast majesty, and both of us feel a clutch at the heart at the sensation of a live deck beneath, with all its promise of adventure and excitement. That first deep scend of the bows outward bound — the "curtsy to Neptune" every ship must make on entering His realm. The contraction of your world into the ship's comforting, never-changing rhythms — so different to life ashore with all its distractions.

In the course of this book I revisited Sheerness, the bleak setting of this most awesome of mutinies. As I looked out over the cold, drab wilderness of the Nore one particularly raw winter's day, seeing back into time to those great events, into my mind, too, came remembrance of myself as a very small boy looking out from that very spot to low, gray shapes slipping out to sea, disappearing over the horizon and taking my imagination with them. You can still walk out at low tide over the mudflats and find clay pipes of Kydd's time, but he had quite a different experience — this was where he first set foot on the deck of a man-o'-war, and met his future.

As ever, this tale has materially benefited from the time and kindness of people at the various locations I researched; I think particularly of Lorna Swift, at the Garrison Library of Gibraltar (which still exists), who found for me priceless documents of the time; Admiral Lorenzo Sferra, conservator of the Naval History Museum at the Arsenale in Venice, who at short notice deployed the full resources of his museum for me; and David Hughes, a local historian in Sheerness who was able to reveal to me fascinating hidden facts and color of this underrated part of the naval history of

England. To the many others I consulted, my deep thanks.

I'm blessed with a knowing and professional literary agent, Carole Blake, and Susanne Kirk, my editor at Scribner, heads an enthusiastic and hardworking team that is bringing the world of Thomas Kydd to life for so many.

As each book is finally launched on the world, it only increases my respect and admiration for my creative partner and wife, Kathy, who was originally responsible for my embarking on the voyage of my life. And it is certainly time I acknowledge my parents-in-law, Keith and Cressey Stackhouse, who believed in us both from the beginning.

The end of this book marks a watershed in the series; Kydd is now an officer and in the next book he begins the transition from the fo'c'sle as a common seaman to the quarterdeck as a gentleman. It will not be an easy journey . . .

About the Author

Julian Stockwin was born in England in 1944 and was sent at the age of fourteen to *Indefatigable*, a tough sea-training school. He joined the Royal Navy at fifteen, before transferring to the Royal Australian Navy when his family emigrated. He served in the Far East, Antarctic waters, the South Seas, and in Vietnam, where he saw active service in a carrier task force. After university, he became a teacher and an educational psychologist and lived for a number of years in Hong Kong, where he was commissioned into the Royal Naval Reserve and received Britain's MBE award. He retired with the rank of lieutenant commander. *Mutiny* is Julian Stockwin's fourth novel, following the successful launch of the series with *Kydd*, *Artemis*, and *Seaflower*. He lives in Devon, England, with his wife, Kathy, where he is at work on the fifth Kydd adventure, *Quarterdeck*. His website is www.julianstockwin.com.

We hope you have enjoyed this Large Print Edition. Other Thorndike, Wheeler or Chivers Press Large Print books are available at your library or directly from the publishers.

For more information about current and upcoming titles, please call or write, without obligation, to:

Publisher
Thorndike Press
295 Kennedy Memorial Drive
Waterville, ME   04901
Tel. (800) 223-1244

Or visit our Web site at:
www.gale.com/thorndike
www.gale.com/wheeler

OR

Chivers Large Print
published by BBC Audiobooks Ltd
St James House, The Square
Lower Bristol Road
Bath BA2 3SB
England
Tel. +44(0) 800 136919
email: bbcaudiobooks@bbc.co.uk
www.bbcaudiobooks.co.uk

All our Large Print titles are designed for easy reading, and all our books are made to last.